BREAKING NEWS

Waiting in the condo lot for the traffic to break, Jack hit the scan button on the radio. It stopped on a Baltimore Orioles game, with the Birds leading the Tigers 10-2. That was about the last thing he was in the mood to hear; he hit the scan again and it flipped over to the CNN Radio News stock market recap. The Dow Jones had gone up more than a hundred points in the past week, said the announcer; good news for mutual fund owners—a group that did not, unfortunately, include Jack.

And then came another item that wasn't good news for anyone.

"In a press conference we will carry live on CNN in a few minutes, the FBI is expected to announce that they are looking for an American scientist working for the Defense Department in connection with an espionage investigation. Dr. Daniel Ferico is considered an expert in an esoteric niche of science dealing with stealth aircraft, and may be working with an unnamed foreign government, providing them with stolen technology. . . ."

Other Leisure books by Jim DeFelice:
WAR BREAKER
HAVANA STRIKE

BROTHER'S KEEPER

JIM DeFELICE

LEISURE BOOKS  NEW YORK CITY

A LEISURE BOOK®

June 2000

Published by

Dorchester Publishing Co., Inc.
276 Fifth Avenue
New York, NY 10001

ISBN 0-8439-4740-3

Printed in the United States of America.

BROTHER'S KEEPER

The near future

The technology described in this book exists or is under development. The places, people and politics described are entirely fictional.

I changed some of the train stations, especially.

I

"Wroth"

Gen. 4/5

Chapter One

Over Central Russia

He moved through the night the way a knife moved through flesh, plunging, dividing, caressing. He had honed his body to pure metal, shorn of impurities, an infinitely sharp edge penetrating the sky. His eyes were part of his hands were part of his legs were his heart pumping the blaze of his soul.

Adrik Rashov's plane was an afterthought, a container that propelled Adrik's mind through the darkness. The heavily modified MiG-21 moved now without a shudder through a violent wind shift at 26,000 feet, following as Adrik nudged his eyes in the direction of the single flashing beacon on the tail end of a Yakovlev Yak-42 airliner, headed toward eastern Siberia. The red light high on the tail of the airliner pulled him in, a red dot growing in his brain.

If the ancient Russian airliner he was following had

once been equipped with rear-looking radar—not necessarily a given—it was now inoperative, like the wing lights it was supposed to be flashing on its flanks. But even the newest avionics suite aboard an American AWACS would have missed Adrik and his black MiG. The MiG was as stealthy as a U.S. Air Force F-22—more so, since its airframe was considerably smaller.

Adrik did not understand all of the changes that had been made to the MiG, beyond the obvious physical alterations to the trailing wing edges and tail assembly. He knew that the electronic devices packed into the dorsal tube behind his cockpit were critical to his stealth, capturing radar signals and returning perfectly matched waves of empty air, but he did not know precisely how the device worked. Nor did he care. He existed only for his mission, only for his duty. He pushed his plane toward the airliner, slowly but steadily gaining.

When he was fifteen hundred meters away, Adrik began easing back on his power. The airliner's cabin glowed with a faint, pale yellow fuzz, light streaming out like threads of stray yarn pulled apart. The light exaggerated the thickness of the airliner's fuselage. The Yak-42 was a three-engined airliner similar to a Boeing 727, with seats for just over a hundred people, but as he closed in the plane seemed as vast as the *Titanic*.

Adrik's cockpit was a cramped cave, so tight around his body that he could not fully extend his elbows on either side. The iron wall of dials and the immense radar hood that once dominated the plane's dashboard were gone, replaced by three glass screens and thick rows of push buttons. Adrik actually preferred the older indicators, though he would not have relished flying with his head locked against the radar hood.

Adrik pulled himself toward the soft belly of the Yak-42, a shark zeroing in on a swimmer. He reached his left hand to the panel above his knee and uncaged a toggle activating the GSh-23 23mm twin-barrel cannon stowed in the MiG's fuselage. The panel was brand-new, but the weapon was as old as the airframe, installed at the factory in Nasik more than three decades before. The GSh-23 was notorious for being dependable only at very close range. This was not a problem tonight; Adrik was now barely one hundred meters from the airliner, riding the eddy of its slipstream.

The Yak's high tail sat right below the gun's crosshairs. Adrik tightened his grip on the stick in front of his chest, thumb hovering over the deceptively thin button at the center as he edged his nose into position for the attack.

His heart pounded in his chest, and for a moment Adrik's metal dissolved back into flesh; the vibrations of the Tumansky R-13-300 turbojet behind his back fell away and he was a person again, not a machine, a soul and not a soldier with a duty to fulfill.

Among the people aboard the plane there would certainly be several children. He thought of his two daughters.

For a solitary second, his gaze wandered downwards. It was involuntary, a quirk, a reaction to thinking of his girls, lying far away in the warm earth where they would never be disturbed.

Adrik caught himself, tried pretending he was looking at the lights on the large master caution panel at the head of the dashboard, checking his orientation on the artificial horizon.

As if he might lie to himself.

The Yak-42, oblivious, lumbered onward, unaware of how short the line of its fate was drawn. Adrik's hand was tight on the stick. If he pressed the square button, the bullets from the MiG's cannon would lace downwards, sheering off the rear stabilizer, continuing across into the Lotarev D-36 engine over the fuselage, across again and into the left wing, lingering there before continuing through the front portion of fuselage. Each bullet would sear through the thin metal of the plane, a hundred targets at its disposal. The incendiary tracers would ignite a half-dozen fires as he swept the MiG in a killing arc. The gas tanks in the wings and center section would explode.

If God were merciful, most aboard would die at that moment.

In Adrik's experience, however, the Creator was rarely so kind. Even with its wings shot off, it would take the Yak at least thirty seconds to reach the ground, perhaps considerably more. It would seem a long time to those aboard, contemplating their deaths.

Adrik eased off slightly on the throttle, settling his MiG into perfect position, dead-on behind the plane, which was fat in the aiming circle on the heads-up display. His passive radar detectors sounded a warning that two other planes were approaching, but he ignored them—he had known that they would be here, and in fact they were part of his brother's plan.

He heard something in his earphones, a stray sound like the faint cry of a child, his younger daughter Anna waking from a bad dream.

Adrik felt a spasm in his hand and chest. His thumb froze over the trigger as the aiming pipper at the center of his windshield twitched upwards. He took a long, slow breath and narrowed his eyes, edging the plane back onto course as the targeting cue slid inexorably toward the airliner's tail.

Chapter Two

Near Goshen, N.Y.

It figured that Ziorella would pick a diner near a garbage dump for the meeting.

Jack Ferico cranked the Impala's window closed, but it was impossible to escape the smell. The FBI agent had been sitting in the lot of a tool outlet across from the diner for nearly two hours, downwind of the county landfill. By now the stench had undoubtedly worked itself into the seat fabric. This was one bucar—FBI slang for bureau or official car—Ferico would be glad to get rid of.

One good thing at least—the stink had driven his boss, U.S. Attorney Jacqueline F. Sherman, into one of the backup cars a few miles down the road. Jack didn't have to listen to her slurp tea or complain about Ziorella's sorely lacking trustworthiness.

Not that she didn't have a point. Ziorella was both a

land developer and third cousin to a mob capo; it was hard to say which would be more damning in a jury's eyes if the bust actually came off. And even without the dump's luscious aroma, the operation was heavy on farcical elements. Jack and eight members of the grandly named Federal Task Force on Local Government Corruption were waiting to get the goods on a town supervisor who had asked for a bribe in exchange for "streamlining" a development across the river. The grand total of the bribe: two thousand dollars. The surveillance team's overtime came to more than that. Considering that the development in question had 546 lots, the bribe worked out to about three and a half bucks a house—less than the gold-plated numbers that would be screwed on the mahogany front doors. Hardly the sort of crime Jack had envisioned fighting when he left his post in the Bureau's Intelligence Division for the special assignment roughly nine months before.

But both he and the U.S. Attorney were under considerable pressure from Washington to prove that the local government task force was worth the twenty-five people assigned to it. They needed the bust.

And they'd get it, assuming the scumbag showed up. Jack put his hand over his ear as Jimmy Greene, one of his men planted inside the diner, used the team's beta-test discrete-burst com equipment to bitch about how bad the coffee was.

Greene had been in the diner nearly three hours, so he was an expert on it by now. That and the rest room.

Jack was just about to order a rotation, shifting the surveillance members around so they wouldn't die of boredom or food poisoning, when one of the pickets sighted their suspect coming down the highway.

"Looks like Milton borrowed a car just for the

prom," said Melissa Curry, who was parked three miles away in a used-car lot. "Check out the Crown Vic."

Instantly, the bitching stopped and the adrenaline started flowing. Even Jack felt his heart thumping in his throat as he slipped down in the seat and eyed the mirror, spotting the gray Ford Crown Vic as it began signaling to turn into the lot across from him. Jack spotted its driver, Town Supervisor Harry Milton, glancing nervously around the lot as he parked.

Milton heaved his bucket of a stomach from the car, smoothing the wrinkles from his light-tan polyester suit as he slammed the door shut. He bent to tie his shoelace—probably a ploy to make sure no one he knew was in the diner. Satisfied, Milton walked up the diner steps, pants sagging around his shoes, shoulders stooping as if weighed down by his stomach. This was Jack's first look at him in the flesh, and the truth was he couldn't help feel a little sorry for him. Milton was paid less than twenty thousand dollars a year, and though in theory the job was part-time, the reality was that it was anything but. The guy had two ex-wives and owed about thirty-five thousand dollars more on his two-bedroom fifties-era ranch house than it was worth. No wonder he had his hand out.

Jack listened over the wire as Ziorella greeted Milton. They'd coached him a million times on what not to say, but even so Jack was surprised that he actually followed the script, saying, "Hey, how are you?" and acting as if he did this all the time.

Which maybe he did, except not for an audience.

If anything, Ziorella sounded too cool, talking about eggs and suggesting Milton try some.

"I'm not staying," said Milton gruffly. He added something else unintelligible.

Jack jerked upright in the car seat. Ziorella's mike

had been taped to his chest and until now had worked perfectly.

Ziorella said something else it missed. Milton's voice broke in and out.

Fuck, Jack thought.

"What's the problem, Harry?" Ziorella said, his voice no longer cool.

"We're not talking here," said Milton. He added something else that broke up

There was a muffled sound; Jack guessed that Ziorella was getting up.

"They're moving," said Jimmy Greene. "Something's screwed up. Milton's pissed."

They couldn't make the bust without Milton taking the money. Ziorella had left it in his car so they'd be sure to get a good picture—a tiny fiber-optic lens was fixed to the dome light.

So maybe they were going to Ziorella's car. Or maybe not.

"Where we going?" Ziorella said loudly as he came out the door.

"Just come with me," said Milton. At least the mike was working properly.

"Which way?"

"Just get in," said the town official, pointing to his car.

Don't, Jack thought to himself. But there was no way to tell Ziorella that, outside of rolling down the window and shouting. Ziorella pulled open the door to the Crown Vic.

"Hey, Boss, what we doing here?" Greene asked over the com system.

"I say we grab him," said Bruce Goldfarb, who had a car just up the highway.

"You see a weapon?" Jack asked Greene.

"Negative. But with that stomach he could hide an M-16 in his jacket and it'd be hard to see."

"He'll be unarmed," said Melissa. She'd done the background checks and had the best feel for Milton's personality.

Jack agreed with her. Still, it was a difficult moment—for Ziorella. Jack had been there himself on his last assignment, an undercover weapons deal in Russia. Three or four times, he'd been sure he was a dead man.

Not counting his visits to Moscow restaurants.

"All right, let's hang with it. Follow Ziorella's lead. He's in the car. We'll stay close," Jack told the team. He unholstered his main pistol—an oldish but still effective Sig automatic P-220 chambered for .45-caliber slugs—and placed it on the seat next to him as the FBI agents swung into a preplanned routine, cars trotting into a standard surveillance pattern as the Crown Vic set out. Jack had second position, a few hundred yards behind the suspect on County Route 213.

Either the mike had gone dead again or neither Ziorella or Milton was talking. Finally, Ziorella burped loudly.

Nobody on the surveillance team laughed.

"Excuse you," said Milton tightly.

"Yeah. Sorry. Must've been the sausage. What's this about?"

"Guy wants to talk to ya."

"What guy?" Ziorella said.

Milton didn't answer.

"Now this is getting interesting," said Greene, who by now was in his own car.

"Shit. Where'd that fucker come from?" screamed Goldfarb.

Even before Goldfarb described the truck that had cut him off, Jack mashed his foot on the accelerator and began shouting over the com circuit for the team to move in. Two black Suburban SUVs were barreling down the road, zeroing in on the Crown Vic. Goldfarb, in a brown Taurus, tried swerving in front of one of the SUVs, but missed, losing control and going off the wrong side of the road.

Jack was about a hundred yards behind them. Left hand stiff against the wheel, he reached under the dash and hit the cutoff switch for the airbags as the Crown Vic veered off the road into the lot of a Mexican restaurant. Something—Ziorella, most likely—flew out of the Crown Vic. One of the SUVs skidded nearby, a pair of gunmen climbing out with M-5 submachine guns. Jack yelled and cursed and threw his pistol back onto the seat, holding on with both hands as he rammed the vehicle just as the gunmen began firing. A black shadow loomed behind him as the Impala tore into the SUV; Jack ducked in the seat as the second Suburban grazed his rear bumper. Bullets and dirt flew in the air. Somehow Jack managed to yank the Impala free of the two Suburbans. The gunmen jumped into the first as its driver fought off the damage to the rear and skidded onto the highway. The other careened up the sidewalk to the restaurant and into the large plate glass at the front of the building.

Jack grabbed the Sig—miraculously still on the front seat—and rolled out of his car a few yards from the Crown Vic. He waved the gun in front of him as he tried to sort the frenzy into something approaching order. Ziorella was on the ground a few yards away, on the other side of the Impala; Jack leaped over the crushed hood of the car and ran to him as two of the team's other vehicles skidded into the lot.

Ziorella was hunched over, face in the dirt. Jack grabbed his shoulder and flipped him over as if he were a rug.

Only to find a snub-nosed .38 revolver in his face.

"I'm on your side, dickhead," he told Ziorella, pushing him backwards as Ziorella's gun fired aimlessly toward the sky. Jack kicked the gun away, and just barely stopped himself from kicking his erstwhile collaborator in the face.

"What the hell are you doing?" Jack demanded.

"What the hell are *you* doing?" Ziorella answered. "You set me up with these mob guys."

"Fuck you," said Jack, still unsure exactly what the hell was going on. The com set in his ear was screaming with three different conversations. The U.S. Attorney, Sherman, was on there somewhere, barking something about constitutional rights and processes.

"Everybody shut the fuck up," said Jack, talking into the mike at his sleeve. "We have one SUV on the road. Suburban, with two machine guns, M-5s, in it."

"I have it," said Greene. "High rate of speed, west toward I-84."

"Call in the state police," Jack said.

"Done," Greene answered. He kept talking, but Jack had already turned his attention to the restaurant, where the back end of the second Chevy Suburban protruded from the window. Melissa was walking slowly toward it, gun drawn. Another member of the team, Kevin Willet, was covering her from his car nearby.

Melissa ducked near the window, then cursed.

"We got a fucking fire," she screamed.

In the next second, the Suburban and much of the restaurant exploded.

As explosions went, it wasn't the biggest. On the other hand, it wasn't the smallest either. Two-thirds of the restaurant's front dining room, along with the Suburban and its driver, were diced into slices the size of taco chips. Jack and the others managed to pull out two cooks and a busboy before the smoke got so thick they had to move back. Fortunately, they were the only people in the restaurant, which didn't open until five.

Sherman had a characteristically useful remark as she surveyed the scene as the firemen arrived.

"This how you did surveillance in Russia?"

Ziorella's line was better.

"Maybe the whole thing was a setup for an insurance scam."

As near as they could piece it together four hours later, the ambush had been intended as a retaliatory hit on Ziorella for squirreling out of a mob deal some months back. Ziorella, in fact, had probably originally gone to the U.S. Attorney's office with the idea that the government would help bail him out of that mess—though he had somehow forgotten to mention it. The guys with the M-5s weren't talking, but Milton was—so much, in fact, that they'd nearly run out of tape.

That at least guaranteed the mess would be salvaged. Government corruption and tie-ins to the mob were oldies but goodies—more than enough to placate the bosses when the shit hit the fan.

Actually, the shit had already hit. Tom Pelham, the Associate Deputy Director/Investigations—Jack's boss's boss and an old family friend—called Jack personally to find out what the hell the Attorney General was screaming about.

"Jack. Jack. Shit, Jack. Two thousand bucks? Shit, Jack. You have an informer who's mobbed up? Shit, Jack. Jack. Two thousand bucks? God."

Jack considered telling Pelham that the cost of living was cheaper in upstate New York than in D.C. Instead, he opted for the "tip of the iceberg" cliché Sherman was preparing for the press.

"Don't give me that crap, Jack. Two fucking thousand dollars? You know how much that car you wrecked was worth?"

"They told you about that already?" Jack wheeled the wooden desk chair backwards in the large but sparsely furnished task force office, borrowed from the National Guard at Stewart Airport in Newburgh.

"God, Jack. You know the Attorney General himself called me this afternoon?"

"I'm sorry to hear that," said Jack. He decided nolo contendere offered the easiest and quickest way out of the conversation.

"How's your father?" Pelham said.

"Uh, well, about the same," said Jack, caught by surprise. "Still in the hospital."

"Maybe you ought to take some time off to be with him," suggested Pelham.

Jack sat up and put his elbows on the desk, pressing the phone close to his ear. "I don't know how to answer that, Tom."

"What do you mean?"

"Are you ordering me to take time off?" Jack asked.

"I'm expressing concern for your father."

"Look, I know we look a little bad on this," said Jack.

"Bad? You look like the Keystone Kops. Shit, Jack, you look like an asshole. You. On top of that fiasco on the B-3 assignment, this is going to crimp your career."

"Wait a second." Jack felt his temples flare with heat. "What fiasco? What the hell are you talking about?"

"I heard you messed up on B-3."

"Like hell. Jesus, Tom, what the hell did you hear?"

Jack's record on the inter-agency task force, assigned to help buy weapons on the Russian and Middle Eastern black markets, was exemplary.

At least he thought it was.

Shit. He knew it was.

"Tom? What did you hear? It's bullshit. Bullshit. What did you hear?"

Pelham made a kind of blustering noise, pushing air out the side of his mouth, a sound he habitually made when he was wrong but wasn't planning on admitting it.

"None of this has anything to do with your dad," Pelham said. "Look, I want to make sure that you know if you need time—"

"I appreciate your concern." Jack shifted around noisily in the creaking chair, as if someone had walked into the empty and cavernous room. "I have to wrap up some paperwork and make sure Sherman has what she needs for the press conference," he said. It was a lie—he'd finished that nearly an hour before; his deputy was wrapping up the nitty-gritty. "Got to go."

It took Jack sixty-seven minutes to drive from the task force office to the hospital where his father lay waiting for a liver transplant that even the doctors said wouldn't come in time to save him. It took every minute, every bump and pothole of the ride for Jack to prepare himself; it was as if his body needed to be bludgeoned into a dull buzz to face the pale ghost laid out against the bright white sheets.

During his eight years with the Bureau, Jack had stared down a would-be assassin and dealt with any number of murderers, thieves, and generic criminals; while there had certainly been moments of trepidation and doubt, he had never felt anything approaching the panic that pumped his heart every time he pulled off the interstate and began making his way to the hospital. He didn't want to watch his father die, yet he worried that he would arrive and the glass-enclosed ICU room would be empty. Within the past week his father had had two strokes—"exceedingly minor," according to one of the specialists taking care of him. But Jack and his sister Brianna—everyone in the family called her Bree—were now measuring his life in days, if not hours.

Turning off I-287 for the county highway that led to the hospital, Jack remembered the day he'd finally decided to join the Bureau. He was still in the Army, though on leave; he'd spent two days with friends in Pennsylvania rehearsing different ways of telling his dad, who had once been head of the FBI's New York office, unarguably the most important Bureau operation outside of headquarters. They said his father would be proud; Jack worried that the old man would tell him to his face he wasn't good enough.

It had taken him forever to mention it. They'd gone out for a long walk along Basking Ridge, a preserve thirty minutes from the house where they'd grown up. His dad spent hours there, "hunting" turkey and pheasant with a long-range camera. Jack tagged along, not saying anything when he'd had a dozen chances. They ate sandwiches they'd bought at a local deli, shared a beer, walked. He said nothing.

Finally, he blurted it out in the most awkward sentence imaginable.

"Dad, I'm signing up. With the FBI, I mean. They want me."

His father had nodded and pointed to the sky, where a hawk was slowly gaining altitude. "Red-tail. You can tell by the markings."

Jack realized later that one of his dad's cronies must have told him. In a way, his changing the subject was a compliment, as close to congratulations as the old man ever got.

Daniel, his older brother, was the one who got the congratulations; Daniel was the standard by which Jack and Bree were measured.

And yet that wasn't entirely fair. Daniel had had his problems with the old man, and obviously still bore the wounds, even if they were mostly self-inflicted. Jack's relationship with Daniel had been strained for many years now—ever since Daniel had gotten in over his head gambling during college—but the complex melange of emotions Jack felt toward his older brother included love, absolutely.

He parked, thinking about Danny, wondering what to say when he finally showed up here.

Might be upstairs already. Up for the weekend.

Visiting hours for most of the hospital population were just ending, so it was easy to find a parking spot near the entrance. Patients in intensive care could be visited at any hour, but technically, legally, Jack should have stopped at the security booth near the visitors' desk, not just to obtain a pass but to identify himself as a federal agent, entitled to carry his gun. But there were no weapons detectors on any of the floors, and Jack knew no one would stop him if he simply acted as if he knew where he was going. And he did, all too well. Jack went straight to the elevator, consciously pasting a bored look on his face.

It melted when he stepped off the elevator and saw his sister Bree pacing the wide hallway upstairs.

"Hey," he said.

"Hey," she said, stopping her pacing and coming over to kiss him. At five-four, she was a foot shorter than he was, and Jack had to lean his cheek down to accept her greeting. As she stretched to kiss him he noticed she had an unlit cigarette in her hand.

"So?" he asked.

Bree shrugged.

"You talk to the doctor?" Jack asked her.

"I talked to his nurse."

Jack nodded. Bree didn't say anything else.

"So I guess I'll go see him," he told her.

"He's asking about Danny," said Bree. "It's like an obsession."

"You call him again?"

"I keep leaving messages and he doesn't call back."

"Yeah." Danny lived in Maryland, not far from D.C. and about four hours away. But it could have been Asia for all the contact he had with them.

Bree pulled up her pocketbook and slipped the cigarette back inside. "Come on. I'll go in with you."

"You sure?" Jack asked, but Bree had already started walking. He followed her past the glass-fronted half rooms, where the light came mostly from small TV sets and the green glow of machines that tallied vital signs. Jack felt his throat constricting as he walked; by the time they reached the room where his father lay, he could barely breathe.

Jack's father's head lay propped against three pillows. His body lay off kilter below it, to the side, deflated and shallow on the bed, as if it were a sack of potatoes left to fool the nurses into thinking he was still there. Was this the man who had once carried two fellow agents down three flights of stairs and out a burning building? Or ducked through a hail of semiautomatic bullets to grab a four-year-old who'd wandered past a police barricade?

Or even the disappointed widowed single father who'd spotted the C on the report card and instituted a month's worth of math review sessions, conducted every morning at six before he went to work?

He still had his cold stare, and his voice could drain the juice from Jack's stomach. But the thinness of his arms, the blotched skin and dark bruises from the nurses' gentle handling, was more unnerving now than even his worst scolding.

"Danny." For a moment Salvatore Ferico's eyes

grew wide and animated. Then he recognized it was Jack, not Daniel; he smiled still, but the disappointment was unmistakable. "Giacomo," he said. "Giacomo, come in."

"What's with the Italian?" Jack reached for his father's hand, though it hurt to feel how soft it had become. "You think you're Grandpa now?"

"Giacomo's a good name, Jacky."

"How come you didn't use it on the birth certificate?"

"You get your tomatoes in yet?"

"Weeks ago," Jack lied. Unlike Italian, his father's gardening was an old obsession. Jack had learned a great deal about growing vegetables and flowers from him, but didn't have the time or the yard to actually plant a real garden. The tomatoes he talked about now existed only in his mind.

"How tall?" his dad asked.

"Foot, eighteen inches. No flowers yet."

"I'm behind. I was going to Adams. Haven't had a chance." His father meant the garden center near his house. "Think it's too late?"

"Nah. It's only June."

"So where's Danny?"

"I don't know, Dad." He glanced up at the TV, where CNN was on. They'd just gone to a commercial, denying him a chance to change the subject.

"I want to see him, Jack. Before I die. I want you to get Danny here."

"You're not dying." He said it emphatically, almost desperately.

"Jack, get Danny. Do that for me."

Bree stirred behind him. Somehow that helped Jack stifle the sudden surge of jealousy he felt.

"Jacky, you do that for me," said his dad. "Bring Daniel here. I want to see him. You want me to call somebody, get you time off?"

Jack shook his head.

"So you'll get him?"

"Dad—you know the last time I saw Danny? Two years."

"Jack, we saw him last Christmas," said Bree.

"Yeah—last Christmas two years ago."

"A year and a half," she said.

"He wants nothing to do with us," said Jack.

"That's not true," said Bree. "He's probably busy."

"Then how come he hasn't called you back?"

"Bring him here, Jacky," said his father. The old man's eyes were large circles, silent moons in a familiar but twisted landscape. "Be a good boy."

Jack would always wonder not why he gave in, but why he decided to leave that night, that instant, without prompting and without a plan, except to go and drag Daniel back, if necessary.

Maybe part of it was that he just couldn't stand the machines in the room anymore, or the knobby flesh lying flat around his father's elbows on the bed. Maybe it was jealousy of his older brother, who'd always been his father's favorite. Maybe it was fear of disobeying his father's order, or falling short in his eyes, or grief. Maybe it was relief to be told to do something that would take him away from the filtered air of the small room, take him away from the fact that his father was disappearing before his eyes.

Whatever it was, it plunged him into the fading twilight of the New Jersey Turnpike, stabbing the gas pedal of his Malibu. He was nearly to Delaware when he realized he was doing over ninety, and even with the FBI credentials in his jacket pocket, he better slow down.

Chapter Three

Over Siberia

Thirty years' worth of flying fatigue choked the muscles in Cal "Crow" Bain's chest, pulling at his neck and shoulders as the bird colonel blew a wad of air into his flight mask. It wasn't rust—on the contrary, the fifty-three-year-old interceptor pilot had spent more than twice as much time in the cockpit this month than the average Air Force fighter jock; he'd done that last month as well, and for a slew of months stretching back beyond the horizon. It was more like sheer experience wearing him down, his bones starting to grind together like unoiled wheel bearings. Metal fatigue ate away at the strongest wing structure like acid. Something similar worked on Crow's bones and joints and muscles, insidiously breaking them down.

Not that he'd admit it to anyone. The jet-black hair that had helped make the nickname apropos had long since turned gray, but he still stood cocky, pitched forward on bandy legs so that even at rest he seemed in motion. Crow had just aced a physical exam as well as a "mental proficiency assessment," the latter amounting to an hour's worth of jawboning with a rather loopy government shrink who pronounced him "psychologically peaking," an assessment Crow figured was probably intended as positive. Three weeks before he had won the new Gunfire Air-to-Air Games, an inter-service contest pitting the military's best pilots against each other in perfectly matched F-5's, old stick-and-rudder war birds that relied on physical and mental skills, not cursor controls. If there were better pilots than Crow in the U.S. Air Force, there weren't many of them.

But as he flexed his hand on the control stick, Crow thought to himself that maybe, just maybe, he was getting too old for this baloney/crap.

Baloney/crap being the colonel's personal designation for horseshit.

Crow's F-22 Raptor was the first of its kind, a new-age interceptor that until this week had been serving as a tester for the rest of the fleet, due on-line in the next several months. The cutting edge of American technology, the air-superiority fighter was without peer when it came to stealth and aerial performance—and, to Congress's great consternation, price. In supercruise mode as it was now, the silver-gray war bird churned through the sky at roughly 1.6 times the speed of sound, burning less fuel than most fighters in subsonic mode. Its array of sensors, which included conventional and infrared radars, covered the sky as effectively as an AWACS, giving the pilot the chance to take out enemies before they even knew he was there. As he flew tonight over southwestern Siberia at 33,000 feet—actually, 32,987.5 according to the overly precise readout on the heads-up screen in front of him—those sensors assured Crow he had the cloud-filled blackness completely to himself.

Which was the problem. He was supposed to have rendezvoused sixty seconds ago with a French Eurofighter, a Russian Sukhoi Su-37, and a Chinese J-10. The impressive collection of new-millennium aircraft was rehearsing for a dog-and-pony show three days from now. The show had been arranged for commercial as well as political purposes, and the real star was the new ATSF9 Super Concorde III passenger jet. Unfortunately, the Concorde was still experiencing what translated from the French as "problems of birth"—crews were frantically overhauling the Russian-made hydrogen cryogenic engines at an airport in northern China for its planned flight.

Maybe that was where the rest of the escorts were as well. The Raptor's high-band radar sweep picked up the airborne flight controller in a Russian Ilyushin A50 Mainstay about a hundred miles due north; the only other plane in the sky was a lumbering YAK-42 airliner trudging eastward from the Ural Mountains about seventy miles ahead at just over 25,000 feet. Crow clicked his radio into the command frequency, dialing up the Russian airborne controller and his American interpreter.

"Flight, this is Raven One. I'm beyond Charlie and no sign of the rest of my birds." He began to bank, slowing into a relatively lackadaisical orbit around the rendezvous point.

The Russian Ilyushin A50 Mainstay—essentially an Il-76 with a radar dome—was the equivalent of an American Sentry AWACS E-3, circa 1985. Among its deficiencies was a static-laden com circuit; the controller immediately asked him to repeat his message.

"Where are the other planes?" Crow asked. He

hated politics, whether it was geopolitical or the more vicious Air Force crap he had to put up with just to keep drawing his pay. And he especially hated flying in circles, figuratively or literally.

The Raptor's superefficient engine design meant that he spent about the same amount of fuel whether he was sub- or supersonic, but there was little point whipping around central Siberia at Mach 1.5. Crow eased his throttle down, the plane shuddering slightly as its speed fell down to Mach .9.

"Euro's intercept point has been changed," said the controller. "The plane will meet you near Moscow."

"That a permanent change?"

"Affirmative."

Crow snickered; the French jet was actually the oldest of the escorts, but had the most problems. Despite the billions spent on its development, its range and capabilities were severely limited.

"And my other friends?" the pilot asked.

"Uh, we're not sure about Ming Flight. We have Red Dog coming at you from the north three hundred klicks bearing, uh—"

Crow only half paid attention to the bearing numbers as the Raptor's own radar finally spotted the Sukhoi. An advanced export version of the Su-27/30/35 family, the single-place plane had undoubtedly been selected to showcase its worth to potential customers, since it was optimized as an attack plane rather than a fighter escort or interceptor. It lacked a powerful radar and its avionics couldn't compare with those in the Raptor; its air-to-air capability was rather primitive.

Crow pulled the F-22 back onto its course five miles due west of the planned intercept point, returning to the track of the Concorde III's flight. He flexed his shoulders back one at a time, stretching his muscles to keep them from cramping. A special flight suit had been developed for the Raptor; it helped pilots cope with six-g-plus turns, but did little to make long patrols more comfortable. Crow considered himself lucky to be wearing a standard flight helmet—he had been testing one with a three-D projection array the last few months, which added nearly three pounds to the pressure on his neck. While the projections put more flight graphics in front of his eyes, he didn't think it was worth the extra weight on any flight lasting more than twenty minutes.

The Raptor's stock "dashboard" was almost entirely glass. An eight-by-eight-inch multiuse video screen sat in the middle, flanked by a pair of slightly smaller displays; these had an infinite array of colors and could be slaved to any of the Raptor's systems, including the flight computer, AN/ALR-94 electronic warfare system, and the target acquisition center or TAC. Another set of smaller three-color displays sat above them; the front portion of the glass bubble windshield was filled by a heads-up display that had several display sets, depending on the pilot's needs or desires.

But while they leapfrogged beyond the technology in the previous generation of American jets, the glass-panel controls were actually obsolete—or would be, as soon as Crow and the team working with him completed functional testing of "F1," the onboard supercomputer that was essentially a silicon backseater.

And more.

Actually a set of programs and additional computing and data storage modules integrated into the Raptor's versatile "stock" flight computer, F1 performed the functions of an airborne squadron—everything from repair to intelligence to tactics. F1 reviewed mechanical, electronic, and computer functions and could repair problems in-flight. Its voice command mode—Bitchin' Betty with 'Roid Rage—translated the pilot's plain language directions into complicated flight instructions for the plane; if Crow wanted or needed to, he could fly entirely by voice. In combat, F1 could analyze an opponent's present flight state as well as its capabilities, not merely pointing out vulnerabilities but predicting what the enemy would do. It carried a tactical library with performance data on every plane flown since the Korean War, and could guide a nugget through a shoot-down of a pair of MiG-45s—the as-yet-unbuilt Russian superplane that was the nearest thing to a rival for the Raptor.

Contrary to rumors, however, F1 could not dial in NBA games off the satellite, though Crow suspected the crew of techies that served as his ground crew was working on it.

The enhanced computer brain would be added to the other 330-something F-22s scheduled to join the Air Force only if it won final approval from the Congressional panel assembled to review it. Which was why Crow and his Raptor were here—trying to add a few talking points to the dry if impressive data that would be reviewed behind closed doors in a secret Congressional briefing set for next week.

Crow's own resume had been the major reason he'd been chosen senior pilot for the Raptor/F1 project, but the fact that he was a true believer in computer-assisted piloting didn't hurt. He'd helped the programmers perfect the tactical warfare modules in the computer, and had even made some unexpected contributions to the interface. And if he'd helped the computer develop, it in turn had helped him. His flying reflexes had diminished somewhat over the past few years—something he barely admitted to himself, and never out loud. F1 more than made up the difference. In many ways, F1 was the best backseater he'd ever had.

Just now that backseater was using another of the special-edition Raptor's experimental modules to connect via satellite with an external Air Force database known as AFDI, for Airborne Flight Data Information, or "Alfie." Alfie aimed at tracking every commercial and private flight airborne on the planet; there were vast gaps, but in this case F1 was able to fill the left multiuse screen with information about the Yak-42 airliner it had spotted ahead. Vnukovo Airlines Flight 35 had originated in Moscow with a stop at Kazan; it was headed toward the far east of Siberia, with three more stops before reaching the Pacific. F1 used flight data from the Raptor's sensors as well as the plane's filed flight plan to plot a situation map on the right screen, laying out the Yak's course against Crow's and the Sukhoi's.

The controller in the Mainstay asked him to slightly alter course and drop his altitude to 25,000 feet. Even before he gave F1 the new numbers, Crow realized the change would take him fairly close to the airliner.

Not almost, said F1. Dead-on, if he dropped speed as directed.

A trick?

The Russians were very interested in the Raptor's capabilities. Crow was under strict orders not to say or do anything that would give them away. In fact, he wasn't even allowed to broadcast information about radar intercepts, since those would give valuable data about the F-22's powerful sensors. His orders were to wait for visuals on other aircraft before noting their presence.

On the other hand, he wasn't supposed to hit anything either.

Crow acknowledged the order and shifted to the new heading. Waiting until visual range would make things tight.

The Russian controller, who ought to have the Yak on his long-range radar, hadn't even painted the airliner for him yet. Interesting. The Russians weren't above using nonmilitary planes for spy missions—was this incompetence or design?

Or high-altitude chicken?

The Raptor's systems showed that the Sukhoi was running "passive"—using its detection systems but not sending out active radar, standard procedure for the Russian. The Yak ought to be equipped with at least a bare-bones radar, but it didn't seem to be operating. Which meant they couldn't see each other.

Another trick?

Crow eased back on the throttle, riding the power down until his speed was at a veritable dawdle—420 nautical miles an hour. He fell into a nasty run of clouds, obscuring his forward-looking infrared radar, which had trouble peering through water vapor. But the pulse repetition unit had a strong hold on the Yak, and F1 whined in his ear, warning that he was going to "violate the proximity protocol of an approaching civilian-identified aircraft."

In other words, he was going to fly right through the sucker's windshield.

And soon. The HUD flashed an urgent message predicting intercept in 32.3 seconds.

Was the Russian controller blind? Or did he have a thing against Vnukovo Airlines?

F1 had the Yak-42's flight data on the left MUD. There were 118 passengers aboard.

According to the Raptor's computer, Crow would miss the Yak by 152 feet—damn close if he didn't do anything.

The Sukhoi, on the other hand, was going right into the civilian's wing 3.2 seconds later.

Somebody was going to have to yell chicken.

Crow felt his chest tighten. Acid gurgled in his stomach and his fingers cramped on the stick. Twenty-five seconds. The civilian plane was just over eight miles away, nearly dead ahead, obscured by the clouds.

Crow strained his eyes to make out the airplane's lights. He had tremendous faith in the Raptor's instrument set—much more faith in the silicon than in his own tired eyes. The plane ought to be dead ahead.

He'd kick upwards and clear the airliner. But what would the Su-37 do?

The Sukhoi commander hailed him in a thick accent. Crow flicked his mike on to acknowledge.

Twenty seconds. The Raptor bucked ever so slightly as it hit the edge of an odd windstream. F1 hit full whine, worried that her pilot had lost his mind and was going to collide with the Yak. Crow steadied his right hand on the stick and tensed his body, ready for evasive maneuvers.

He ought to be able to see it. He'd lost a few seconds in his reflexes over the past few years, but his eyes were still perfect, 20-20 uncorrected.

The Raptor's passive sensors didn't detect any radar from the airliner. Poor slob didn't know what was coming his way.

Who was going to know whether he'd seen it through the damn clouds or not? Crow pressed his mike button to warn the Su-37, revving the motors and yanking the stick at the same time. In that instant he saw a glow and a hulking shadow ahead.

Then all hell broke loose.

The Raptor shot upwards like ground lightning reaching for the clouds. The Russian controller in the A-50 Mainstay yelled a collision warning. The Sukhoi tucked its wing into a rolling dive.

Crow counted three, then snapped the plane's climb

off and rolled into a tight turn. Gravity tugged at his body, nudging his old, worn bones against the thin fabric of the ejector seat. He flattened his wings, spinning the F-22 around in a training-video maneuver so precise that even F1 cooed with praise. Or at least it would have, if its programming allowed idle chatter. Crow's turn positioned the Raptor behind the Sukhoi and about a thousand feet above the Yak-42.

Which gave him a perfect view as the airliner exploded in flame.

Chapter Four

Maryland

Jack had been to Daniel's house only once before, but finding it wasn't hard; the entrance to the subdivision featured a pair of low-slung brick walls with the words "Clintondale Farms" highlighted by enough yellow-glow spotlights to land a small plane. Beyond the signs, a collection of neo-Georgian facades in alternating red and gray brick climbed the gentle hill at odd angles. Even though it was well past eleven, every third or fourth house had a sprinkler system going; overanxious motion detectors highlighted faux Japanese gardens along the sides of the driveways as he passed.

Sitting at the end of a cul-de-sac, Daniel's house was comparatively modest—merely two stories, without columns at the front, and only a three-car garage. The landscaping was mostly wood chip and rhododendron, though Jack had no doubt the rhododendrons hadn't come from the local Home Depot.

The lights flared on as he pulled into the driveway. Jack felt a slight flicker in his chest. He turned off the car engine and sat for nearly a minute before getting out. He thought about what he might say—*How come you never answer your phone?* or *Dad's dying, you know*—then just sighed without a plan and undid his seat belt.

When was the last time he'd seen Danny? Christmas a year and a half ago? They hadn't talked much. He remembered a barbecue at their father's house a few months before that. Some chance comment about a horse race made Jack think he was gambling again, but Danny hadn't used the phone obsessively. That was a sure sign; maybe he wasn't or maybe he was just hiding it.

If he was gambling again, he'd avoid the rest of them because he didn't want them criticizing him. He'd certainly avoid their father.

On the other hand, if he was gambling, sooner or later he'd hit bottom and need cash. And knowing Danny, he'd have run through his wad months ago.

So maybe he wasn't gambling again. Maybe Danny just hadn't bothered keeping in touch because he was Danny, and didn't feel like it.

Or maybe Bree hadn't left explicit enough messages on his phone. She wouldn't have used the words "Dad's dying." She couldn't. She'd make it sound like he had a cold or something.

No one answered when Jack rang the bell. He stood back on the front lawn, wondering whether to break in or not.

Serve his brother right if he set off the burglar alarm. On the other hand, Danny might not even be home; it wasn't all that late.

Jack leaned on the doorbell. He could hear it ringing inside. He rang again, waited, rang again.

He could get in through one of the windows, but if Danny wasn't home the alarm would probably bring the police.

Odds were, Danny kept a spare key handy. At least if Jack used that and the police came, he could make up some BS about not remembering the PIN.

Actually, the burglar alarm was right near the front door and he might be able to guess the PIN if it was four digits: Danny's birthday, backwards. He'd used that all the time when he was a kid.

Jack stood in the light in front of the door, examining the lawn for the spare key's hiding place. Daniel wouldn't put it in the obvious places—over the door, or under the flower pots on the small brick patio. Jack thought of the mailbox, and the lights.

Nothing there, and too obvious.

Trash cans?

Ditto, but he checked them anyway.

The rain spout?

Again, too obvious—and then he realized that Danny might put it in the gutter, but in a spot where only someone like him—six-four, with longish arms—might reach. Jack went back to the front door and reached up to the roof. He had to stand on his tiptoes to feel inside, and at first he couldn't find it. But then his finger slipped against the edge of a metal box taped to the plastic; he pulled it up and brought down the key.

Jack pushed open the front door and found the alarm box right next to it in the foyer. He flipped down the panel, scanning the plastic box first in case the code or some hint was written there. As he did, he realized it was blinking green—the alarm hadn't been set.

The light switch next to the alarm box had more switches and sliders than the control panel for a power plant. He pushed five buttons before the lights in the foyer came on.

"Hey, Danny. It's me. Jack. Yo," he yelled.

He didn't hear anything. The foyer was about as large as his bedroom, but the only furniture in it was a large Chinese vase near the door, which held a fairly battered umbrella. A pair of hiking boots with heavily scuffed toes lay next to it.

Jack tried remembering his last and only visit, trying to decide if Danny had hocked his furniture. It was too long ago to remember.

"Danny? Hey, Daniel."

Jack began walking through the house, calling his brother's name and flipping on lights as he went. He found the master bedroom at the back of the first floor of the house. It was a large suite, with an elaborate bathroom and large closet at the far end, but like the rest of the home only sparsely furnished. Besides the queen-sized bed there was only one dresser. A single, plastic-framed photo was the only thing on the wall; it was a very old picture of his father and mother, one Jack didn't recognize.

"So where the hell are you, Danny?" Jack asked the empty room.

Just to make sure his brother was out, Jack went upstairs. Only one of the three bedrooms had furniture, an obviously uncomfortable single bed where Jack would probably have to spend the night.

Back downstairs, he wandered through the living room to a cavernous suite off the side of the house. One end led to the garage and laundry room. The other contained a den and some mostly empty storage closets. Jack sat at the fake cherry desk and glanced at his watch; it was a few minutes past eleven.

The den was the only room that looked truly occupied, though in typical Daniel fashion, the dark cherry shelves and cabinets were carefully arranged and very neat. There were many photos, including several of Jack, which surprised him.

On top of the desk in front of the computer screen was a picture of the entire family taken when Daniel was about eight and Jack three or four. The sun cast long shadows; everyone squinted toward the camera. There was dust on the shelves and most of the desk, but not on the photo.

An answering machine sat in the left-hand corner of the desktop, next to an elaborate phone. The light was on, showing it was working, but the indicator said there were no calls.

So he'd listened to his messages. Maybe he'd been planning to come up at the end of the work week all along, and just being Daniel didn't bother to tell anyone. Maybe Jack had passed him on the highway. Which would figure.

Bree's phone was ringing before he remembered she usually went to bed around ten.

"Bree? Hey."

"Jacky? Where are you?" she asked. She sounded tired, but not as if she'd been sleeping.

"At Danny's. Is he there?"

"Here?"

"Did he come up or call you?"

"No," said Bree. "What's going on?"

"Aw, shoot, I'm sorry. I thought he called you back and went up there."

"I just came from there. You want me to call them?"

"Nah. Don't bother. How's Dad?" Jack asked.

"The same. Maybe a little better. He was happy about you going to get Danny, Jack. That was good of you."

"I'm sorry I woke you up," he said. "I'll see you tomorrow."

Jack hung up the phone, then punched the replay button on the answering machine to check messages. Nothing happened. He opened the lid and saw that there was no message tape. The machine had been set to deliver only an outgoing message.

More than likely, Daniel hadn't gotten any of Bree's messages over the past few days. He didn't know their father was in the hospital.

Stupid fucking genius.

Jack glanced at the family photo, probably taken only a few months before their mom passed away. The sun must have been streaming into their eyes; they were all squinting and their faces were washed out. But they were all smiling, even Danny.

Jack looked kind of dumb, standing next to his big brother. In those days, he had idolized him.

"Stupid fucking genius," he told the picture. Then he went to make himself some coffee.

The clock radio woke him up with a story about a Russian airliner crash, 123 people dying the day before in Siberia. Search teams were just getting to them now.

Jack's head felt as if he'd been drinking. He was lying on Daniel's bed, his clothes and shoes still on. His cup of coffee, barely touched and now very cold, sat on the floor near the bed.

The red numbers on the clock radio said 5:55 a.m. Daniel hadn't come in.

Probably out gambling, no?

Jack reached under the bed, retrieving his gun and shoulder holster. Then he went to the bathroom to shower. It wasn't until he was soaking wet that he realized there was no soap. Cursing as if Daniel had purposely sabotaged him, he used the shampoo instead, lathering thickly and then rinsing.

If Daniel were gambling again, it would probably be blackjack or poker. Those were his games. Jack remembered Daniel teaching him how to play Let It Ride in Atlantic City when he had just turned eighteen. He remembered one hand in particular—three kings.

The game guaranteed a payoff with two tens or higher, so Jack knew he would win. But the really big payoff would have come if the dealer gave him another king.

His heart had started to pound, and for a second he felt sure he was going to get it.

He got a three and an eight.

He'd laughed and started to leave.

Danny grabbed his arm. "You're on a roll," he said. "Come on."

Some roll. They blew three hundred bucks, Jack's entire stash from his birthday. And that didn't count what Daniel lost on his own.

That cured Jack from gambling forever. He still felt that empty failure in his stomach whenever anyone asked if he wanted to play cards. He didn't even play Lotto.

Jack rinsed his body and wet his hair, glopping the shampoo onto his scalp.

Maybe Daniel had spent the night with a girlfriend. Jack was an FBI agent; he ought to be able to figure this kind of stuff out.

Dressed, Jack went back to the den to check the telephone's quick dial. Apparently his brother didn't believe in automated dialing, or didn't know how to use the machine—none of the buttons were programmed. The phone had a caller ID window, though—Jack scrolled back through it, looking for a recurring number.

There weren't any, except for Bree's. Most of the ninety-nine stored numbers were the ubiquitous "unavailables," the phone solicitor's ID of choice. The others fell into no predictable pattern.

Not that he'd ever exactly been his brother's keeper, but Jack didn't even know what Daniel did for work these days. Daniel had a Ph.D. in some sort of engineering field. Fresh out of grad school and out from under the gambling goblin, he had helped patent something that worked like Teflon; he'd even gotten some big bucks for it. But that was all Jack knew. Bree had mentioned something about a scientific think tank with vague government connections, and Jack knew that Danny gave lectures at George Washington University; they'd met for coffee there once three or four years before. Beyond that, he didn't have a clue.

There was something tempting about the closed drawers of his brother's desk, as if he were a little kid warned away from his brother's room by a KEEP OUT sign. But Jack put off the pleasure, thinking about how he would feel if Daniel broke into his house. He went to get breakfast; when he found there were no eggs in the refrigerator, and no milk for cereal, he decided he might just as well go out and get something real to eat.

It took a while to find a place that did breakfast. Finally he passed a small dump of a diner placed almost catty-corner at the front edge of a Wal-Mart mall near the highway. If the outside seemed to date from the fifties, the inside was from the thirties. And the waitress who pushed a full cup of steaming coffee down in front of him looked even older.

"Drink," she commanded.

Jack looked up, guessing she mistook him for his brother. "You know me?" he asked.

"No."

"How do you know I take it black?" Jack asked.

"I can tell. Drink."

He did. The coffee was as good as the waitress was

surly. The blueberry-strawberry-banana pancakes—"only reason to come here before lunch"—were even better. Jack couldn't finish the entire stack, let alone the side order of bacon.

Besides breakfast, there was one other good thing about the morning—the fiasco in Goshen hadn't made the national papers. Which probably meant that it had played well enough back home that he still had a job.

And the Yankees won. Three-game winning streak.

Danny used to take him to Yankee games all the time when he was in junior high. His brother looked after him a lot after their mother died. But things changed when Danny went to college. Danny changed. It wasn't just the gambling. Part of it was that they didn't do things together like they used to; there wasn't the opportunity to. But he'd become quieter and more withdrawn, not talking.

More like their father, in a way.

When Jack finished the newspaper, he decided he would go back to the house, give Daniel another hour to show up—tops—then hit the road. He'd leave a note on the kitchen table and let his brother decide whether he wanted to see their father before the funeral or not.

He didn't like to think of it that way. He paid, left the frosty waitress a good tip. He took a wrong turn going back, and for ten minutes or so thought he'd never find the house. When he did, there was a year-old Lexus GS400 in the driveway.

He felt his anxiety about what to say choked back into his chest as he walked to the front door. He started to knock, then decided to just go in, just see his brother and get it over with, discharge his duty so the prodigal son could return home and be feted.

The door wasn't locked.

"Dan. Danny," he yelled inside. "Hey. It's me, Jack."

The front hall and living room were empty. He started for the kitchen, then heard the muffled sound of the shower at the other end of the house.

Just the thing. Surprise his hairy butt.

Scare the piss out of him.

Jack slipped into the steam-filled room quietly, barely able to control a laugh as he approached the figure behind the thick frosted glass of the shower door. Daniel's back was to him, obscured by the steam and a towel hanging on the door rack.

"Hey!" he yelled, reaching and pulling the door open.

But the person who yelped in surprise wasn't his brother. It was a woman, who jumped around and smacked her head and back against the stall.

If it weren't for her nose, she would have been model-beautiful. As it was, the slightly off-kilter angle of her face drew attention to her eyes, oval glimmers of pure sapphire. The rest of her body was molded like a sculpture, glistening with the water of the shower.

"Who the hell are you?" she demanded.

Jack managed to mumble that he would wait outside, and took two awkward steps toward the bedroom. She slammed the door behind him, emerging a few seconds later with a thick robe wrapped around her body and a towel on her hair.

She looked even more beautiful, and possibly even more angry.

"I'm sorry," he told her. "I'm Dan's brother, Jack. I'm sorry. I thought, um—I thought that was him in the shower."

The corners of her mouth folded back and she frowned at him as if he were something like sour milk. She stood about five-eight, a little lean but definitely beautiful. Even the off-kilter nose.

"And you'd just burst in on him like that?"

"Well, uh. It's kind of a kid thing, like when we were young."

"Do I look like him?"

"No." Jack paused, scratching his temple with his finger, and trying to smile weakly. "My father, our father, is dying."

"You're Jack?" She pulled the robe tighter around her body.

"Yeah."

"I'm Cara," she said without any hint of friendliness. She turned and walked out to the kitchen. He followed, watching as she made herself a pot of coffee. "Where's the milk?" she asked, looking in the refrigerator.

"There was none," said Jack.

"What did Danny put in his coffee?"

"He wasn't here. Does he take milk?"

"You look like him, or I'd think you were lying about being his brother." She slapped the refrigerator closed, took down a coffee mug from the cabinet, then put it back, deciding against having any.

"Of course I'm his brother."

"You don't know if he takes milk in his coffee?" She shook her head with disapproval, as if it were the sort of knowledge imparted by genetics. "Where is he?"

"I don't know. I thought he was with you."

"I haven't seen him in more than a month. I just got in from California."

"You an actress?"

Cara laughed. "I'm a systems analyst. Your brother didn't tell you all about me?"

"We're not, uh, that close."

"Oh."

"Seriously, do you know where he is?" Jack asked.

"Seriously, no. Have you tried him at work?"

"On Saturday?"

She shrugged.

"Let me ask you a question," he said. "Is Danny gambling again?"

"Gambling? He buys a lottery ticket every so often. Is that what you mean?"

"He play blackjack?"

"Not that I've seen."

"Where is he?"

"Not here." She shrugged. "I don't know. He's a workaholic. Maybe he's out of town or something. Sometimes he has to go to conferences and things."

"He told you he was leaving?"

"Well, no—"

"Would he?"

"Sure he would," she said.

"Take me over to his office," said Jack

"Me?" A thin wisp of wet hair had fallen from behind her ear. She picked it up with the tips of her fingernails, slipping it back in place as if it were a thread in a tapestry. "I just got back. I'm tired."

"You live with him?"

"Of course not."

"Come on. Take me to his office," said Jack. "I really need to talk to him."

"Call him. It's Turlow Industries." Cara pointed to the phone and began reeling off digits.

Daniel's voice snapped onto the line so quickly Jack didn't realize it was his voice mail at first.

"Danny, it's me, Jack. You have to come home, back to New Jersey. Dad's not too well. He needs a liver transplant and on top of that, he's had a stroke. Two. It doesn't look good." He glanced at her, then turned his back, as if that might give him some privacy. "He's dying," he said, the words choking out. "He's dying. Yeah. It's St. Anthony's Hospital in Madison. I don't know the number off the top of my head, but it's got to be in information. Or call Bree."

By the time Jack hung up, Cara had started out of the kitchen. He grabbed her arm to stop her, felt her biceps stiffen as her face flared.

"Let go of me," she told him.

Sweat erupted from at the top of his chest and the back of his neck, as if the temperature in the room had gone up ten degrees. Jack immediately loosened his grip.

"I didn't mean anything," Jack said. "I just wanted to know where you were going."

"First I'm getting dressed, then I'm going home," Cara said. "Is that all right with you?"

"Show me where his office is."

"Find it yourself."

Her bare feet slapped against the hard tiles like the paws of a lioness returning to her cubs after the hunt.

Turlow wasn't in the phone book, but it didn't take an FBI special agent to find out where it was located. Jack simply changed the last digits of the phone number for his brother's office until he got someone live to answer. Then he asked which building he'd gotten in the middle of a harangue about whether or not he was calling the right person.

But he had considerably less luck at the building itself, which was located in a Maryland industrial park. The doors were pass-locked, and when he was finally let in by a smoker, a security guard met him in the front hallway.

"Who are you?" asked the guard.

Jack sighed, then flashed his FBI creds. The man's demeanor instantly changed, but no one answered at his brother's office upstairs when they knocked. And the guard claimed not to have a key. He offered to call his supervisor to see if he could get a passkey, but Jack settled on leaving a note on a piece of paper and sliding it under the door.

"You know my brother?" Jack asked the guard as they walked back downstairs.

"Can't say that I do. I mean, probably by face, and you look a little familiar, but to tell you the truth, these scientist types, they don't mix, you know what I mean?" The guard was an older man who'd explained—twice—that he only worked on the weekends as a retirement supplement.

"What exactly does Turlow Industries do?" Jack asked.

"Your brother never told you?"

"I didn't realize it was a secret."

"It is," said the man. Unlike Jack, he wasn't joking, but it took Jack a second to realize that. "Think tank. I guess they have a lot of contracts with government agencies. I figured, you being with the FBI, you'd know that. Or at least your brother would say."

"You'd think so, wouldn't you?"

"Maybe he's kind of shielding you or something."

Outside, the humidity had built exponentially. It felt ninety degrees instead of seventy; it also felt like it was going to pour any minute. Jack looked up at the heavy clouds as he reached for his car keys.

He had just noticed how dark the clouds were when something poked him in the ribs.

Something that felt suspiciously like a gun.

"This way, Jack," said the man holding the weapon. "And please don't protest. I know you left your pistol in the glove compartment. Nice old gun, by the way."

Chapter Five

Western Siberia

Adrik shifted his weight on the thin metal folding chair. His eyes drifted slowly across the wall in front of him. The plasterboard had been taped and spackled some months before, but never painted. The screws had worked themselves through to the surface in a dozen places; one panel had slipped away from its steel support, exposing the rest room behind it. Since Adrik was the only person who used this hangar—since he was the only person allowed here at all—there was little concern to repair it. Adrik himself did not care.

When he first arrived at the base more than a year before, there was no plasterboard; the entire empty hangar, something over six thousand square feet, served as his ready room, command post, and quarters. His brother, the commanding general, had directed the workers to add partitions. At first Adrik thought Lev was looking out for him, as he had when they were younger; he appreciated the gesture. Now he thought that Lev had been planning on adding more pilots to his large private army.

If he still had those plans, Adrik couldn't tell. He was the only person who flew the Black Eagle, the stealthy MiG housed in a large hangar three times this size across the pockmarked concrete apron. And the MiG was the only combat plane permanently stationed here, though Lev commanded the loyalty of several squadrons' worth of planes at bases throughout northwestern Siberia. The only other pilots on the base handled transport and civilian-type aircraft, not interceptors. Adrik had twice suggested that the MiG have a backup pilot; Lev had nodded both times but changed the subject.

Its tail section looked like something out of a comic book, a jagged circle angling slightly upwards instead of a conventional wing-and-fin arrangement. Its main wings had triangular cuts in them, sharp indentations that looked like oversized sawteeth on the trailing edges. Still, the MiG was not particularly difficult to fly. Adrik thought it considerably "truer" than the Sukhoi Su-27M, and that plane was nearly perfect. The Black Eagle was smaller and with far less power than the Sukhoi; at heart it was still three generations older and not as maneuverable. It could not carry, much less fire, the advanced missiles of the Su-27M. In an equal fight, it was decidedly unequal.

But the Black Eagle had not been designed for an equal fight. It was designed to be nearly invisible. The odd shape of the rear helped. So did the coating of a plasticized carbon hybrid over the entire surface, including the canopy, where it cut visibility by about fifty percent. But the biggest advantage came from an array of antennas installed throughout the fuselage and controlled by a device about the size of a large lunch pail in the avionics bay. The device was able to detect and mimic different radar patterns, effectively blanking an enemy radar.

Since he activated it from the com panel, Adrik called it Radio B. He made no pretense of knowing precisely how it worked. He often spoke to the mechanics who worked on the plane before taking off and after a flight, but never to the men in charge of Radio B. They weren't off-limits—no one on the top-secret base was off-limits to him—but he had no interest in the device, beyond knowing that it worked. And he had no interest in any of the men.

He had only a bare interest in flying, actually. He was here out of duty, and he would follow orders until he was released. That substituted for interest, and would suffice.

"You've done well, brother."

Adrik jumped up, standing at attention as his brother Lev entered the room behind him. It was an old habit, rising for the commanding general, though Lev was his brother and he would be alone.

"Relax, sit," said Lev, grasping him around the shoulders. He pulled up one of the two other metal chairs and sat down, his large frame overlapping the seat. "We should put better furniture here," said Lev. "You deserve it."

Adrik shrugged. "Why?"

"Getting a nap?"

Adrik shook his head. He spent most of his time when he didn't fly here, but spent very little of it sleeping. Sleeping was very difficult.

Lev's body seemed to deflate as he sat on the chair. He did not complain of his duties and responsibilities, and only rarely spoke of his dreams and ambitions, but

Adrik saw how heavy they were in the way his brother's shirt sagged at its collar. It was as if his clothes—like his responsibilities and plans—were a size too big for his large frame.

He was still Lev to Adrik, not the leader of the White Bears. He gazed at Adrik with their father's eyes—soft and compassionate.

"I will be leaving for Moscow in the morning," Lev told him.

Adrik nodded.

"We are at the crisis point," Lev said.

Adrik nodded once more. Lev was telling him that he might not see him again. The plan was full of risk; once in Moscow, the general might be arrested or assassinated.

"I imagine all of the white birds are rustling on their perches," said Lev, referring to the generations of Siberians persecuted by the old regimes—Czar and Communist alike—and whose spirit lived on in the White Bear movement. "And the Cheka ghosts rolling in their graves."

"Let us hope," said Adrik. He shared neither Lev's political ambitions nor the poetic bent that let his older brother view his personal struggle for dominance as part of Siberia's struggle against European Russia. But Lev was his brother, and Adrik felt it his duty to encourage him, just as it had been his duty to come here and fly the Black Eagle.

Lev suddenly jumped up, clapping his hands as enthusiastically as he once had when his team scored in a hockey match. It was his one blind spot, misinterpreting his brother's encouragement. He swung his fist through the air like a boxer, then instantly became more serious—another of their father's traits.

"I thought, perhaps, you would like to go to Serov," said the general. "There is time."

Adrik's little girls were buried in Serov. So was his wife, but it was the girls he thought of. He saw them, three and five, on the last day they were alive—running in the small yard, splashing in the mud. Anna, the younger girl, had her mouth open, giggling. Lara, always so serious, folding her arms around his leg for a kiss.

He bent down and asked them if they had had enough to eat.

"Oh, yes, Daddy," they lied.

Oh, yes.

Their mother appeared behind them, her face already pale.

"Come on, girls," she scolded them, telling them to leave their father alone; he had to go.

He was angry. He wanted to stay. He wanted them to kiss and hug him. She wouldn't let him.

Or was that merely memory playing a trick? Perhaps he had wanted to leave that day, wanted to get away. That was often how he had felt. Perhaps he was to blame for their deaths.

Adrik looked up at his brother. "Thank you," he told Lev. "But I will not return to Serov."

Lev nodded. "The flight will be in two days," he said. "It should be easy. Colonel Bashkin will go over everything for you."

Adrik said nothing, returning his eyes to the exposed screws on the wall.

Chapter Six

Maryland

Jack's first thought was that he was being kidnapped by a pair of thugs who held his brother's markers. But these guys were too clean-cut for that. In fact, if they hadn't used a gun, Jack would have sworn he was caught up in a Bureau operation. They were smooth, quick, and they drove a crappy car. The back seat fairly reeked of *odeur de bucar*—spilt coffee.

Lo and behold, the supposition turned out to be correct. The car turned into the parking lot of a small office building in the middle of a highway strip of car dealerships and fast-food joints. Around the back, it stopped in front of a glass door with a Bureau insignia.

"Hey what's going on?" he asked as the goon who'd poked him opened the back door. "What was with the gun show?"

"Just shut the fuck up," said the man.

Heckle and Jeckle led Jack through a short, narrow hallway to an empty conference room. The furniture was government-issue gray, and the place looked like it would fit in the middle of every Bureau office suite Jack had ever seen. But the location was odd; the Silver Springs office wasn't all that far away—nor was D.C., for that matter. So what were they doing out here nestled between McDonald's and Dunkin' Donuts?

Besides the obvious.

A short, slightly overweight woman with shiny black hair trimmed almost to a crew cut entered through the far door. She wore an FBI tag on a chain around her neck as if she'd just come back from a bust or serious photo op. She held her hand out and identified herself as Special Agent Amanda Boyle.

"One of your schoolboys put his pistol in my kidney," Jack told her, ignoring the offer to shake hands.

"Where's your brother?" was her answer.

"Danny?"

"You have another brother?"

"What does he have to do with anything? One of your schoolboys just broke the law."

Boyle reached into the pocket of her thick tweed suit. At that point Jack wouldn't have been totally shocked if she pulled out a gun. But all she did was slip out a business card. "If your brother contacts you—when your brother contacts you—I'd appreciate hearing about it." She slid the card across the table.

"You know I'm FBI, right?"

Boyle gave him a sardonic smile. She straightened and walked back toward the door.

"I really would appreciate knowing what's going on," Jack told her. "Or do I have to call your boss?"

"If you leave now, the schoolboys will drive you back to your car. Otherwise, you walk."

Fingers balled into fists under his folded arms, Jack sat silently in the back of the Chevy as the two agents drove him back to his car. He realized that he was being treated to some sort of command performance, but couldn't begin to decipher it.

His brother?

If Boyle had been older and the circumstances different, he might have figured this as some sort of elaborate joke having to do with his father and his old cronies. But that obviously wasn't the case.

His brother?

Why didn't Boyle care about the gun in his ribs? Pulling a weapon without cause on a subject, let alone a fellow agent, was a serious infraction, potentially a "four-bagger"—an internal-discipline matter that called for censure, transfer, suspension, and probation.

To say nothing of a good ass-whipping.

Jack resisted the urge to comment on Heckle and Jeckle's boyish charms when they pulled up behind his car at Turlow; he didn't even bother asking for their names. The driver handed him the Sig, saying the clip was in the Impala's backseat. Jack tucked the gun into his holster without retrieving the bullets and started the Impala with a delicate click of the key—the thought that a bomb had been planted flicked through his head the moment before the engine caught. But there was no bomb, and as far as he could tell driving to the Beltway, he wasn't being followed.

He got off the highway after three exits and found a McDonald's with a phone next to the entrance. His first call was to Boyle's number, to make sure she was for real. He clicked down when she answered. Then he took out his address book and called the agent in charge of the western Maryland offices, who in theory ought to be her boss.

Billy "Beef" Bozzone had been a "first-office agent" or rookie under Jack's dad. By now well connected with the hierarchy, Beef was good for advice on everything from Bureau lore to single-malt Scotch. Beef had told him to accept the transfer out of Intelligence and into the special task force position with grace, arguing that it was meant as a serious career booster.

Maybe Jack ought to hold that against him.

Bozzone's wife's voice was on the answering machine, announcing that they weren't home.

"Beef, this is Jack Ferico. Listen, I just had a bizarre experience with a special agent in your territory. I don't know that she's working for you, but I sure as shit want to find out."

He flipped the page in his book to get his brother's phone number, and left it on the machine. Then he tried Beef at his office and left the same message.

Jack considered calling Pelham, but decided not to, at least until he figured out who Boyle was and what she had up her ass. The Deputy Director wasn't going to appreciate being bothered on a Saturday with anything less than an assassination plot against the President.

Even then he'd probably ask if shots had been fired.

Jack bought a quarter-pounder with fries and a shake—no sense letting a McD's go to waste—then drove back to Daniel's house. He checked the house carefully, gun drawn, wondering how paranoid he should be.

The caller ID unit blinked with Bree's number. Jack called his father's hospital room, where his sister picked up on the second ring.

"Hey," he said.

"Hey," she said back.

"How's Dad?"

"Sleeping."

"And?"

"Menza-menz," she said. "The doctor was in before I got here. He told the nurse he was unchanged. I think Dad's slipping. He keeps asking for Danny. That's all he talks about now. Where's Danny, where's Danny. It's driving me nuts."

"Yeah. You called."

"Yes. So where's Danny?"

Jack wasn't sure what to tell her. "I can't find him," he told her. "He tell you anything about a girlfriend?"

"I don't think we've said more than five words in the past six months, maybe longer," said Bree. "You know Danny."

"What's up his ass, you figure?"

"Jack."

"I met his girlfriend. She told me he works at Turlow Industries. It's a think tank or something. He tell you about that?"

"The last time I talked to him, he said something about Parm or something," said Bree. "He was a consultant. I think he mentioned the Energy Department."

"The Federal Department of Energy? Parm? You don't mean DARPA, do you?" said Jack. Usually pronounced "dar-pa," the acronym stood for the Defense Advanced Research Projects Agency. It was a major defense research group connected with the Pentagon.

Suddenly the meeting with Boyle made sense.

Very bad sense.

"I thought it was Parm," said Bree. "Like the cheese. I think it was, because he made a joke."

"You know what he was doing?" Jack asked.

"Whatever he does. Weird science." Bree intended it as a joke, but her voice was so drawn and hoarse it sounded like a complaint. Jack could almost see her turning toward their father as she spoke, her lip starting to quiver as she watched him inching steadily toward the end.

"He's asking for Danny again, Jack."

"Yeah, okay, listen, Bree, let me see if I can run down something," Jack told her. "I'll come back tonight."

"Make it soon, all right, Jacky?"

"No sweat, girlie."

The words were out of his mouth before he could stop them. It was his father's expression, not his. Bree took a soft breath through her lips before hanging up.

The wooden filing cabinet next to Daniel's office in the den contained two dozen hanging folders, more than half of them empty. The thickest file held bank statements dating back five years and stopping eight months ago; according to the bank statements, his brother had less than three thousand dollars all told in his bank accounts. That was a hell of a lot less than Jack expected. There were no other papers, no mortgage coupons or reconciliations, no credit card receipts, no pile of bills that might give a clue about Daniel's whereabouts, or what he was up to these days.

Jack went through the desk and the rest of the den—quickly at first, then doubling back more slowly. He found a few old brochures in the drawers, an enclosure for buying Savings Bonds on the Internet, a catalog of sports clothes. Daniel was neat, but no one was this neat—Jack couldn't imagine why he didn't find a stash of receipts somewhere, or even a worn *Penthouse.* He went up to the bedroom and checked the drawers there; the clothes looked more or less fresh and certainly folded, and while he couldn't tell what might or might not be gone, there were no signs that the closet or bureau was understocked. The kitchen also yielded no new information, beyond the already obvious fact that Daniel had not gone shopping in a while.

Being an FBI agent—and having worked in the Intelligence Division—Jack couldn't help but jump to conclusions about the Bureau's interest in Danny. His scientific work probably had a great deal of commercial value. The Bureau had several sections concerned with commercial espionage; Boyle might be working with one, at least temporarily. It would explain why she was using the satellite office and not Silver Springs.

The idea was a bit out there—Teflon substitutes didn't strike him offhand as worthy of federal investigation—but Jack knew from his own experience that many things that appeared trivial from a distance were actually very important. Or at least worth big bucks.

He went back to the den and tried Beef again. Still not home. Jack thought of calling Cara—Boyle probably would have talked to her, and maybe given her more of an idea of what was going on. Her goons would certainly be less careful talking to her than to him; they'd drool the whole time, and undoubtedly at least hint at what they were up to, trying to impress her.

She hadn't told him her last name, so he couldn't look her up in the phone book. But he had written down her license plate number when he'd moved his car.

Thinking Daniel's phone was bugged was surely paranoia. Nonetheless, Jack left the house and went back to the diner where he'd had breakfast, to use the pay phone. He called the weekend desk sergeant in the Newburgh Police Department and talked him into calling Maryland to run the plate.

"Gonna cost you a spaghetti dinner," said the sergeant, Mike Marg.

"Done, Mike. No problem."

"Hey, you look pretty good in this morning's paper."

"I do?"

"Finally nailed Milton, huh? I wouldn't have figured him for a mob guy. You know, I voted for him. Twice, I think."

"Sorry to hear that."

"Hey, he got us pay raises two contracts in a row. What can I tell you?"

It took nearly twenty minutes for Marg to get the information, and when he did, Jack had him double-check it—the car came back registered to a Stephen Karn.

"Surprised, G-man?" asked the sergeant.

"Interested is a better word," said Jack, hanging up the phone.

"Who's Stephen Karn?" Jack asked when Cara answered the door.

"What are you talking about?"

"Let me in."

"Why?" she asked, pulling her body close to the condo door, which still had a chain lock on it.

"FBI talk to you?" Jack asked.

Cara gave him a quizzical look, then slipped open the door. If she'd come here to take a nap as she'd told him earlier, she must have changed her mind. She was dressed—a short cotton skirt that emphasized how smooth her legs were—and her expression was anything but sleepy. She scowled as he closed the door, turning away quickly and leaving him to follow her into the kitchen.

Jack's shoes squeaked on the marble tiles of the foyer hallway. The kitchen had a cathedral ceiling; its elaborate stove, granite countertop, and cherry cabinets looked like the stage setting for a television cooking show.

"Still looking for your brother?" She didn't use a lot

of makeup—she didn't need to—but her pale red lipstick made her mouth seem softer, even more inviting.

"Your car is registered to Stephen Karn. I checked the phone book. He lives here."

Cara laughed. "You see him anywhere?"

"You married? Or is he your sugar daddy?"

Her eyes became narrow points, and for a moment Jack thought she might actually reach across the counter to take a slug at him. She'd be giving up close to eighty pounds, but there was so much fury in her face that Jack felt a twinge of fear.

"Stephen is my ex. The divorce came through three weeks ago. I got the condo; he got the house in Connecticut. Frankly, I think I got the better end of the deal. The damn house always collected dust and Connecticut's too damn cold in the winter."

"What about the Lexus?"

"He has the Mercedes. And the Expedition. The registration is still in his name. It's in the glove compartment. Go check it. Be my guest."

"Where does my brother work?" he asked her.

"I told you. Turlow."

"Doing what?"

"How the hell would I know? He's a consultant. Something with metal or film or something. God, he's your brother. I'm just his girlfriend."

"For how long?" Jack asked.

"Long enough."

"He mention something about Parm to you?"

She shook her head.

"How about DARPA?"

"Got me."

"Did the FBI come to talk to you?"

"The FBI? Why?" Cara backed against the counter. "You work for them, don't you? What's this all about? Is Danny in some kind of trouble?"

"I haven't a clue. What did you do when you left his house this morning?"

"I took a nap."

"You don't look like you've been sleeping."

"If this is a trick to get me into my bedroom, it's not going to work."

"Very funny. Call Daniel now," he said, pointing to the phone on the wall.

"At home?"

"At work."

Cara stamped her long fingers on the phone keys, pounding each number. She listened to it for a moment, then abruptly handed the phone to Jack.

He heard his brother's voice announce that he wasn't at his desk, but would call back if a message was left at the beep. It was the same message he'd heard earlier.

"Where's Danny?" Jack asked her again, hanging up.

"You tell me. You're his brother."

"Has he been gambling?"

"What is it with you and gambling?"

"When Daniel was younger, in college, he used to gamble a lot. It got him in big trouble. Has he been gambling lately?"

The anger in her eyes softened; for the first time since they'd met she looked worried as she shook her head. "I don't know. Not that I know. I mean, I don't know. Should I be worried about him?"

Jack wasn't sure what to tell her; he wasn't sure what to tell himself. He took a business card from his wallet and put it down on her counter, then grabbed it back and wrote Bree's number, his own home number, and the name of his father's hospital down.

"I'm taking Monday off. Until then, try my sister Bree first, then the hospital. I don't know what the hospital's number is, but it's easy enough to get. My dad's first name is Salvatore. Tuesday, and after that, try me at work first. Then my house, then the hospital. If you see him. And if anyone from the Bureau contacts you, cooperate. But let me know, okay? My dad—his dad—really wants to see him, and there isn't much time."

Waiting in the condo lot for the traffic to break, Jack hit the scan button on the radio. It stopped on a Baltimore Orioles game, with the Birds leading the Tigers 10–2. That was about the last thing he was in the mood to hear; he hit the scan again, and it flipped over to the CNN Radio News stock market recap. The Dow Jones had gone up more than a hundred points in the past week, said the announcer; good news for mutual-fund owners—a group that did not, unfortunately, include Jack.

And then came another item that wasn't good news for anyone.

"In a press conference we will carry live on CNN in a few minutes, the FBI is expected to announce that they are looking for an American scientist working for the Defense Department in connection with an espionage investigation. Dr. Daniel Ferico is considered an expert in an esoteric niche of science dealing with stealth aircraft, and may be working with an unnamed foreign government, providing them with stolen technology. . . ."

Chapter Seven

Hokkaido, Japan

Of all the things Crow might have expected when he landed his F-22 several hours after the Yak blew up, being surrounded by two-dozen Air Force Special Ops troops on the runway was probably the last.

"You expecting me to hop back in the cockpit and turn the cannon on you?" he growled, stepping off the crew ladder at his temporary base near Nayoro on Hokkaido into their small semicircle. His maintenance crew—ordinarily waiting for him with a small army of support vehicles—was nowhere to be seen.

"Excuse me, sir, but I have to request that you turn over your personal weapon," said the captain in charge of the security detail. Flanking the six-foot-eight captain were two sergeants with M16A3s held across their chests.

"I don't carry a gun," Crow said. He put his fists on

his hips, more than a little annoyed by the look of disbelief that spread over the captain's face. Technically, an Italian NATO general was in charge of the Raptor mission. But that was a paperwork fiction. Crow had seen him exactly once. *He* was responsible for the plane, its flight, and the crew; the security people at least nominally worked for him.

Tell that to their guns, which snapped forward to challenge position as Crow took an annoyed step toward the captain. He had to pull his head nearly straight back to return the taller man's scowl. But before the pilot could ask what the hell was going on, a pair of Humvees shot down the tarmac, stopping so close the security detail flinched.

"Admiral needs to see you right now, sir," said a young Navy ensign, hopping out of the first vehicle. He was wearing full combat gear.

"Admiral?" said Crow, even more confused than before.

"Sir, yes, sir."

Crow looked at the Air Force Special Ops captain for an explanation. "We will secure the plane, sir," the man told him.

"You're to carry all relevant documentation with you. Your tapes, sir," added the ensign, just in case Crow didn't understand he was to bring the flight recording media—actually minidiscs—from the plane.

"What f'ing admiral are we talking about?" Crow asked.

"Admiral Mober, sir," said the ensign.

"Who the devil is he?"

"The devil would be the top cheese in the Pacific Fleet, which somebody at the Pentagon has decided we're attached to, apparently so the Russians have an important uniform to scream at." Major Fred Rosen popped his head over the top of the Humvee and gave him a sardonic grin. "Hey, Crow. Looks like we're going sailing."

The major tossed Crow a small bag that looked like the type used by banks for cash transfers. It had a cable lock at the top.

"You have to grab the disc box and seal it, Okay?" Rosen added. "Get one of our Navy friends to watch and see you don't have a demagnetizer in your hands when you do it, okay? I know it's all a pain in the ass, Crow," he added in a more respectful voice, "but I'll dope you out on the way. Russians are screaming like they want to go to war. They're claiming you smoked the airliner."

The Seahawk helicopter bucked like a pickup truck driving down a dry creek bed. Crow, hands balled into his armpits, stared toward the open door of the helo, exhausted, confused, and angry—though not necessarily in that order. The bag with the recorded flight data and images—part of a special recording suite that helped the techies work out the bugs in the new plane—sat on the floor between his legs. The Yak's inexplicable explosion was threatening to become an international incident, and it didn't take Rosen's cold analysis for Crow to realize it could lead to the forced retirement he'd been ducking for nearly a decade.

That or a Russian firing squad.

"You didn't shoot it down, right?" Rosen asked as the Navy helo skimmed over the choppy sea toward the admiral's flagship, an aircraft carrier about fifty miles out to sea.

"Screw you," said Crow.

"That's what I figured," the intel officer replied cheerfully. "But I know how you guys like to blow stuff up, so I figured I ought to ask."

"Screw you."

"It's because of this Siberian thing," Rosen said. His voice had two tones—completely sarcastic and almost naively reverential. He switched back and forth freely, sometimes in the same sentence. Mostly he was reverential when he talked about world politics, which he did now, his eyes glinting wide in the shadowy interior of the helicopter. "The Siberians are making all this money from their oil and gas and coal, but they don't have autonomy and they're pissed. See, if you look at this in the historical context, it's just one more working out of what the Soviet states have gone through for the last thirty years, basically catching up with the rest of history. Except that the people on the airliner probably feel a little short-changed by the process. I mean, if they could feel anything."

Rosen launched into a long explanation of the Siberian faction's grievances. Crow listened silently, his fury continuing to ferment. He wasn't particularly interested in becoming a scapegoat in a conflict that dated to the Czars.

"They call themselves the White Bears," said Rosen, summing up the present alliance of Siberian rebels and semi-rebels, all of whom held positions in the legitimate government. "They control something like two divisions in the army, which is nothing, and a great deal of the air force, but not the plane that met you. Otherwise, I think the rest of the government would be blaming them for the shoot-down."

"What in God's name does it have to do with me?"

"Nothing," said Rosen. "It's a diversion."

"Nothing?"

"The Siberians want to delegitimize the present government, so they don't want the peace treaty to go through. They're using this as evidence that the Americans are out to kill Russians. Meanwhile, the government wants to divert attention from the split with the White Bears, and at the same time show they're macho enough to stand up to the Americans. Plus they haven't a clue why the Yak went down so they have to blame something. Or excuse me, almost blame something—they just want an investigation. You're not charged with murder."

"That's nice."

Rosen shrugged and pulled a thick folder from his briefcase. "You know, I did a briefing paper for you on the background political situation before we came over to Japan. Didn't you read it?"

Crow shrugged. It was the intelligence officer's job to worry about crap like that.

"Well, relax. The discs will show you didn't do it." Rosen paused. "Right?"

"Fuck you, right."

"Ow," said the major, with mock hurt. "I thought you didn't use those dirty words."

Crow shook his head and leaned back in the webbed canvas rack that served as a passenger bench in the utility helicopter. He'd nearly been bitten by a diplomatic conflict once early in his career, when a Soviet reconnaissance plane he was assigned to intercept near Alaska developed engine trouble. He had led the plane to a civilian airfield—to the consternation of both the American and Soviet governments. Fortunately for him, it was just after his brief tour in Vietnam, where he'd shot down a MiG-17; his stock was high enough to ride out the trouble, which was total baloney/crap to begin with.

How was his stock these days? He had a lot of friends with stars on their shoulders, but there were also plenty of people who felt he was too old to be flying. A few might actually resent the fact that he'd side-stepped their offers to help get him promoted to general—a promotion that would have meant stepping down as the Raptor's lead pilot.

One of the papers in the stack Rosen had been studying slipped to the floor. Crow bent to retrieve it.

He'd expected some briefing paper on Siberia or Russian politics. This was anything but. The quality was poor, but it looked like a photocopied picture of a bound man hanging from a barn post.

Minus his head.

"You want to talk about this?" he asked the major.

Rosen laughed and stuck the sheet back in his pile. "Oh, this. Don't worry. Just one of my cases."

"Cases?"

"Murder in Seattle. Could be a good true crime."

"You're a detective now?"

"Nah. I'm going to write a true-crime book. At least I'm thinking about it." Rosen pushed his legs out along the helicopter floor, then cocked his head around as if he were lounging on a deep sofa and confiding a dark secret. "I'm thinking of going into the reserves. You know I have twelve years in?"

"You're not old enough to retire."

"Hey, I'm thirty-two. I'm thinking of getting married." Rosen had a very serious look on his face; he'd been hanging around a lot with a female lieutenant who worked with the press office.

A lieutenant whose face made a Great Dane look handsome, but Crow wasn't one to talk. His ex-wife's haircut made her look like a poodle.

It was her yapping he couldn't stand.

"Everybody's got to leave home sometime," said Rosen. "Even you."

Crow grunted as the helicopter turned abruptly and began to descend.

"Uh-oh," said Rosen, stuffing his papers into a

manila folder and then back into his canvas briefcase. "Looks like we're not going to see the admiral."

"What do you mean?"

The intel officer got up and went to the large window across from them, grabbing onto an overhead strap as the helicopter bucked into a descent. "I may be pretty dumb about the Navy, but I do know admirals live on big ships like aircraft carriers. And I'd say we're landing on something more like a tugboat."

It turned out to be a minesweeper. And the man they met in the captain's quarters—slightly bigger than a pantry, with a cot where the canned peas should be—wasn't an admiral. In fact, he wasn't military at all. Dressed in an ill-fitting gray sports coat, he plucked at a thin goatee with one hand and held the other out to the two men as they joined him.

"Sorry about the accommodations," said the man, who nonetheless ushered them inside with the flair of a maitre d' at an expensive restaurant. "This is the best the captain could afford us, and I didn't want to insult him. I'm Dr. Blitz." He pushed back against the door after making sure the two Marine guards outside were standing sufficiently far away. "I'm Deputy Director of the NSC and a special, uh, unofficial representative for the President."

Rosen nodded solemnly. "I've heard of you."

"Nothing bad, I hope," said Blitz. He smiled like he was making a joke no one in the world had ever heard before. Then he pointed at the security bag in Crow's hand. "The flight recorder from your mission?"

"Something like that," said Crow, irked by the civilian and his casual attitude.

"Very good. Hold on to it, Colonel."

Blitz squeezed by them and leaned against a narrow fold-out desk. He sighed, lifting his head up so strongly that his wire-rimmed glasses nearly bounced off the bridge of his nose. With the gesture his entire demeanor changed.

"Colonel, you're going to be debriefed about the incident with the airliner by some of Admiral Mober's men on the aircraft carrier. The helicopter will take you there when we're through." Blitz worked his hand like a jackhammer, poking sharp holes in the air. "The things you and I discuss right now will not come up. Is that understood?"

"I'm not quite sure I follow."

"Your debriefing about the flagship will be conducted with Russian officers present." Blitz's hand slashed away. "Obviously, you have to be truthful. You will not lie. But I'm sure I don't have to remind you not to extend their knowledge of your plane."

"I'm not stupid," said Crow.

"Yeah, I realize that. But let's not fuck up, okay? No offense, Colonel, but consult with Rosen if there's a question of what's in the clear and what isn't. And if you have any doubts," he added, pointing to Rosen, "tell him to keep his mouth shut. Period. You're the bad cop, he's the good cop." He turned back to the colonel. "The man who analyzed the flight telemetry and satellite data for me says that you were 3.2 miles away from the airliner when it exploded. Is that correct?"

"Sounds about right." Crow started to ask why the flight had been tracked by satellite, but Blitz cut him off.

"You told the Russian flight controller you saw nothing."

"I saw it explode."

"You saw nothing near the airliner, as in another airplane," corrected Blitz.

"The Sukhoi, I believe, had cut off to the south. It'll

be there. I picked it up at a hundred miles, maybe a little before. I wasn't in distant scan."

"You have a chance to review the radar imagery?"

"Why would I?"

"I take that as a no. Turn the discs over to the admiral if he directs you to do so. He's been briefed on the security details."

"There was nothing else on radar, if that's what you're getting at," said Crow. "I'm positive."

"That's the problem," said Blitz. "This is code-word material. Alpha Ruby." He turned to Rosen. "Major, I assume you've never heard of that combination, or of Shadow R?"

"No way," said Rosen, shaking his head.

"You either, right, Colonel?"

"Haven't a clue."

"Shadow R is a CIA designation for a low-observable Russian interceptor project. A very stealthy plane. It's been in development for some time outside the normal Russian Air Force channels by what is easiest to describe as a breakaway faction of Siberian generals. I'll spare you the political details; the Russian power structure is as byzantine as it gets."

Blitz glanced at Rosen. Crow had the feeling that Rosen wanted to ask for the full lecture, but Blitz rushed on before he could.

"Suffice to say, the main Russian government either is unaware of the project or sincerely believes it's years from going operational," Blitz told them. "We have good intercepts and humint on that. But they're wrong. It's flying now. The Russians who are working on Shadow R call it the Black Ghost or Black Eagle. We have extremely little information about it, but we're confident that it achieves its low profile both mechanically, like your jet, Colonel, and electronically. It carries a device that is able to fool radars, and I have to tell you that it is very, very effective, as your discs will no doubt prove."

"You're telling me this thing shot down the airliner?"

Blitz nodded. "Absolutely."

"There was nothing in the air between me and that airliner," said Crow.

"It was most likely behind the Yak," said Blitz.

"At close range, active radar will pick up a Raptor or a B-2," said Crow. "I've been there. I've seen it. I've painted F-117s with an APG-70 in an F-15. Stealth just narrows the detection envelope; it doesn't remove it. Five miles away and anything's visible to radar."

"Depending on the actual angle of attack, I'm told the MiG could have been as far away as two miles when the airliner exploded. It may have been much closer. We believe it can be detected by the Raptor's AN/APG-77 radar at three miles," added Blitz, "but of course we haven't had a chance to field-test that. We've had a satellite trained on the area for several months now, but the data is extremely difficult to interpret. Two teams are working on new radar detection modes, neither one of which, I'm told, will boost detection much past ten miles. Your discs may help, once we copy them. In any event, that work won't help us in time."

"Time for what?"

"We believe Shadow R will try to disrupt the Concorde III's flight. The Siberian forces who call themselves White Bears—I'll spare you my tortured pronunciation of the actual Russian words—are hoping to shoot down the Concorde and unbalance the four-part alliance it's supposed to be showcasing. They want to disgrace the present government as a way of gaining power. They're also not particularly fond of the Russian Premier, who'll be on the plane."

"So will our Vice President," said Rosen.

Blitz said nothing, squinting instead as if something were in his eye.

"What's this plane like?" Crow asked.

"It's like a MiG-21," said Blitz. "As a matter of fact, that's what it is. A MiG-21 version J, at least back to the tail."

"A Fishbed?"

"They've made a number of changes," said Blitz dryly. "And I may have the base version wrong. In any event, Shadow R remains small, maneuverable, and can go like hell if it has to. It's also relatively cheap to convert into a stealth plane, which, while of little consequence to you, is another reason we want you to shoot it down if it gets off the ground. If it succeeds, every terrorist with half a million dollars and access to an airfield will want one. To say nothing of Libya, Iran, Iraq, China—even Russia."

Rosen laughed as if it were a joke, but Blitz didn't even crack a smile.

Crow had come up against a MiG-21 during his brief stint in Vietnam at the end of the war. He hadn't done very well; in fact, he'd almost been shot down. Though in theory outclassed by Phantoms, the planes had been deadly in the hands of an experienced pilot.

"No sweat," said Rosen. "We'll just put a pair of heat-seekers in the Raptor's belly and nail the little bastard from behind."

"That will be a problem," said Blitz. "As the admiral will no doubt tell you, the Russians are fairly well convinced that you had nothing to do with the Yak going down. As far as we can tell from our intercepts, they believe the airliner was destroyed by a time bomb planted by the Siberian extremists. But publicly, they're obliged to take a more neutral tact; they can't accuse the White Bears without engendering the outright split they fear. They're going to insist you and the other planes take off unarmed, and they're going to want inspections to make sure that's the case. And they'll be monitoring the flight the whole way."

Chapter Eight

Maryland

He listened to the press conference the whole way back to Danny's house. There wasn't that much to listen to; the press conference itself consisted of a short statement and three questions, about as informative as the label on a soup can. The man in charge of the investigation, a senior agent from the West Coast Jack didn't know, said Daniel was wanted "in connection with" an investigation, but offered no details about an indictment, let alone what the specific charges might be. Nor did he say what country or company Daniel was allegedly assisting, though he answered yes when asked if it would be fair to characterize the investigation as one involving "some form of espionage and important secrets, proprietary and otherwise."

A commentator who came on afterwards with obviously leaked information supplied the gory details:

Daniel had been involved in stealth technology, and had been working on the manufacturing process of high-tech polymers. He was suspected of selling or giving secrets to "a private group" that might or might not be connected with the Russian government. He had bought an airline ticket to an "unspecified location in Europe" four weeks ago, and had not reported to work since.

The commentator also noted that Daniel had been arrested for illegal gambling twice—though he conveniently left out the fact that both arrests were nearly twenty years ago.

The man also said that, if his sources were correct, Daniel would eventually be charged as the first American since the end of the Cold War to "defect" to Russia.

"Assuming, of course, my sources are correct," he added with a snicker, implying there was no question they weren't. The newscaster back in the studio answered in sententious tones that the FBI would hardly have held a press conference if they didn't have strong suspicions that something illegal was "afoot."

Jack had never heard the word "afoot" outside of a TV dramatization of Sherlock Holmes. He flipped the radio off in disgust.

Why hold the press conference with so little information to release?

There were only two reasons he could think of. One was to screw some newspaper or TV station before it could put out the story as a "scoop."

The other was to sweat someone connected with the case.

Inside Danny's house, Jack marched to the den and grabbed for the phone. It took information an eternity to find the number for the hospital. Bree answered his father's phone with a shaky "Yes?" and Jack knew they had been watching on TV.

"It's Jack," he told her.

"Oh, Jacky, what's going on? Daddy was watching CNN. He wants Danny back. What's happening to us?"

"I don't know, Bree."

"This can't be true, can it? It can't be. Daniel—he could never be a spy. Never. Not Danny. What secrets does he have?"

"I don't know," Jack told her. "I'll have to talk to some friends of mine. I don't understand what's going on yet."

She lowered her voice to almost a whisper. "Do you think he's gambling again, Jack?"

"I don't know," he said. He felt defensive, instinctively defending Danny just as he would have years ago, even though it was the most logical explanation—the only one, really.

"Daddy wants to talk to you," Bree said.

"Aw, Bree. I don't know what the hell to tell him."

"Here, Daddy. It's Jack."

Daddy. She was reverting to childhood too.

"Jack? Where's Danny?" His father's voice was a distant but demanding rasp.

"I don't know, Dad."

"He didn't do this thing. Bring him back. Clear his name and get him back here. I want to see him before I die."

"You're not going to die," said Jack.

"Bring him back, Jacky. You can do that, can't you?"

"I don't know that I can."

"You need me to make some calls?"

"No. It's okay."

"Get me Tommy Pelham's phone number," his father told him. "Tommy'll straighten it out."

"I can handle it myself, Dad," said Jack.

He could have been ten years old, talking about a bully in school.

"Bring him back," said his father.

"All right, Dad. Relax."

"Promise."

"You want me to promise to do something I can't?"

"You can, Jack. Promise me. Go clear his name. You're in the Army."

Jack nodded silently, holding the phone, barely breathing. When Bree came back on, he told her that he would try to find out as much as he could before coming back to Jersey.

"Can you straighten it out, Jack?" she asked. "It's got to be a colossal mistake. That's the only explanation."

"I'll find out what I can," Jack said.

"Daddy wants—"

Jack hung up before she could complete the sentence.

A lot of things made sense to him now, beginning with the suggestion that he leave B-3 for a post that didn't match his background and training. "Federal Task Force on Local Government Corruption." What a hunk of flaming bullshit. He'd been shunted away from intelligence because they were watching his brother, and probably suspected him as well.

No wonder Pelham had suggested he take time off yesterday.

The bastard. And Jack had thought he was being nice for his father's sake.

Why the hell didn't they talk to him?

Would *he* have, though? If it were Beef's brother, say?

Shit, yeah.

Probably.

Jack sat at Danny's desk, calling every agent in his little address book. Not one answered the phone.

Hell of a coincidence.

As he hung up after one more futile round, Jack

accidentally slapped his arm against the picture frame of the family photo on the desk. It sailed across the room, plastic splintered into several pieces against the wall. Jack sat at the desk, looking at the shards.

So where the fuck was Danny anyway? He'd obviously cleaned out all his papers.

Maybe there'd be some clue in the computer. He turned the PC on, mesmerized by the memory count at the top of the start-up routine. The CPU was a big gray box, several years old; the screen was oversized at twenty-one inches—pure Danny.

He scanned the programs. There wasn't much here—a spreadsheet program, a Web browser, and some games.

No word processor?

There ought to be more—the system utility totaled hard drive capacity at over twelve gigabytes, with barely a twentieth of it used.

Probably erased.

Jack was just starting to fiddle with the programs to check for deleted files when the phone rang. The ID gave a Maryland area code. He snapped up the phone, answering with his sharp agent-who-doesn't-take-shit voice.

"Yeah?"

"Jack, it's Beef. What the hell's going on?"

"You hear about this shit with my brother?"

"Not officially." Bozzone sighed on the other end, as if he were figuring something out—or maybe there was someone in the room with him, or on the line listening. "You ought to talk to your boss," he told Jack finally.

"I tried. He didn't answer the phone. What's going on?"

"I'm not really sure. You're supposed to be off-limits. Seriously."

"Me?"

"Yeah. This is your brother's house I called, right? This line's probably tapped, you know? I mean—it's an active investigation."

"Look, Beef, I haven't seen my brother in months. The only reason I came down here is my father's dying." He pushed back the desk chair, waiting for Bozzone to say something, but he didn't. "Does Boyle work for you?"

"Boyle? Who's he?"

"It's a she. Special Agent Amanda Boyle," he said, double-checking her business card.

"Never heard of her."

"You don't have an office out in Claptonville?"

"Nah. Nothing but car places out there."

"Who does?"

"An off-site?" Bozzone thought about it a moment, pushing air through his teeth as if he were mimicking a marching band. Despite everything else, Jack laughed.

"I don't know, Jack," Beef said. "I mean, you know, if it's undercover, I don't know. But it's not mine and offhand I'd say, well, I would have said there isn't one. This operation—I'm not in the loop."

"But you never heard of Boyle?"

"It's not like I know everybody. She good-looking?"

"Ugly as shit. A real fucking witch," Jack told Beef. "Sent two farm boys after me. Didn't bat an eye when I told her they pulled a weapon."

"They pulled a gun on you? Holy crap. That's out of control. You have to report—"

"Oh, yeah, right. Like I don't have enough trouble," said Jack.

"This is bullshit."

"Thanks for the support."

Bozzone did the marching band thing again. "You ought to talk to your old boss."

"I told you, I tried already. I was thinking maybe I'd call Pelham, but he's not going to be in a good mood."

"I mean Buzz Eagleton. He's got a lot of juice."

Buzz was the CIA's Deputy Director for Operations, Norman "Buzz" Eagleton. Buzz had headed B-3, and while he and Jack had never gotten along particularly well—Buzz was a bit too slippery, though of course that was exactly the sort of thing that would make him valuable in covert operations—he was perfectly positioned to know what was going on. Or to be able to find out.

But he'd have little reason to help Jack.

"Look, Beef, you got to help me," he told his friend. "Am I under suspicion or what?"

"I'm real sorry about your dad," he offered.

That was it?

If the phone was bugged, what more could he expect?

"Call Buzz," Beef suggested.

"Yeah, thanks," said Jack, hanging up.

Buzz wasn't particularly hard to locate—one call to the DDO's duty desk at CIA headquarters in Langley got him bounced to some sort of desk assistant, whose laconic tone gave no hint that he recognized Jack's last name. The man took his number and said the DDO would call him, if he called; Jack knew better than to ask when.

He'd barely hung up when the phone rang back.

The voice was young, feminine, and to the point. "Jack Ferico?"

"Yeah."

"Hold the line."

"Jack, how the hell are you doing?" Eagleton's voice boomed so loud Jack had to hold the phone away from his ear. "You still running?"

"Running?"

"I run every day at four o'clock. Every day, Saturdays included," said Eagleton. "Start up on J Street and run down to the Lincoln Memorial. Hell of a workout. Every day."

Then he hung up.

Jack would have had to be truly stupid to miss the suggestion that he hook up with Eagleton outside the intelligence building in D.C. It was already three-thirty, barely enough time to make it. He found a pair of cross-trainers in Daniel's closet that fit perfectly. But Daniel's shorts were several inches too wide. The only thing Jack could find to fix them were some paper clips, and even though he poked the metal through the waistband, he still worried about losing them as he trotted to the car.

Great shot for the surveillance team, if he was being tailed. He didn't seem to be.

They wouldn't tail him. They must trust him to some degree since they didn't make a serious effort to question him.

Or maybe they had intended to, and Boyle had cut it short because of the gun thing. Anything he said after they displayed the weapon would be tossed out as coercion. Somebody pulls a gun on you, you're going to go along with their suggestion. Jury'd buy that.

Jack kicked himself. He was already thinking of juries.

Saturdays in D.C. tended to be fairly quiet. Jack found a parking spot on the street a block from the intelligence building, a nondescript brick office building where Buzz and some other agency execs had offices. A suite of high-tech secure offices had been installed in the third-level subbasement several years before, and when he worked with B-3 Jack had been headquartered there. He was still familiar enough with the area to nod at the guy who owned the delicatessen near where he parked his car.

As he turned the corner in front of the building, he saw a jogger start down the steps. Jack pulled his baseball cap—his brother's Mets cap—down to nearly his eyes, took a breath, and fell into the pace, trotting as casually as possible, keeping himself back, figuring he'd overtake him on the next block. The blue, baggy T-shirt was easy to follow, billowing with the wind as the jogger reached the end of the block and turned right.

Only then did Jack realize it wasn't Buzz. He cursed to himself but kept running, did a pirouette at the end of the block, and came back, as if he were just warming up.

He almost ran Eagleton down, coming out of the building.

"Jack." The CIA deputy director, stretching to warm up, didn't seem particularly surprised.

"Buzz," he said. "Running without a trail team?"

"You're my trail team today, Jacky." Eagleton plunged into his trot, a leggy stride that belied his fifty-odd years and his overindulged appetite for fine food. Jack, in good shape himself, nonetheless struggled to keep up.

They ran towards the Mall, Eagleton pushing hard. Jack had run with him once or twice before. Contrary to what he'd said on the phone, Buzz didn't run at the same time every day, and surely wouldn't take the same route twice, but he was still a potential target; two dozen people would have reason to do him in, and that was only in the CIA. But running without bodyguards was very Buzz. He was competent enough—or so it seemed—but his ego was oversized.

Eagleton veered to his right. They crossed the street, barely making the light before a flood of traffic. They dodged through tourists and ran straight toward the Lincoln Memorial.

"Steps," said Eagleton.

Sweat streamed down his back as Jack followed. Warm air radiated from the monument like heat off an old steam radiator, and the glare of the day attacked his eyes. They dodged through a school group, Jack nearly losing his balance and bowling over a third-grader. He no longer worried about being followed or seen; he didn't even think about his brother or the reason he'd come. His only goal was to stay close to Eagleton.

Buzz hit the stairs without pausing. "Started doing stairs last year," he said, about a quarter of the way up. "Better than sprints."

Jack grunted.

"Capitol's more of a challenge," added Eagleton. "But I wasn't sure you'd be up to it. It's an acquired taste." He reached the top, then paused, running in place for a second. "You're here about your brother."

"I'm wondering where he is," said Jack.

"You don't think I'm keeping track of him, do you?"

"No, sir."

Eagleton plunged downward. Jack cursed but followed. His knees were going to feel torn to shit tomorrow.

Maybe even in five minutes.

Buzz pounded all the way to the bottom, then started up again without saying anything.

"Your brother's a real scumbag," said Eagleton about halfway up.

"Tell me something I don't know."

Buzz snorted. He stopped at the top, stretching out his legs in a long, awkward stride that was halfway between a stretch and a walk.

"We know where he is," said Eagleton.

"Where is that?"

"Russia. St. Petersburg. Leningrad," he added, as if Jack were stuck in the Cold War. "Working with some scumbags there."

"Russian government?"

"Not exactly."

"What was with the press conference?"

"Unfortunately, the FBI is the lead domestic counterintelligence agency," said Buzz—his way of saying the press conference wasn't his idea.

"Is this why I got bagged from B-3?"

"I wouldn't say you were bagged, Jack. Bad connotations. Everyone likes you. I like you."

"You knew at the time that this thing was going on?"

"Not exactly. The FBI wanted you back. They told me it was a career opportunity for you. Pelham over there told me he had his eye on you. I thought you had juice, so it made sense."

Jack didn't necessarily believe Buzz—the DDO was a consummate insider, always angling for political position, with a finger in every pie and an ear at every door. But Pelham and others in the Bureau had told him the same thing, so it was likely Eagleton was telling the truth.

Buzz finally stopped moving. He put his finger to his neck, counting his pulse against his watch. "You don't want to be involved in this, Jack."

"No shit." Jack tried to keep his legs limber, but he could feel the muscles tightening into massive knots.

Eagleton shook his head as he finished his pulse count, then plunged down the stairs in a zigzag pattern, working between two groups of tourists. Jack followed as Buzz trotted along the reflecting pool, easing his pace.

"He's a valuable man, your brother. Smart. The problem is, we can't touch him."

"Why didn't anyone tell me what was going on?"

"Come on, Jack. Your bosses probably are shitting bricks that this is going to get them fired. They're covering their behinds."

"Am I under suspicion of something?"

"I doubt it. Why would you be?"

"Who's Boyle?"

"Boyle?"

"She work for you?"

"I have more people working for me these days than the Director." Eagleton edged left, angling back around in the direction of the Wall. "What is she? NSC?"

"Said she's FBI."

"Boyle? I don't have any Bureau people, Jack. Liaisons maybe. You were our last B-3er."

"How do I get my old job back?"

"You want to come over to the CIA, I'll try and swing something down the road. I have to tell you, Security Committee is going to be a bitch and a half, you know what I'm saying?" Eagleton had the pace nailed solid, easing his upper body back and forth with the rhythm of the run. If he was sweating, Jack couldn't tell. "This isn't my turf, Jack. If they're screwing you, there's not much I can do. I'd make it worse. You know the attitude. Talk to Pelham. He likes you. I know he does."

"Come on, Buzz. You can help. I'm being screwed."

Eagleton stopped short. He cocked his arms back as if he were going to take a swing. "Your brother screwed you when he started working with the Russians."

"So why didn't you tell me when I could have done something about it?"

"Yeah, right."

"Why did he do it?"

"You tell me."

"Show me where he is and I'll find out."

Eagleton frowned as if he thought Jack was putting him on. He started running again, slowly, almost shaking his thigh and calf muscles to keep them loose.

"I know he liked to gamble," said Jack.

"Stay out of this, Jack. This isn't for you. I don't blame you. But you have your own things to worry about."

Jack wondered if that was supposed to be a reference to his father—and if it was, how or why Buzz would know.

"Buzz—how involved in this are you?" he asked.

"Not at all." Buzz quickened his pace. "Two, three weeks, everything will blow over. Who knows—maybe he'll show up on your doorstep."

"Yeah, right."

"Don't worry about it. I hear you're bowling them over in Poughkeepsie."

"Newburgh."

"They're near each other, aren't they? In New York? My first wife went to school up there at Vassar." Eagleton changed direction back toward the business district. "I have to go back to work, Jack. Remember what I said. Leave it to the pros."

Something in Jack rose up, some piece of bile he couldn't deny. "That an order?"

Buzz didn't bother answering. "Take care of yourself, Jacky," he said as he quickened his pace into a sprint.

Jack, suppressing both his anger and his competitiveness, dropped into a walk.

Driving back to Danny's, Jack decided it could have been worse—he could have pulled a muscle running with Buzz.

Cara's Lexus was in the driveway when he got

there. She was sitting in the living room, watching CNN. The network anchors were talking about a shooting in Texas.

"What are you doing?" Jack asked.

"Trying to figure out what's going on. What happened to Daniel, Jack?"

"I don't know."

"You must," she said, clicking off the TV. "You work for the FBI, right?"

"I'm the last person they're going to say anything to. They think I helped him."

"Did you?"

Jack just shook his head and went into the den. He picked up the phone to call Bree to check on his dad, but decided not to bother. The news was bound to be bad, and he'd risk having his father beg him to bring Danny back home again.

The computer's screen saver was on. He pushed the mouse and clicked on the trash can, picking up where he'd left off before Beef had called several hours ago. There were no deleted files in the trash can—which alone seemed suspicious. He opened up the Web browser, which was set to automatically dial into the network. Jack sat back as the computer buzzed away.

"What are you doing?" Cara asked from the doorway.

Jack didn't answer. The provider's generic home page unfolded slowly on the screen. He rolled the cursor up over the favorites; most were preset, except for the sports file.

Yankees home page, along with two fan sites.

Since when had Daniel followed them? He'd always been a Mets fan.

The mouse's trackball was dirty and the cursor moved jerkily across the screen. Jack opened the favorites folder; two columns of gambling sites spread across the screen.

The history window showed another interest. Daniel had accessed more than dozen sites having to do with Russia. Half were generic; the rest were connected with St. Petersburg in some way.

Jack went back to the home page and clicked on the local news. The *Washington Post* "late-breaking electronic edition" came on the screen. His brother was the second lead. A sketchy photo, probably made from a security badge, ran with the story, which began with a rehash of the press conference.

The reporter wrote that the government had declined to say what secrets Daniel was privy to. But he quoted an unnamed expert who speculated that, since Daniel was an expert on high-tech materials and held at least one patent for applying them, the secrets must be related to stealth technologies. If so, the expert said, the loss would be "significant."

Family members were unavailable for comment.

Off-line, Jack checked the dates on the cookies left by Web sites. The last access was dated three and a half weeks ago. Daniel had visited two airline sites as well. Jack's simple search of the computer files didn't turn up anything newer than those files.

Three and a half weeks ago. His father wasn't in the hospital yet.

Would it have made a difference?

So how much trouble was Danny really in? In theory, an American citizen could work for any company in the world, but someone like Danny would undoubtedly be tied down by various non-disclosure agreements, and possibly by a direct contract to the government, maybe through Turlow, maybe directly to the Energy Department or Defense. Leaving abruptly might mean that he had been giving—or rather, selling—information to someone and then got caught. It might also mean that he suddenly got a good job offer and jumped. Either explanation was theoretically possible, though obviously the latter was potentially more benign.

He could also have been kidnapped or blackmailed. Granted, that didn't fit with the FBI's actions—or what Buzz had told him.

Cara watched him with her stony blue eyes, her expression someplace between concern and fear. Her knit shirt was cut high enough to reveal her flat, tanned belly above the waist of her short skirt; her legs looked muscled enough to have withstood Buzz's workout without complaint.

Jack could understand Danny distancing himself from the family—but leaving her?

"You're a computer expert?" Jack asked.

"Systems analyst."

"Can you retrieve deleted files?"

"What do you mean?"

"I'd like to see what was on this disc. It's almost empty. My guess is that it's been erased."

She walked over, moved the cursor around the menu, selected the Windows program manager, and clicked open a few files.

"Maybe it was erased," she said finally.

"Can you get it back?"

"I don't know." She put her long fingers to her mouth, smoothing the moisture of her lips onto her thumb. "Maybe. I think I have a program on my laptop. It's in the car."

"Let's try it," said Jack.

She nodded, but continued to stare at the screen for a few seconds more before going to get the laptop. Jack went to the kitchen and made himself more coffee.

Cara's program resurrected two interesting things on Daniel's computer. One was a collection of E-mails, which remained only in bits and pieces.

The other was an encryption program, good enough to be covered by export controls.

"I couldn't get the whole program back," she said, "but it's very similar to EnCapU8, which, as it happens, I do have."

Cara's soft, silky skirt rolled up against her legs as she sat at the computer. Her top revealed the shadow of a camisole or slip-top without a bra beneath, nipples clearly outlined; Jack had a hell of a time forcing himself to look at the computer screen.

"These E-mails were encoded," she continued. "This should show them in the clear, but something's wrong. I've tried running them through a second and third time, but nothing."

"Did he change the key?" Jack asked.

She shrugged. "Maybe. This is the one that was saved. It's possible that there are other variations. But if you look at this old file that I recovered, the text is the same as this one. I'm assuming that he decoded it, since it's gone through the program."

Jack stared at the text windows on the screen. About two dozen letters and numbers ran together in a seemingly random pattern.

"It's a simple code," he said. "What month was it sent?"

"Last month. March?"

Jack opened his datebook to the year-at-a-glance section. He took a piece of paper from the desk drawer and worked up a grid based on the calendar. It took a minute for him to remember the simple transpositions in the middle, and then fill out the grid.

"We used to do this when we were kids. It's a calendar code—you change with the month," he explained, starting to decode.

Except that it didn't work right.

"It's not that complicated," Cara said suddenly,

grabbing his paper. "It's not encoded, just interspersed with gibberish." She skipped every other letter in the middle line, and found:

—STPETEON4—

"Saint Pete on the fourth," she said. "Florida?"

"No, St. Petersburg, Russia. The fourth of May." Jack looked through the rest of the E-mail, but found nothing significant.

"Is that where he is?" Cara asked.

"Maybe," said Jack. "It's odd, though. He knows a lot better codes. We used to send messages when we were kids."

"Remember, it already went through an encryption program," she said.

"Yeah," said Jack. Working through the rest of recovered E-mails, Jack found two things he thought might mean something. One was "St. Catherine"—a reference, he thought, to a hotel, which was listed on one of the Web sites Daniel had accessed. The other was a name or code name, "Ivan Gizbertov." The only other thing that seemed significant was a message with the words "df ministry," which Jack interpreted as Defense Ministry. But there was no other information in the message, or at least nothing that he could find.

Sum total—more evidence beyond what Buzz had told him that Daniel had gone to St. Petersburg, might still be there, made contact with or had something to do with the Russian Defense Ministry, itself a labyrinth that could lead anywhere. He had at least thought of going to a hotel named St. Catherine.

That was enough of a lead, if Jack were working a case. He'd go to St. Petersburg and start nosing around.

He could. The Bureau obviously wouldn't like it,

but there were plenty of industrial security people who could help him. Bill Schenck, the IBM Overseas Security specialist. He was right in St. Petersburg. Mike Dee was with Texaco, outside of Moscow, and he owed him big—Jack's B-3 team had helped smuggle an accountant out of one of the southern provinces the year before.

Mikey was a guy you could work with. Loved the Giants and the Yankees.

But hell, if Jack were going to Moscow, the person to talk to was the Milkman.

He was known to his employees as Alfred Jones, but it was anyone's guess what the Milkman's real name was. He was well known as a black-market arms dealer and free-lance "expediter." He had extensive contacts in the Russian military and the Mafiya. An expatriate American with a flair for the bizarre, the Milkman also owed Jack big-time.

Jack had saved his goddamn life. Though how much that counted for was anyone's guess.

But the Milkman was in Moscow. Danny was in St. Petersburg.

And Jack was here.

"Jack?"

He glanced from the screen at the desk chair, surprised to see it empty. Cara was standing at the doorway with a Coke. "Are you okay?"

"I'm thinking."

"About Danny?"

"About my dad. I got to get back to him." He glanced at his watch—he'd told Bree he'd be back hours ago.

"Oh."

"Look, I got to go back to New Jersey. You still have that card I gave you?"

She nodded. "What's going to happen to Daniel?"

"Nothing good."

"Can we help him?"

"I don't think so." He turned off the computer. "I have to go, okay? You call if you hear anything."

She nodded again. Then she leaned over and gave him a soft kiss on the cheek.

A very sisterly kiss, but it still nearly stopped his heart.

Chapter Nine

Washington, D.C.

Norman "Buzz" Eagleton didn't shower immediately when he got back to the intelligence building; instead, he went to his secure office in the subbasement and began a computer search to find out who Boyle was.

He suspected—knew—Boyle must be Russian, but that in itself told him nothing. Discipline and paranoia demanded that he first dismiss the infinitesimal possibility that she was indeed working for the FBI, and so Buzz had the computer search the Bureau and national security personnel lists first. In the time it took to glance at his watch—he was due to see the President at Camp David at eight—the computer completed the search, coming back with only two significant hits: a middle-aged forensic accountant with the Defense Department Intelligence Agency and a young man with the first name of Dante who did criminal investigations in Oregon for the FBI.

Obviously not the Boyle he was interested in.

Buzz slid his long legs under the desk and passworded himself into the foreign agents file. He had to give the computer a new retina scan before the information came up, cursing as the awkward visor nearly slipped out of his sweaty hands. The computer whirled, checking against aliases and using the very limited physical description Jack Ferico had provided to sort through a list of known and suspected foreign operatives, double-checking the list against their last known areas of operation and expertise. The juiced-up Cray supercomputers took about three minutes to look through the collective wisdom of the country's top intelligence agencies, but didn't come up with anything Buzz didn't know off the top of his head already.

Boyle could be any one of three operatives, each of whom worked for a different segment of the fractious Russian intelligence commands. The one he suspected was a former low-level GRU clerk whose combination of English skills and Siberian ancestry—and large breasts—had obviously placed her on the fast track with the White Bears, a loose association of Russian and Siberian military men angling for a bigger place in the government. If that were so, her interest in Jack was a good sign.

Or maybe a really bad sign.

The press conference had been the right move, at least, enough to keep his operation one step ahead of them, even though it made things with Jack very complicated. He would undoubtedly try to help his brother.

A potential problem. But also a potential plus, since Buzz now suspected Boyle would be watching. In all likelihood, that would seal the deal.

It might also get Jack killed. It definitely might, if

he left the country and went to Russia. Buzz didn't have enough people to protect him.

The only alternative was arresting Jack, which Pelham had already vetoed twice.

Buzz opened up the secure PROD-FS system, checking through the recent intel bulletins on the Yak-42 shoot-down. Buzz had a full report in his safe upstairs; he knew exactly what had happened. What he wanted to know was who else in the Administration knew. The information would help him decide how best to lay it out for President Jack D'Amici at their meeting—for which he would have to leave in twenty minutes.

Judging from the NSC bulletins, National Security Director Richard Thompson was still pushing engine failure. That was understandable—the NSC's top staffer, Dr. Michael Blitz, was in Asia on a special assignment for the President, and therefore not available to steer Thompson to the proper conclusions.

Too bad Buzz was no longer interested in Thompson's job; this would have clinched it. The evidence was now overwhelming, the reason he'd already given the go-ahead for Blue to proceed.

Buzz knew that the President would insist that the Concorde flight go on as scheduled, no matter what. It made sense—the international stakes were so high, the geopolitics so well balanced that even a hiccup would screw everything up. Blue would bail them out.

Besides, D'Amici had never really liked the Vice President.

Buzz snickered as he got up from his desk to go take a shower.

Chapter Ten

New Jersey

Jack thought about Cara's kiss on his cheek all the way back to his father's hospital room. It was far better than the obvious alternatives—his brother and his father. And the Yankees were getting creamed so badly he turned off the radio.

It reminded him of other kisses. There had been enough years between them growing up that he shouldn't have been jealous of his brother's girl-friends, and Danny had never done anything as overt as stealing his women.

Once, almost. It was Judy Kay, or Kaymon, or something.

No, it was definitely Kay. And she wasn't exactly a girlfriend and Danny hadn't stolen her.

But she had perfect lips—and big, loose-swinging breasts. Judy was a year older than Jack and he had a crush on her in the worst way. And it turned out she had a crush on Danny.

He didn't know that the one time he'd gotten up courage to ask her over to go swimming. She said sure and laughed, and within an hour she was diving from the wooden platform into the four-foot pool, arms extended in front of her head as she knifed under the water. She surfaced at the far end of the pool, water running off her hair, the top of her suit hanging low over the plush white skin of her breasts. She giggled and hooked her thumbs into the fabric to pull it back up.

Nothing else he'd ever seen, explicit or not, had seemed nearly as alluring.

And then Danny came out of the house and did a cannonball into the pool.

Jack had come under mortar attack during his brief stint in Haiti in the Army, but those explosions didn't have half the impact of Danny's splash. He stood frozen, stunned, baffled, dazed, lifted away from his body. Danny surfaced and said something along the lines of "hey," kicked across a time or two, then climbed out and left.

Judy didn't do anything more than say hi back, but Jack watched the way her eyes trailed his brother. Her nipples swelled under her suit as Danny climbed over the side.

Maybe her nipples hadn't really swelled. And Danny most likely hadn't done it on purpose. But that was the end of Jack's hopes, if not his crush.

They swam for an hour or more after that, but Jack was too hurt and too smart or maybe too proud to say any of the things he'd planned to say. He never invited her back after that, though she hinted a few times that summer about how hot it was.

After she left, Jack threw his basketball as hard as

he could at the garage door. The ball shot off one of the windows that ran across it, shattering the glass. He caught the rebounding ball and heaved it again, this time directly at one of the windows. He didn't stop throwing the ball until all of the windows were smashed.

Fortunately, there was a large pane of glass in the back of the garage and his father was working late; this was long after his mom had passed away. Jack spent the night replacing the windows. If his dad noticed they'd been replaced, he never said anything.

No, actually he had—but it was subtle, totally his dad's way. They'd played one-on-one together a few days later, a Saturday or maybe a comp day. His father asked how things were going.

"That Judy Kay's nice," he said.

"Yup," Jack replied.

They kept on playing. Thinking about it now, more than half his life later, Jack realized his father had taken a few rebounds close to the garage door, dribbling around to give him an opportunity to say something about the windows. Jack hadn't gotten the hint.

Maybe Danny had said something. Or more likely Bree. Or maybe his father had just figured it out—the guy was an FBI agent, after all, a hell of a detective according to everyone who worked with him in the early days.

A good father too, especially considering the times and the difficulties of raising three kids without a wife. Close to them, but not a talker.

His father never talked to him about sex. He didn't talk to him about a lot of things. He did teach him how to shoot. And how to change the oil on a car. Jack remembered that very clearly. He remembered holding the flashlight one night as his father pulled a balky filter out.

Funny to remember that as a good time, his dad getting pissed because the damn filter wouldn't unscrew and it was dark and he needed the car. One of the few times Jack ever saw him come close to losing his temper.

Jack hit the heater now and flipped on the radio, checking to see if maybe the Yankees were doing better.

An hour and a half later, Jack pulled off the Jersey Turnpike and threaded his way north to the hospital. The closer he got, the slower he went, finally driving up the long hill in front of the hospital so slowly the Impala was in danger of stalling. The parking lot was nearly empty. Jack parked, got out, and walked in slowly, even stopped at the visitors' desk and took a pass to the ICU. Upstairs, he thought of bagging it and going home as he neared the first glass-enclosed room in the intensive-care suite. But Bree turned the corner in front of him.

"He sounded so desperate, Jacky," she said, running to him. "Like people were chasing him."

"Is Dad? Did?" The idea choked him. "Did Dad, is he alive?"

Bree pushed back away from him. "No. No. He's fine. I mean, he's the same."

"What do you mean then?"

"Danny called."

"Danny?"

"Just now. Ten minutes ago. Fifteen maybe." Her body shook. "They had given Daddy a shot already, thank God. He was calm. He talked to him."

"You sure it was Danny?" Jack asked.

"Who else could it have been?" Bree grabbed his arm. "It was him, Jack. What are you going to do?"

"What do you mean, what am I going to do? Where'd he call from? Is he under arrest?"

"He's in Russia."

Jack walked past her to his father's room. His father moaned slightly, but his eyes were closed. The monitors kept a steady beat in the corner. The phone sat on the rolling nightstand in the corner.

"You were going for a cigarette?" he asked Bree.

"Yeah."

They walked back to the elevator in silence. The first car that stopped had two nurses in it; Jack held Bree back. The next was empty. As soon as they were inside and it started downward he popped open the emergency override panel and froze the car.

He was luckier than he'd hoped—there was no audible alarm. Most likely a light was flashing in the security booth downstairs, but by the time they realized it and sent someone to check, Jack and his sister would be gone.

"Are you absolutely positive it was Danny on the phone?"

"I only talked to him for a second," said Bree. "But Daddy talked to him. He knows."

"Dad called me Danny the other day," said Jack.

"This was different. It was definitely Daniel. It had to be. He's in Russia, Jack. You have to get him back."

"How?"

Bree pressed herself back against the wall of the car. "Aren't you going to go help him?"

Jack looked at his sister, her body small in the yellow light of the elevator gondola. She had always been the peacemaker in the family, soothing problems over whenever there was a fight or disagreement.

Why did she think that was her job?

"Did he ask for help?"

"No. He said he's fine, but you know that's a lie. It has to be."

"Yeah," said Jack.

"They kidnapped him," Bree said. "I know they must have. That's the only thing that makes sense."

"I doubt that," said Jack. "I think he started gambling again. He probably owes somebody money, and this is how he's paying off the debt."

"Jack, Danny hasn't gambled since grad school."

"I looked at his bank statements, Bree, going back more than a year. He has no money. How else would you explain any of this?"

"He's been kidnapped," said Bree. "We have to help him."

"Did he say he was kidnapped?"

"He said he was dealing with something."

"What else?"

"I don't know. Daddy said the line went dead."

Jack put his back against the wall of the car and told her about Boyle and Buzz. "More than likely, they'd arrest him the second he came back."

"Daddy said you should go get him. You have to bring him back, Jack." Bree sounded like she was telling him to do his homework.

"Even if I knew where he was, Bree, why should I? The government will crucify him, for christsakes. They ought to—he's a goddamn traitor. This probably broke Dad's heart."

"Dad wants him home."

"Bree—"

"He was crying. Daddy was crying."

"Dad was crying?"

"I've never seen him cry, Jack. Never. Not even when Mommy died. Can't you do something?"

Jack had a friend at the telephone company who tracked the call down for him while he waited outside, watching Bree smoke. The call had been routed an unusual number of times—enough so his friend couldn't be positive where it had come from. But it had traveled through Russia and probably originated there.

CNN was beamed all over the world, and it wasn't exactly difficult to imagine Danny seeing it in St. Petersburg. Tracking down his father at the hospital wouldn't have been impossible.

Why, though? To apologize to his father? Even if Danny truly was all right, he'd know how their dad would react. He'd jump to conclusions like Bree, and tell him to come home.

The hallway to the ICU seemed darker, the lights fading progressively as he walked toward the room where his father's life was ebbing away. Jack opened the door and saw his dad lying helplessly on the bed, eyes closed. He felt his breath start to leave him, then realized the monitor above his dad's head was still pinging steadily.

"He's sleeping," said Bree.

"Yeah," said Jack, pulling over a chair.

"Maybe there'll be a miracle and the transplant will come."

Jack didn't say anything.

"Are you going there?" she asked.

"I can't just drop everything and go to Russia," he told her. "Even if I knew where the hell he was."

Part of Jack wanted to hop on the nearest airplane, fly straight to Russia, find Danny, and bring him back. He'd show his father exactly what his favorite son was—a traitor.

And another part wanted to bail him out of this mess and prove that he was innocent.

"I can get you the papers," Bree told him. She was a customer rep with Lufthansa. "I can get you comp tickets. You can leave in an hour."

"Bree, if Danny was so easy to find, don't you think the FBI would have brought him back themselves?"

"Maybe they can't. Maybe there's some complication."

Jack got up from the steel-backed chair, went to the more comfortable foam-filled one in the corner.

Eagleton had been very careful about what he said. He had specifically urged Jack to stay out of it. But was that what he was really saying? If he didn't want Jack involved, why meet with him in the first place?

If somebody wanted to hide in Russia, it would be impossible to find them. Since Yeltsin had resigned—even before—the country had become the Wild West.

If the right people were holding him, Jack could work out a trade. Easier for him to swing something than the FBI. Maybe Buzz wanted him to.

But did Danny really want help? He'd called and said he was okay; why not take that at face value?

Jack felt his eyes growing heavy. He shook himself, staring at his father.

"Jack?"

Jack turned to find Cara standing at the doorway.

"Jack?"

"Who are you?" asked Bree.

"I'm Daniel's girlfriend," she said, striding toward her. "Are you Brianna?"

Bree took her hand warily.

"I thought, maybe, Danny would be here. Or that you knew something. I'm sorry about your father." Cara was wearing plain, baggy jeans and a leather bomber jacket. Her green eyes shone brighter than the life support machines, but the rest of her seemed thin, almost wispy. Jack thought it must be the hospital—everyone who came through its doors was pulverized somehow, as if the air ate at your flesh.

"I don't mean to intrude," said Cara. "The people from the FBI called me a few hours ago in D.C., Jack. A man named Johnson asked me questions about Russia."

"Did you tell him about the E-mail?"

She shook her head. "He didn't ask. I thought I shouldn't volunteer anything."

"What E-mail?" Bree asked.

"We found some messages," Cara told her. "We think he's in St. Petersburg. At a hotel called St. Catherine or St. Catherine's."

"So you do know where he is." Bree's face flushed red as she turned toward Jack.

"No, I don't."

"That's not a good enough lead?" demanded Bree. "You have a hotel. For christsakes, Jack. If you're not going, I will."

"Bree."

"Somebody has to. Daddy wants him here. Someone has to. Someone has to tell Danny to come home."

"It's not as easy as that, Bree. Jesus." Jack curled his arms against his chest.

"He bailed you out of so much, Jacky," said Bree. "Now he's counting on you."

"What did Danny bail me out of?"

"I mean Daddy."

"If you're going," Cara said to Jack, "I'm going with you. I'm very good with languages. I studied Russian a little in high school."

"I'm not going."

"You can come with me," Bree told her, "I can get us both plane tickets." She took her phone from the table where Jack had placed it and started dialing.

"Bree."

"Hi. This is Brianna Sullivan. Hi. Can you give me Fred Gers? Right. Of course."

"Bree, come on," said Jack.

"Do you have a passport?" Bree asked Cara.

"I brought it," said Cara.

"What do you mean, you brought it?" said Jack.

"I always carry it with me, for my job," said Cara. "We do overseas consulting."

"I need the spelling of your full name for the visa. You need to be invited," Bree explained to her. "It's a bureaucratic fiction to help the country make money. But you can't get in without following their procedure. Fortunately, I work for Lufthansa. We have some forms ready for emergencies. We may have to fax your passport. Fred can take care of it."

"Bree, hang up the phone," said Jack.

"Someone has to talk to Danny. In person. He has to understand what's happening here."

Jack grabbed for the phone to cut the connection when his father groaned loudly. Jack's and Bree's eyes met before they turned together toward the bed, where the old man had propped himself up on his elbows. He shook his head almost imperceptibly, as if they were toddlers and he was warning them not to fight or make any noise because their mother was upstairs sleeping.

He groaned again, then sank back slowly, eyes open. Jack and Bree and Cara came closer. The machines monitoring his heartbeat peaked momentarily, then slid back into a steady pulse—not vibrant, but enough.

"Get your brother, Jack. I want him here more than anything," said the old man. He groaned again, and closed his eyes to rest. They stared at him in silence, the only sound the steady beat of the monitor behind him.

Jack told himself he still hadn't decided to take Cara as they drove to Newburgh in her Lexus. But the truth was she might come in handy. She had a wallet filled with credit cards in her ex-husband's name, which was unlikely to be on the FBI watch list.

And there were the many places in the dark labyrinth of Russia where beauty opened doors quicker than a crisp hundred-dollar bill.

Go all the way to St. Petersburg on a rumor and an E-mail. What would he really be able to do there?

But the truth was, he had to go. His father wanted him to. And Bree would if he didn't.

The truth was, Jack didn't want to be in the hospital room when his father passed away. He didn't want to see the blinking line on the machine run flat.

Cara took his directions off the Thruway, driving quickly—far too quickly, actually, if there were any local cops around. She tracked off the county highway onto a road barely wide enough for a motor scooter. Branches brushed against the window as she took the curves, finally finding the driveway of Jack's rented raised-ranch. He jumped from the car, adrenaline starting to pump into his legs—something he hadn't felt in a long, long while. Inside, Jack ignored the blinking light on the answering machine, walking through the living room down the hall to his bedroom in the back. He got his passport—the plain-Jane "civilian" version—from the large strongbox beneath his bed. He stashed his gun in the box—no way he'd get on the plane with it—trading it for a small, battered pocket-sized notebook. The notebook contained contact information for people likely to help him throughout Eastern Europe. He also took out his maps—finding useful maps in Russia would be harder than finding his brother. He threw a pair of pants, some underwear, and two shirts in a small overnight bag. He opened the window a crack—there was nothing here worth stealing, and the place tended to get musty after a few days.

Back in the living room, he found Cara eyeing the striped sofa as if it were a foreign animal.

"Monkey Wards. Five hundred bucks for the whole set," he said, gesturing at the furniture.

"Good deal."

"I was impressed." Jack picked up the twelve-inch-high statue of St. Francis of Assisi that he kept near the TV.

"I didn't know you were religious," she said.

"I'm not," he told her. He hurled the statue against the floor, where it broke into a thousand shards, revealing a thick wad of hundred dollar bills. "My life savings," he said. Even though it was hardly a joke, he laughed as he scooped the money from the floor.

II

"A fugitive and a vagabond"

Gen. 4:12

Chapter One

Over the Atlantic

Cara Ciello locked her legs against the bottom of the seat in front of her and twisted her upper torso until her vertebrae cracked. She leaned back in the seat, sighing loudly as the muscles in her body relaxed.

Jack didn't move. His head was turned toward the window, but he seemed to be asleep.

"Jack?" she asked anyway, just to be sure.

Nada.

She got up and slipped down the aisle of the darkened plane to the lavatory.

She really did have to take a pee. Her abdomen felt like it was going to explode. But that wasn't why she'd come.

When she was done, Cara stood quietly and removed a small, rounded wand from her pocketbook. At first glance it appeared to be a plastic tampon holder; passed through an airport X-ray machine, the three microscopic circuits wrapped in a spiral at the base of the holder showed up as delicate, decorative lines of metallic paint. The long spiral of metal looked like a spring, but was actually a battery. Spring-loaded tampons would be tough to explain to a female guard, and had she run into one boarding, Cara would have insisted on a visual search. Men, on the other hand—they took one look, realized what was inside, and quickly moved on. Slap the words "sanitary napkin" on an AK-47 and you could carry it anywhere you wanted, no questions asked.

Cara pulled the holder apart, dumping the tampon into the trash and refitting the sections together piggy-back-style. She took the headphones from her Walkman and undid the earplugs, revealing a bare wire that fit snugly into a hole in the base of the holder. Then she inserted the headphone wire's RCA plug into her cell phone, hit the star key twice, and listened to the register tone as she swept the restroom for bugging devices.

The wand was powerful and versatile enough to intercept any transmission within a mile and a half radius, even through the airplane's metal hull. Its purpose here, however, was not to eavesdrop but to detect someone else eavesdropping; it broadcast a series of tones and listened for echoes. Finally, sure that there were no bugs to pick up her conversation, Cara punched a second sequence into the cell phone, placing it into discrete-burst mode, and made her call.

Buzz—not the desk operator she expected—came on the line.

Not too happily either.

"Where the fuck are you?"

"Aboard BOA Flight 547, halfway to Frankfurt," said Cara. "You weren't following us at Dulles?"

"We lost you at Stewart. What the hell are you doing?"

"You lost me at Stewart? God." Cara shifted on the toilet seat, trying to get comfortable. The bathroom had obviously been designed to discourage long stays.

"Don't give me that. I told you we're undermanned. And I have a complaint here about your driving."

"So arrest me." Cara leaned to the sink and turned on the water. Less than thirty-six hours ago she had been looking forward to a week's vacation, visiting her aunt in Virginia Beach. Buzz had literally grabbed her by the arm as she was going out the door of the Executive Office Building and sent her directly to Daniel's house with a half-baked cover story.

"What are you doing on that plane?" Buzz demanded.

"You told me to stay with him."

"I told you to keep him in America. I'm sending you back to the goddamn Navy."

"Wire a ticket to Frankfurt," she told him. "I'll catch the next flight home."

"No, you won't," said Buzz, as if she were seriously contemplating it. "Don't be a wise-ass."

"You told me that was my best asset." Cara stood up. She tapped the volume on the phone down and stood near the door, listening as someone shifted in the passageway outside. "Jack asked me if an FBI agent named Boyle had called me. Who is she?"

"A problem." Buzz's tone made it clear he wasn't going to elaborate.

"Is she really FBI?"

"He bought the St. Petersburg thing?"

Buzz simply wasn't going to give her information he didn't want to give, whether she thought it important or not. Cara disliked being kept in the dark, but there was nothing else to do but trust—hope, really—that Buzz and the others had things under control.

As much as that was possible.

"That's where we're going, isn't it? But your phone call backfired."

"What phone call?"

"You didn't have someone call his father at the hospital and pretend to be him?"

"Shit."

When Cara had come over to the NSC on loan from Naval Intelligence, she had thought that covert operations always worked with something approaching precision. She wasn't naive—she knew that real life, let alone the military, and forget about the CIA, was never truly precise or ordered. But it was difficult to understand how many variables there were, and how contentious fate could be, until you were there.

It was also difficult to understand how emotion, not intellect, could play such an important role in things. She liked Jack—more than liked him—a lot. Cara hadn't expected that. She worried it clouded her judgment.

"By the way," she told her boss, "you were supposed to keep him in D.C. longer when you went running. He nearly caught me screwing with the computer."

"Call me from Frankfurt," Buzz said, then hung up.

Cara leaned against the sink as she redid her lipstick. This was her first trip to Europe; as a Naval Intelligence officer—her language abilities had helped make her a Russian specialist—Cara had barely left the States. She'd hardly even been aboard ship. Probably her longest sea duty was a sixteen-day stint in the Atlantic, posing as a petty officer on loan for an internal counterintelligence operation aboard a destroyer.

That assignment culminated in the arrest of two

chief petty officers for a half-baked plot to hijack the ship, though not before one of the assholes nearly managed to throw her off the ship. The fact that he ended up in the drink instead—and the quick convictions that followed—led to an assignment with the NSC, where she'd worked for Buzz on a number of minor assignments.

Which this had started out to be.

It would help to know precisely what the hell Buzz was doing. She wasn't in on the operation, whatever it might be, and in fact didn't know much about Jack or his brother. Cara guessed that Daniel really was in Russia somewhere, but where was a mystery—aside from the fact that he wasn't in St. Petersburg.

Was he really a traitor? Cara had her doubts. Jack obviously thought so, but could brothers be so different?

Cara put her lipstick back in her purse. She put her phone back inside, then placed the pseudo-tampon holder on the floor. With her heel, she crushed $2.3 million worth of very fancy electronics into high-tech dust, then began scooping the ground plastic and metal bits into the commode.

Four years of college on ROTC scholarship and several years of intensive Navy training, and she had still ended up on her hands and knees cleaning floors.

Chapter Two

Near Japan

Crow had now been awake for nearly twenty-four hours. Had their transport back from the admiral's flagship been anything but an old Seasprite—a Kaman SH-2 that had probably entered service before he did—he might have fallen asleep. The helicopter bucked tremendously in the heavy wind—or maybe Crow's fatigue amplified even the slightest nudge as the aircraft whipped over the whitecaps at 120 knots toward the large Japanese island of Hokkaido. The damp sea air stiffened his knees, and he had a knot in his neck the size of the air base they were approaching.

Rosen, on the other hand, seemed absolutely cheerful. Sitting next to the pilot on the thankfully fully padded passenger bench in the crew compartment, the major tossed out suggestion after suggestion on how to deal with the renegade MiG. He seemed to have ingested several air combat encyclopedias, dropping references to the most famous along the way. Just now he was praising Robert L. Shaw's *Fighter Combat*—an excellent work, though Crow was hardly in the mood to say anything that might encourage Rosen; he was still angry at the intelligence officer for prolonging the admiral's debriefing session with his own questions about the Yak.

Besides, Rosen didn't need any encouragement. He veered from a suggestion to avoid a front-quarter attack—had he been talking, Crow would have said "duh"—and began hypothesizing about how a gamma-ray weapon could be used to neutralize the electronics aboard Shadow R, rendering it uncontrollable.

That was too much.

"You ought to write science fiction instead of true crime," Crow told him.

"It's a great idea, don't you think?"

"Share it with Cleveland. I'm sure he'll love it."

Cleveland was the Raptor's crew chief, a master sergeant with nearly thirty years' experience who knew more about the plane than many of the engineers who'd designed it.

"Cleveland would probably try and figure out a way to do it," said Rosen.

Blitz had told Crow that two flights of Navy F-14 Tomcats would be assigned to shadow the flight at extremely low altitude, where they would be undetected by Russian radars. At the first sign of trouble, they would scramble to deal with it, Shadow R. Crow would keep his sensors at full blast, painting the enemy plane for the interceptors. The F-14s' air-to-air missiles had a handoff mode that could use the Raptor's radar to find their way to the target.

The MiG's range and the Concorde III's flight plan

limited the danger area to roughly two hundred miles, or about sixteen minutes, assuming the flight followed its script.

Crow didn't like the plan very much, and not least of all because the Tomcats would have to stay out of range of the Russian AWACS that was helping coordinate the flight; depending on where the Russian was, that would put them at least fifty miles away from missile range—more likely much more. The Navy fighters would be flying from the Indian Ocean, refueling over Pakistan, and if things got tight would have to rely on their tankers to violate Russian airspace so they could fill up for the trip home. They would have to worry about Chinese as well as Russian air defenses. The pilots would have spent a minimum of three hours in their cockpits before they got close to the intercept point.

Last but not least, he'd have to stay close enough to the MiG to paint it with his radar, and yet sit there helpless the whole time.

Crow figured that he could have been as close as two miles to Shadow R and still not detected it—the MiG would have had to get very near to the Yak in order to be sure of hitting it with its notoriously inaccurate cannon.

This encounter would be daylight, giving his eyes as well as his radar a chance to spot the plane. But the MiG-21 was a relatively small fighter difficult to see under the best of circumstances. And hours of staring at the F-22's screens tended to wear his eyes down.

It didn't do much for the rest of him either. His knee gave him a sharp twinge to remind him how much it appreciated the helicopter ride. Flexing it didn't help; he ran his thumb slowly down the inside of his thigh, working some of the tension out of his muscles.

He'd see Shadow R. The question was how far

away. Drawing up the game plan as optimistically as possible, he figured it would take the F-14s nearly a minute to complete the interception once he alerted them. That meant he had to see the MiG when it was still eight miles away, or risk having the Concorde shot down right in front of him.

If he could carry even a single Sidewinder in the weapons bay he'd be fine. The heat-seeking sensors on the missile wouldn't be fooled by any high-tech radar gizmo; they'd just run for the MiG's exhaust.

But his weapons bays were going to be inspected at takeoff. There was no way that he knew of to hide a Sidewinder onboard.

"Too bad you can't snag a missile during your refuel," said Rosen, as if he were reading his mind. "Have a wing-walker tie it on for you."

"You volunteering?"

"Oh, yeah," said the major. "Just as soon as I get a set of magnetic boots."

With something like forty percent of the plane built from a silicon-titanium composite, even Rosen's imaginary boots wouldn't have kept him glued on at high speed. Crow didn't bother pointing this out. He looked out the window and picked out boats in the distance, mentally measuring them off—three miles, four, five. They were smaller than the Fishbed.

"Was that a MiG-21 you shot down in the Gulf?"

"I shot down two planes in the Gulf," Crow snapped.

"I wasn't trying to offend you."

"Yeah, I'm sorry." He shrugged. "One was a MiG-29, and the other was a Mirage. The MiG-21's a much older plane. I came up against a few in Vietnam."

"Oh, yeah," said Rosen, as if he knew all about it.

"What did you do, study my personnel record?" Crow asked.

"Nah. Everybody knows you're a hero."

"I'm not a hero."

"Ace or whatever."

"I'm not an ace either," said Crow. Five shoot-downs was the traditional mark of an air ace; Crow had only three. And if truth be told, he'd been lucky to get the Vietnam kill, an ancient MiG-17. He was a newbie paired with an experienced backseater, who had done everything but fly the plane and set up the radar-missile kill.

The Gulf shoot-downs were different, solely his. They were heavily lopsided affairs, executed from long distance with textbook precision against enemy pilots who frankly had no clue.

"I wasn't trying to insult you," said Rosen.

"MiG-21 almost nailed me once," Crow told him. "It was my second mission over Hanoi. This was real late in the war, early for me, but I think it was two or three weeks before Nixon shut everything down. Anyway, I was escorting a reconnaissance flight and I went lost airman."

"Lost airman?"

"I got separated from my flight leader. Basically, I didn't know what I was doing. The Reds sent up a pair of MiGs and we started to take evasive action. I saw one of them and, man, I got hot to trot. I started to follow it, figuring I was going to put a Sidewinder up its tailpipe. Except that he had a buddy trailing behind him."

It was a classic combat tactic. Essentially, the lead plane suckered him in, taking him low where the Phantom's technological superiority was largely negated. As the decoy twisted away, Crow realized he had another MiG on his tail, zooming in for the kill. He tried jinking to his left, rolling at the same time to trick the enemy ahead of him in a turn. But the North

Vietnamese plane was more maneuverable than his, and the pilot was experienced enough to stay inside and behind. In fact, Crow would almost certainly have been shot down if his wing commander had not realized what happened and dove into the fray, managing to nail the MiG behind him just as it began firing its cannon. When Crow returned to base, he saw that about a third of his rear stabilizer had been perforated.

"You're a much better pilot now," said Rosen. He jumped forward, as if pushed by the physical force of a new idea. "Hey, maybe you could hand-load the cannon yourself. Climb back and slide a few rounds into the magazine."

"Just take out the forward fuel tank and crawl right back there, huh?" said Crow.

"That's all it would take?" asked the intelligence officer. He didn't actually seem to be joking.

Crow leaned his head back against the seat cushion. "Sure. I'll twist around the ejector seat, squeeze through the avionics access panel, remove the AC, swim through the fuel tank, and open the magazine. Piece of cake."

"There's a way to do it, though, isn't there?" said Rosen.

"Fred. No."

"Maybe you can talk one of the other escorts in. The Russian plane."

"They're going to be unarmed too."

"You think the Russians will really be unarmed?"

"I think they were planning to be unarmed," said Crow. "Besides, the Su-37's radar and avionics are a lot less capable than ours."

"Look, all you need are a few incendiary rounds to scare him off, right?" said Rosen. "You fire a few rounds and you spook the crap out of him. That's all you have to do—break his attack and give the Concorde time to run away."

"They'll inspect the gun, right? So where do the bullets come from?"

"Sure, they'll inspect it. You load up in the air."

"Fred, you're into science fiction again. There's no way to do it."

"Shit, there's got to be a way," said Rosen. It was tough to tell if he was being serious or stubborn. While he didn't know a huge amount about the plane, he ought to know enough to realize what he was suggesting was impossible. But it wasn't like him to give up. "I bet Cleveland wouldn't think it was ridiculous."

"I want to be there when you ask him," said Crow. "Just to hear his laugh."

Cleveland didn't laugh. His round black face did turn light purple, however. And his head nearly fell off as he shook it.

And then the master sergeant got an idea.

"Who's ever inspecting the plane won't check past the magazine," said the sergeant. "So if we could find a way to have some bullets in the barrel of the gun itself, we might be able to get it to fire. It's far-fetched, but if you want to try something, we can get Jacky Bauer in here. He knows these cannons better than anybody who hasn't been shot down by one."

"What the hell," conceded Crow. "Better than being a damn spectator."

Jacky Bauer served on the traveling F-22 flight crew at the survival shop—supervisor, workhorse, and flunky, all rolled into one. In most operational squadrons, the survival shop—which would include several if not dozens of men and women—was responsible for making sure the parachute and other emergency bailout equipment worked; they tended to flight gear and handled other odds and ends as well. Bauer was not only good enough to do all those jobs himself, but in a previous life the crusty old sergeant had been a weapons expert. He knew the Raptor's M61 Vulcan cannon well enough that he could overhaul it blindfolded. Used on both the F-16 and the F-15, the cannon worked somewhat like an old-fashioned Gatling gun; its barrels revolved to accept rounds from the magazine at the rear, allowing for a rapid rate of fire as they changed position and discharged their bullets.

Bauer realized immediately that Cleveland's idea wouldn't work, since there was no way to get the bullets back into the firing area once they were in the barrels. But he thought he could rig a small clip to slide up into the magazine after the inspection, as long as he could line it up outside the weapons bay properly.

Crow soon found himself standing in the Raptor's maintenance hangar, holding a worklight while Bauer, Cleveland, and two of their assistants played catch with access panels and airplane parts.

It was when the acetylene torch was wheeled over that he asked for an explanation.

"Here's kinda what it is," said Bauer. He ducked under the belly of the plane, pointing to the roundish cylinder that ordinarily received the shells. "We got the magazine here, belt, you know, zip-zip-zip, pack this part up and then like it's a conveyer belt right on up here to the gun. You're going to inspect it, you look here, and you can see this here, and maybe you even rap the guide here to make sure it's empty." Bauer banged on a large flat piece of metal that fed into the rear part of the cannon. "Hell, maybe you put your fingers in, if you're crazy enough. Whatever. We have to figure that who's ever inspecting it will. So the trick is going to be to have something down here where no one's looking, right? And then prime its way into the gun. No one's going to notice that."

"Of course not," said Crow. Bauer was pointing at about three feet of open space. "It's impossible."

Bauer smiled. "No. We just have to be clever about it, that's all, Colonel. We have to push the rounds up into the chamber here after the plane takes off. It's doable. I think." Bauer gave the plane a somewhat wistful look, as if he were a teenager eyeing the family car and making a mental list of how to set it up for drag racing. "We can get the Tinman to rig some sort of lever thing to use the landing gear pressure to push it in. Because you see with this space, it's got to go right there—it's already lined up."

"I don't see it."

"Well, it's lined up or everything falls apart, which is a possibility if we screw it up. But we won't. We'll use the landing gear. Gear doesn't close, you got a problem. Otherwise, you're ready to go. We're going to have to figure out a way around the programming in gun mode that tells F1 the gun's out of ammo."

"That's a bitch," said Cleveland. "Dommie's the only programmer with us, and he's no weapons system expert."

"We can do it," said Bauer. He started nodding vigorously. "Yeah, man, we can do it."

"The landing gear?" asked Rosen.

"You want to try, Colonel?" asked Cleveland.

"We may only be talking about twenty rounds," added Bauer. "But I guarantee it. They're in there already."

"Something's better than nothing," Crow said. Two dozen bullets wouldn't be much. But F1 could make those two dozen all he'd need. The computer could analyze the enemy's flight characteristics so well that it would be impossible to shake the Raptor off its tail. And F1 would show precisely where the MiG was vulnerable, line up the shot, do everything but pull the trigger.

Hell, it could do that too if he let it.

"You think messing with the landing gear's a good idea?" asked Rosen. "What if you can't land?"

Cleveland looked at Crow. The plane they were standing under had cost something like $210 million.

"I've never had to bail out of a plane yet," Crow said. "I don't intend on starting now."

"Famous last words," said Rosen.

"The problem will be folding the gear up," said Bauer. "It won't affect them locking in place. We'll work it all out, don't sweat the mechanical stuff. It's the computer crap I'm worried about."

Crow looked back at the cannon nestled in the weapons bay. He'd be damned if he could see how they could rig anything up.

But he couldn't think of any other solution. There was no way to hide a missile in the weapons bays, and he certainly couldn't carry one on the wings. Putting in a second cannon would be a neat trick.

What the hell. Might as well let them try. Worst case, he'd be back with Blitz's plan.

"Go for it," Crow told them. "You have twelve hours to pull this together."

"Ten and a half," said Rosen, glancing at his watch.

Crow nodded and began walking toward the Humvee waiting to take him to bed.

Worst case, he'd paint the little bastard for the Navy boys and watch it get nailed. Best case, he'd smoke the MiG himself.

Unless, of course, it got him.

Chapter Three

Frankfurt, Germany

Jack made the surveillance team about twenty feet into the airport. He caught a nod, paced himself, watched a reaction across the hall.

Prematurely bald fat guy and a woman who looked like she was carrying a bowling ball in her butt.

Bureau was falling on hard times. But it had never been very good at overseas operations. He continued to the Lufthansa ticket desk, annoyed with himself because he had engineered an elaborate airline dance from Stewart to Logan and then down to Dulles, with a stop in Paris before coming here—only to end up with a Bureau tail. He'd have been better off using Bree's flight, booked under her husband's sister-in-law's name, from JFK to Berlin. Less time, less money.

Even if it was Cara's money. Jack hooked his arm around hers, keeping her close to him as he came to the Lufthansa information desk. A trio of well-groomed men stood behind it, crisply turned out in dark blue suits with identical black handkerchiefs in their breast pockets. They moved with just the slightest hint of stiffness, perfect embodiments of German "correctness."

They were also pleasantly efficient; the man on the far right produced a thick envelope for Jack as soon as he mentioned his sister's name.

The documents included two visas and travel passes through the Ukraine and Belarus as well as Russia, along with additional company documents and something with an official-looking letterhead written entirely in Cyrillic. Jack had no idea what that was about. Stuffing the documents back in the envelope, he looked to the right, as if absentmindedly gazing through the terminal.

Boyle. Passing behind a line of passengers to his right.

Boyle. Jesus H. Christ. She'd come herself.

Was it her, though? He only had a glimpse and now he wasn't sure, worried that he was jumping to conclusions.

He *was* jumping to conclusions. It wasn't her. Couldn't be—they'd never have her tail him this close; he'd seen her close up, could easily make her.

Could he, though?

Jack stared at the spaces between the people in the line, trying to conjure her face in his mind. She'd had fat cheeks, but her hair was the thing—black and very short.

He'd lost the woman somewhere in the crowd. He stepped back, craning his neck slightly, trying to see.

"Sir?"

Something in the man's voice startled Jack, as if he'd been grabbed from behind. He fought the impulse to spin back, moving as calmly as he could though his heart had begun to race.

"Your tickets," said the attendant.

"Oh, yeah." Jack nodded at him apologetically and took the envelopes.

"You are checked in. Your flight to Berlin boards in an hour," added the man. "The VIP lounge is upstairs. Should I show you the way?"

"Nah, I can find it," said Jack. He glanced at the tickets, the words barely registering.

Berlin? Why not directly to St. Petersburg?

If it had been Boyle, she'd moved deeper into the terminal. He couldn't see her.

There were any number of ways to get to Russia from Berlin, but there were more direct flights from here. Why hadn't Bree arranged one?

Did she know he would be followed? Was she worried about Russian customs and her airline documents? Had the Bureau stepped in somehow?

Was he really being followed, or was he just out-of-his-mind paranoid?

Jack took a few steps into the middle of the floor and stopped to nonchalantly fiddle with the ticket documentation, all the while scanning the terminal from the corner of his eyes. No one seemed to be watching him.

"Jack? Are you okay?" asked Cara, standing at his elbow. She had both bags, one over each shoulder. The terminal lighting made her eyes seem almost blue.

"Yeah, come on," he said, starting toward the wide staircase that led to the second level.

The VIP lounge reeked of furniture polish and overly thick leather upholstery. As they pushed open the glass door, Cara and Jack were greeted by a pair of older women who showed them to a pair of club chairs in the corner of the large but empty room. They offered slippers and drinks, as well as the latest newspapers.

Jack tried waving them off, but Cara ordered a Chardonnay.

"Not thirsty?" Cara asked him when he repeated for the third time that he wasn't interested in anything.

"We're not staying."

"I'm glad you slept on the plane or you'd be in a really lousy mood," she said, slipping out of her shoes and curling her feet up beneath her on the couch.

Jack hunched in the chair, considering what to do. One thing he knew—he didn't want the FBI trailing him all the way to St. Petersburg. For one thing, they'd stick out terribly. For another, they'd arrest Danny the second he and his brother got on the plane for home.

Not that Jack didn't want to see his brother strung up by his thumbnails. But only after he faced his father.

The old man would probably be pleased as hell to see him. Even if the Bureau arrested him in the hospital room. His father would smile and pat Danny on the arm, tell him how proud he was of him.

Jack curled his arms at his chest, pushing into the leather couch. He hadn't even found Danny yet, let alone figured a way to get him home, and already he was fantasizing. Good way to get himself shot.

"You giving me one of those visas or what?" Cara asked.

"No," said Jack.

"What if we get separated?"

"Better stay close to me then," he said.

She pulled her feet under her, leaning on the oversized arm rest. She'd changed to jeans or he'd have found it impossible to control himself.

What the hell did she see in Danny anyway?

Cara flicked her head so that her short hair fluttered in the light breeze of the overhead air conditioner. She leaned forward, and for a second he thought she was going to come over and kiss him, but all she was doing was shifting so she could take the glass of wine from the approaching waitress.

Jack jumped to his feet.

"Where are you going?" Cara asked.

"Don't ask questions. Just follow me."

"My wine—"

"Suit yourself," said Jack, pushing open the door and heading back toward the stairs. He didn't bother to look behind him, walking across the terminal to Scandinavian Airlines. He bought a pair of round-trip tickets with his credit card to Helsinki.

An arm brushed against his back as the clerk handed him the packets.

"What took you so long?" he asked Cara.

Except it wasn't Cara. It was a girl about ten or eleven, who had accidentally bumped into him while playing with her brother.

Jack took the tickets and retraced his steps slowly, going back upstairs. Either his tails had passed him off to much more accomplished agents, or they had enough people to watch the gates and the entrances without bothering to stay on his butt.

Or he wasn't being trailed at all.

He could see through the glass door that Cara wasn't in the lounge. He continued to the end of the hall, looking for her, trying not to let the adrenaline that was building in his body take over. A fire exit with a wired glass panel stood at the right; the outside overhead light cast no shadows. Jack turned down the hallway at left, saw a set of rest rooms at the far end in front of him near an office suite. He walked to them, lingered, and checked his watch—the hallway was empty, and if he was under surveillance they were giving him a lot of space. Jack pushed into the men's room, scanned it quickly; when he saw it was empty he went to the wall near the women's room, listened for her.

Nothing.

He debated going into the women's room, realized that would be foolish.

Best thing to do was take another turn through the terminal. And then?

Page her, like any tourist. What the hell. If he was being followed, there was little hope of wiggling away.

What was the sense of the Scandinavian tickets then?

Just let her go. He didn't need her money or her credit cards. The trail team was probably watching her.

He'd made a mistake letting her come. Sucked in by her beauty, and maybe the mistaken notion that she was interested in him.

Or the even wilder idea that he could steal her from his brother.

Right.

Jack pulled open the men's room door, took a step, and rebounded off someone.

"Miss me?"

Jack grabbed her by the arm, walking quickly to the fire door. He rolled his back against the panic bar, pushing her outside with him onto the metal landing.

"Don't ever do that again," he said.

He looked down into her face. Her eyes were closed and her mouth was edging toward him. It was an invitation he couldn't resist.

Jack's lips pressed against hers. For a second everything else disappeared; for a second he wasn't worried about his father or his brother, about Boyle or the Bureau tails or the fact that he was a pawn in some game he didn't understand.

Jack caught himself. He pulled his head up, felt her cling a moment before letting go.

"This way," he told her, grabbing her overnight bag

and practically pulling her down the metal stairs. He walked quickly along the side of the building, the lay-out of the airport flashing into his head. A big Airbus jet began edging away from one of the gates ahead; Jack reversed course, heading around toward the gate where Rusfak—one of Aeroflot's more reputable successors—was boarding a plane.

"What are we doing?" Cara asked.

"Giving them something to think about," said Jack.

"Who?"

"Whoever." He spotted the door ahead. He saw some Cyrillic letters on a display through the glass.

"I didn't get lost," she told him. "I had to pee."

"Whatever," said Jack. He pushed the door open, pulling her along as he walked around the service counter in front of the departure board.

A flight to Moscow was just boarding.

He quickly scanned the line. Two kids, obviously students, were standing with backpacks a third of the way back.

British kids. Barely twenty.

"How much did you pay for your tickets?" he asked one.

"Excuse me?"

"Your tickets." He reached into his pocket and pulled out his roll of money. "How much were they?"

"Got them cheap," said one of the kids. The other punched him in the shoulder.

Perfect.

"A thousand," Jack said, "for both."

"Make it two," said the one who had punched his friend.

Jack shook his head.

"I don't know," said the first kid.

Jack spun and started to walk away.

"Excuse me," said the second kid. "Here we go. One thousand American dollars."

The transaction wasn't exactly unnoticed, but Jack didn't care. He took the two tickets and pulled Cara along.

"They'll just go and buy other tickets," he told her before she could say anything. "The plane's always half empty."

The ticket taker—a woman who looked nearly as pretty as Cara—frowned at him, but took the tickets and waved them along.

Cara took her bag from him as they walked through the door and out onto the tarmac. The airliner—a small and very old Yak-40 with room for about forty people—sat about fifty yards away.

"This is going to get expensive if we keep changing planes," she said.

"Wait until we get to Moscow," said Jack.

She started to say something. Jack took her arm again, pulled her aside as the others continued toward the plane.

"If you don't want to come, you don't have to," he told her.

She opened her mouth to speak, but nothing came out.

"Look, things are going to get a lot trickier from here on out. If you want to go home, go. It's okay." He shook his head, softened his voice. "I realize this isn't the kind of thing you're used to. You're in over your head."

Her lower lip quivered and she looked like she was about to cry. "I'm not," she said.

"You still love Danny?"

It seemed to him it took her a moment before she nodded.

"Why don't you stay here," Jack told her.

"No. I'm coming," she said, wrapping her fingers around the handle of her suitcase.

Jack was climbing the stairs to the plane before he realized he was glad she hadn't gone back.

Chapter Four

Washington, D.C.

If life worked the way Norman "Buzz" Eagleton had thought it did when he headed for Yale as a sixteen-year-old math and political science whiz, he would be sitting in a cabin in the Smoky Mountains, writing the memoir of his recently completed two-term Presidency. He'd be about halfway through the book by now, just starting the meaty chapters on Asia and Russia. On the shelf above the desk would be an earlier book covering his meteoric rise from Congressman to Secretary of State to President at thirty-six; on the wall behind him would be the framed letter from the Nobel Prize commission alerting him to the fact that he was to be honored for his so-called four-corner alliance of the world's great nations, which had ushered in an unprecedented era of prosperity beginning his second year in office.

But life rarely if ever measured up to anyone's teenage fantasies, a fact Buzz had been dealing with for many years. The Deputy Director of Operations for the CIA would be happy, in fact, if it merely ran on track with his present ambition to become the junior Senator from Maine. As he gazed out the window of the Marine helicopter as it lifted off from the back of the White House and headed for Camp David, that ambition seemed well within his grasp—if he could just get past the next few months without something blowing up in his face.

Like Shadow R. He'd ordered Plan Blue into effect before boarding the helicopter. A team was already moving into place to sabotage the plane.

It was a risk, throwing the switch before the President approved it. But he knew D'Amici would; there was no choice.

A pair of small ducks flew in the distance, paralleling the helicopter. Buzz, sitting alone in the passenger compartment behind the flight deck, stared at them a moment, trying to make out the color of their head feathers in the dim light of dusk. He suspected they were buffleheads, common along the Eastern Seaboard, though in his experience rarely such high fliers.

Buzz watched the birds veer off, back toward the water. It was common knowledge that his nickname had been shortened from Buzzard, and in fact quite a large number of people in the agency called him Buzzard, not Buzz—though not necessarily to his face. But almost no one knew that he'd had the nickname since high school, or that he had gotten it, not because he picked out enemies' or subordinates' gizzards, but because he was fascinated with birds—ducks, vultures, grosbeaks, songbirds. And, in fact, one of the items in the briefcase at his feet was a well-thumbed Peterson's *Field Guide* to North American birds.

When the birds were out of sight, Buzz turned his gaze toward the city disappearing in the distance. The setting sun cast a yellowish beam across the mall, bathing the Capitol dome in red.

Why exactly did he want to be a Senator? Was it a substitute for being President?

Part of him thought he wanted to serve his country—truly. His father had been a Lieutenant Governor and his father's father a Congressman. But Buzz also had to admit that his goal was tied up with an emotional impulse for power, for feeling important—for *being* important.

He was DDO of the CIA and damn important right now. He could stay on with the agency for a long, long time if he cared to.

Well, at least until the next Administration.

A Senator had a different kind of power, one that had more to do with prestige than actually getting anything done.

Even so, a Senator could change things, could play a role on the right committee. He'd be on the short list for Foreign Affairs as well as the Intelligence Committee; he had a long list of things he wanted to do on both.

There were other reasons, a lot of them. One was even to make the world a better place, as corny as it seemed. Eagleton believed it, even though what he'd seen over the past decade and a half with the CIA proved the world wasn't something that could be saved by any one country, let alone any one man.

He did like prestige. Yes. He was a conceited son of a bitch and he knew it, even though it got him in trouble.

There would be an undeniable pleasure in defeating

the Democratic incumbent, Senator Calvin Malcomb. The old geezer had killed two favorite projects of his by tinkering with the budget.

They called Malcomb "Hands Off." The Senator told voters it was because he had kept a previous Administration from cutting aid to the state, but in reality it was the common refrain of his female aides. And, rumor had it, one or two of his male assistants as well.

Few of his constituents had heard those rumors, but more might before the election. Politics was dirtier than espionage.

The helicopter thudded down sharply at the landing pad at the Presidential retreat and weekend office. Buzz bolted upwards, practically jumping down the steps as he jogged toward the low-level staffer sent to greet him. He smiled at her—whatever she said couldn't be heard over the roar of the helicopter taking off, and continued running all the way to D'Amici's hideaway office, deep in the compound.

Eagleton wasn't particularly fond of the President—practically a job requirement for top-ranking CIA officials. D'Amici devoted most of his attention to domestic problems and was constantly behind the curve on foreign problems. While Buzz enjoyed the opportunities that provided, he couldn't help feeling superior not just to D'Amici but to the cabinet-level officials who were supposed to be keeping the President better briefed, including his own boss. But Buzz was careful to mask his feelings, as well as his political ambitions; Jack D'Amici was an effective, efficient, and ruthless Chief Executive.

He could also be appropriately deceitful. Buzz was enough of an insider to know that the plainclothes Secret Service agent posted outside the door of the office was there not for security purposes, but in case the President needed a cover: On the record, he hadn't touched tobacco in twenty years. The agent nodded at Buzz and stepped aside to let him enter the room. Debbi Fleming, D'Amici's long-suffering secretary, sat at the far end of the room, her notepad open. She hated tobacco smoke.

"Hello, Buzz. Have a seat," said D'Amici. "Okay, Deb, you dot the i's and get them out."

"You want to hand-sign them?"

D'Amici waved his short cigarette in front of him. "Nah. Pretty routine stuff, don't you think?"

"Yes, Mr. President." Petite and attractive though well into her forties, the secretary got up from the chair and nodded at Buzz. Her husband was one of D'Amici's few cronies who didn't work for him, a novelist who hung out in the upstairs quarters some weekends watching baseball and football games with the Chief Executive. Buzz actually liked him, more so since he was convinced the writer had modeled the hero of his last espionage thriller on him.

And maybe the villain as well.

"You want something?" D'Amici asked. "Leftovers from dinner? We had sole. Very nice."

"No, thanks," said Buzz.

"Cigarette? Coffee?"

"No, thank you, sir," said Buzz.

"Deb, could you get me a refill?" D'Amici asked. He pointed to an espresso cup at the corner of his desk, then got up and began pacing as his secretary left the room. "Shadow R definitely took out the Russian plane, yes?"

Officially, that was supposed to be still in doubt, as the State Department and NSC E-mails and memos Buzz had reviewed before coming over clearly showed. Two assistants had labored for several hours to prepare a report on the incident, filling a thick manila folder with satellite photos, infrareds, and meticulously detailed analysis that Buzz had hoped to present as a trump card, enhancing his position with the President and justifying Blue. Now all he could do was admit that, yes, he read the evidence that way, though as the Director of the National Security Council pointed out, anything was possible.

"Come on," said D'Amici, waving his cigarette dismissively. "Thompson doesn't think that at all. He's convinced it was Shadow R. Where have you been, Buzz?"

Obviously, the NSC director had planted the memos on the E-mail system to sandbag him. Scumbag.

"The question is, why?" D'Amici folded his arms in front of his chest. He was in his shirtsleeves, tie loose at the collar, cigarette in the corner of his mouth. He looked like a broker trying to psyche out a stock deal, or maybe a pool hall regular unraveling a rival's strategy. One by one, he pocketed his cuff links and began rolling up the sleeves of his white shirt.

"They had to make sure the plane works," Buzz suggested.

"More. They want to use it against the Concorde," said D'Amici.

"Well, of course," said Buzz, annoyed that the President had obviously kept on top of the situation without his help. "And since they're mobilizing their forces—"

"Why take the risk that we'll find out about it?" D'Amici's question was rhetorical.

"We already know about it," said Buzz.

"No. They don't care. Why? Because they're in a no-lose position. They can't be sure that we don't know about it, unless we tell the main Russian government. If we do that, the government cancels the flight and the Siberians win because there's no way that news stays quiet. If we don't, they go ahead and shoot down the Concorde and they win even bigger."

Buzz nodded. D'Amici took one last draw on the cigarette, pulling the flame almost to his fingers before stabbing it out in his ashtray. He reached into the top drawer of his desk—Thomas Jefferson's desk, actually—and pulled out a fresh pack.

"We have to make sure the Concorde flight goes off as scheduled," he told Buzz, banging the pack on his desk before unwrapping the cellophane. "And we also have to make sure it lands in Moscow."

"Blue's in effect," said Buzz. "Shadow R won't fly."

The President pulled away the wrapper and tossed it in the burn bag next to his desk. If he was angry that Buzz had already started the operation without authorization, he didn't show it. But then he wouldn't have. Nor did he tell Buzz to reverse his order.

There was a knock on the door. Palming the cigarette pack, he said, "Come," loud enough for Debbi to hear and open the door. She set down a tray of fresh espresso on the edge of the desk and left.

A lemon sat next to the coffee cups, along with a paring knife and a demitasse spoon. D'Amici picked up the knife and slowly cut away a piece of the peel.

"Sure you won't have any?"

"No, sir."

"Little luxuries, Buzz. You have to remember to appreciate them when you're a Senator."

"Senator?" he said blandly.

"Come on, Buzz. Everybody knows you're running for Senate. You had that poll done. I know they didn't use your name, but your brother-in-law's cousin or whatever the hell he is paid for it. Come on. Looks like Hands Off's finally vulnerable, eh?"

"Well, I'm interested in the seat."

"I didn't know you were a Republican." D'Amici—

a Democrat—leaned back in his chair. "I mean, I expected you leaned that way, but I didn't think you would register."

"I haven't."

"You will, though, right?"

"I'd have to, if I run," said Buzz, who of course had chosen to enroll in the party where he had the best chance of winning the nomination.

D'Amici propped the tiny cup of Italian coffee against the tips of his long fingers, bringing it slowly to his lips as if it were a thimble of magic elixir. He savored the espresso—or maybe Buzz's squirming.

"You're aware, I assume, that the Russians are demanding that the escorts fly unarmed. There's nothing to do but agree, especially since that was the original plan. We're preparing some Navy planes for a long-range intercept, and I've alerted the F-22 that's accompanying the Concorde to what's going on," said D'Amici. He put down the coffee and reached for his cigarettes and matches.

"Do you think that's wise?"

A match flared in the President's hand. He cupped his fingers together and lit the unfiltered Camel. "Done deal, Buzz. I couldn't afford not to. For one thing, what if the Raptor is shot down?"

"That's not going to happen," said Buzz.

"If they had one of our cannons in Shadow R it might have," said D'Amici. "We can't count on detecting the plane outside of visual range until we analyze the radar deflection device. You've said so yourself many times. It was, I believe, the basis for your original estimate on the covert project, if memory serves."

"Shadow R won't get off the ground."

"The Professor tells me Blue has a low coefficient of success," said the President. "I hate it when he does that, don't you? Makes it sound as if you could make an operation into a mathematical equation."

The final indignity. Not only was Dr. Michael Blitz—an NSC assistant and the President's personal friend—involved in the operation, but he was passing judgment on Buzz's operations. Blitz had supported the Shadow R project originally, but that hardly softened the blow.

"I don't know that I agree," continued D'Amici. "Even though the Professor has a tendency to call these things in advance."

"I thought Blitz was in Australia."

"I hustled him north as soon as the Yak went down. I couldn't afford to wait. The Professor has been talking to the Russians, and by now he should have finished briefing the pilot. All the elements will be in place in a few hours."

"With all due respect—"

"Don't worry," said D'Amici, obviously enjoying Buzz's contortions to keep from exploding. "I told Blitz to cut back on the length of his dissertations. It's perfect medicine for the Pentagon windbags, but can't have our pilots falling asleep in the middle of a briefing, right?"

"That wasn't quite my objection," said Buzz, straining to be polite. "Shadow R was my operation."

"You run the military now? And the State Department?"

"I could have dealt with the pilot," said Buzz. "As your representative."

"You were busy," said D'Amici. His large brown eyes flickered as he puffed out a massive smoke ring. "That's why you couldn't come out here yesterday, or today for that matter, until this evening."

"Well, I—"

"Don't worry, Buzz. No hard feelings. This is just the kind of job the Professor loves. Besides, you're going to be tied up for the next day or so. I think your Senate campaign needs a boost. I want you to join the Vice President in Beijing tomorrow for the Concorde flight."

"Tomorrow?"

"You're taking off at nine a.m. local time. Don't worry, you can catch some sleep on the plane ride. Just make sure you're awake when the Concorde lands in Moscow. Wouldn't want you to miss the toasts."

"But—"

"Buzz, one thing you'll have to learn as a Senator is to jump on opportunities. And this is a real opportunity for you. Headline material, one way or another."

There was a knock on the door; the President ground the cigarette out in the ashtray and rose. "Better get moving. The Air Force has a plane waiting. You're going to be in the air all night just to get there. By the way, if this is my wife at the door, tell her you were the one smoking, right?"

"Okay," said Buzz weakly.

D'Amici laughed and slapped him on the back. "Just kidding. But I'll remember you were willing to take the fall when the election rolls around."

Chapter Five

Moscow

Major international flights arriving in Moscow used Airport Sheremetyevo II, a relatively modern facility about twenty miles outside the city. Rusfak Airlines had an arrangement with Domodedovo Airport, which lay due south of the capital and catered, as far as that word might be used for anything in Russia, to domestic airlines. The arrangements were considerably different than at the large international airport—though much more typical of Russia in general.

Customs consisted of a sawhorse in the middle of a long corridor. Only a third of the overhead lights in the hallway were working; two halogen work lights had been commandeered to provide light for the officers checking bags and papers. The terminal behind them was ostensibly undergoing renovation; large flaps of thick plastic were stapled against the walls, and steel beams were exposed everywhere. The airport had been this way when Jack last used it nearly two years before.

Whether it was a victim of the government's chronic economic problems or equally endemic bureaucratic wranglings was impossible to tell, and irrelevant; Jack knew that it would be a mistake to mention the surroundings, let alone give off any hint of superiority when dealing with the guards. Using a Russian airline to enter the country meant that they were regarded simultaneously with suspicion and boredom—they stood out as Westerners, Americans especially, but on the other hand were regarded as cheap or at least poor, in either case not good marks for a shakedown.

Jack took care of the visas, unfolding the pink-colored forms and handing them to the guard so the first third—the actual entry portion—could be torn off. He realized belatedly that the forms probably bore Lufthansa's name somewhere in the support section, a discrepancy that could potentially cause problems. If so, the guard either didn't notice or didn't particularly care. The man, in his early twenties with small round glasses that made him look like he should be in a library poring over an early Tolstoy text, merely nodded as he handed back the paperwork needed to get out of the country. They moved along to the next spot at the sawhorses, where Jack filled out the currency forms and wrote out a token sum—five hundred dollars—rather than the several thousand they were carrying. It was a gamble, for if the guards suddenly decided to search them and found the extra money, it would be theirs. But Jack took the chance; putting down a larger sum would attract attention far beyond the airport.

He could have written zero, and the man wouldn't have noticed. He was too busy eyeing Cara.

Not in a particularly benign way either.

"My fiancée," said Jack, putting his arm around her proprietarily.

She caught the cue and kissed him. A deep, penetrating kiss.

"Yes, move, come on," said the man, waving them beyond the sawhorses.

"What did he want?" Cara asked as he walked her down into the main terminal. Things seemed more settled there—thicker plastic covered the construction areas.

"Strip search, probably," Jack told her.

"That's all?"

"Depends on whether he's married or not. If he was, you could really have had problems. This way."

Jack led her past a pair of security guards with dogs to the main door of the terminal. There was a long line of official taxis waiting at the curb. Jack began walking in the other direction.

"Where are we going?" Cara asked.

"We don't want a taxi."

"Why not?"

He stopped suddenly, spinning around. "Look, if you're going to ask me questions every three seconds, I'm going to leave you behind."

"It's just a question."

Jack saw what he was looking for—a group of private sedans with drivers parked at the far end of the lot. The vehicle of choice for these private cars had apparently become Nissan Sentras, about five years old; otherwise, everything was exactly as it had been the last time he was here.

Even the price.

"Twenty American for a night?" he said loudly as he approached.

"Fifty," came the answer. There would be no bargaining between the drivers; they worked according to a strict order and would not undercut each other. But whoever was up next was expected to haggle with the clients, or lose face.

"Twenty-five," said Jack.

"You've got more than that," said the man.

Jack swung his canvas overnight bag further back on his shoulder. "I can go to thirty," he said.

The man shrugged and turned back to the other drivers. Jack shrugged as well, turned, and started away. Cara started to say something, but Jack tightened his grip on her arm. They took five or six steps, then he swirled around.

"Forty," he yelled. "But you will have to help the girl with her bag."

"I will always help a woman," said the man. He pointed to his car. Jack and Cara walked over quickly.

Jack stopped him as the man took Cara's bag to put in the trunk. "That won't be necessary," he said. He uncupped his hand so the man could see that he had not two twenties but a one-hundred-dollar bill. "We're not going far, but we want to go quickly. And we want you to wait."

"Where?" said the man.

"The Club Circus."

The man snorted, as if he had suspected this all along. "Get in then."

"The Club Circus?" asked Cara as the driver pulled from the curb. He drove as if the gas pedal were an on-off switch, accelerating with a sudden burst.

"Club Circus is a nightclub," Jack told her. "You bring a dress?"

"Of course."

"Is it short?"

"What?"

"You'll have to change."

"Where?"

"Here's fine."

"You're kidding me, right?"

"You want me to close my eyes?"

She reached immediately to her pants and undid the zipper. She pulled them off, then yanked her shirt over her head.

Jack noticed the driver gawking in the rearview mirror. He leaned forward and pushed the mirror flat. His arm brushed against her bare breast as he leaned back. He turned and looked out the window.

Hadn't Daniel forfeited her by leaving?

A gold glow rose from the city in the distance, the lights hazing together. The Kremlin spirals stood as if on a cloud of light, Emerald City above the plain of sleep-inducing poppies.

Except that Moscow was hardly in Oz, and certainly not ruled by a wizard. It was more an animal than a city, wounded and dazed, but growling, ornery.

Before his first visit to Russia, Jack had been briefed by an old CIA hand, who'd emphasized the great religious tradition of the country; he'd said there was nothing more important than the spiritual life of the Russians, which had lain buried under Communism but thrived nonetheless. It made everything possible—not merely endurance or generosity, but the great leap into the cauldron, the chaos of Russia's medieval modernity. The economy had been wrecked since the great crash at the end of the 1980's and might never recover, but dreams continued, and that made the country very dangerous. Moscow was now a place where anything could be purchased, but always at a tremendous price both to pocketbook and soul. Someone with money could buy any dream imaginable, and many that were not. From the street corner vendors to the illegal arms dealers, from the cart restaurateurs to the technology merchants, Muscovites walked with their souls in their faces and their hearts in their fists. To succeed here, you had to be a Muscovite yourself—ready to react from feeling, not thought, to move with the night and survive on little more than will and hope.

Even a voyeur, such as himself, felt it. And perhaps beyond everything else, that was why Jack had come back. He wanted the thrill of Russia again, the edge that came from being in the game. His brother, his father, as important as they might be, provided only the motive, not the desire.

That was how he could do it—the spytrons.

The idea crashed at him from the lights of the city: the spytrons. Assuming they were still there, they'd be worth whatever his brother's keepers wanted to release his debts.

On his last mission, Jack had carried a dozen of the ultra-high-voltage krytron switching devices, intending to swap them for smallpox stolen from a Russian facility. The deal had gone bad and the exchange hadn't been made—the B-3 team came out with the germs, but left the spytrons behind.

They were very valuable pieces of equipment—high-tech tubes capable of switching twenty kilovolts of energy in under twenty nanoseconds, even in the presence of nuclear radiation. The switches could be used for an array of applications, including, and most especially, triggering nuclear bombs.

They were sitting at the bottom of a shallow lake in the Ural foothills. Or maybe they weren't. He'd have to make sure.

Doable.

A dozen triggers would make a lot of bombs. He'd be responsible for that.

But Buzz himself had approved the exchange on the earlier mission. For all practical purposes, the government already assumed the devices had entered the black market.

Certainly, it could be interpreted as theft or worse. If anyone found out about it, it would end his career.

But wasn't his career already over? The transfer to the task force hadn't turned out to be a shift to the fast track. With his brother a wanted man, who was going to back his promotion?

And wasn't his brother worth the risk?

He wasn't doing this for his brother—he was doing it for his dad.

It wasn't as if spytrons were impossible to obtain. Difficult, but not impossible.

Just expensive. A dozen would be more than a fair exchange for a deadbeat U.S. scientist.

Assuming he could find Danny.

Jack continued to stare at the city's lights as they drove northwards. Near the Kremlin was St. Basil's Cathedral, Ivan the Terrible's monument to God intended to be so beautiful and unique that he blinded the architects who designed it so they couldn't build another.

Or so the legend went. Jack wondered what God would think of that.

Trade the spytrons for his brother.

It was an act of treason, just the same as his brother deserting.

How else would he get Danny out, though?

"Satisfied?"

Jack jerked his head back toward Cara. She wore a black dress with a plunging neckline, its skirt barely covering her crotch. She could not have looked more perfect.

"Yeah."

She slapped him hard across the face. "The next time, you tell me to change in the ladies' room."

* * *

Not quite halfway to Klin, the driver veered off Highway M-10, his tires squealing as he just barely held the macadam of the turnoff. Though well-traveled, the road they took was unmarked and narrow; the driver worked the power steering hard as they swept first up and then down a succession of twists that seemed to have been carved as part of an obstacle course. As his hi-beams caught a dirt road off to the right side, Jack reached to hold Cara back; the next second they were taking the turn at practically ninety degrees, gravel and sand spitting everywhere.

Five hundred yards later, the width of the road widened as the surface changed to perfectly poured concrete. Ahead on a hill, yellow-tinted spotlights illuminated the hulking ruins of a great complex of buildings.

"That's where we're going," Jack told Cara, pointing to the shadows. "It was a monastery. The KGB took it over under Stalin, and used it to torture people."

"Really?" she asked.

"It's true," said the driver, speaking for the first time. "My father died there."

Jack realized that was most likely a lie—according to the CIA agent who had briefed him on his first visit, the facility had only been used for foreigners. But it was common for drivers to make such claims, and contradicting the man was out of the question.

"That's terrible," said Cara.

"Yes," said the driver. "I think his ghost haunts it sometimes."

"There would be many ghosts," said Jack.

"Why did they kill him?" Cara asked.

"He was a medical experiment," said the driver dryly. "We are not sure which one."

"Probably botulism," said Jack. According to the

CIA agent, the experiments had attempted to see if strains of the bacteria could be used as a weapon.

"I doubt he was important enough for that," answered the man. "The botulism experiments were only on foreigners, and my father was from the Ukraine—foreign to a Russian, but not the regime."

He laughed, as if that were a joke. He slowed to take another turn, this one for the road to the club.

Cara pulled her arms across her chest, nearly shivering, though the heat was going full blast and the night was already warm. But it was too late to regret taking her; Jack gave her leg a reassuring pat as the driver stopped in front of the ruined steps marking the entrance to the club.

"You wait," Jack told the driver, dropping a hundred-dollar bill on the seat.

"You have to have the valet call for me from the desk." Private cars and drivers had to sit in a parking area behind the ruins; though there was security, leaving the car was considered very dangerous. The driver would spend the next few hours staring at the walls and their shadows.

"I've been here before," said Jack, opening the door.

Cara was already out of the car, walking tentatively up the stone steps. Before Jack could catch up to her, two apelike men stepped out from the side of the staircase. "They're not going to hurt you," he said. "Hold your arms out so they can wave their metal detectors."

Cara complied. The men were quick and silent; after wanding Jack they stepped back into the shadows, practically disappearing. Jack took Cara's arm and pointed her to the right, across a long limestone passage to a new flight of stairs. Crumbling walls, now less than two feet high, met them at the top. Past the threshold, soft yellow lights illuminated a vast floor mosaic depicting a lion jumping through a flaming hoop. Jack led Cara across it to what seemed a casual pile of rocks marking the start of another staircase, this one leading downward. At the base, another pair of silent guards checked them for weapons, then stood back to reveal the way to a third set of stairs. These were carpeted with a thick red material, and led down into the vast catacombs of the former monastery. A carved pair of mahogany doors—another circus scene—swung open as Jack and Cara reached the final step.

"God, this lion is eating the acrobat's hand," said Cara, studying one of the doors.

"Yeah. I wouldn't look too closely at the other door if that turns you off," said Jack. He led her past the doors onto a platform of solid Italian marble that seemed to float in the air, hovering in front of a laser-lit, fog-enshrouded dance floor. A throng of people—mostly men and women in their twenties, related in some way to the Russian power elite—worked to the beat of a retro-techno dance mix. The music was Western, but would have been considered several years out of fashion in Berlin or Paris.

"The first circle of Hell," said Jack as a young woman dressed in a skirt but no top ushered them toward the side of the platform, where a set of steps were roped off leading into the club. As they walked, an X-ray system several times more sensitive than the devices Israelis used to keep plastique explosives off their planes examined them. On the first step down toward the dance floor, a set of eye-scanning lasers studied their retinas, checking them against a list of personae non gratae, as well as filing them away for future interest.

"I seem to be overdressed," said Cara as they reached the floor level.

"Easy to fix," said Jack.

"Good evening, and welcome to the Circus," said a short, zoot-suited man, materializing from the crowd in front of them. He came to Jack's chest; his face was a good third as long as the rest of his body. Thinning hair slicked back, pinkie rings on both fingers, he held his thumb to his mouth at the beginning of each sentence, as if he were pushing the button that made his mouth operate. His English had the heavy strain of Brooklyn, New York, 1940s vintage, though he himself could be no older than thirty.

"Good evening, Johnny," said Jack. "We'd like a table in the casino."

"Oh, the casino is very busy," replied Johnny. He had no reason to be surprised that Jack knew his name; everyone who came here knew him.

"That's the attraction, isn't it?" said Jack. He slipped out a hundred-dollar bill.

"Oh, hey, that isn't necessary," he said, glooming the bill. He lifted his hand in the air, motioning with one of his fingers. "Kersten will show you the way."

A blond waitress with perfect breasts and a low-slung miniskirt appeared before them, standing at the edge of a rising cloud of artificial smoke.

"One more thing," Jack said to Johnny, touching his shoulder as the short man turned away.

Johnny hated to be touched. He stopped, visibly shuddered, turned stiffly.

"The Milkman. I'd like to see him," said Jack.

"Milkman? Oh, hey, I don't know what you're talking about," said the maitre d'. He took a step backwards and vanished behind the smoke.

"This way, please," said Kersten.

This section of the club was an open floor, marked off by the lasers and cloud machines from a second level one step down. Here the mood and music changed, becoming less disco, more circus, though this too was a dance floor. Trapeze artists could be seen doing their thing over the crowd. They worked without a net; generally they didn't fall, but the idea that they might was part of the attraction, at least for the people who danced beneath them.

And there were other things.

"Oh, my fucking God, that's a real lion," Cara screeched, grabbing Jack as the animal loomed two feet away.

"Yeah," he said. He did his best to remain nonchalant as they followed Kersten through the writhing crowd. The animal took a step toward them, sniffing vaguely, then walked away.

"It had teeth," said Cara. "Jesus."

"Yeah. Wouldn't be fun without teeth. But it's the rhino you have to watch out for," Jack told her.

He wasn't kidding.

They picked up a trail of blinking red lights in the floor, and followed them to an Escheresque black and white bull's-eye. Kersten stopped. Jack had to grab Cara as the floor suddenly plummeted downward.

"That's not very safe," she said when they stopped.

"It's not supposed to be," said Jack.

The smoke and heavy pulse of the disco music was replaced by the softer, though no less frantic, beat of neo-Big Band jazz. The music soaked into the heavy carpet, absorbed and dulled by the crowd of gamblers who knotted tables every few yards. The cigar and cigarette smoke hung thicker than the artificial clouds above. Kersten, boobs pert, led them in a diagonal between the roulette and twenty-one tables, past a section for a game called "Killjoy," a quick-hit version of War played with three cards that was a specialty of the house and routinely featured six-figure pots. The money on the tables was all American; Euros, yen, and even the occasional ruble were exchanged at the cashier for real American dollars, fifty-, hundred-, and thousand-dollar denominations only.

Kersten showed them to an empty table for six about thirty feet from the band. "To drink?"

"Scotch, neat. And a Partagas four," Jack said.

"Only a four? I would have thought bigger," said Kersten.

"I'll have a water," said Cara sharply.

Jack put his hand up to stop Kersten. "Make it a Chardonnay for the lady," he said.

Kersten smiled and left them.

"I don't want wine," said Cara.

"Water here means Nectar Vodka," Jack said. "It's something like white lightning. About 195 proof. You can't get real water, not even as ice."

"Oh." She folded her arms in front of her. Jack watched her pout deepen as she scanned the club. "Well, at least the males are bare-chested too. Who's the Milkman?"

"The owner. One of them. An American, or at least he was," Jack told her.

"He must be pretty rich."

"Yeah. He sells things. Like black-market MiGs and Sukhoi fighter planes, BM-27 rocket launchers and the odd T-72."

"He's a friend of yours?"

"I helped him avoid a few pieces of lead last time I was in Russia. That ought to be worth a car to St. Petersburg." Jack leaned back in the chair. "Maybe not. Depends on his mood."

"That guy Johnny didn't act like he was here."

"He'll show up eventually. That's why we got the big table." Jack scanned the card tables. He wouldn't have been completely surprised to see Daniel at one—was it possible that the Milkman had snagged him?

If so, things would be even more complicated.

"You've been here before, I take it," said Cara.

"I've been here." Jack spotted the bald-headed man as Kersten approached, and leaned across the table and suggested that Cara fix her makeup.

"Where?" she said.

Before Jack could point out the rest room, he was lifted from his chair.

"Jack Ferico, how the hell are you?"

The Milkman, wearing a faded Yankee baseball cap and a blue sweatshirt beneath a beat-up leather jacket, appeared at his left. He grinned at Jack, who despite being six and a half feet tall, was being held over his chair by one of the Milkman's henchmen. Then the Milkman turned to Cara, wrapping his fingers around the top of her shoulder and kissing her cheek as if they were old friends. Jack couldn't tell if the pain on her face was from the kiss or the pressure of his fingers.

"You can put him down, Ti," the Milkman told the Mongolian giant who was holding Jack. "Not too gently."

Jack fell back down into his chair. Even if he hadn't realized this was the Milkman's idea of a floor show, he would have taken a careful approach to Ti, whom he'd seen grab the rhino when it got ornery during his very first visit there.

The Milkman let go of Cara and sat down next to her. As she started to get up, he grabbed her hand at the wrist. "Don't go," he said.

"She's not part of this," said Jack.

"Part of what?" said the Milkman. Despite the rigors of his business, the Milkman had a soft, babylike face that never, to Jack's knowledge, betrayed tension or even moderate concern. It was difficult to tell how old he was; his eyes gave nothing away, and the only hint that he was anything other than a pampered playboy was a dark red mark on his neck about the size of a nickel, apparently a souvenir from someone who didn't like the terms of an early deal. Though he stood only five-eight, he had a way of filling space that made him imposing even with his bodyguards out of sight.

"I have to pee," said Cara weakly.

"By all means," said the Milkman. He let go of her arm, smiled at her as she left.

"Jack, it's been too long," said the Milkman. "I've missed you."

"I think about you too."

"I hear the FBI's pissed off at you for some reason. I thought you did a good job for them last time you were here. They weren't angry that the people you were dealing with all died, were they?"

"Not that I know."

"Bad coincidence, that. I hope it's not catching."

"It may be."

The Milkman had a soft laugh, the kind other people used when they knew only they would find something funny. "So why are you in Russia, Jack? Taking in the museums this time around?"

"I'm here to find my brother," said Jack. The best way to deal with the Milkman—the only way when you needed something—was to be direct.

"That wouldn't be the famous turncoat, would it? Daniel Ferico?"

Jack wasn't surprised that the Milkman knew about Daniel—even if the FBI hadn't had a press conference on CNN, the Milkman was the definition of plugged-in. But it was difficult to hear other people talk about Danny like he was a piece of dogshit, even if Jack might share that view at the moment.

"He's in St. Petersburg somewhere and I want to get him home," said Jack. "It's a personal thing."

"I wouldn't have thought anyone related to you

would be a traitor. You're so—patriotic. Gung ho."

"Can you help me get to him?"

This time the Milkman's laughter was very loud. "Why would I?"

"Out of the kindness of your heart?" he said.

The Milkman laughed again. He reached into his pocket and took out a silver cigar case, slowly unscrewing the top.

"I imagine there could be something in it for you," said Jack, not sure what else to say.

"Like?"

"I'm sure my brother must be doing something worthwhile."

"Your brother, yes. High-tech materials. Ceramic Teflon or something, right? Makes those radar waves just slip right off the plane. Is that it? I was never very good at chemistry." The Milkman glanced over Jack's shoulder. Instantly his mood changed, though whether it was because of something he'd seen or decided, it was impossible to tell. "Cut the bullshit, Jack. Why are you here?"

"I told you. I'm here for my brother."

"The FBI sent you to arrest your own brother?"

"No. I'm here on my own. My father's dying. He wants Danny to come home to say good-bye."

"Buy your father the liver and be done with it," said the Milkman.

It was impossible to keep surprise from his face.

"Funny what things you can find out in just a few minutes if you have the right resources," said the arms dealer. He removed the cigar from the case and produced a pocketknife, whittling off the end with a flick of his thumb. Few knives were so sharp. "You want me to help you do that, Jack?"

For just a second, the temptation loomed. Jack's father would never, ever agree to something like that—

in fact, he had made it clear to Jack and Bree that he didn't want them to use any influence to get him moved up on the waiting list. Jack had held off asking his dad's old friends in the government for help because of that. But now—the Milkman could obviously deliver, and even though his father had other problems, a new liver would greatly improve his odds of living longer.

Would his father want to live, knowing that the organ had been stolen—perhaps from a living person?

"Tempted, Jack?" asked the Milkman, lighting his cigar. "You're not letting ethics or morality get in the way, are you? It's your father we're talking about. I mean, a liver's a liver."

"We're on a waiting list," said Jack.

The Milkman's laugh was soft. "You know how those things go. But Jack, why care where it comes from?"

His father would care, but there must be ways to keep him from finding out.

He could trade the spytrons. Surely it was worth it.

Jack saw the old man floating on the white sheets in the hospital room. He was ready to die; it was Jack who couldn't accept it.

"I'm just here to get my brother," he said finally.

The Milkman took a long pull on the thick cigar before nodding thoughtfully. "Your brother is helping some not very nice people. Apparently they want to coat an airplane with a radar-avoiding plastic and ceramic compound. I have to say I'm surprised, because I thought they knew how to do that already. In fact, I know they did. But apparently he made them an offer that was too good to be refused. They've taken him on as a consultant."

"What did he get in return?"

The Milkman shrugged. "I imagine they helped him

pay off some debts. This is only of tangential interest to me. I don't even know if he's helped them yet. He may, if they keep him around."

"I'd like a car that I can use to get to St. Petersburg."

"Your brother's in Siberia, Jack, not St. Petersburg. I know FBI agents in general are woefully ignorant, but I expected more from you."

"Siberia?"

"A complex near a place that used to be called Norabk. Not terribly far from Surgut, given the fact that we're talking about Siberia."

"How do you know?"

The Milkman considered the cigar, ignoring the question. Obviously, it was his business to know. When he finally spoke again, Jack felt almost relieved.

"I have to say, Jack—the people your brother is involved with: not top shelf. Dangerously deranged. That's not my opinion solely. Others feel that way. I have a hard time doing business with them, and you know I do business with everyone."

"Who are they?"

"Different people. Many Siberians. Army and Air Force people. They want to be the government. That is what makes them dangerous. But then, why not? What is the government, after all? Me, you—we're as legitimate as Shrankov or Yeltsin's nephew or any of the dozen pretenders who parade through the Kremlin. And the Parliament." The Milkman took a long puff from his cigar, then waved his hand dismissively. "Each company commander in the Army is his own boss. That's where the power is. Though I prefer to spend my money on the sergeants. I've always gotten along with sergeants."

"Can you help me get to my brother?"

"What? For a reunion?"

"He's in trouble."

"He should have thought of that before he went to work for the Siberians. They're very committed." The Milkman leaned back in his chair, his eyes wandering across the massive room. "Is he really helping them, you think? Or is he up to something else?"

"I'll ask."

"I heard they pay scientists with unmarked Swiss bank accounts. They've been checking around about Daniel, though. They had some people looking into him. And you."

"Me?"

"That's what I hear. But of course, I heard everything. Rumors. Innuendo. Cute girl, your girlfriend." The Milkman paused to take a thoughtful puff on his cigar.

"She's Daniel's girlfriend."

"Oh, yeah?"

"Can you help me get to him?" Jack asked.

"You think it's like buying a train ticket? All I have to do is write down the destination in Cyrillic letters? You think these people would even flip open a cell phone to take my call?"

"I can get money, if that's what you want."

The Milkman laughed. "If you sold everything you owned, you wouldn't have enough to make it worth my while."

Kersten approached with the drinks. She grew noticeably nervous when she saw her boss sitting at the table, but the Milkman—whom she knew as Mr. Jones—didn't even turn his head in her direction. He looked only at Jack, watching Jack take the small cigar in his hand. The waitress left a cigar guillotine in the ashtray, along with a gold lighter, then quickly found other business.

"Small cigar," said the Milkman.

"I didn't figure I'd be here long," Jack lit the hand-rolled Cuban. It had a strong taste that belied its size. He grinned at the Milkman and pocketed the lighter.

"Your brother's new employers may object to his leaving," said the Milkman.

"We'll work something out."

Jack saw the flicker in the Milkman's eye, a hint of interest that quickly slipped behind the furl of smoke.

"And the FBI is not involved? Or the CIA? Or B-3 or the ad hoc groups your boys like so much?"

Jack shook his head.

"So what's with the sailor girl then?" asked the Milkman.

"Who do you mean?"

The Milkman's eyes squinted ever so briefly. In the next instant, he was on his feet. "Come with me," he told Jack.

Jack hesitated.

"I like you Jack, that's my problem," said the Milkman. "I like you and I actually trust you. So I'm going to do you a favor that maybe you don't deserve."

He started walking and Jack jumped to his feet, leaving the cigar in the ashtray. Ti lumbered behind him as the Milkman angled beyond a row of computer slot machines. A pair of uniformed policemen—they were on the state payroll as well as the Milkman's—stood aside to let him down a short landing, where another officer swung open a bombproof door. The exotic trappings of the club abruptly ended; Jack's feet scraped against steel-reinforced concrete laced with tread inserts to assure traction. He followed a few feet behind the Milkman down a long, industrial-like corridor past yet another set of guards, these in ninjalike black. The Milkman disappeared around a corner, but the way was obvious. Jack caught a glimpse of a pair of additional bodyguards trailing Ti as he turned through a series of sharp zigs, obviously a precaution against a mass attack. No medieval castle was better protected.

Jack felt almost dizzy when he completed the last leg of the double W. The corridor opened up again; there were rooms lining the hall ahead. Ti stood near the door to one. As Jack walked toward it he again felt the empty weight where his gun should be, though he knew he'd never have been allowed to carry a weapon into the club.

The Milkman was waiting in a small room midway down the hall. There was no pretense at decoration here; the walls were bare Sheetrock, taped but not painted. The ceiling consisted of metal framework but no tiles; in their place wires ran everywhere. There were wires scattered along the floor as well.

The room was hardly forgotten storage space or an insignificant utility closet. Three massive tables held several banks of computers and associated equipment in the exact center. There were at least twenty additional monitors and CPUs clustered nearby. Three men squinted at the different displays, occasionally tapping keys and moving quickly from one unit to the other. The Milkman stood in front of a twenty-one-inch flat video screen at the far end of the tables, pointing to the display.

"You told me her name was Cara, but it's really Maryanne. A nice name."

Cyrillic letters filled the bottom band of blue on the set. The rest was a U.S. government personnel data screen, with a digital shot of Cara and information to the left.

Maryanne C. Gillespie. DIA assignee from the Navy. Ensign rank. On loan to the NSC. Assigned project: classified.

"Fuck me," said Jack.

"Yeah," said the Milkman. "Fuck you. Boffing an ensign. I don't trust this DOB either. Twenty-seven? No way. I doubt she's even old enough to drive."

Chapter Six

Hokkaido, Japan

Sleep wouldn't come. His neck hurt, and even four Extra-Strength Tylenols couldn't cure the throb in his knee.

Crow tried an old trick, replaying a World Series game he'd seen as a kid, reliving it pitch by pitch. Usually it knocked him out before the second inning, but tonight he was too wired.

Yet his body felt like an anchor, ready to fall right through the bed into the earth. The pilot slid his arm under his thin pillow. He imagined himself the pitcher, rearing back to deliver a fastball.

The batter nailed it into the right-field bleachers.

Not exactly the way he remembered the real game. Not the way he wanted to imagine it either.

If that was what sleep would bring, he wanted no part of it. Crow rolled himself off the bed and went to the window. He and the other officers assigned to the Raptor were staying in a hotel a few miles from the airport. He considered calling Rosen or maybe Jerry Fernandez, a captain who'd put in a great deal of time around Japan and was always ready to suggest a club or more serious diversion. But Crow wanted to be alone, at least for the moment, and besides, he did need to sleep at some point. He went to the window and pulled open the curtains, gazing down at the hotel swimming pool twenty-two stories below. The water shimmered perfect blue in the late-night darkness, its underwater lights giving it an eerie glow. A shadow moved slowly across.

A naked swimmer.

No, just the shadow of a bird or something fluttering by one of the terrace lights.

And he was going to see a MiG-21 from eight or nine miles off? Or even five?

No way. It wasn't possible, even if he were thirty years younger. Guys used to talk about seeing them three miles off, and they called that luck.

Fishbed's a hell of a flier, turns like a dream, runs circles around an F-4 Phantom. Don't ever let it behind you, don't ever try to follow it into a turn, don't ever try and stay in an invert with it.

They tell you not to turn into him, but you can if he's balls-out; he's got to muscle the shit out of the stick and if he's really moving it's too much work.

Keep your turn wide enough so you don't lose energy and he can't close inside.

Worst thing you can do is be predictable. Gomer sees where you're going, his bullets'll get there first. And they love to fly in pairs—always watch for the trail. Always.

* * *

The veteran pilot's warning thirty years before replaced the hush of the room's air conditioner. Crow sat uneasily in the foam-cushion chair next to his bed, remembering the advice and then the flight. Sweat poured from his neck again, his stomach queasy with the yanking g turn as the MiG's cannon sprinkled slugs into his rear. If the Russians had put a better gun in the plane, he'd be dead now.

If, if, if. No sense playing that game. Things happened and you moved on.

The MiGs did well in Nam because the Vietnamese and Russian pilots had learned to dictate the terms of engagement. Low-altitude furballs took away the Americans' major technological advantages. As bad as the MiG's cannon was, it was better than nothing—which was what most F-4 Phantoms carried until late in the war.

The F-22 was even bigger than the Phantom. As conceived, it aimed to defeat enemies from long range—launching missiles before its prey even knew it was there.

That wasn't going to happen with Shadow R.

But the engineers who had designed the Raptor had been mindful of the lessons learned in Vietnam. Not only had they put a serious gun in its belly; they had designed the plane to be highly maneuverable in combat at high and low speeds. Thanks to thrust vectoring and computer-assisted flight controls, the Raptor could cut squares out of circles and outdance anything in the sky. Including a MiG-21.

At least in theory.

Crow would only have a few dozen rounds at most. But F1 would help, showing him where to put those BBs better than any gray-haired backseater.

Besides, all he had to do was scare the bastard off and wait for the F-14s.

Unless the MiG saw him first.

No way. Even the Raptor, with all its cutting-edge stealth technology, wasn't invisible to sensors, let alone the naked eye. The F-22's radars would pick up the MiG in time.

So what was he worrying about? The ache in his knees and the crink in his neck?

The fact that he'd blown it so bad thirty years ago?

Or just because?

He wanted the MiG. He was going to get it. It wasn't enough to paint it for the Navy fighters. He was going to take advantage of everything—his experience, his plane, F1, everything—and he was going to smoke that son of a bitch. It was his job and his fate, and the fact that he was old for a fighter pilot sure as hell didn't mean he was washed up.

Crow picked up the phone on the table next to the bed. "I'd like a pot of coffee up in 22D," he told room service. Then he got out a pad of paper and started calling anyone he could think of who might be able to tell him something about MiG-21s.

Chapter Seven

Moscow

Cara wasn't particularly surprised that Jack wasn't at the table when she got back from the ladies' room. She sat at the table, eyeing the wine, debating whether it was drugged.

What the hell, she decided. She was in so far over her head it probably wouldn't make a difference.

The bimbo who'd followed her into the rest room took a seat four tables away. Cara tried to ignore her, sipping slowly at the wine.

It was extremely good California, Chateau Woltner. Cara took another, letting the flavor soak into her tongue.

She hadn't been briefed on Club Circus or the Milkman, but it wasn't difficult to guess he'd be among the last people Eagleton wanted Jack to hook up with. She was fairly powerless to do anything about it, and in fact wasn't exactly sure what she was supposed to do from here out. When she'd called the operations desk from the airport rest room in Frankfurt, Buzz had been unavailable; the assistant handling the desk had told her the mission had gone to Plan Blue. He'd said it as if she'd know what the hell that meant, hanging up quickly. Her line was open, and even though she'd used a dummy phone number that routed her call halfway across the world and back, she couldn't ask for an explanation. Since she'd never been properly briefed, she had no clue what Blue was.

Buzz didn't want Jack near his brother. Did Blue reverse that? Should she help him or hinder him? Why did Buzz let him go to Russia in the first place?

She had no contact agent in Moscow. As far as she could tell, they were on their own here. Buzz knew they were going to St. Petersburg, so she had to hope the trail team would pick them up there.

Assuming there was a trail team. And assuming they were smart enough to watch the hotels planted on Daniel's computer.

"How's the wine?"

She looked up into Jack's face, trying not to show surprise. "Acceptable."

"It ought to be for a hundred bucks." Jack slid his chair out and sat down. "We'll have to find someplace to stay the night," he said. "I'm starting to feel jet-lagged."

"Fine with me. Do you have someplace in mind?"

"I have some ideas. You drinking that?"

Cara studied his face, trying to decide whether the Milkman had told him anything useful or not. It was a handsome face, betraying only a bare hint of wear and worry.

"I'm drinking it," she said, picking up the wine. "What's our next step?" she asked.

"Sleep."

"Leave for St. Petersburg in the morning?"

"We'll see."

Something about the way he leaned back in his chair and frowned made her think—made her realize—he wanted to sleep with her. Cara felt her heart jump, and for the barest second forgot who she was and why she was here.

She wondered if it wasn't time to just come clean.

"Some floor show," she said.

Jack stood up. "Come on. Take the glass with you. They can spare it."

The driver shrugged nonchalantly when Jack told him to pull off the highway to see if they were being followed. Then he pulled a U-turn across traffic at about sixty miles an hour, driving the wrong way until finding a divider. He narrowly missed a black Mercedes before careening across to an exit. Cara put her hand on her throat to keep the wine from coming back up.

"Thanks," Jack told him.

"Of course."

It seemed to her that the two men communicated in a secret language, most of it on a subconscious level, as if they were performers in a theater troupe ad-libbing through technical difficulties. It was all improv, yet they understood each other perfectly.

"We're looking for a place to stay," Jack said. "Someplace quiet. Not in the main tourist area."

Cara felt his weight against her as they made another turn. She pushed back gently.

The driver recommended two small hotels south of the Moscow River in the city.

"Take to me the cheaper one," said Jack.

"Make it the cleaner one," said Cara.

Jack snorted but agreed. The driver said the hotel was near Lenin Hills.

"You can do some sightseeing there, lady," said the driver. "It's the highest point in the city."

"Just what we want," said Jack sardonically. He turned to the window, staring at the shadows that crossed the highway like a giant swatting his long arms at them. The highway wound through hills haunted by the ghosts of broken Panzers and Frenchmen cursing their starving nags. A thousand years of Russian history peeked out from the hulking darkness lining the road, gawking at the billboards and the thick, tangled ribbons of telephone and power wires.

"What are you thinking?" she asked him.

"I'm not thinking," he said, his eyes still fixed outside.

"Your father must have been some man."

Caught by surprise, Jack turned from the window and found her face practically next to his.

"Yeah," he said.

"I didn't know my father, except as a folded photograph. He died when I was little. My mom too. Together."

Jack nodded. His eyes probed hers, and it seemed to Cara that he wanted to ask her something, but instead he said simply, "My mom died when I was nine."

"So your father was everything, mom and dad."

"He's just my dad. Mom was Mom."

Jack's voice was hard, the words as dismissive as anything he'd said back in D.C. Cara tried to tell him she was sorry, that she hadn't meant anything, but he had turned back to the window and wouldn't look her. It made her feel hopelessly distant and cold and in love, all at once. She only barely kept herself from telling him everything.

They drove the rest of the way to the city in silence.

Off the highway, the driver pulled onto a wide boulevard, through the shadow of the Lomonosov or

Moscow University, skirting through the edge of the vast campus. The driver spoke in his best English, telling them about the circus building nearby. "The *real* Circus," he said with emphasis, "*Novi Tsirk,* the new circus."

Cara wanted to ask if he had seen performances there, but Jack's sullen glare warned her off. The driver fell silent.

The building he stopped in front of had no sign outside, no marking that declared it was a hotel. Jack got out confidently nonetheless, as if he'd been there dozens of times before. Inside, the driver led them through a small lobby to a desk manned by a bent old lady. The carpet was old, well-worn, but clean enough.

Cara felt another bump in her pulse when Jack asked for a single room.

Walking up the two flights of stairs to the room, Cara realized she'd made a major mistake not correcting him. She was supposed to be hot for his brother, not him. She had to fall back into character or he would surely realize something was up. This was a job, not a date.

"One bed?" he said when he opened the door. It sounded as if he'd expected two.

"Yeah."

"Well, at least there's a bathroom. You go first."

She knocked her elbow against the wall closing the door. The sink took up half the room, more space than the shower stall and toilet together. She slipped off her short black dress, leaning against the sink to take off her panty hose.

The bare yellow incandescent bulb over the mirror showed thick, heavy eyelids. There was fear in her eyes as well, or at least apprehension.

Cara furrowed her hair back, resisted the temptation

to add a little makeup to soften her eyes. She pulled on a T-shirt, then pulled a sweater over it. She stepped into some jeans and put socks on and shoes before stepping out of the room, chaste, or at least reserved, back in character. She'd sleep in her clothes.

Jack was sitting on the bed, watching her. While she was in the bathroom he had pushed the bureau in front of the door; Russian hotel workers had a notoriously limited sense of privacy.

She took two steps and was in front of him, felt him standing, and then pulling himself around her.

Cara gave in and began to kiss him, lost her balance momentarily as he twisted her down onto the bed.

"Jack," she said, intending to protest about his brother.

He put his finger over her lips, was on top of her. She closed her eyes and kissed him again.

Then Cara felt the sharp edge of a knife at her throat.

"Tell me, Ensign, exactly what the hell am I doing here? And where the fuck is my brother?"

She couldn't speak for a moment. He had her completely pinned; even without the knife at her throat she'd have been helpless.

"You can feel how sharp this is," he said.

"I don't know."

"He's not in St. Petersburg."

"Probably not," she admitted.

Jack pulled the blade back, but kept it near her throat. "What were you going to do, seduce me?"

"I have all my clothes on. Even my shoes."

"What is this all about?"

"If you let me up, I'll tell you what I know."

"How can I trust you?"

"I'm on your side, Jack. I'm working for Buzz Eagleton. You can call him."

"Yeah, right, just pick up an open line in Moscow and call the CIA's covert operations desk." Jack snorted contemptuously. "You didn't even tell me your right name, Maryanne."

"It's not Maryanne. I never use that. I use Cara. Maryanne is on the birth certificate, but I never use it. Check. Contact Buzz. Christ, we can go to the embassy."

"What about Gillespie?"

"I told you I was getting divorced. You never asked what my name was."

"You said your husband's name was Stephen Karns."

"That's who the apartment belongs to."

She winced as he put the blade back to her throat.

"I could slice your damn neck right off with this," he told her. "I'll blame it on the Russians."

"Buzz won't believe you," she managed.

"Screw him," said Jack—but he eased off on the knife.

"He didn't want you to go to your brother."

"Why not?"

"I don't know. Maybe they're afraid you're going to kill him."

"Really? Or do they want me to find him so they can kill him?"

"If that were the case, wouldn't I have been helping you find him?"

"Not necessarily."

"Look, I'm being honest. Please let me up."

Jack let go of her. "Where did he call from?"

"I don't think it was him."

"Who was it then? One of Buzz's people?"

"I think so. I might be wrong." Cara pulled herself up, feet dangling over the edge of the bed. "I got into this about fifteen minutes before you found me in the shower. All I was supposed to do was make sure it was you."

"How come you're still around?"

"Buzz wanted me to change some things in the computer. Then I was supposed to watch you."

"What things? St. Petersburg?"

She nodded.

"What about Boyle?"

"I don't know who Boyle is. Buzz wouldn't say. He told me Boyle was a problem."

Jack snorted. His eyes seemed to have narrowed and flattened, as if he were looking at the world through a permanent scowl. "What is Buzz up to?"

"I don't know. I'm not CIA, I'm Navy, assigned to the NSC. I don't even know who the CIA station chief is in Moscow."

"Art Sandborn."

"See? You know more than me."

"Why were you trying to seduce me just now?"

"I wasn't trying to seduce you. God. I've got my clothes on."

"Yeah."

"Hey, screw you."

"Wouldn't you like to."

"I just told you everything I know. Buzz will kill me when he finds out that I've told you all of this. My career is toast."

"It's toast anyway."

Something came over him suddenly, his body lifting up as if a tornado had burst into the room behind him. He scooped down toward her, and Cara threw her arm up to ward him off.

Then she realized he wasn't attacking her but pulling her off the bed as rifle fire ripped through the room.

Chapter Eight

Western Siberia

Colonel Bashkin had flown Sukhoi Su-25 ground-support planes in Afghanistan; he had come under fire several times, taken a few slugs in his wings, and come home intact. He was not, however, a particularly good pilot. Adrik Rashov sensed that the colonel regarded him with some resentment, both because of his skills and because he was Lev's brother. The colonel spoke of Lev as "my general," and only in terms better reserved for God. Adrik, while he would do whatever his brother asked without question, no longer believed in God, and exhibited reverence toward no one.

Bashkin most especially. He ignored the hovering colonel behind him, completing his walk-around of the Black Eagle. The technicians had tinkered with Radio B's antenna system, and the captain in charge of the maintenance team had asked the pilot to take it on a brief flight, just to make sure all of the mechanical systems were at spec. The flight would also give him an opportunity to practice the takeoff that would be necessary on the day of the mission: He would taxi and lift off under a large Tupolev bomber, a TU-95, so he could escape American satellite surveillance.

Until now, his missions had started during nighttime windows when the optical satellite had difficulty picking up the flight, but this would not be possible tomorrow, since he would have to launch in the morning. The maneuver called for modest coordination and required that he alter his normal takeoff procedure, since he could not use the usual rocket-assisted packs. The rockets, mounted beneath the wings and falling away once he was airborne, helped make up for the decreased wing area and lift characteristics that were by-products of the MiG's stealth modifications. Still, the plan was not technically difficult; the TU-95 Bear was a large, stable plane that had been practicing the slow runway passes all morning. Once off the ground, flying beneath it was not much more difficult than lining up for a refuel; he had no doubt he could do it for the planned ten miles. And while the men on the Bear were undoubtedly top professionals, he had heard it said that the big turboprop bombers practically flew themselves.

"My general places great trust in you, and in your airplane," said Bashkin as Adrik bent to look over the cannon muzzle.

Adrik straightened. "It is not my airplane, Colonel. I fly it only. I am a truck driver."

"Come, Captain, you are too modest. We know what an excellent pilot you are."

Was there a time when flattery had worked with Adrik? Perhaps when he had joined the service. Certainly, if someone he had respected in his youth, his first flight instructor for example, had talked about his skills, his head would inflate.

His first flight instructor had augured in three weeks after Adrik was promoted. Probably it had been a mechanical failure, though the instructor's nightly vodka-soaked discussions with his old flying comrades would not have helped.

"A hundred men fly better than I," Adrik told the colonel.

"Our American tells us the carbon surface can be improved," said the colonel. "Do you believe him?"

"I know nothing technical," said Adrik. He had not bothered to meet the American; like most of the others on the base, he did not trust the man, though Lev had gone to great lengths to make sure he was authentic. Apparently the man had some kind of difficulty with gambling, all the more reason to despise him.

"The American is quite valuable. He has given us several suggestions for improvements in our next plane. We were not sure that he was genuine, but now we have proof," added Bashkin proudly. Perhaps he had had something to do with the man's "enlistment." In any event, improvements weren't important to Adrik; they were irrelevant to his mission.

Adrik paused at the back of the MiG's wing. The flap seemed slightly off-kilter, as if it were adjusted a hair higher than its partner on the other wing. It ought to be perfectly parallel with the wing surface, yet it seemed slightly off.

Imagination?

Adrik fought off the impulse to climb on top of the wing and check it. The coated surface could be easily scratched. He ducked under the fuselage instead, practically crawling on his hands and his knees because of the low clearance.

The other flap did seem straighter. Gently, he put his fingers against the surface. It felt warm.

Anna's cheek, the last day he touched her.

"I want to check these flaps," he told the colonel.

Alarmed, Bashkin barked for the mechanical crew. Instantly the plane was surrounded by a dozen men. Adrik explained that it was little more than a whim, but the men quickly retrieved micrometers and a torque wrench to make sure the flap was precisely at spec.

His first flight instructor would have keeled over, seeing that. Even without vodka. He would have laughed for hours, never imagining that even a meter's difference would affect him.

And probably it wouldn't. He had great stories about flying in North Vietnam under the guise of teaching pilots there. He had used an early version of the MiG-21 to shoot down an American Phantom.

Sometimes two, depending on how much vodka he had.

Probably, it was only one. But the man had been an excellent pilot.

As a flight instructor, he was only so-so. He lacked the patience and knack for detail that Adrik later realized set the better instructors apart. He was not content to be a teacher, and it made him drink all the more.

But the man had taught Adrik the most important things, and he had paid him the highest praise.

"Better than," said the instructor, raising his finger. He meant that Adrik was a better pilot at that stage than *he* had been when he shot down the Phantom. It was high praise—and an admission of how far his skills had deteriorated.

The man must have been a very, very good flier.

When the flap was cleared, Adrik completed his inspection. Nothing else was out of place. Bashkin circled behind him as he walked to the rack where his flight suit and helmet hung. Except for the helmet's visor, both were coated with material similar to the black polymer that covered the plane, though Adrik couldn't imagine why this would be important.

"After your flight, you must join me for dinner," said the colonel. "My wife insists."

"Your wife?" Adrik hadn't even known the colonel was married, much less that his wife was at the base with him.

"She is a very good cook," said the colonel. He lowered his voice. "We have no children so you won't be reminded. You have lived in isolation too long."

Caught off guard, Adrik nodded almost in slow motion, then began to dress for his mission.

Chapter Nine

Moscow

The *dezhurnaya* or hall attendant was pounding on the door before Jack realized the shooting had stopped.

"We're okay," he yelled in English, slipping the knife quickly into his overnight bag. His Russian was too rusty to make out more than the gist of what the woman was saying, but that was enough—open the door.

Cara, hunkered down on the floor behind the bed, looked at him expectantly as the woman pounded again. The chain and chest of drawers he'd pushed in front of the door was probably enough to keep the woman out, at least until he was sure what was going on.

"We're okay," Jack called again. He motioned for Cara to stay down, then climbed onto the bed, rolling over it and onto the floor in front of the shattered window. He reached gingerly and pushed the frame upwards; fortunately, it slid easily, pulled by old-fashioned counterweights in the casings.

The flat roof across the street had a clear view of the hotel window. A short wall of bricks lined the front; the gunman had probably stationed himself there.

He could still be there. The street lamps threw more shadow than light at the top of the building.

There was a fresh voice out in the hallway, this one belonging to a male, and Jack heard it say something along the lines of "Which room?"

Jack pushed his head through the window. There was a fire escape there; no one was in sight below.

Anyone who really wanted to shoot him would have killed him by now. The light behind him made him an easy, well-framed target.

"Let's go," he yelled to Cara. "Grab your bag. We're leaving."

"My clothes are in the bathroom."

Jack leaned back into the room and grabbed her. Cara just managed to drag her pocketbook over the bed as he pushed her to the window.

"Come on, damn it."

"My clothes are back there," said Cara, but she started down the rungs of the fire escape.

"Put in a voucher," said Jack.

Cara jumped to the sidewalk and ran toward the end of the long block where several of the streetlights were out. Before he jumped to the ground Jack lost sight of her; he almost missed her in a doorway near the end of the block. She was crouched in the shadows, waiting for him.

"What the hell was that about?" she asked as Jack slid in next to her, catching his breath. There was just enough space for him to stand between the street and the building's closed wooden door without being seen from outside.

"You tell me."

"I haven't a clue," she said.

"Yeah, right. That wasn't a message from Buzz?"

"Buzz wouldn't shoot at us."

"He had Boyle's thugs pull a gun on me."

"I told you, Boyle's not part of the operation. Buzz said she was a problem."

"What exactly is the operation?" he said.

"I don't know."

"Well, obviously, someone's trying to scare us, or me at least," he said. "And to me, that can only be Buzz."

"Maybe the people who have your brother don't want you to get him. Or maybe it was Milkman."

"It wasn't the Milkman," said Jack. He leaned against the wall, resting his head for a moment on the damp, open-pored bricks. If it was Daniel's employers, that wouldn't bode well for a deal.

"Why doesn't Buzz want me to find Daniel?" Jack asked her. "He's alive, right?"

"Buzz wouldn't kill him."

"I don't know what Buzz would do." Jack leaned his head out of the doorway just long enough to spot a man near the entrance of the hotel down the street.

Cara zipped her shoulder bag and put it under her arm. "We leaving?"

"Not just yet."

"The guys in the hotel are going to come looking for us."

"You're an expert now, Ensign?"

Cara realized what he had seen, and slipped to the ground to look from the bottom corner of the doorway. Jack studied her, trying to decide exactly whose side she was on, and how far he could trust her.

"One guy. He's got a gun at his belt," said Cara. "In the belt. No holster. Kind of fat."

Jack pulled her up roughly and looked into her face. "You're with me?"

She didn't say anything. He had no choice but to trust her, at least for the moment.

"Start down the street in that direction," Jack said, still gripping her arm. "Let him catch up to you. I'll jump him."

"You don't think he'll check the doorway?"

"Not if you walk right."

Cara stayed frozen as Jack loosened his grip. He began to put his hand back to push when she flicked out from the doorway. But instead of walking she stopped.

Shit.

She said something very loud. She was acting drunk.

Jack saw the shadow of a man approaching, stopping right in front of him. He jumped forward, pushing his knee up and landing square in the man's back.

Taken by surprise, the man fell immediately to the pavement. Jack pushed him around and flailed with his fist, connecting with the man's jaw as he pinned his upper body with his knees. The man was short and somewhat fat; Jack felt no resistance after the punch, and started to get up as the man's head fell back against the cement sidewalk. But suddenly the Russian sprang up and out of Jack's grip, catching him by surprise with a kick in the side before he could react. Jack fell back against a car, warded off a blow, and then fell to the ground. The Russian grabbed at him and kicked at his face, barely missing.

Then he stopped.

Cara had swooped in and grabbed his pistol. She told the man in what sounded to Jack like very good Russian to stand back and put his hands up or he would never make love to his wife again.

The man backed away, his hands up.

"That's far enough," Jack told him in English. "Tell me what's going on."

The man said something in Russian. His face, lit by the faint light of a street lamp half a block away, seemed confused.

"You speak English?" Jack asked the man. "Who are you?"

The man launched into a long dissertation in Russian, his words jangling so fast that Jack caught maybe every fourth or fifth one. He could have been talking about dinner.

"He says he works in the hotel down the street," said Cara. "Someone fired on some guests, and he thought we were the shooters," said Cara. She undid the clip of the pistol, removing it and checking the chamber to make sure it was empty before handing it back to the man. She told him in Russian that she would leave the clip at the end of the next block if he didn't follow them.

The man nodded.

"Let's go," Cara said, walking toward the doorway for her pocketbook.

Jack, somewhat bruised from the man's kicks, resisted the temptation to extract retribution. He caught up to Cara as she crossed the street.

"You speak Russian," he said.

"I told you I did."

"You speak it better than I do."

"That's not saying much."

"That's why you're here?"

"No. I'm pretty sure Buzz picked me because I was the first person in the hall he saw," she said. "Or it may be that he figured I'd seduce you."

When they reach the curb, Jack grabbed her shoulder and spun her body so he could see her face in the light.

"Why wouldn't Buzz want me to come here?" he asked.

"I don't know."

He glanced down the block, toward the Russian, still standing and watching them. Jack let Cara go and began walking toward the end of the block.

He found the Metro station more or less by accident. Jack thought he was heading toward the river, hoping to find the elaborate Metro stop near Lenin Hills. Instead they nearly fell down the escalator to a somewhat more modest one in the heart of the residential area well beyond the park and the university.

A bright mural met passengers as they came down to the platform. A tall farmer loomed protectively over a pair of small children, the tails of his blue coat flapping backwards in a way that suggested an angel's wings; it was as if the Metro sheltered the real spirit of Russia, worn and beaten as it was by the brutalities of the last two hundred years, but still vibrant.

A train pulled into the station as they got through the turnstiles; Jack ran for it, aware that Cara was following but not paying a lot of attention to her. Wondering if they had picked up a surveillance team or if the shooter was still following, he got off two stops later, waiting on an empty platform for the next train to arrive. Only two old women came before the next train arrived; Jack decided they were on their own, though it was impossible to know for sure—a sophisticated team with enough people could have been following along on the street, and there was always a chance that one of the *babushkas* was in fact a spy or member of the federal security force.

"Where are we going?" Cara asked as the next train began moving.

"I have some errands to run," he told her. "I don't know where you're going."

"Jack, I'm on your side."

"Yeah, right." He folded his arms and stared blankly ahead, trying to keep as much of the car in view while seeming to be thinking about something else entirely. Most of the other passengers seemed to be university students, and though it must have been obvious he and Cara were Americans, they paid little attention to them. Maybe that was because of the hour, or maybe it was his stare and cold manner; he jumped when they reached the first stop beyond the brown loop, practically running from the train and up into the grand Novokuznestskaya terminal, rushing through and out into the center of the city, walking as if he were absorbed in a single-minded mission, though all the time carefully looking around him to make sure they weren't being followed.

"Is the Kremlin near here?" Cara asked, trotting to keep up.

Jack grunted noncommittally. There were a good number of people out, more than he'd thought. It was a mixed blessing, providing some protection but making it more difficult to tell if they were being followed. Assuming they weren't, he had to find a place to spend the night until he could meet with the Milkman's man in the morning. The Milkman had promised him a ride to the region where his brother was, but no more than that.

The real problem was what to do with Cara. She could easily find the embassy from here on her own—and for all he knew, she knew Moscow much better than he did. But she knew he'd seen the Milkman, and he wasn't sure whether Buzz and the others knew enough about the renegade American's operations to stop Jack.

He walked a ways more, sure now that they weren't being followed, but still without an immediate plan.

"You got a gun?" he asked her, turning sharply.

"No."

"So why the hell did you give that jerk his pistol back?"

"You wanted him to call the police on us?" She pulled her shoulder bag up defensively, holding it in a way that reminded him of a submachine gun. "Where are we going?"

"We?"

"You still don't trust me, do you, Jack?"

"Of course not," he told her. "You've been lying to me since I met you."

"I'm not lying now. I want to help you."

A small Russian-built Fiat roared off the boulevard, barreling down the side street so close it nearly swept her off the curb. Cara ignored it.

"I want to help you get your brother back."

He wanted to believe her, but knew he couldn't, knew he mustn't. It was an urge he had to resist, sex he couldn't have.

Like not stealing his brother's girlfriend.

If she was lying, she was too dangerous to cut loose. If she wasn't lying, she might be valuable.

Or not.

She pulled at the front of her jeans, hiking them under the longish sweater. For some reason the bulky top made her look skinnier.

He was just about to tell her she could stay with him when Cara turned suddenly and began walking away. For a second, Jack felt like he was out on a date, and had just said something inappropriate.

Then he saw a vehicle approaching from the other

direction. It was a dark, boxy Russian Fiat, exactly like the car that had passed before.

One person in it. Unlikely to be an American trail team; it was generally SOP to ride two to a car in a foreign country.

"Hey!" he shouted to her, starting to run.

She kept walking. By the time he reached her, the car had passed by. Jack grabbed her shoulder and pulled her around. They were standing in the shadow between the arcs of two street lamps, but he could see her face clearly, her lips pursed, anger in her eyes, nose slightly crooked.

"Look, you lied to me and I don't see how I can trust you now," he told her.

Cara pulled her arm away. "I'll help you. We're on the same side."

Jack said nothing. For a second he thought he might kiss her again, but the feeling quickly passed. "All right. Don't screw up."

The spytrons were in a lake about twenty kilometers north of Gari, not far from the Ural Mountains—assuming, of course, no one had gotten them in the nine months since he'd been there.

Flying out to Gari to make sure the waterproof cases were still there would be somewhat inconvenient. But there were other ways to check the lake.

"Ask that guy over there where we can play chess," he told Cara as they walked through an area of small cafes not far from a college.

"Chess?"

"You speak Russian, right? Ask that guy."

"He'll know?"

The man had a beard and glasses—in Jack's opinion, the very image of a Russian intellectual. But he didn't know, or at least claimed not to know, where a chess game could be found.

"Ask for an access club," Jack told her. "It's a place where people go to play chess on-line. Go ahead. Use the word 'access' in English. Ask."

"Why?"

"Just do it."

The man claimed not to know. Maybe Cara's Russian wasn't as good as Jack thought. Or maybe she wasn't really using the right words. He crossed the street, walking to the corner. A group of students were milling around a stall that sold used books, including a number in English. Jack tried asking two girls about chess and on-line computers; they just laughed, obviously thinking he was trying to pick them up.

He found Cara standing next to a large man with a scraggly beard.

"He's writing down directions for us," she said. "It's a walk."

Jack glared at the man as he put his arm around Cara before handing her the directions. The Russian said something to her and she laughed, slipping away.

"What was that about?" he asked after they had crossed back in the direction they'd started.

"He wanted to marry me, and when I said no, he asked for just a favor." Cara smirked. "Down this street, I think. It's seven blocks, according to this."

Vaguely Gothic buildings loomed on both sides of the street; there was a heavy smell of cabbage or maybe rotting garbage—or more likely both. Exactly seven blocks in, Jack finally spotted hand-drawn chess pieces on a cardboard sign propped in a first-floor window of a six-story walk-up. The front door wasn't locked, though the only light in the lobby came from a naked bulb in the stairwell immediately to the right of the entrance. They went up slowly, hesitating on the third story until Jack heard the murmur of voices above.

On the fifth floor, they found an apartment with an open doorway. More than two dozen people were inside; one or two actually sat at tables playing each other. The rest were working computers.

Jack paid the club-master fifty American, the standard fee for foreigners. That allowed him to stay at a computer as long as he wished, but didn't actually pay for his access time. That was paid on the computer with a credit card. Jack had Cara help him through the sign-in; the Cyrillic words really asked only one important question: Visa or MasterCard?

The machine sent the credit card number into cyberspace, chewed on it, and made the connection. Each site accessed cost $1.25 beyond the initial fee of fifteen dollars; chat rooms were thirty dollars a half hour. It was rumored that the owners of these access clubs were among the richest people in Moscow, even if half the students using them had hacked bogus credit cards.

Jack figured that by now the Bureau would be tracking his credit card, but he knew from experience it would take more than a few hours for it to bounce back to anyone in the field. By then, he'd be out of here.

"Go see if you can get us some coffee," Jack told Cara as an old but still operative version of Microsoft Explorer filled the screen. "We passed a shop two blocks back. It'll still be open."

She hesitated, maybe thinking that he was going to leave before she came back, but then she nodded and left.

Jack thought about whether he would leave as he pulled out his small notebook and thumbed to a page. Several Web sites offered near-real-time satellite photos. While most required preregistered accounts, Jack knew he could get recently archived photos of Russia from the Western Indian Satellite Company, a Cayman Islands firm owned by the Israelis. The images he wanted were at one-meter resolution and taken by IRS-7D—an Indian government satellite that was only coincidentally lined up for surveillance of the Urals. Because of India's relationship with the Russians, some sections of the region were blacked out, but the ones he needed, only a week old, were there, at seventy-five dollars a pop.

Twenty-five more than his team had paid nine months before for the same region, but under the circumstances, a considerable bargain.

Compared to the state-of-the-art American defense system satellites, the commercial optics were primitive—they could only focus on objects about a meter wide. They also could only penetrate relatively clear water to a depth of about five meters. But neither parameter was a problem. It took several tries to find the lake, and when he did he ended up with an image obscured by clouds; he backed out to images archived a week before and ended up with the same problem. Six hundred dollars worth of image-accesses later, he saw the outline of the boat in the muck. There was a dark shadow at the back, which had to be the trunks with the spytrons.

Was it, though? Was he positive this was even the right lake?

"Well?"

Jack stood, trying to block the screen from Cara, who was standing behind him with two ceramic mugs of coffee. Both were filled to the rim; she'd somehow managed to get them back all the way without spilling.

"Go over there," he told her.

"Jack, I'm on your side."

"Go."

She made a face. For a moment he didn't think she'd move, but then, slowly, almost imperceptibly, she stepped back and pretended to be interested in her coffee.

Jack looked down at the computer screen. The trunks were only about two feet long and fairly narrow; their shadows were fuzzy and imprecise.

That was going to have to do. He reached his hand down to the keyboard, hitting the alt and F4 keys simultaneously. The window closed, returning to the browser screen where he had started.

Quickly, he pulled down the favorites file and hit one of the chess sites. Then he selected another and another.

Anyone who really wanted to find out what he'd looked at could study the history folder and figure it out without any great difficulty. But there was only so much he could do. He paged through a few more selections, filling the small buffer until the satellite radar site no longer appeared in the recent hits. Jack killed the browser and started walking from the room.

"Hey, you want your coffee?" asked Cara, practically shoving it in front of him as they walked.

Jack took the cup, then gave it back to her without saying anything.

"Where are we going?" she asked as he started down the steps.

He stopped and looked back. She stood at the top of the steps, a cup in each hand, her eyes tired and hair hanging forward at the sides of her face, hips and breasts obscured by the oversized sweater.

No one had ever looked so beautiful.

Sex made you do bad things.

"Give me the coffee," he said. "And don't ask any more questions."

The Metro had closed at one. They spent the night huddled behind a garbage dumpster at the back of a restaurant in one of the city's tourist sections near the river. The wind picked up as they slept, rattling garbage cans and kicking papers and dirt everywhere. Cara fell asleep almost instantly, leaning her head against his shoulder. Jack, his back straight against the wall of the building, drifted in and out fitfully for hours.

He thought he'd dream about his brother, or maybe his father. Instead he saw himself running through a dark maze of a city, not Moscow, not any place really, just looming shapes and narrow alleyways. It was a dream he had first had when he was little.

Then he dreamed about his mother.

She was in her bed at home. She was dying. The dream began as a memory of her last day at home—it really had happened the way he saw it in the dream, the home-aid nurse ushering Danny and Bree and him inside. His nose stung with the smell of mothballs and medicine. As the kids got nearer the bed, he saw his mom's lips were very red; she'd put on makeup for the first time in months, if not years.

"Jacky, take care of your brother," she said in the dream. "He's all you have."

That wasn't what had really happened—his mother hadn't said anything at all. But even though part of him knew that, in the dream Jack began to shake his head. How could he take care of his older brother? Shouldn't she be saying that to Danny, not him?

Danny punched him in the arm and laughed.

Then Jack woke up.

The sun was just rising. Cara was huddled against him. His eyes barely focused enough to let him see his watch. It was a little after six.

"Come on," he told Cara. "Come on."

She mumbled something.

"Come on," he said. "We'll go somewhere warm."

She groaned, got to her feet, and absentedmindedly checked the zipper on her bag to make sure it was still closed.

Obviously not a morning person.

They got to the Kazansky Train Station nearly a half hour before the appointed time, but the Milkman's contact was already waiting. He had a carton of Hershey's chocolate milk in his hand to identify himself—a typical Milkman joke—and smiled grimly at Jack and Cara as they approached. Then he started to walk out of the station.

Jack recognized the man. The last time he had been in Moscow, the man had been one of the Milkman's bodyguards—and had, in fact, screwed up the night Jack saved the Milkman's life, getting so drunk he couldn't go out with him.

So either he was here to do penance, or to extract some sort of revenge.

The man led them to a red panel truck. Opening the back door, he gestured for them to hop inside. Cara hesitated for a moment and Jack froze, eyes glued on their contact.

"Your plane's not going to wait," said the man, taking a step back.

Cara looked at Jack. The van itself was empty except for a pair of blankets on the floor.

Once they were inside, they'd be trapped.

Jack had assumed the meeting was at Kazansky because they were going to be put on a train; the station was a nexus for lines eastward. This had the smell of a double cross.

But what were the options?

"We'll ride in the front," said Jack.

The man frowned, but pushed the door closed. "Do not speak if we are stopped."

Cara and Jack had to squeeze into a bucket seat, propping their arms against the dashboard as the man drove wildly to an airport southeast of the city. To call it an airport was to exaggerate its importance; it was more a narrow parking lot off a side street an hour and a half outside of Moscow. Four or five small planes were parked in a row at one end of a hangar that looked as if it had been built before the Great Patriotic War. Their plane stood in the high grass at the end of the concrete, a two-engined Antonov An-14 Pchelka dressed in faded brown and green camo.

The Russian word "Pchelka" meant "little bee," but the Cold War-era NATO reporting name was much more descriptive: "Clod." The fifties-era craft looked like a VW Microbus with wings and a tail. As the van approached, Jack saw the engines crank to life; the pilot hopped out, removing the chucks from the wheels as Jack and Cara got out of the truck. The plane inched forward with no visible restraints as the pilot ran up and took Cara's arm, helping her through the propeller wash like a footman ushering the queen to her carriage.

Jack closed the van door and started for the plane.

"Hey!" said the driver. It was the first word he had said since they got into his car.

Jack turned around and saw the man had leveled a Russian pistol at his gut.

He had no time to react, not even to close his eyes.

Time hollowed out, a space in his head created by an imploding star. He remembered the dream he'd had of his mother a few hours before.

"Milkman says thanks."

The man pushed the gun into his hand. He gave Jack

the stiff, forced smile of a man doing a job he hadn't wanted, and went back to the van, leaving Jack alone next to the Pchelka's wing as the engines revved and the pilot struggled to keep the plane from taking off without him.

Chapter Ten

Over the Pacific

Buzz grunted at the young airman and took the cardboard cup from his hand. The coffee sloshed as the Boeing RC-135M hit fresh turbulence. Buzz just barely managed to confine the spill to the dirty linoleum floor. The corrosive liquid was doing a number on his stomach; odds were it would have melted right through the console he was sitting next to.

Not to mention ruined his new Cardin suit pants, which was his real concern.

The Air Force had detailed a Rivet Card RC-135M electronic reconnaissance plane for the flight, most likely because it had secure communications gear and could go from the East Coast to China with only one refueling. But Buzz swore the reason had more to do with the fact that the big, converted transport had no passenger amenities; he imagined some well-padded

Air Force officers chuckling to themselves at the idea of the DDO trying to get comfortable at the small workstation with its narrow desk surface and narrow chair.

But at least Buzz was able to communicate with some of his people. The team responsible for Blue had made contact and was proceeding against Shadow R. He was confident the MiG would never get off the ground.

Jack, on the other hand, was becoming a real problem. He had apparently switched planes in Frankfurt and gone to Moscow with Buzz's borrowed female agent in tow. With Blue in operation there was no one available to chase them down in the city, and the Moscow station had thus far been unable to locate them. Meanwhile, a check of the flight manifest on Jack's trip to Germany revealed a former KGB operative now associated with the Siberian breakaway faction. That was in addition to Boyle, who was now positively identified as a White Bear operative. Buzz guessed they had been assigned to find out if Daniel was a legitimate defector or not, and had begun following Jack as a kind of bonus or maybe insurance policy. It was anyone's guess what they intended to do if he insisted on trying to find his brother.

They might already have done it.

It was a shame, because Jack was a damn good operative. Even considering that he was an FBI agent.

"Ugh," Buzz said, tasting the coffee. "This is cold and it tastes like rusted piss water."

"Sir, I'm sorry," said the airman, rushing back. "I, uh, I can ask my sergeant if I could make some fresh coffee."

"So do it," said Buzz, practically throwing the cup at the poor kid.

"Scrambled call coming in for you, highest priority," said the sergeant who handled the communications. He looked to be all of nineteen.

Buzz turned to the console and pressed a green button, holding his headset to his ear.

"Blitz here," boomed the NSC assistant director from a ship somewhere off Japan. Maybe the ocean didn't agree with him—ordinarily he took at least three sentences to say hello. Now he got right into things. "Interesting set of problems."

"It's under control," Buzz told him.

Blitz snorted, not without malice. "Hardly. Despite what the Navy says, I think the odds of the F-14s arriving in time are about ten to one."

"Ten to one? Can't you arm the Raptor that's going with the flight?"

Blitz launched into a complicated explanation about the various pressures on the Russians, basically reinforcing what the President had said about their insistence that the escort fly unarmed.

"That's probably the Siberians, pulling strings," said Buzz.

"No. It's the Prime Minister. We have good intercepts," said Blitz. "We're boxed in. There's no way to get out of it without letting them know why. Surely you don't want to do that."

"Of course not. But—"

"Are you recommending we cancel the flight?"

That was not a serious option. Never mind what it would do to world politics. It would also expose a clandestine operation and advertise Shadow R—stealth on a shoestring for every tinpot despot around the world.

It would make Buzz look like a coward.

"Of course not."

"If you can suggest an alternative to the F-14s, I'm all ears," said Blitz. "I have a message here from the President that says they're just a backup anyway."

"They are," said Buzz.

"Think Blue's going to work, eh?"

His nemesis seemed to be laughing. "Damn straight I do, Professor."

"Then we won't have to worry, will we? Talk to me from China. Signing off."

"Blitz. Shit." Buzz banged at the com panel angrily, then threw his hand up in disgust.

Unfortunately, the airman had chosen that moment to appear with the thermos carafe with fresh coffee.

Which was fresh and very hot, and blotched his new pants in a stain that few people would consider flattering or strategic.

Chapter Eleven

East of Moscow

"We're only flying as far as Surgut," the Pchelka pilot told them after they'd taken off. The man was German but spoke fairly good English. "There are tickets in that envelope on the floor for a train from there. There are also papers you will need. My name is Helmut. It is two thousand kilometers to the field, so it will take us some time to get there. I have Cokes in the cooler back there. And thank you for not smoking."

He laughed. German humor.

The Pchelka's cabin had once been divided into crew and passenger areas, but the divider had been removed and the backs stripped off the benches; Jack sat next to the pilot, while Cara huddled on the floor behind him. The two engines flanked the top of the cabin and were fairly loud. The craft had been modified to carry extra fuel, greatly improving its range, but apparently speed was not much of a priority; it barely topped a hundred knots.

Most of the people the Milkman employed were not particularly talkative. Helmut was positively loquacious in comparison.

"Siberia is an interesting place. Very much like the Wild West of America, very John Wayne," he told Jack. "Anything goes. If you have money and connections, you can do very well."

"And you have both?" Jack asked him.

Helmut laughed. "I have none of either."

"What about the Milkman?"

"Our Mr. Jones?" Helmut rolled a laugh so deeply in his throat that it sounded like he was choking. "Our Mr. Jones has no friends. And yet he is everyone's friend. That is his paradox. But he is my employer. I am like a day laborer."

"And your job today is to transport us?"

"No, you're just along for the ride."

That didn't seem to be another of his jokes. Helmut touched his left ear, and then became very interested in the controls of his plane. Before Jack could ask what had happened, the plane lurched into a dive. It fell quickly from about five thousand feet to something less than two hundred.

"Sorry," said Helmut, pulling level barely above the trees. "Watch over there." He pointed to the right as he nudged the airplane even lower.

Jack saw two large black dots appear in the very top quadrant of the windshield, moving together in an arc to the south.

"Fortunately, their radars are not very effective, even head-on," said Helmut as he juiced the throttles and nudged the nose back upwards. "They are not with the main Air Defense Force."

"Who were they?"

Helmut shrugged. "Hard to say. It's best not to find out."

Jack had been warned during his previous visits that air piracy was common. MiGs from one or another Russian Air Force units would intercept non-military planes and "escort" them to bases under their control. Ostensibly the planes would be inspected for air safety and fined for noncompliance. They were, of course, being held up for bribes, sometimes with the cooperation of the flight crews, who would urge passengers to chip in. Even official airline flights were not immune because it was difficult to pay off everyone in advance.

"How did you know they were there?" Cara asked, her voice edgy as if she expected a trick.

"My radar warning receiver," said Helmut cheerfully. He turned to show her the small hearing-aid-like device in his ear. "My little plane has several upgrades from the standard model."

"I'll bet," said Cara.

Helmut began listing the plane's assets, sounding much like a salesman. Besides the French RWR, the ancient Pchelka had been equipped with a state-of-the-art Australian ECM or electronic countermeasures pod in its belly. This was effective against several types of radars, including those in the J-band, the detector of choice for Russian-made surface-to-air missiles. Flare and chaff dispensers were located in the rear fuselage. Helmut also noted that the plane did not carry parachutes.

"That the Milkman's rule?" Jack asked.

Helmut shrugged. "There would be no sense having a parachute. I don't even know how to use one."

Jack wasn't sure whether that was meant to be reassuring or not.

* * *

The Ural Mountains rose before them like a giant unfolding himself from bed. Helmut slid the airplane close to a skinned peak, angling the wings as if he were sneaking between the giant's neck and outstretched arm. The plane shuddered in an eddy of rough mountain air, and for a moment the pilot's demeanor froze in a grimace. But then the Pchelka shot forward and he leveled off smoothly. They had passed into Siberia.

To most Westerners, Siberia was a frozen wasteland broken only by the occasional gulag. The reality was considerably more complicated. The immense region covered nearly a fifth of the Asian land mass with geography as varied as any on earth.

They were heading northeastward, short of the permafrost in the swampy but oil-rich northwest beyond the Urals. An early spring had taken hold; green stretched before them in every direction, streams and rivers coursing in brown spiderwebs. There were roads and rail lines, and settlements and the gray shapes of oil rigs, but they blurred in the distance, overwhelmed by nature—or at least nature as visible through the small windows of the plodding Pchelka. The world seemed bright and green, prosperous and undisturbed.

Then the Ob River appeared, and the illusion dissolved into the dark blackness of hell. Gutted factories, abandoned work sites, vast stretches of rusted-brown oil equipment, and seemingly endless expanses of dumps lay everywhere, smoke billowing up indiscriminately. Houses and buildings appeared, scattered first in a jumble, then arranged in neat grids near rail lines. Roads started and then stopped; open pits of mud and bogs of gray mangled tree trunks stood like pustules between them.

The airport was a small, blackish runway near three or four large buildings. Helmut did not bother communicating with the control tower, if there was one; he made his approach dead-on, smoothly skimming in for a landing.

"Pay the driver you will find at the terminal building with the bill in the envelope," said Helmut as he taxied toward a large concrete building off the runway. "He will take you to the train. If he suggests the highway, shoot him."

"I'd prefer not," said Jack.

"Too bad," were Helmut's parting words.

The driver spoke only Russian. There was no question that he was the right man—he was the only person in the terminal.

The only person. There were no government officials, no airline representatives, no vendors selling refreshments. The terminal's design dated from the 1950s—heroic bland in tasteful though substandard concrete. The walls were water-stained and gutted with chips and cracks. Jack showed the man the Milkman's hundred-dollar bill and the train tickets; the man nodded, not even bothering to reach for the money, which, of course, Jack would not have given him until they arrived at the train station.

Cara complained about the chill in the air as they followed the man to the black, 1950s Russian-made sedan in front of the building.

"This is warm," said Jack, honestly surprised.

"I think you're just having hot flashes," she told him.

"Better me than you."

While there had been considerable road-building in western Siberia over the past few years—most of it sponsored by private companies for their own purposes or to charge tolls—trains were still the primary means of transportation. The local rail lines had recently been improved, to judge by the thick ties and shiny rails Jack saw as they drove toward the rail station. He paid off the driver quickly and led Cara around to the platform. Unlike the airport, the station was crowded; two dozen people milled around beneath the elaborately carved and carefully preserved platform roof.

Though not dressed particularly well, the two Americans obviously stood out. No one pointed a finger at them, but Jack felt uncomfortable, pacing a few steps back and forth near the north end of the platform. A large faded mural poked through the painted whitewash on the warehouse building across the tracks. The grim smile of a worker tilling the soil had been swathed with black paint, as if the man's mouth had been taped shut.

A trio of perfectly matched and immaculately clean diesels pulled in, hauling a long train of cars behind them. The blue of the passenger cars was so bright it seemed to belong to a movie set, something done in the early days of Technicolor. Jack looped his arm through Cara's as they waited for the train to stop. Two stiff security types in plainclothes made small talk about fifty feet away; beyond their shiny suits and shoulder-harness bulges, their leering glances at nearby women made it obvious that they were policemen or government agents of some sort—private security men would have been much more discreet.

A couple in their twenties materialized on the other side of Jack. In a very proper British accent, the woman asked Jack whether he thought it was going to rain.

He shook his head, trying to ignore them. Cara leaned across in front of him and said she hoped it wouldn't.

"Could I have a cigarette?" she asked, and despite Jack's attempt to warn her off with a subtle squeeze, she unhooked herself and walked around him. Jack contained his anger only by jumping onto the train as soon as the conductor opened the car door. He walked to the second car in the first-class section, saw an open compartment, and pushed inside it.

"From Dover," said Cara when she finally found him.

"They your team?"

"Which team?"

"Your trail team."

"Are you going to trust me or what?"

"Why should I?"

Cara pushed her head back so that she was looking up at the sky. Her hair hung down in a blond curtain over her neck. "I'm on your side, Jack."

"Well, then don't go talking to Russian interior security agents."

"Security agents?" Cara laughed. "They're English."

"You think tourists are going to be out here?"

"He works for an oil company. Jesus, you're so suspicious."

"It's the only fucking way to stay alive."

"Jack, I'm sorry. That was stupid of me." She curled her arms around her stomach, pushing into the corner of the bench seat across from him.

"It was stupid," he told her, still not sure who the people were. It seemed almost inconceivable that they could have been followed all this way—unless the Milkman had given them up.

To who?

No. More than likely they were what they said they were.

The train turned out to be extremely crowded. Three other passengers came into the compartment. Neither Jack nor Cara spoke, acknowledging the others with nods only. The others were Russian, and while it was customary for passengers to talk, no one seemed ready to start a conversation.

Jack certainly wasn't planning to. He looked out the window as the train slowly got under way, thinking about his father, thinking about Danny, thinking about how the hell he was going to work something out of this mess.

He was in over his head. The spytrons might get Danny out, or they might get him killed.

Was Danny even being held against his will? The Milkman made it sound as if his being here was completely voluntary.

No. Not really.

The spytrons could be used for bombs; it was, in fact, what they were best suited for.

Buzz had cleared the earlier deal for them. But that had been meant as a trade for what they thought was the world's only uncorralled smallpox—infinitely more dangerous than a handful of bombs.

Jack's team had been bargaining for bio-warfare canisters stolen from a depot in a place code-named Peca far to the north. Jack was second member in the team. He'd been given money and a laundry list of items for barter; it was easier to pay for the germs than try to take them by force.

They'd offered a quarter of a million dollars to buy the canister outright, but the men who had them, a group of former paratroopers, weren't interested in money. They wanted leverage for some kind of internal political maneuvering Jack only vaguely understood.

There had been several meetings before Jack brought up the spytrons. The men became very interested. Eventually, arrangements were made, and Jack flew to a small rural town with two boxes of the devices. He and the key Russian went out on the lake in a boat to make the exchange. The plan was to deposit the Russian in a second boat where the spytrons had been placed; Jack would motor across to the other shore. Meanwhile, another member of the American team would be completing an exchange for the canister a few miles away.

The wind came off the lake so cold and hard he swore he was going to get frostbite though it was late summer. The Russian sat with his back against the gunwale, sucking a bottle of vodka. By the time they sighted the boat with the spytrons, the Russian was three quarters of the way down.

The scumbag pulled a gun. Jack was wearing a bullet-proof vest as well as a microscopic bugging device feeding audio and his location to a monitoring team in a helicopter just over the horizon. Even so, he was in a tight spot, and his heart jumped into his mouth when the Russian motioned him toward the water.

"That's not the plan," Jack told him, first in English, then in his halting Russian.

The man motioned again. Jack shook his head, hoping the backup team was listening—and moving.

The Russian aimed the revolver at his chest. Even at this range, the bullet wouldn't go through the Kevlar lining beneath his shirt. But falling into the icy water could well be fatal.

The man moved the gun upwards, leveling it at his face.

Jack shook his head again. "We go through with the plan, or everyone's sorry."

The Russian took another swig of vodka, then glanced across at the boat where the boxes with the triggers were plainly visible.

Jack thought of jumping him, but the man looked back too quickly. Their eyes met, and Jack realized something had changed. The Russian took another long swig of the vodka, then tossed the bottle to Jack.

As he caught it, the Russian leapt across into the other boat. He went to the motor, starting it up without checking the boxes. As it caught, he straightened and waved to Jack. Then he fired a shot into the lake.

Probably, the shot was a signal to his compatriots waiting nearby. But it made the B-3 monitoring team go nuts—the helicopter roared in from behind the trees on the far shore.

It took the man only a few seconds to realize he was in big trouble. He tried racing the helicopter—a "rented" Russian Kamov Ka-27 Helix—to the shore. The squat, double-bladed chopper waddled over the water, its stubby rudders working to hold it steady in the heavy crosswind. The helicopter wasn't particularly fast, nor heavily armed; a relatively simple single-barrel machine gun had been installed beneath the cockpit in place of Soviet-era antisubmarine-warfare equipment. But the 30mm gun was more than enough to perforate the bottom of the boat; weighed down beforehand for just such a contingency, the small craft slid into the water as if it were riding an escalator to hell.

Jack had turned his own boat to follow the Russian, though he was careful not to get close. As the foam receded, he found the man's body floating in front of him. He leaned over the side to fish out the dead body, and puked instead.

The boat with the cask of spytrons lay below, in the muck at about twelve feet. There wasn't time to retrieve it as the operation began to unwind; the dead man was the only Russian who knew where it had gone down.

The smallpox turned out to be a harmless strain incapable of reproducing.

* * *

The train would take roughly an hour and a half to deposit them at Norabk. Once they were there, they would have to hire someone to show the way to the complex where Danny was working—which, according to the Milkman, should be about ten miles away.

Fifteen minutes of staring out the window didn't advance Jack's plan beyond the vaguest outlines—essentially, show up, sniff the wind, and offer the bribe if he thought it would work. Assuming, of course, that he found Danny, and that Danny was willing to come back with him.

When the conductor came for tickets, Cara asked in Russian if there was a dining car. The man practically salivated, telling her about the food but staring at her jean-covered crotch. Maybe he had X-ray eyes.

Cara didn't seem to mind. Or maybe she just didn't show it, thanking him and getting up to find the car. Jack waited a second, sighed, then went after her.

"There are ruby grapefruits," she said when he caught up.

"Bullshit."

"The conductor told me."

"He was talking about your tits."

"Bet you ten bucks."

"I don't bet."

"It's an expression, Jack."

"Uh-huh."

There were grapefruits. And in fact, they were very good, at least to judge by the look on Cara's face as she savored each bite.

Jack stuck to tea. He would have preferred coffee, but they didn't have any. One of the conductors came through, announcing the next town; apparently it was a junction with a western spur of the line, for the man rattled off a series of destinations, each more slurred than the last.

As he passed down the aisle, Jack noticed a man in the booth at the far end of the car, pretending to read a newspaper but obviously watching them.

Jack waited until the train slowed to a stop. "I'll be right back," he told Cara. He touched the gun the Milkman's contact had given him in Moscow, hidden beneath his shirt, making sure she caught the gesture. Then he began walking toward the far end of the car. He threw his eyes around the train without focusing them anywhere, sweeping, trying to find the man's partner, if he had one.

The two security types Jack had spotted on the platform were here, in the last booth. One of them stared at him.

Jack passed the man with the newspaper. He was Russian, wearing a thick wool shirt, the kind an American wouldn't even pretend to wear, no matter what his cover was.

Could be a contract guy, working for Buzz.

Or whoever shot at them in Moscow.

Jack pulled open the door and stepped between the cars. He continued into the next car, an excursion coach that served as an annex to the dining car. He kept walking, as if he were really looking for the rest room.

The door opened behind him when he was about halfway through the car. He squeezed sideways to let someone else through as the train stopped moving.

An old lady.

Behind her, one of the security types, in his shiny suit, definitely eyeballing him as he walked.

The rest room was on the right. If he stopped and went into it, he'd be trapped. But if he didn't, he'd give himself away. The cars ahead were all compartments with no where to go.

The rest room was occupied. He paused, glanced

uneasily at his watch as if trying to decide whether to wait.

The old woman kept coming. So did the security man, who was now trying to appear nonchalant.

Jack leaned his ear toward the door, as if listening to something inside. Then he pulled open the door at the end of the car and stepped through.

He nearly lost his balance as the train jerked into motion. He caught his hand on the door handle, struggling with it for a moment before getting the door to swing open. He had to fight the sense of panic starting to burn in his chest.

The security man was definitely following. There was a rest room directly inside the door; Jack pulled it open, slammed the lock home.

He stood beside the door, gun ready, trying to listen. The noise of the train was too loud. He gave up, leaned over, and flushed the toilet, then ran the water. As he pulled open the door, the train lurched sharply, the wheels locking in an emergency stop.

Jack was thrown out into the aisle of the car. He rolled on the floor, expecting to find the security agent staring at him, probably with his gun drawn.

But he wasn't.

There was no one else in the car, or at least in the narrow corridor bisecting it.

Cara.

Jack pushed to his feet, got up, and grabbed for the door. The train was still trying to stop, and he felt like he was swimming in a riptide, running against its momentum as he pulled himself between the cars. The exhaust from the engines was sucked down into the space between the two coaches; Jack coughed as he entered the dining car, the train finally stopping. Glass and shards of china as well as food littered the floor in front of him. He ran forward, dodging one man who was sprawled across the aisle, blood trickling from his nose. Jack kept his hand at his stomach, the gun still covered by his shirt.

People were screaming in the dining car. A girl of nine or ten sat in the middle of floor near the door, crying hysterically. Jack stepped around her, saw one of the conductors at the far end of the car trying to calm people.

Cara wasn't there. Neither was the man he'd seen reading the newspaper. Jack stepped around the girl, began running again, heading toward their compartment beyond the car.

"Jack. God, are you okay?"

He turned around and saw Cara climbing from beneath the table where he'd left her.

"Come on," he said, taking her hand. "Let's get the hell out of here."

The conductor blocked the aisle, talking in loud, quick Russian.

"I think he's saying we should remain in our seats," said Cara. "Don't you think that's a good idea?"

He didn't, but Jack slid into the booth anyway, Cara next to him. At least it gave him a chance to check the car for his friends.

"What happened?" he asked Cara, glancing around. "What was the conductor saying?"

A head popped between them from the next booth. "The train stopped to avoid a truck on the tracks," said a woman. "Excuse me. You speak English?"

"Yes," said Cara.

The woman, who seemed to be in her early twenties, said she was a German student visiting friends from the university. She also said this sort of thing happened a lot, and predicted the train would be moving shortly, assuming the truck hadn't been hit.

She seemed genuine, but Jack was so paranoid now

he believed everyone on the train was a spy. He looked out the window near him, but saw no one nearby; he didn't know whether that was a good sign or a bad one.

A steward came by with fresh cups of complimentary tea. As he placed a cup down in front of Jack, the train started moving again.

"Let's go get in our compartment," Jack told Cara.

She nodded and got up. As Jack followed her into the aisle, he sighed, trying to force himself to relax. He was getting paranoid. It was unlikely that they'd been followed. Frankly, it was unlikely anyone gave a damn about him. Or his brother.

Jack had reached to open the door when he saw the reflection of the security goon in the glass. He was walking toward them from the far end of the car, his suit jacket wrapped over his hand.

Precisely the way someone would hide a pistol.

When he realized Jack saw him in the glass, he smiled and quickened his pace.

Chapter Twelve

Hokkaido, Japan

The laugh shook the telephone practically out of Crow's hand.

"Shit, Bain you old goat—you're still in the Air Force?"

"Hey, Blaze," Crow told the pilot on the other end of the line. "How are you?"

"Well, I'm just fine. When they paged me I had a déjà vu flashback, as if I were back in Riyadh."

"Been a long time, huh?" said Crow. He lay back on his hotel room bed, propping his head on the pillows.

"Seems like yesterday," said Blaze, who had flown F-15C Eagle interceptors in Crow's squadron during the Gulf War. A section leader, Blaze had led a two-plane formation that had killed a pair of Iraqi fighter planes on the second day of the air war. One of the planes was a MiG-21. "Jesus—you know who I saw the other day? B. J. Dixon. Remember him? The A-10 pilot? He drives a 777 now. Hell. I told him I wondered how he stayed awake."

Crow smiled. B. J., a young lieutenant at the time, had been an absolute cowboy during the war, flying his ground-attack airplane almost literally through Hell. The kid had bragged about how he'd never go to work for an airline. Too boring, he'd said. What was the use of flying if you couldn't shoot something up?

"You sound like you've done pretty well for yourself," Crow told Blaze. "They were telling me how you were some senior flight trainer or something."

"Ah, just a BS title so they can get more hours out of me. So what's up? You looking for a job?"

"Believe it or not, I'm looking for a little information about MiG-21s," said Crow. "But, uh, what we're talking about—strictly off the record."

"Since when is bragging off the record?" asked Blaze. His voice grew serious. "Hey, what's the story here?"

"I really can't go into details. But if you could remember that tangle of yours, I'd appreciate it."

After a few seconds of silence, Blaze began recalling the encounter. His words were precise and analytic, the account far from boastful, but his voice quickened as he spoke, the memory growing more vivid. Crow felt himself getting excited as well, as if he were reliving the war.

Blaze and his wing mate had an escort assignment, flying protective air cover well over the Iraq border. The air war had gone on for two weeks by then; Iraqi defenses had been pretty well neutralized. The planes Blaze and his wing mate had escorted had just completed their bombing run and turned for home when the controller in an airborne E-3 Sentry AWACS alerted the fighters that two bandits—enemy airplanes assumed to be hostile—had just taken off from an airfield twenty miles north of them. Blaze turned his Eagle to face the threat.

"We were at about thirty thousand feet. Things started happening real fast," Blaze told Crow. "AWACS is trying to get an ID on them and I've gone to the armament panel, you know, I've got the AIM-7s ready to rock."

The AIM-7 or Sparrow III was a radar-guided missile with a range of approximately thirty nautical miles. Crow's experience with the Sparrow dated to the Vietnam War, and was not particularly positive, but twenty years of refinements had turned it into a deadly efficient weapon by the early 1990s.

Blaze and his wing mate got their planes nearly head-on to the two Iraqis, which by now had been identified as MiG-21s. A cue on Blaze's guidance system indicated the missile had locked on the first MiG, and he fired.

"Sparrow plunked him," said Blaze. "We were five miles off when he splashed. I never saw him."

"Five miles."

"Yeah. I mean, I fired well before that, you know, got them on radar after the AWACS alerted us. The Sparrows worked perfectly."

"Did you see the missiles hit?"

"Five miles is a long way," Blaze told him. "Saw the fireballs, though."

Crow nodded to himself. The Americans would have been maneuvering to avoid any missiles from the Iraqis, as well as positioning themselves for a follow-up attack if the radar-guided missiles failed. They'd have been far too busy to watch the splash, even if they had been so inclined.

Still, they hadn't seen the planes.

"You know anyone who flew against them up close?"

"Exactly what are you up to?" Blaze asked again.

"A mental exercise," Crow told his friend.

"Nobody I know, outside of Red Flag. They're little suckers. Thank God for radar, huh?"

Red Flag was a training exercise. "How close do you think you'd have to be to see one?" Crow asked.

"How close to tallyho?" Blaze said the words in a singsong voice, but then got serious again. "Figure it's about the size of an F-5. You'll have it on radar way before you see it. Way before."

"Five miles?"

"To see it? I guess it depends on where you're looking. This a bet or something?"

"Something like that," said Crow.

"Realistically, head-on or almost head-on, I'd say five miles would be possible, but optimistic. Two miles would be damn good," said Blaze.

"Yeah, I was worried about that."

Whether he saw it with his eyes or waited until the radar finally picked up the plane, there would be less than thirty seconds before the MiG closed in for the kill. Thirty seconds was too little time for the F-14s, and quite possibly too little time to engage Shadow R before it opened up on the Concorde.

"I wouldn't worry, even if he gets to come in close on you," said Blaze. "Eagle can fly circles around a Fishbed. As long as you keep him off your tail when you do see him, you're fine."

Crow grunted noncommittally. He felt he couldn't even tell Blaze that he would be in an F-22; in any event, the Raptor was more maneuverable than the older fighter.

His friend repeated the stock advice for dealing with a MiG—try to keep him high where you had a serious performance advantage, remember that he would try to stay inside you on turns, where he could yo-yo behind you for a shot.

"You'll waste him, man," concluded Blaze. "Even if you are over the hill. That was a joke, Colonel," he added quickly.

"I'm laughing," said Crow. He glanced over at the clock—he ought to have gone to sleep hours ago.

"You know, you want a job flying with us, you let me know. I'll set you up. They love Air Force pilots. Seriously," said Blaze. "You combine a salary with your pension, you're living large. Even though, uh, you're up there, I can get you in. No sweat. Put a couple of years in flying, then we'll get you moved over into Administration. Easiest job in the world. Fly anywhere you want for free."

"Thanks."

Crow wondered what the mandatory retirement age was for active airline pilots. He was probably damn close to it.

Drive an airliner. He agreed with B. J.—rather be a bus driver.

Why, though? It was a respectable job and it paid damn well.

Usually when someone suggested he leave the service and go to work for the airlines, he made some wise-ass remark, something about how he didn't think he could handle the strain of being a professional baby-sitter. Tonight, though, he just thanked his friend and hung up.

Crow leaned his head back on the pillow, closing his eyes for a moment before pulling the phone toward him and dialing the next number on his list.

Chapter Thirteen

Western Siberia, near Surgut

Jack pushed Cara out of the dining car, holding her on the platform between the cars as he grabbed the door handle and yanked it open. "Run," he told her, shoving her ahead.

"Jack?"

"Go!" he commanded. Cara's first two steps were barely a trot; Jack pushed again, and finally she started running. By the time the door to the car opened behind them, they were at the far door.

"Faster," he said, once again practically throwing Cara between the cars. The Russian behind them was heavyset and didn't seem to have a good sense of balance, but he made less and less pretense of nonchalance as they continued through the train. The gray-blue steel of his gun flashed in the shadowy light of the corridor. They passed their compartment and kept going.

The train rounded a sharply banked curve as they entered the fourth car. Jack slammed against the door frame but twisted through, bouncing against the walls like a ball finding the chute in a pinball game, and running on. The curve slowed their pursuer, and they managed to get a car and a half between them.

Then they ran out of train.

"Here," said Jack, seeing the caboose in the window of the door ahead. He yanked open the door of a compartment and pushed Cara inside. At the same time he pulled his pistol out from his belt.

Three women and a man were sharing the compartment. One of the women screamed. Jack ran to the window at the end of the aisle between the two seats. He planted one foot and tried twisting into a kick with the other, hoping to smash it. The window didn't budge.

The man in the car started to get up. Jack turned quickly and pointed the gun at him. As the man sank down, Jack took the pistol and rammed it against the glass. It took three hard smashes to get it to crack, but then the window disintegrated into rounded pellets.

Someone in the corridor yelled something in Russian and grabbed the door handle.

"Go," Jack told Cara, grabbing her and pushing her next to the window.

"Where?"

"Just go!"

The door shuddered. Jack yelled, but before any of the passengers could react one of the women slumped back. Bullets smashed through the lock and frame, the sound of the bullets echoing like immense firecrackers exploding behind them. Jack dropped to his knee and pumped three or four bullets through the door.

As he stood up a fresh spray of bullets slammed into

the cabin. Jack fired twice more, then felt the revolver click empty. He threw himself on the left seat, rolling over the passengers as Cara's leg disappeared out the window and another round of gunfire passed through what was left of the door.

A fire extinguisher was attached to the side of the door frame. His pursuer kicked the door open, but Jack threw himself against the frame. Two bullets whizzed by his head as his fingers grabbed the plastic tie holding the red canister to the wall. The door opened and the shooter took a step forward. Jack fumbled for the trigger on the extinguisher, realized he hadn't removed the pin, threw the extinguisher instead, hitting the Russian in the face. The pistol fell and Jack plunged into the hallway on top of his pursuer, ramming his knee into the man's side. Jack slammed his elbow into the man's neck, heard a shout, and looked down the corridor, where the other security agent and the guy with the wool shirt from the dining car were just coming through the door.

Throwing himself back into the compartment, Jack flew to the window and dove into the open space. He stuck halfway, scraping on the sides, unbalanced, twisting toward the top.

Something whacked his head.

Cara.

His body turned to liquid, paralyzed by the idea that she was part of this, that she and the Russians were working together.

"Take my hand," she yelled. "For Christsake, grab on, damn it. Use your hands. I can't pull you up by the head."

She wasn't working with them. She was trying to help him up.

One of the passengers grabbed his leg inside. Jack

kicked back and at the same time reached for Cara, grappling like a swimmer caught in a stiff current beneath the waves. Cara pulled; his stomach scraped against the window, but he pulled free, then was with her on the top of the car.

"Are you okay?" she asked.

"Go!"

"Where?"

"Just go!"

They scrambled toward the front of the car, moving on all fours. The roofs of the cars had flat work areas along the middle; Jack and Cara stooped forward, pulling and pushing and somehow keeping their balance as the train took another curve. Cara threw herself across the gap and Jack followed, wrestling his legs up behind him.

"Your arm is bleeding," she said, stopping to help.

"Yeah, you don't look too good yourself." His forearm and elbow had been cut by the glass on the side of the window.

The train started going uphill. They couldn't see what was going on in the car they had escaped from, but Jack guessed that the goons would soon be following.

"How far are we going?" said Cara.

"I don't know," said Jack, pushing her.

The top of the next car was smooth, with no railing or anything to help them balance. As they stopped to consider what to do, a head appeared over the far end of the train, near the caboose.

"What we need is a tunnel," said Cara. "Or a low bridge to knock them off."

"We need a machine gun," said Jack.

The train sounded its horn. Jack saw another train, a freight, coming in the opposite direction on the parallel tracks.

"Think you can jump on?" he asked Cara.

"That's got to be ten feet away."

"No. Five or six," said Jack. "We can do it."

"Shit, Jack."

"It's either that or jump to the ground."

"I don't know which is worse."

The Russian didn't seem to be in any particular hurry to chase them down. He climbed to the top of the car at the end of the train, then turned to help a friend. The approaching freight was moving fairly quickly, heading downhill.

"We'll never make it," yelled Cara as the engine passed. "It's suicide."

"Worse to stay here," said Jack. He crouched. The cars at the front, passing them now, were boxcars. But a set of coal cars were coming up.

Then two tankers. Then the caboose.

Go for the coal cars.

The goon's friend reached the top and the pair began walking gingerly along the train's roof. A machine pistol with a tubular metal stock hung from the second man's hand.

"You comin'?" Jack asked.

"What if I say no?" said Cara.

Jack grabbed her arm, jumped to his feet, and pushed. But she was already springing across. He caught his balance, managing to leverage his legs just enough to clear the gaping void between the cars. He bounced against her and then down, into the interior of the open-top coal car.

One piece of luck—the car wasn't filled with coal. It was filled with garbage.

Jack felt the stench sting his nostrils.

Then the smell faded into the dull rattle of pain that closed over his head.

* * *

Jack woke to the pop of automatic gunfire and the low thunder of mortar shells.

He couldn't open his eyes. Something splashed against his face.

Shrapnel.

He was back in the Army, back in Haiti. Under mortar attack.

Not shrapnel. Water.

Rain.

A thunderstorm. He was soaked, lying in a pile of garbage, somewhere in Siberia. Because of Danny.

Because his father was dying and he felt obligated to fulfill his last wish.

Because he was out of his mind.

Jack pulled his head and chest up. The train had stopped. Cara's leather boot was next to him, empty. He rolled over, got to his knees, slipped on something, and fell face-first, nearly retching with the smell.

Cara lay on her side at the very edge of the car, face turned away from him. Even in a pile of garbage, her body had a grace and beauty to it that made his hand reach to her. He turned her over, not sure what he would see, bracing himself for a mangled wreck of a face, bashed and battered by the jump.

But it wasn't. He saw her again as he had seen her the first time, nearly flawless, just the slight hitch in her nose.

She took a slow breath through it.

Rain pelted his back. Jack grabbed her boot, pushed it onto her foot, and then lifted her over his shoulder, draping her limp body across his back and moving on his knees to the ladder at the edge of the car. He couldn't get his legs out from under him without using both hands, and had to put her down; she lay across the garbage like a broken doll. He managed to scoop her back over his shoulder with one arm and began pulling upward. By the time he remembered he ought to check if there were guards in the train yard, he was over the side of the car and starting downward.

He couldn't see more than a few yards away in the grayness of the rain. There didn't seem to be anyone, and at this point he hardly cared.

The ladder ended several feet from the ground. Jack leaned forward, took hold of Cara's arms, then pushed off like a skydiver leaving a plane. Landing, he started to lose his balance, tried to counter it by pulling forward, and ended up rolling on his side, partly on top of her.

She groaned.

Jack took that as a good sign. He got up, steadied her on his back again, and began walking down the long line of railroad cars. He could see the roof of a building jutting from the ground behind the siding to his left; as he got closer he realized the rest of the building had collapsed completely into rubble. Stubby telephone poles, wireless, splintered, and gray, stood in a line leading from the roof toward another grouping of rails where a flock of relatively new freight cars were parked. Jack made a quick circle on the rock-strewn ground; there was no one nearby, at least not that he could see.

There was a fence in the distance, and beyond it a brownish-gray field; otherwise, there were rows of tracks and train cars. Jack decided to try a row of older freight cars that stood on a rail ahead on his right. With Cara strung on his back, he had trouble reaching up to the handles on the door locks of the freight cars. The first car door was either locked or too rusted to move; the same with the second. The third had a chain lock guarding the opening pin.

The fourth was already open a crack.

He put Cara down gingerly, turning her face to the

side to avoid the worst of the rain. Peering through the crack he saw nothing inside the freight car; he pulled himself up on the rung and pushed the door open another two feet. When no one rushed him, Jack clambered inside. There were cardboard boxes piled on one side and scattered around the floor, but nothing else, at least not that he could see in the dark. He jumped down and scooped Cara into his arms. Her arms hung down like a toy's and there was no gentle way to put her into the freight car; her head thumped as he lifted her inside. Jack pulled her toward the back on some of the cardboard, then made a pillow with his sodden jacket. Finally he ripped some cardboard into a crude, stiff blanket.

It would hardly keep her warm, but it was the most he could do for her. She was barely breathing. Maybe she'd broken her spine or her neck jumping into the car.

She needed medical attention, but Jack had no idea where or how to get it. He went to the door and saw the rain was slowing to a stop. His watch said it was about two o'clock Moscow time. While it was several hours later here because of the time zones, it was still much earlier than he'd thought.

He still had his wallet. That meant two credit cards and about a thousand dollars, along with a few hundred in his pocket.

Passport and watch. Keys. The false IDs and papers the Milkman had given him. That was it.

And the spytrons. Though they weren't with him.

Would be nice to find a gun somewhere. Or even a map.

His clothes were a mess. The side of his shirt had a thick mass of crud on it. Poking at it, he wondered what the hell it was. Oil or something.

Blood. Cara's?

No, it was his, from his arm. He'd scraped it getting out of the train. Otherwise he was intact.

Good day to play the lottery.

The clouds moved in heavy masses above the train yard, rain slackening off to a haphazard drizzle. Jack jumped from the car, walking to the side, where a bent ladder led to the top. He jumped to catch the lowest rail and banged his shins against the bottom of the car. As he tried to steady himself he lost his grip and tumbled down, smashing the back of his head on the rocks.

For a minute, it didn't hurt at all. Then pain surrounded his head, gripping his temples with sharp pincers. Jack tried to shake it off, groping his way to his feet and shakily walking to the ladder, where once again he had to jump to get the ladder. His head pounded so much he screamed and cursed, but he was able to haul himself upwards. At the top, he hunkered over his knees for a minute to let the pain recede.

Freight cars and coal carriers were arrayed in groups of five to eight long nearby; beyond them were longer lines of cars obscured by the haze. On his left were several rows of what he assumed were garbage cars like the ones they'd jumped into. Beyond them there was a swamp with several piles of debris and an ancient, half-yellow, half-rusted bulldozer.

Behind him, maybe fifty yards away, were empty tracks, and then a row of buildings. He could make out the steep slope of what might be a passenger terminal a bit further on.

So at least he had a direction to go in.

The rain had been warm, not cold; even the wind that began to pick up as he stared from the top of the car was warm. He slapped at his face as a mosquito buzzed nearby; he realized he'd soon be inundated by them, and decided to get moving again.

Jack was about twenty yards from the freight car when he heard Cara's scream.

He flew back to her, legs and arms pumping. Gripping the side of the door, he whipped it open, the wheels that held the large panel on track moving more freely than he'd expected.

Something flew through the air, nearly whacking him in the face.

A dead rat.

"Where the hell were you?" demanded Cara, emerging from the dark interior of the boxcar. "Why'd you leave me with vermin?"

"You're okay?"

"Were you just going to leave me for the rats?" Cara jumped down.

"I didn't know there were rats. I wasn't leaving you. I was just checking the place out."

"My ass."

Jack leaned up into the boxcar to retrieve his jacket. Meanwhile, Cara walked to the rat on the ground and kicked it beneath the train. Jack thought it was better not to ask exactly how she had killed it.

"I think there's a passenger station that way," he told her. "We can figure out where the hell we are, then catch another ride."

"What happened to our friends with the guns?"

"I don't know. Still back on the other train. When I came to we were in a garbage car parked up there." Jack gestured with his thumb.

"They'll be trying to track us."

"Probably."

"Okay," she said, starting to walk in the direction of the station.

Jack quickly caught up. "You okay? You break your back?"

"No. All my ribs are broken, but I'm okay."

"I wasn't leaving you."

Cara stopped. If she believed him, it didn't show in her face. She pulled off her sweater and threw it to the ground with about the same expression she had used kicking the rat. Her thick flannel shirt was nearly as soaked.

"We can't take a train," she told him. "We stink like shit and we look like we drowned."

She had a point. They'd have to find some fresh clothes, as well as figure out where they hell they were. Their friends would undoubtedly be coming for them; they had to get moving.

"Let's find a car," said Cara.

"Yeah, I think there's an Avis at the terminal." Jack started to laugh. Cara pressed her lips together and started walking again. He took a step to follow, to explain that it was just a joke, just tension—to tell her he hadn't been leaving her. His head began to pound again, pain pulsing around the lobes of his eyes. Jack stopped and rubbed his fingers against his skull so hard he thought he scratched the bones, then bent his neck back and forth, hoping to loosen the muscles and maybe trick his body into thinking he was merely tense.

It didn't work. He followed Cara toward the building area. Clearing the last of the parked trains, they saw a group of ramshackle buildings off to the left, a kind of squatters camp. On the right, station buildings were lined in a haphazard jumble. Cara started for them, then veered sharply to the south, perpendicular to the end building. She headed toward a lot of parked cars, protected by a chain-link fence topped with barbed wire maybe ten yards from a squat cinder-block building.

If she'd hurt herself in the fall, it didn't show as Cara jumped onto the fence, clambering up the fourteen feet like a squirrel scaling a tree. Jack followed more slowly, dividing his glances between the building and the barbed wire at the top.

She picked her way gingerly over the wire and scurried downward. One of the barbs sliced through the side of Jack's palm as he reached the top; another ripped through his shirt as he pulled himself over. His pants stuck, and for a second he thought he was going to end up hanging upside down, dangling from the top.

Instead, he just fell.

About six feet from the bottom of the fence he managed to grab the side. His legs swung partly behind him as he did a flip that would have impressed a circus acrobat. He tumbled around, quickly losing his grip. The maneuver probably saved him from breaking his neck or at least an arm, but the pain in his side and knee as he landed blacked him out. He rolled in the mud, blind, his body surrounded by a circular wall of fiery pain, his head unconnected in the fuzz below consciousness.

It took a few seconds before he could see again. Jack found himself on his back, staring up at the gray Siberian sky. He got up slowly. Cara crouched nearby, studying the door of an ancient Mercedes, a car nearly forty years old, though the body itself seemed in perfect shape. She stood and undid her belt.

Jack wondered what she was doing until she wrapped the leather around her fist. Then she hammered the glass of the triangular vent window at the front of the car door.

It took three blows before she had worked it far enough from the frame to get her fingers into the crack. She pried it open and snaked her arm inside to unlock the door.

"See. That's why this car," she said, as if in answer to a question he'd asked.

Maybe he had asked a question. The pincers on his temple squeezed so hard, he bent forward as he watched her slide back and forth in the front seat, then get out and walk to a nearby truck.

"What are you doing?" he asked.

"Jump-starting the Mercedes." She unlatched the truck's hood and leaned into the engine compartment, emerging with a long wire. Then she checked something in the Mercedes' interior, opened the hood, and crawled under the bottom of the car. Sparks flew and Jack heard her curse. He got up, but before he could steady himself on his legs the Mercedes roared to life.

"I'll drive," she told Jack.

"Yeah," he said, walking to the passenger side.

He was still fumbling for the seat belt when Cara slammed the car into second and aimed for a weak part in the fence.

"No seat belts," she said.

Jack turned to look at her. In the next second they crashed through the chain links and he heard something pop in front of him.

"You blew the tire," he said.

"No, that's just those guys shooting at us," Cara said, pulling the wheel hard to dodge the shards of the fence and then accelerating for the hard-packed road. "Don't sweat it. We're home free."

Before Jack could turn back to look, he felt the dizziness and blackness return. He slipped his head back against the top of the seat, nodding into oblivion.

Chapter Fourteen

Western Siberia

Colonel Bashkin's wife was perhaps half his age, with a stout face that hinted of native ancestry. She was in no way attractive, with clumps of facial hair beneath her chin and a mouth that hung down slightly at one side. But she treated Adrik at dinner as if he were an ancient hero risen from the dead, constantly filling his glass with water—he declined anything stronger—and spooning him the best pieces of beef from the stew she had labored over much of the afternoon. The meat was not the best cut, nor the freshest, but it was rare here, even for officers, and Adrik found it impossible to eat it slowly.

Colonel Bashkin looked on with some amusement, carefully draining his tall, clear glass at regular intervals and waiting for his wife to fill it—with vodka, of course, not water. He pushed his empty plate aside for her, smiling as she brought it to the sink. The floorboards creaked and shook as she walked, the entire house swaying with her movements. A faded white and red curtain hung across the small kitchen window across from Adrik, obscuring the view of the auxiliary east-west runway; he imagined the house shuddering terribly every time a plane took off.

"I would not be surprised if one of my old MiGs is out back," said the colonel. By "out back" he meant the large boneyard or plane cemetery that lay at the edge of the house. It extended around two thirds of the air base; several hundred airplane carcasses were parked there.

"I didn't know you flew MiGs," said Adrik.

Colonel Bashkin nodded vehemently. "Oh, yes, but not like you. My assignments were all in obsolescent craft."

The colonel began describing a MiG-17 he had flown in a ground-attack unit assigned to Poland, a craft that dated to the 1950s. Bashkin spoke of it with a mixture of nostalgia and scorn. The plane was truly from another era; a pilot muscled its stick through a tight turn, and entered a dive cautiously. The colonel had watched a squadron mate crash after losing his airbrakes. His eyes grew wide as he described the MiG's wing kicking into a spiral as something flew from the fuselage. He thought it was the canopy; he stared at the plane, waiting for the pilot to follow.

Bashkin shook his head, his hands pausing over the table as they re-created the flight.

"I almost inverted, like a stupid ass," he told Adrik. "I was behind my plane, very far behind it at that moment."

His wife filled his glass. The colonel abruptly began talking about how much he admired Lev.

"To be my general's brother, it must be an honor."

"I owe my brother my life," said Adrik. He sipped his water. "He raised me. He is my brother."

Bashkin nodded solemnly as he took a gulp that emptied half the glass. He would not be considered a heavy drinker among other Siberians.

"To you, he is a brother. To us, a lifesaver and a leader of the future," said Masha Bashkin. They were her first words of the night, beyond the greeting at the door.

Her husband held his glass up to toast Lev.

Adrik had seen this sort of reaction to his brother before. Lev was nearly fifteen years older than he was, and had taken care of him from the day his mother died in childbirth. It was his brother who had told him to go into the Air Force; it was his brother who had brought him here. If Lev had asked him to jump into the Ob River, Adrik surely would have. But he did not understand the reverence in others; he could not understand why someone who did not owe their life to Lev would think him a god. In his heart he doubted that his brother's plan—for it was Lev's as much as any of the other White Bears'—would succeed in toppling the main Russian government and put the Siberians in power. Shooting down the foreign plane would anger the foreigners as well as Russians; while it would get rid of the Premier, Lev's faction would ultimately fail. The White Bears had much money and control of key Air Force and Army units, but the Moscow forces were ultimately much stronger. Like others before them, the White Bears were doomed to sink back into the chaotic cauldron that had characterized the country for the past decade and a half.

So too would Siberia. With even more depressing results.

"I drink to the prosperity of our children," said the colonel, lifting his glass.

The words were out of his mouth before he realized that the expression he had meant symbolically—he and his wife had no offspring—might be taken literally as some sort of insult by Adrik. Turning beet red, Bashkin glanced at his wife for help. She immediately grabbed for Adrik's plate, saying she would refill it.

"No, thank you. I'm full. It's all right," Adrik said in a very soft voice. He had underestimated these people, the colonel in particular, and now felt truly ashamed. "Please, Colonel. I was not offended by your words. The children do not haunt me."

Bashkin nodded, but the lie did not put him or his wife at ease. Masha fumbled around in the kitchen while the colonel drained his glass, then rose and got a fresh bottle from beneath the sink.

"You'll join us now?" Bashkin said, gesturing with the bottle.

"As I said, I cannot," said Adrik. "My stomach is tender, and it would not do to get sick for tomorrow."

The colonel nodded. "Have you ever visited America?" he asked, looking for some neutral subject.

Adrik shook his head.

"It is an interesting place. We visited New York a few years ago. I thought it would be like Dallas, but it seems dirtier. No one tried to shoot us." He laughed and sat down, then took a long sip from his drink.

"It was too hot," said his wife dismissively.

"Their television is different," said the colonel.

"You're a dirty old man," said his wife. They laughed; obviously it was a joke between them.

Adrik's wife had always talked of going to America.

"I think I should be getting to bed," Adrik told them. "Thank you for dinner; it was the best meal I have had in a year."

He shook her hand gratefully.

"I told you she was a good cook," said the colonel.

"Yes," he said. "Better even than you said. Though I would not have believed it possible."

Masha grabbed his arm and put her nose practically against his. "Succeed," she said. "I was in Kolpashevo. I was four years old when the bodies floated from the riverbank. You and your brother, everyone—you must make things right. You will. I am sure of it."

Adrik understood immediately. Nearly thirty years before, many miles to the south in the Siberian city of Kolpashevo, the Ob River had changed its course, eating away at the frozen soil to reveal a mass grave of NKVD victims, prisoners put to death decades before by security forces under Stalin's decree. For days bodies floated in the river, the dead come back to remind the living of debts that could not be erased.

"I will do my duty," he told Masha.

She took it as an affirmation. Tears edged into her eyes as she pulled her arm around her husband. Adrik let himself out into the damp night.

"Good night, Colonel," he said, snapping off a smart salute, perhaps his first for Bashkin since arriving here. Then he began walking slowly toward his quarters, aware that he would not find any sleep tonight.

Chapter Fifteen

Western Siberia

The pressure in her right rib had four points, like the knuckles of a fist being pressed against her skin. The thing she was driving down—she wouldn't deign to call it a road—wove back and forth, obviously engineered to hit the worst features of the landscape. Every rock and boulder in the pockmarked surface reverberated in the soft, overworked shocks of the ancient Mercedes. It was dusk and the headlights were just barely strong enough to catch the drop-offs at the roadsides.

Cara's grandfather had had an old car just like this. She remembered being driven home from his house with her mother one Sunday night, going over the bridge to Philadelphia. She was spread across the backseat, half sleeping, half looking at the shadows of the lights against the interior.

Snap out of it, Cara told herself. You're falling asleep. Snap out of it and drive the damn car.

Where was she going, though?

Wherever. Toward Surgut, like the sign had said.

Just drive. Stop out here and God knows what will happen. You're in the middle of Siberia and the natives are restless.

Jack shifted in the seat next to her. He'd been unconscious for an hour now. As near as she could tell, it was just exhaustion, though it was possible he'd broken something jumping from the train and falling over the fence.

She sure had. Her ribs were on fire.

Big, beefy guy. He ought to have more stamina than she did.

Nice body. Feel good lying next to her in bed.

Snap out of it.

They were going to need gas soon. There were oil fields nearby but no gas station that she'd seen. Cara hadn't seen anything that would pass for a store in the U.S., and had only passed two or three cars since getting off the main road near the highway. If she hadn't seen a sign for Surgut a few miles back, she would have thought she was heading toward a deserted swamp.

She might in fact be. The truth was that Cara not only had no idea where she was, she wasn't sure what exactly she should be doing. She was starting to have second thoughts about helping Jack—maybe she should try to make her way back to Moscow.

Cara turned her full attention back to the road in time to take another S curve. Her ribs poked for a moment, then settled down as her weight fell off them.

"Where are we?"

Cara nearly jumped out of her seat.

"Where are we?" Jack repeated. He slowly raised his head from the back of the seat. "Do we know?"

"You've been sleeping about an hour," she told him. "I took the road west from the station. It forked south, kinda, and that's the way I went. There was a sign for Surgut a few miles back."

"South, kinda?"

"I don't have a map. The markers were the same, so I went that way." She glanced at him. He seemed to be taking stock of his injuries. "You okay?"

"More or less." He was silent for a minute. "How about you?"

"Hurt my ribs."

"How bad?"

She shrugged. "I broke my nose when I was nine. That was worse."

"How'd you break your nose?"

"My cousin whacked me with a baseball bat."

"Nice."

"Yeah. It was an accident, I think. In Philadelphia you can't be too sure of anybody."

"That where you learned how to steal cars?"

"Yup." She laughed. "Same cousin. We got caught by the cops once. I'm not going to tell you how I got out of going to jail."

Actually, the policeman was her cousin's father, but the story had more juice without the details.

"We have to head northwest from Surgut, not south. We're going to a place called Norabk," Jack told her. "The guys in the train must work for the people who have my brother. They must be trying to keep him here. Assuming they're not working for him."

"I doubt they were."

"Why doesn't Buzz want me to help Danny?"

"I'm not sure he doesn't want you to help him. He may have been worried you'd get hurt."

"Unlikely," said Jack.

"Anyway, I'm helping you."

"You sure?"

"Yes," she insisted, as if he had overheard her considering driving back to Moscow. "Yes."

A military-type Ural truck approached in the distance. It didn't have its headlights on, but it was clearly in the middle of the road, its thick shadow edging well over into their lane.

"Buzz must be afraid I'm going to screw up something," said Jack.

Cara didn't answer. There was about two feet of shoulder before the ground fell off into a rough bog. If she went off, she wasn't getting back on.

The truck kept coming.

Cara pushed the horn and yanked at the wheel; one of her tires slipped off into the soft tundra bordering the road. The Ural veered out of the way and she held the pavement, barely, scraping the rear bumper against the back of the truck as it continued on.

"Just a drunk," said Jack.

"Yeah," she managed. Her ribs were pounding. Now it was worse than her nose.

"You didn't answer my question," said Jack after a while. "What am I going to screw up?"

"I don't know," she said. The words gasped from her chest. She felt faint and hungry.

"Why don't you guess?"

When Cara didn't answer—guessing was impossible—he folded his arms in front of him, then leaned over to look at the fuel gauge. "We need gas."

"You see a station, you let me know."

"There'll be something over there," said Jack, pointing toward a clump of buildings far off in the distance. "You see tire tracks heading in that direction, follow them."

They did better than a trail—a four-lane macadam highway led directly to the tiny town, which backed against an empty railway siding. At the end of the road, a hand-scrawled sign with one word, *"pettrol,"* pointed them down a dirt path that ran over one set of tracks toward a group of private homes.

Using the word "homes" loosely.

Cara spotted one with a pump in the front yard. As she pulled up, she saw it was connected via a snaking garden hose to a gas truck around the side. An old man with thin white hair reaching to his neck approached the car warily.

Jack got out and said the Russian words for filling the tank—they sounded like, *"Na-poll-ne the back."* But the old man didn't react until Jack took a hundred bill from his pocket and snapped it in the air.

The man jerked the hose out of its holder like it was on fire, practically ramming it into the Mercedes as quickly as Jack could open the cap.

"Kapta?" Jack asked when he had finished filling it up.

"Kapta?" repeated the man.

Jack mimed the unfolding of a map. Cara realized the man knew what he was saying, but was debating how to answer—maps were fairly precious in Russia, and possibly dangerous. She opened the door and started to get out; the pain in her side was so intense she had to sit back down, the blood rushing from her head.

The man said something in Russian. His accent was unfamiliar; Cara's mind worked in slow motion, translating.

Why do you want a map? Where do you want to go?

She turned to tell Jack, but he had disappeared. So had the man.

Fear replaced pain in her side.

She took three long breaths, pulling herself together, then stood and looked through the growing shadows in the yard for a weapon. A long iron bar was propped near the gas pump. She grabbed it in her hands, swung it to feel its heft.

Jack appeared on the porch, the man following closely behind him.

He must be holding a gun on him.

Cara swung the bar behind her back and edged against the hood of the car.

"You gonna try for my nose?" Jack asked hopping down the steps.

By the time she realized it was a joke—he was referring to what she had said about her cousin—Jack had slid in behind the wheel of the Mercedes. "You look pretty beat," he said. "I'll drive."

"Okay." Cara didn't move. The old man said something to her from the edge of the porch.

"You probably ought to leave the crowbar," Jack told her, rolling down the window.

"I thought—I thought he had kidnapped you."

"Nah. We were just haggling on a price. You getting in?"

Cara dropped the bar and walked around to the other side of the car. Jack had unfolded a yellowed piece of paper and put it on top of the dashboard. "He drew us a map. There's a neighbor we can get some dry clothes from down the road. Men's clothes, but she's got a teenage boy about your size. And he sold me a gun."

He pulled his shirt back to reveal the handle of an ancient weapon tucked into his waistband.

"Outside looks like hell, but I checked the works. I think it's okay. Bullets seem to fit."

Cara nodded.

She was with him, she was definitely with him. But what did that mean? She sat silently as he drove to the house with the clothes; Cara started to get out, but Jack told her he would handle the transaction with a note the old man wrote for him. He returned in a few minutes; Cara was so exhausted she let him help her change into the rough but dry pants and shirt.

His hands felt soft and warm. He slammed the door next to her; Cara felt herself starting to fall asleep as he came around and got in.

"Jack, I don't know what Buzz is doing," she told him. "Does Blue mean anything to you?"

"It's a color."

"It's a plan or something for the operation."

"Could be anything," Jack told her.

"Why do you think your brother is in Nojarb'sk?"

"He's not in Nojarb'sk," Jack told her. "It's Norabk. It's not even there; it's an air base about ten miles to the east. It'll take us a few hours to get there. Old man knew about it. Not nice people up there, but there's a ton of money. Of course, to him a hundred dollars is a ton of money. Map cost me twenty bucks, and it turns out there's only one road, and that's along the train tracks. We didn't even need a map."

Maybe Blue was an escape plan.

Buzz must have planted Daniel. If he was a scientist, he must have planted him.

Stealth. Siberia.

Buzz had been trying to keep Jack from spoiling some sort of infiltration operation.

Blue would be an extraction. Had to be.

Daniel was probably home by now.

Cara opened her mouth to tell Jack it was too late, but nothing came out.

"I also got a painkiller," Jack told her. He held a small jar in front of her. "Homemade painkiller."

The stench was as fierce as the trainload of garbage. She managed to shake her head before passing out.

Chapter Sixteen

Western Siberia

Jack gripped the wheel of the Mercedes so tightly his fingers felt like pieces of metal stabbing the base of his wrists. Outside the car, fog furled upwards, shrouding the earth in a chiffon curtain, wisps parting as he drove. They were the veils women wore at funerals.

Jack thought about his dad, lying in the hospital half a world away, waiting for a transplant that wouldn't come, waiting for his prodigal son to be returned to him.

It was likely his father was dead already.

So why bother then? Why drive deeper into Hell?

Giving them the spytrons for his brother wouldn't change the balance of power in the world, not even in Russia. It was a fair trade—more than fair. Jack would immediately tell Buzz. They'd be able to get them back before they were sold or used.

Or maybe not. Jack would take his punishment, deserve it. His father was worth the sacrifice.

But his dad wouldn't have wanted him to do it. He'd be appalled. He'd think Jack betrayed his country, or at least his oath and duty to uphold the law as a member of the FBI.

His honor.

Salvatore Ferico was an ethical, moral man. He had adamantly told Jack not to use any influence to push him up on the transplant list. Even if it meant he would die.

Jack hadn't even considered going against his father's wishes. As tempting as the Milkman's offer of a black-market organ was, he hadn't taken him up on it.

Why not?

Because his father wouldn't allow it.

Goddamn Danny might not even want to come home. Trade the spytrons for him? Screw that. Let him rot in this soggy outlaws' slum.

No, better to drag him back, bring him in front of the old man, let him get arrested there, let his father see once and for all who Danny was—see who the worthy son was. That was worth the spytrons and the fallout, worth spending twenty years in jail for.

He'd have to find another way, figure something out when he got there. If he got there.

Jack drove on, bile worn down by fatigue. The old Siberian at the gas station had tried telling him a great deal, but most was indecipherable. Jack thought it wasn't advice on what he would find, but rather words of how much the country had changed and who was to blame. The man had grown angry at points, and kept talking about Moscow. But most of what he had said was incomprehensible. Jack was just thankful that the old man had been right about the woman with the clothes, and that he'd drawn out a good map with careful illustrations of landmarks and signs.

A blank but lit billboard appeared along the side of the road just before a turnoff, exactly as predicted. Jack took it, and noticed that the road under the furls of fog was brand-new and very wide. Three miles later, four blinking red lights appeared to his right, looming out of the night like UFOs. Jack almost hit the brake before realizing they were aircraft warning lights on radio towers.

The airport that formed the center of the base and research facility must be nearby. Jack stared in the direction of the lights as he drove, but in the dark and fog he couldn't even see the towers they were mounted on.

He looked back at the road in time to see a reindeer running across ahead of him. Jack slowed, but nothing else came out of the fog.

Two miles later, the fog parted to reveal a roadside strip straight out of his New Jersey childhood. Buildings lined the highway. A few were old, but most seemed very new. Prefab houses and trailers were parked pell-mell next to motels and warehouse buildings; as the roadway curved, Jack realized he was driving around the edge of the airport. Old planes were parked in a line right next to the macadam, ghosts in the haze. He took another turn and the road straightened out; the fog cleared and he saw a group of cranes standing in a field to his right. A car appeared behind him, the first one he'd seen in almost an hour. The vehicle's headlights grew rapidly in his rearview mirror; it flashed by him, going so fast it might have flown. The driver pulled back into the lane, then hit his brake lights, turning to the left.

Jack followed, immediately entering what seemed to be an industrial park lit by numerous overhead lights. Dozens of rusted fire barrels stood beneath the poles; a few glowed with warm coals. Low-slung steel buildings sat along the street, punctuated every so often by empty lots of heaving asphalt. Jack turned a corner and began driving parallel to a freshly painted chain-link fence topped with barbed wire; beyond the fence was a swamp. As he neared the end of the road, the fence stopped and the swamp was replaced by an open and seemingly dry field. Two tractors, one falling into rust and the other brand-new, sat next to each other a few yards from the street. The pavement ended in a pile of dirt; Jack turned left onto a dirt roadway framed by concrete curbs, as if the pavers had forgotten to lay the asphalt. But a few hundred feet later a first-class road appeared below his tires—flanked by sidewalks no less—and Jack found himself driving through a section of a town that could have belonged to any country in Europe. Most of the buildings looked thirty to forty years old, made of thick bricks and wearing turgid facades. But they were clean and carefully painted, more evidence of a booming local economy, or at least a surplus of paint.

Jack turned a corner, passing several fenced-off lots with low bushes and bog grass; near the end of the block was a large grocery store, set back behind a gravel parking lot. Three Ural trucks, two American vans or panel trucks, a beat-to-hell pickup, and a fairly new Audi station wagon were scattered in the lot, parked haphazardly enough to take over almost the entire space. Jack found a spot at the far end and stopped the car. He couldn't turn the car off since he didn't have a key. He reached over to wake Cara up, but decided she looked too peaceful to disturb.

Legs rubbery and back stiff, he swung his arms to each side as he walked toward the store. Without thinking about what he was doing, he balled his hands into fists and took wild roundhouses. Dancing with his feet, he moved like a boxer, his pulse starting to jump.

Here, Daniel, how's your stomach these days? You used to stand with your hand on my head, laughing while I swung wildly at you, a seven-year-old furious and tormented.

How do you like it now?

Jack stopped midway in the parking lot, realizing how stupid he looked punching the air. He was unshaven, probably smelled worse than a pig, and while his clothes were dry, they were at least a size too small, the cloth jacket too tight to button. He hesitated for a second, but his hunger was strong—he could smell some fresh bread or some sort of cake, and then got a whiff of coffee. Rows of canned goods lined shelves at the front of the parking lot, in the open air; he walked past them into the store, brightly lit with harsh fluorescents that dangled from the ceiling a few inches over his head.

As his eyes adjusted to the glare, Jack followed his nose, turning left, then right, spotting a counter at the far end of the store where a young woman in an apron stood waiting to pour coffee or tea. He walked forward, rehearsing his words—coffee was easy, since it sounded more or less like the English word, but the Russian word for "roll" went something like "*botch-key*," and he couldn't begin to remember the specific phrase for the small desserts set out on a tray. He smiled, noticing the woman's obvious apprehension as he approached; he gestured in apology for his appearance. Since he had only a hundred-dollar bill left, he decided to get as much as he could for it, and after taking the filled coffee cup, glanced around to see if there was a bag or basket or something he could pile food into.

Something caught the corner of his eye as he turned. Jack spun back quickly, and saw his brother Daniel, staring at him from the end of the aisle near the front of the store.

III

"Avenged sevenfold"

Gen. 4:24

Chapter One

Norabk, Western Siberia

Jack jumped backwards, stung by disbelief into paralysis. Before he was able to move, Daniel was gone.

For a moment, he thought he'd hallucinated.

He dropped the coffee and felt his eyes pinching the corners of his sockets, everything in front of him dim yellow as he began to move forward.

It was Daniel. He was here. He was going out the door. He was gone.

Someone yelled at Jack, and he started to run toward the front of the store. As he reached the door, the Audi backed from its space and heaved through the potholes, moving quickly but not racing from the lot. Jack leapt after it, shouting for Danny; there were three people in the car, two in the front and one in the rear. The Audi reached the road and accelerated away.

Jack pulled at the Mercedes door and flew into the

seat, mashing the gas pedal of the idling car before remembering he'd set the parking brake. The car lurched forward, nearly stalling before screeching onto the roadway.

The Audi turned down a road just ahead and disappeared behind a pyramid of rusted oil pipes. Cara flew against Jack as he veered to follow, barely controlling the car.

The road in front of him was empty.

He saw something green out of the corner of his eye as he passed a large gravel lot on his left; Jack yanked the wheel, threw the car into a one-eighty. The rear end jumped the sidewalk, the Mercedes fishtailing through the parking lot. A dog appeared from nowhere, barking—he sped past it, reaching the end of the lot, where he found a concrete roadway. The Audi turned down a street ahead and began picking up speed, definitely aware of him now and trying to get away.

"What the hell are you doing?" screamed Cara, struggling to sit up.

"My brother," he told her, barely keeping the car from sliding into an oil-coated drainage ditch at the side of the road. They bounced over a set of railroad tracks embedded in the roadway as the Audi drove past a row of metal sheds now used as a squatters' camp. The Audi's brake lights flashed; Jack couldn't control the Mercedes as he skidded to follow through a turn, and he smashed his front fender through a stack of oil drums. There was a clothesline and then garbage in front of him, people suddenly appearing from nowhere, sleepy and confused but shouting and diving and running for cover. Jack regained control, following the Audi as it shot onto a patch of clear cement long enough to be a runway. They hopped over another set of railroad tracks, and then out onto a macadam roadway that ran between low-slung oil-drilling rigs and pumps sitting on cement pads. There was no place for the Audi to turn off, and the Mercedes's bigger engine started to tell, pulling them steadily closer.

"Who's behind us?" said Cara next to them. "Jack, there's a van or something behind us."

Jack ignored her, spotting the chain-link fence in front of the Audi just as the station wagon started to skid into it. He hit his own brakes as he pulled the wheel, trying to swerve away. But he lost control, spinning in a circle but still moving forward, the car a top whipping across the pavement. He plowed into the back of the Audi as the station wagon crashed through the fence and onto an oil-sodden field of muck.

A dark shape roared past him, bouncing off the Mercedes and colliding with the Audi before rebounding into the bog. Water and steam exploded everywhere. The shape materialized into a van; bodies flew out as something exploded inside the van. Jack threw himself forward and found himself pounding on the Audi, pulling a body, pulling his brother away through the gook.

Cara, choking, grabbed on and helped him back past the fence. The van and the Audi were on fire. One or the other's gas tank ignited with a volcanic hiss, the explosion laying them flat against the asphalt like pieces of paper.

The fall jarred something in Jack's brain; images floated in front of his face. First was his father, lying on the hospital bed, slowly fading into the white oblivion of the sheets. Then his brother's face loomed against the red bricks on an old schoolyard, saving him from some bully.

His brother again, two years ago at Christmas, not talking to anyone.

Jack pulled himself to his knees, struggling to clear his head and get them both free.

"Come on, come on," he said before he saw either Cara or Daniel. "Come on, come on," he said, grabbing the back of Daniel's thick shirt.

Danny didn't move. He was splayed out in the muck, lifeless.

Jack grabbed the prostrate body and dragged him along the roadway as Cara appeared alongside. Jack took maybe three steps before he was thrown forward by another explosion. He tumbled into a black hole empty of mud or oil or fear, rolling in the slime.

All this way, to have his brother die in his grasp.

Jack tried taking a breath, but couldn't; finally his lungs spasmed and he felt his heart jerking to the side, desperate to find some oxygen for his brain.

All this way to fail.

And then some deep reflex kicked in. There was intense pain in his side and his lungs began to work again; his heart pounded fiercely. He gasped and sat up, found his brother Daniel kneeling next to him, alive.

"Thank God," he said to Daniel. "Shit, I thought you were dead."

"You fucked everything up," said his brother, spitting on the ground. "What the hell are you doing here?"

Chapter Two

Norabk, Western Siberia

Nothing she did could make the images focus. Nothing. Cara blinked and shook her head, tried staring at the ground and even holding her breath. She heard the two men breathing, saw their blurs stirring next to her, moving, saw them standing.

"What are you doing here?" Jack's brother asked.

"Dad's dying," Jack said.

"What are you doing here?" Daniel repeated.

"Dad's dying. You have to come home. He needs a transplant and he's not going to get it."

Cara put her hand to her face and rubbed her cheekbone. The images sharpened and she saw the two brothers kneeling in front of her, their faces barely inches apart. Daniel, a bit heavier, hair longer and completely gray, leaned backwards, hands balled into fists on his upper thighs. Jack crouched forward with his head angled away from her.

"What do you mean he's dying?" said Daniel.

"I mean he's dying. Didn't Bree tell you when you called the hospital?"

"I didn't call the hospital. What hospital? What the hell are you talking about?"

"You didn't call?"

"What fucking hospital?"

"St. Anthony's. You have to come home."

"You think I'm here on a vacation?"

Cara started to get up. Her ribs seemed to jab at her heart; she managed to get up, but turned around with the pain, sliding back down in agony. Both men grabbed her, each taking a side.

"Are you okay?" Daniel asked.

"She's fine," said Jack.

"Who are you?" Daniel asked her.

"Your girlfriend," said Jack.

Cara pushed them gently away with her hands, regaining her balance as the pain subsided. Jack told his brother that she worked for Buzz Eagleton, then asked what Daniel was doing here.

Instead of answering, Daniel jerked his head towards the start of the road. A small Fiat had stopped near the intersection; slowly it backed up, coming toward them.

"We've got company," said Jack. He turned Cara toward the start of a log trail that ran out to some machinery in the bog.

"Wait. They're part of the trail team," said Daniel. "My trail team."

"You sure?"

"Jesus, Jack. I'm working for the CIA. For fucking Buzz. Shit. I'm here to steal an avionics device the Siberians developed."

"What are you talking about?" Jack asked. "This doesn't have to do with stealth."

"It has something to do with it." Daniel explained that he had come to Russia and then Siberia to steal an electronic device that made it difficult to detect aircraft at long ranges.

"It resonates and replicates radar waves. It can do it in pulses and across bands. You want a fucking lesson in physics, or are you going to let go of my arm and let me tell these guys you just blew probably the biggest covert operation of the last ten years?"

"You didn't sell out?"

"Figures you'd buy the goddamn cover story. Shit, Jacky, I thought you were smarter than that." Daniel made a snorting sound, not unlike those Jack had used to dismiss comments Cara had made earlier that he'd considered stupid. "The van had two Stinger missiles in it. We were supposed to blow up a plane in a few hours. What the hell are you doing here, Jack?"

The two men stared at each other. Cara waited for them to do something or say something—if she'd come all this way for her sister she'd hug her.

Or maybe she'd slug her, angry because of everything she'd put her through.

But the two men just stood there, immobilized as the men from the Fiat came forward, pistols drawn, and asked Daniel what had happened.

Daniel got up and walked past them to the Fiat. "We had a change in plans."

The men in the Audi and in the van—three Russians and an American—were all dead, killed by the explosions. Cara shuddered as she stepped back from the charred remains of one of the bodies, then squeezed into the back of the Fiat hatchback with Jack and his brother. The driver was an American; the other man a native who seemed to understand English but not speak it. They drove silently for a few miles before stopping to decide what to do next.

The stealthy MiG was due to take off from the White Bear base in a few hours. Its mission; Daniel said, was to disrupt a planned flight by the Concorde III, which was due to cross the country far to the south near midday. The Siberians expected the Russian government to fall in the crisis that would follow.

"Blue was a contingency plan in case the MiG was used against a high-priority target," Danny explained. "I got the word that it was in effect last night. It means I take out the plane."

Shooting down the MiG with the Stingers would have been relatively easy; the heat-seekers had a decent range and could be fired from a field near the airport where the plane had to pass after takeoff. Daniel had come off the base to advise the shoot-down team where and when to position themselves.

He had a backup plan, but it was considerably more difficult.

"There's an SA-16 shoulder-fired missile hidden in one of the lab storage areas," he said. "If I can get to it, it ought to be pretty easy to take out the MiG, even in its hangar. I had some training using one."

"What happens after you fire it?" Jack asked.

"I get out of there."

"How? Run like hell?"

Some of their facial expressions were so similar it was spooky—Daniel's eyes gleamed the way Jack's had when they'd first gotten to the Circus.

"There's an Antonov An-12 transport sitting in the junkyard right next to the auxiliary air strip," Daniel said. "It's in their old plane cemetery, but it's not a junker at all. I've been trained to fly it."

"You're flying? You're scared of heights," said Jack.

"It's not the same thing," snapped Daniel. "The shoot-down's supposed to take place near Omsk. That's just under a thousand kilometers." He leaned back in the seat; his voice seemed calmer now, though still strained. "It's a fairly long flight for the MiG, and he'll have to take off somewhere between eight and nine. That gives us a little more than two hours."

"You don't think that bonfire's going to change things?" Jack said.

"They may increase security. They haven't left many troops back at the base, less than a dozen. Even the scientists and engineers have jobs to do back in Moscow as part of their plans." Daniel shrugged. "They have a lot of the perimeter mined and they have electronic monitors along the fences, so they think they're secure. They'll let me in at the gate. There's no reason not to."

"There's got to be another way of doing this," said Jack.

"You worried, little brother?"

"Screw you. I just don't think we can ride right in without someone catching on."

"Who said you're riding in?"

"You're going to shoot down the plane yourself? And then make it to the Antonov?"

"Yeah."

"And you can fly it yourself?"

"I flew one just like it every day for two months. It's fueled and ready to go. Even has a time-release additive pack in the tanks to keep the octane fresh. We've been working on this a long time, Jacky. A long time."

"I'll bet."

"One person. Too much risk," said the driver. "It's one thing to steal a black box, but you have to shoot down the other plane."

"I agree," said Cara. "I think we should all go."

"Yeah," said Jack. "Or none of us."

"We have to find a way onto the base," said the driver.

"Well, come up with something fast, because I'm going in," said Daniel. "And I will leave without you."

Chapter Three

Norabk, Western Siberia

When he had finished the thick black bread and small tin of water that were his breakfast, Adrik walked into the cool air. He stood at the very edge of the concrete in front of the hangar, watching the crews prepare the MiG. He watched impassionately, the way a man might stand in a harbor and watch boats passing. Then he walked out along the short pathway between the hangar and the experimental labs to the apron that led to the main runway. It was still before dawn, but even had the sun been high in the sky Adrik would have walked slowly, placing each foot carefully in a stroll that had become a ritual.

When Adrik had first learned to fly, he would start each flight with a short prayer. It was a ritual he had continued for many years, until his daughters died.

Walking along the edge of the concrete had replaced that ritual, though it did not have the same purpose.

Or perhaps it did. For he believed now that God did not exist—how could He, to let Anna and Lara die? So what good had it done to pray?

None. It merely marked time, as did walking. Adrik strolled slowly toward the edge of the concrete where the Black Eagle would soon be pushed.

The large Tupole Bear that would serve as his shadow on takeoff was parked on the auxiliary runway about a half mile away, in the boneyard section of the base. Yesterday's practice sessions had gone perfectly, but Lev and Colonel Bashkin demanded perfection—the TU-95 had practiced the flight several times throughout the night, only just finishing. Now the big bomber with its double-bladed engines and its immense tail fin was being refueled and checked for its mission. Or perhaps the notoriously laborious process was complete—he could hear the crew shouting and laughing, boarding a pair of trucks to go to breakfast. A lone figure walked toward the guardhouse a quarter of a mile away, at the edge of the hangars—it was a favorite place to grab a smoke and listen to the radio; the guard there had an enviable collection of American CDs.

Adrik watched as the trucks headed down the narrow road toward the main base, then continued on toward the gate. Obviously the Bear's flight crew and small ground crew had decided to eat in town—probably because no one there would frown if they added some early morning vodka to the menu.

Adrik didn't care enough to shake his head. As far as he was concerned, the TU-95 was superfluous. It was ridiculous to hide from the satellites. More than likely it was unnecessary, and in any event he could not be stopped.

He stared at the fading stars in the sky overhead. He wanted the day to be over. He wanted to embrace his fate, finally.

He stood and he stared in the direction of Serov. In his mind he saw the small mound where the girls were buried.

In a few minutes, he would turn and walk back to the hangar and don his flight suit. He would go to the aircraft and check it very carefully. Then, well ahead of schedule, he would climb aboard the MiG and wait for takeoff. The technical crew would joke with him, or ask if perhaps he wanted something to drink, or suggest a diversion, but he would insist on boarding the plane. There was nothing else he wanted today.

For now, though, he was content to stare into the face of the Siberian wind, marveling at how warm it felt.

Chapter Four

Hokkaido, Japan

Sleep finally caught him, grabbing him as he waited for yet another number from overseas information. Crow, head propped on the pillow, legs bent so his feet were flat on the mattress, heard the operator start to give him the number for a retired Navy pilot credited with downing two MiG-21s and a MiG-19 during the Vietnam War. There was a click, and the next thing he saw was a batter rubbing his hands with the dirt around home base. He looked in, got the sign, and pulled his arm over for the pitch. As the ball left his fingers, he realized he hadn't checked the man on first base. The runner was going, had the base stolen—but it didn't matter, because Crow's pitch was fat, fat, fat, right down the middle of the plate. The batter grinned and swung. Crow turned and watched it sail toward the stands as the stadium erupted with heavy applause, everyone pounding their feet against the concrete.

Someone was knocking on the door.

Getting out of bed was like trying to swim from the bottom of a deep pool with body armor on. Crow made it, barely, his legs so wobbly he had to steady himself against the TV on the bureau.

It was Rosen.

"Hey, Sleeping Beauty," said the intelligence officer. "You ready to do your thing or what?"

Crow glanced at the clock. It was nearly eight. He was due to preflight in less than an hour.

"I need some coffee," he told Rosen. "I'm going to go take a shower."

"I don't know if we have time."

"I can't take off if I'm sleeping," he said, pushing in the bathroom door and fumbling for the light. "Get two pots of coffee up here right away."

"I don't drink coffee."

"They're for me. Full pots, strong as they got."

Crow's mind was a complete blank shaving and showering. It was a complete blank drinking the coffee as Rosen drove. It was a complete blank as they sped through the gate toward the tarmac where the Raptor was parked.

He couldn't remember anything, not even how to fly. If anyone—Rosen, for instance—had asked how to start the plane's Pratt & Whitney F119 engines, he could only have shrugged.

Luckily, Rosen spent the entire drive to the air base talking about a murder he'd seen on an Internet news report. Somebody had left a pair of shoes in a laundromat drier in Poughkeepsie, N.Y.

There were feet in them at the time.

Crow mustered groans at the appropriate places in the conversation. Japan blurred by his window. The only effect the coffee seemed to have had was on his bladder, which screamed with every bump in the road as they headed for the Raptor's hangar in the restricted area of the base. His mind was blanker than blank.

Going blank before a stressful mission was not an unknown phenomenon. Some of the veterans called it a preflight blackout, and reassured victims that it would go away once they juiced the throttle gate up to takeoff.

As they stopped in front of the hangar, Crow realized he was thinking of himself as a young lieutenant or maybe a captain, not an old-dog colonel with more years on him than a battered T-28 trainer. He'd given pep talks about getting past this sort of thing to guys who were now retired.

The blackout had happened to him only twice in his career. The first was on the day he first soloed. The other was right before his first real combat mission during Desert Storm.

Everything had snapped back at takeoff both times. It would now. He just had to push through. He dressed and briefed with Rosen and the others for the flight, exercising his cranky knees as subtly as possible the whole time. His neck felt stiffer than hell and his eyes blurry as he reviewed the map and long list of mission way points for his navigation system as if seeing them for the first time. Not counting reserves, the Raptor's combat radius was 1,500 nautical miles without refueling; without weapons and trimmed for "ferry service," the craft could travel roughly twice that. The flight plan to Moscow was just under five thousand miles. Three "tanks" or refuels were planned, with two contingencies in case something odd happened. His first refuel would come shortly after takeoff, when he'd top off; he'd be retanking about ten minutes before meeting up with the Concorde III.

Crow dutifully recorded all of the information and coordinates on the pad and kneeboard he carried on every flight, even though the information was also programmed onto a minidisc that would be inserted into the war bird's computer. The pad was an ancient relic, a good-luck charm he had used in Vietnam and carried with him ever since. Ordinarily, the ritual of recording every stage of his planned flight on paper relaxed him, but today Crow's fingers moved so stiffly they could have been chopsticks. The numbers were just numbers, his head still fogged. Walking out to the hangar from the trailer that served as the team's temporary headquarters and ready room, the pilot felt his leg muscles pull so tight against his tendons he thought his knees would snap.

The jet sat at the edge of the tarmac. Its dull gray surface looked wet, as if it were a shark arching over the water. Air Force security personnel stood at full attention around it; a small knot of officials were standing beneath the nose, admiring the plane. Crow assumed the group included the Russian diplomats assigned to inspect the Raptor for weapons, though he hadn't been introduced yet.

"I just want to know what I have to do," Crow told Cleveland when the chief and Bauer met him halfway between the hangar and the diplomats.

The sergeant shot a look toward Bauer, then nodded grimly. "Jacky over there will give it a final check just before you taxi. When you pull in the landing gear after takeoff, the gadget we put in will fold up and the clip will be pushed in. You'll have an error message on the master armament panel, but the aiming vectors and everything else should work. We had to close down two modules in the computer. There may be some other errors, but F1 should be able to corral them. It's a bitch reprogramming that sucker on the fly and we haven't had that much time," said the sergeant. "I was tempted to just pull it off-line."

Crow shrugged, as if he didn't care.

He did care, tremendously. He needed the computer to help him shoot down the MiG.

And if his head didn't unblank itself soon, he was going to need it to fly.

"The landing gear's going to work, right?" Crow asked.

"Yeah, no problem," said Cleveland. "All we did was kill the connection with the computer and dump some of the programming. I had the boys modem a workaround in. You want the details?"

Cleveland looked relieved when Crow shook his head. The sergeant probably knew less about the actual programming than *he* did.

"You still have the panel indicators," continued Cleveland. He was talking about the light that said the landing gear was down.

"The tricky part was getting the loading mechanism to disengage," Bauer said. "What we ended up doing was cutting the top off. Our whole contraption will fall out when you open the gear again. So you'll kick out some metal behind you when you land. You'll hear it, but it won't be a problem. Just go on ahead and land. It's no big deal."

Easy for you to say, thought Crow.

"Listen, Colonel." Cleveland glanced toward the Russian and Japanese officials walking toward them. "We got two dozen rounds for you. That's it. I'm sorry."

"That's enough," Crow told him. "More than I thought. F1'll tell me where to put 'em."

He gave the sergeant a punch and laughed as if he'd

just told a joke. Then he stepped forward to meet the officials. His mind raced as the men introduced themselves and complimented him on his flying machine; Crow wondered what he would do if the radar missed the MiG completely, if whatever made the MiG hard to detect worked up close as well as from a distance. F1 couldn't analyze what it couldn't see.

Ought to be easy; just stay with the little bastard and fire at his tailpipe. F1 could use its infrared to detect it at that point. Crow didn't even need a computer for that; hang there and shoot.

The MiG would have the advantage at first, since it could pick the time and place of the attack.

Child's play. He'd done it in a million drills. He'd nail the little bastard with or without F1.

The Russians practically bowed, asking politely that the pilot guide them through the weapons inspection. Cleveland and Bauer joined in as he showed them the empty weapons bays in the Raptor fuselage. Missiles were ejected by a pneumatic assembly that helped preserve the plane's stealth profile during attack; when the Russian officials didn't pay much attention to it, Crow realized they weren't Air Force or intelligence agents. Sneaking a fully loaded cannon magazine right past them wouldn't have been a problem.

But it was too late for that. And in fact the gizmo that Bauer had rigged was extremely clever. Ordinarily, the plane's two rear wheels folded out from the underside behind the rectangular engine fairings on naked assemblies; they looked like pogo sticks with a truck tire attached. But now the gear sported triangular shields above the wheels, with large black boxes angling into the top of the fuselage. Cleveland began bragging about how the plane's new wheel assemblies could handle even pockmarked runways—total bull, of course, but obviously part of his cover story to explain the additional metal if the Russians had studied pictures of the plane.

They hadn't. They nodded perfunctorily and made what Crow assumed was a joke about airports near Moscow. Then they walked to the side of the plane, watching Crow complete his preflight inspection and climb the ladder to the cockpit. Cleveland came up behind him and helped pull on his seat restraints.

"Geez, Cleveland, your fingers are trembling," said Crow.

"So are yours," said the old sergeant. "Been a while since I did this for real, I guess."

"Me too," said Crow.

"You'll nail him."

"Thanks, Chief." The pilot pulled on his helmet. His hands *were* trembling, damn it.

He prompted F1 for the preflight checklist. He started mechanically, adjusting his AC, reading each indicator separately. Before he was halfway through the fuzz had fallen away; he was in the routine and though his fingers were still shaking and his heart pounding, by the time he kicked up the engines to taxi toward takeoff he was in control.

The Raptor's twin engines spun their turbines into a loud whine, sucking the world into a hush around his ears. He lurched into the sky, anxious to get going. He had a smooth few seconds off the tarmac, then retracted his landing gear.

There was a thud and a metallic scraping noise below him. The plane shuddered.

He assumed the sound had come from the contraption that loaded the gun. But the red indicator light on the control panel indicated that the right rear wheel—the one that had been altered—hadn't closed properly. The plane suddenly felt sluggish beneath him. He glanced at the HUD and saw that his forward airspeed was 150 knots.

One hundred fifty knots and steady. Steady was a problem. It should be leaping ahead, galloping to 200, 250, 300. He had full takeoff power selected.

F1 issued a warning—he was going too slow.

Engine indicators showed he had two live power plants, humming at spec.

Drag from the gear? The light was still burning.

Crow pushed his body back in the seat. He was going a shitload faster than 150, he could tell. There was a problem with the indicated airspeed—the instrument, not the plane.

F1 agreed. It canceled its speed warning and announced that it had detected "indicator program anomalies." It flashed a message in the HUD:

Moving to backup instrument system array, Sect. 3 in block 50. Error detected. Error corrected. Core memory locked off.

Crow went through his checks as the computer did its thing. Fuel consumption okay. Altitude still moving in the right direction.

Gear panic light on. If the gear was really open, his mission had to be scrubbed.

Probably something in the loading mechanism had screwed up the indicator. The plane felt clean. He couldn't be accelerating like this with a leg sticking out.

No speed at all on the HUD now. That was one for the record books.

Crow wished for an old-fashioned speedo above his knee, a round clock with glow-in-the-dark dials instead of the infinitely configurable right multimode screen. He was passing through three thousand feet and the geo-positioner on the left screen marked him out precisely on course. The computer plotted him neatly on line with the briefed coordinates.

The HUD's ghost-white screen suddenly flashed with new data. The ladder showed his altitude at 4,020 feet, climbing rapidly. Speed approached Mach .95, and he felt the slight tremble that was a precursor to breaking the sound barrier.

His instruments were back. He thanked F1 and began edging his power back, since he wasn't supposed to hit supercruise and Mach-plus speed until after his refuel.

In the meantime, he had two problems to deal with: the landing gear warning light, and F1. The light was more immediate, but the flight computer was ultimately even more critical. Cleveland's fudge was obviously not working correctly; approximately twenty of the one hundred-odd parallel modules used by the flight computer had gone off-line, apparently as a result of programming problems. F1 announced that it was using those areas to corral unexpected overflow errors, as if its own programming were a cancer it could control. For the moment, it had the upper hand; he'd just have to take the chance that it would hang in there until the end.

The gear light, though, was a problem. Because the connection with F1 had been severed, the computer couldn't check the sensor. Crow knew the flap must have closed, but he wanted—needed—proof. It nagged at him, stealing his attention, making him doubt the plane and his sense of it.

No way was he going to be moving this fast with one of his landing gear extended, or even with the gear door partially open. No way.

But that was the problem—he was assuming the computer wasn't lying. He was assuming he was going as fast as the HUD told him he was going.

It wasn't just the computer—he felt like he was going that fast.

You couldn't fly by feeling. That was a quick way to get killed.

He needed proof. He could wait until he rendezvoused with the tanker, have the crew check the underside of the plane for him.

Anyone listening in would know he had a problem with the idiot light, though. Procedure would call for him to scrub the flight because of it.

He could deal with the flack. Long way to fly with a leg out, though. Then there'd be the question of landing.

Crow's brain ran through up another possibility—if he got through an invert without a problem, that would mean, could only mean, he was going as fast as F1 told him he was going. He could ignore the stinking light for the next six hours.

Anything wrong with the plane and he'd probably end up grabbing the ejection handles. If he could keep it steady.

Crow remembered telling his crew he had never bailed.

Sweat trickled down the hollow behind his ear lobes as he closed his grip on the stick. Controlled by tiny electric sensors, the plane's control stick was a device to be touched, not muscled—it was Zen, not Superman. But every part of him moved for the F-22, bending as if his weight might help the big Raptor roll herself through the sky without a problem.

F1 complained about the angle, then realized what he was doing and began worrying that his computed flight plan did not include "acrobatic maneuvers."

Crow smiled to himself, relaxing ever so slightly as he flew the Raptor onto its back and then over.

Perfect. The gear was stowed clean. Had to be. The

computer—and just as importantly, his gut—were fine.

He completed the invert and took stock, running through his mental checklist, firmly in control. According to the left MUD, which plotted his position against the flight plan, he was running about thirty-five seconds ahead of schedule.

The idiot light was still on. But if that was all he had to worry about the rest of the flight, he was going to get off incredibly cheap.

Chapter Five

Norabk, Western Siberia

Jack didn't particularly trust Daniel's estimation of base security. Even if he was right that there were only a dozen or so troops there, the morning's misadventure would be sure to make everyone nervous. And just the size of the place—the base was several square miles—complicated things. As Daniel sketched things out for him on a pad in the back of the Fiat, Jack was filled with dread. To get to the SA-16 launcher they would have to pass by the area where the MiG was kept. Then they'd have to double back.

"There's no way to get there from this end?" Jack asked, pointing at the side of the base where the auxiliary runway, their getaway plane, and the missile were.

"No. This is a big swamp and this is a minefield," said Danny. "There's only a single guard here." He pointed at a small square next to a roadway that lay between the main area of the base and the auxiliary runway. "But he has monitors that show him that whole approach. It's easier to come at him from the main part of the base. Once we're past, we're home free."

"Not if we have to go back or wait for the MiG to take off," said Jack. "What kind of explosives do they have on the base?"

Danny shrugged. "Why?"

"We just want to go this way once," he said, tracing a line from the main gate through the lab area and MiG hangar and then on to the escape route. "All we need is a grenade launcher or Molotov cocktail."

"Your brother's a fucking comedian," said the driver. "Who do you think you are, Rambo?"

"I'm not the one who wants to blow up the plane," said Jack.

"Jack's right," said Cara. "The SA-16 is a heat-seeker. If the engine's not on, the plane's going to be cold. You won't be able to target it. Waiting for it to take off will be suicidal."

"They always go through a series of tests in the hangar," said Daniel. He had the overly confident, know-it-all tone Jack hated from childhood. Danny was acting like a kid diagramming an impossibly complicated football play, determined to stick with it because it was his idea. "They turn the engine on here. We can get it from this building when it taxis."

"If we have the missile, which you say is way the hell over here."

"I can drive out there and get it."

Even though he was sitting right next to him, Jack had to twist to look at his brother's face in the cramped backseat of the small hatchback. "There are no other weapons on the base?"

"I think there's a weapons locker in this building here," said Daniel. "Maybe there are more missiles there. I don't know. There are definitely guns."

"How about preset defenses?" asked Cara. "Like machine guns or checkpoints? Even if they're not manned, they may have weapons there."

"There are some sandbags and things like that on the roofs, and maybe there are weapons there," said Daniel. Jack noticed that his brother's tone was less condescending and cocky with her. "They're pretty complacent, though. I think all of the Army units out here are under their control."

"And this is the barracks?"

"Yeah, a hundred yards from the gate. That's really the hard part. Once we get in, we're home free. I doubt there'll be more than two soldiers near the plane. I've never seen more than one or two, and that was when they had close to a hundred on the base. There are a lot less now. A lot less. It's doable, Jacky," he added, looking back at his brother.

Jack wasn't so sure—not about blowing up the plane, but about getting out once they did. But he couldn't let Daniel try it himself.

"All right," he said. "We sneak in there and see what we can come up with. Even a machine gun at close range would do the job. Worst case, we fall back to your original plan and get the missile."

"What I want to know is how we're getting the hell out of there once we cause all the commotion," said the driver.

"We just go to Danny's plane," said Jack.

"Yeah," said Daniel.

"I don't like it," the driver said.

"You're CIA, aren't you?" said Jack.

"Yeah," answered the driver.

"Figures."

"Why don't we just drive the truck into the plane and set ourselves on fire?" said the driver sarcastically.

"We may," said Jack.

That still left them with the problem of getting past the gate. Daniel could simply drive the Fiat through, passing Cara off as a local tart. But the rest of them would be hard to explain, and there was nowhere in the small hatchback for any of them to hide.

"Kelb can get us past the gate," the CIA driver told Daniel, "if we can find a delivery van or something like that. Your brother can hide in the back with the rifle."

"Thanks," said Jack.

"Don't mention it."

They pulled back onto the road, heading back toward the convenient mart where Jack had first seen Daniel, figuring they wouldn't have to wait long to find a likely truck. They were still a few blocks away when Jack saw something much better.

"Go back," he said, grabbing the driver's seat. "The ambulance back there. Go."

"It was empty," said the driver, but he hit the brakes and began to turn. "How are we going to start it?"

"Cara's a car thief," said Jack.

"It's Russian," Cara said.

"So use a Russian screwdriver," he said, taking the rifle to cover her.

It turned out a little more complicated than that, but she got it started anyway. The Russian took the wheel. Jack wanted to take the other seat in the front, but the CIA agent argued that his ill-fitting clothes, unkempt hair, and bruised face would immediately raise questions. Jack took the Kalashnikov and went around to the rear of the ambulance, which was empty except for an old-fashioned wooden stretcher.

"Good luck," Cara told him at the door.

"You too," he said.

"You going to give me a kiss for luck?" She said it in a way that made it seem they were on a date in some place like Venice.

"Yeah," said Jack, and he leaned in to give her a peck on the cheek. Cara turned her head to meet his lips with her mouth, and for a moment he might have believed they were on the Grand Canal, cruising toward the Doge's palace.

Then she pulled back, and he climbed into the back of the ambulance, using the AK-74 for balance. Cara slammed the doors shut behind him, and instead of being in a gondola on vacation he felt like he'd been sealed inside a refrigerator. Fatigue rushed over him as he lay down on the stretcher; even with his heart pumping he worried that he was going to fall asleep, so he pulled himself up as the ambulance started to move. The old truck's shocks were gone; it bounced fiercely as it pulled up over the ruts onto the roadway. Jack grabbed the stainless-steel rail at the side, wedging the rifle along the narrow counter as they drove. A dim dawn filtered through the frosted rear windows, silvery shades of darkness passing through the interior.

He was still pissed at his brother, incredibly pissed. Daniel should have found a way to let the family know what was going on.

Would Jack have done the same? In fact he hadn't; all of the B-3 overseas missions had been highly secret.

He rolled his fingers around the steel rail, maintaining his balance as the ambulance turned onto a gravel road. His pants were stiff and his hair was matted to his head. The AK-74 was an updated version of the classic Kalashnikov AK-47, firing smaller rounds and with less recoil than a standard .22-caliber rifle. Jack had fired one once or twice on a range in the Army; the only "trick" to it was remembering that the cocking handle was on the right side of the gun.

He took his hand off the rail and cocked the weapon as the ambulance slowed to a stop. He pushed his head up to the back window and saw the shadow of the Fiat with Danny at the wheel behind them.

They must be at the gate. The ambulance motor rasped at idle. Jack stood as still as possible, listening as the driver said something to the guard.

The guard answered. Everyone sounded bored.

They waited.

The ambulance rocked again. It lurched forward a few feet and stalled.

Jack waited for the starter to wind, then he realized it wasn't going to—they had jumped it and didn't have a key.

Somebody outside cursed. Danny beeped the horn behind them. One of the front doors opened and the ambulance started moving forward very slowly; Jack guessed the CIA agent was pushing.

A second vehicle, obviously a large truck, sounded its horn from behind Daniel's car.

There was more cursing, much louder now. The ambulance continued to move extremely slowly. Jack could feel the springs rocking as the driver jumped out. Someone shouted and Jack heard the Fiat's engine roar, saw the dark shadow grow behind him, and just managed to grab on as his brother's car rammed the rear of the ambulance.

In the same moment, someone outside began firing a gun. Jack fell backwards as bullets ripped across the ambulance from front to back. Jack slid feet-first toward the door, struggling to roll the rifle off the counter and duck the hail of gunfire. He got the gun and kicked at the door; it opened a quarter of the way, then stopped, blocked by the radiator of the Fiat. Jack shouted for his brother as the front half of the ambulance evaporated in steam under the heavy whomp of a serious machine gun. He dove out of the truck, falling into the dirt as the ambulance erupted in flame. He ran from the flames eyes closed, bouncing into a chest-high metal fence a few yards away. He whirled around, opening his eyes to see someone in a striped shirt coming toward him from the other side of the fence. He pulled the trigger on the AK-74, pushing the bullets in the man's direction. Dirt snapped and popped but the man stayed erect, raising a snub-nosed submachine gun in his direction. Jack pulled his rifle to his stomach and gave another burst, a tight one this time, three bullets right through the Russian paratrooper's face.

He swung around, back toward the gate, and saw three men running for a sandbagged position twenty yards away, either for more weapons or to call for reinforcements. Jack gave a burst, aiming left to right; he missed low, but brought the gun back up, pumping the trigger and nailing two of the paratroopers across the legs or lower backs. He dropped to his knee, but still missed the third man, who threw himself over the sandbags.

He'd missed because he was out of bullets. Jack steadied himself in a crouch. The burning ambulance and the guardhouse at the front of the gate were six or seven yards to his left; the Fiat was a foot or so behind the ambulance, though it hadn't caught fire yet. Two bodies lay near the cab of the ambulance. Jack started for them and felt dirt squirting all around him; he dove, losing his gun as he rolled.

A fuel truck had pulled up to the gate; its horn must

have been the one Jack had heard inside. The driver tried desperately to back up, but someone had shot out some of the tires; the truck rocked back and forth, wheels spinning. The base guards riddled the rear with rifle fire; the truck began oozing fuel. Finally the driver opened the door and jumped out. Jack saw him move about three feet before he was cut down by the heavy machine gun, which was posted near the sentry box at the gate.

Someone crawled under the truck. Jack realized it was Danny.

He yelled at him to get away. Then he realized that wasn't what he was doing at all.

The ground in front of Jack heaved, rocks and macadam exploding as the machine-gunner finally saw him. Jack rolled forward across the roadway and into a shallow drainage ditch. He got up, trying to run toward his brother, but losing his balance almost immediately as the ground bubbled with bullets. Before he could get back up he felt himself being pulled backward to a deeper spot in the ditch. He turned his head and saw Cara crouching behind him, holding a stubby grenade launcher in his face.

"You know how to use one of these?"

Before he could answer, the fuel truck exploded.

Chapter Six

Norabk, Western Siberia

The howl engulfed her, wrapping her in the middle of a raging storm of wind. Cara felt herself flying through the air, propelled into a gray void.

Then she saw the grass around her and tasted the dirt in her mouth.

Cara pushed herself to her feet. Jack was doing the same thing next to her. They were only a few feet from where they'd been when the truck exploded, but she'd lost the grenade launcher somehow. Her head rocked back and forth in a swirling frenzy; she felt a dizziness deep inside her brain, as if her frontal lobe had turned into a whirling top.

No one was firing at them anymore.

"Let's go!" yelled Daniel, running toward them.

"How'd you blow that up and not get killed?" asked Jack, scooping up the grenade launcher.

"I stuffed a handkerchief into one of the bullet holes near the top, lit it, and ran like hell," said Daniel. He grinned. "Smart, huh?"

"You're lucky as shit."

"What's that?" Daniel asked, pointing at the grenade launcher.

"Shoots grenades. You got any?" Jack asked Cara.

She shook her head. She'd found the launcher in the car. Why hadn't Daniel said something about it earlier?

"We better move," said Daniel. "They'll be coming from over there, where the barracks are."

Cara and Jack followed Daniel deeper into the complex, through a field, around to the edge of a cinder-covered road. Trucks were rushing toward the entrance as the fire towered into the sky. There were three or four other vehicles behind the fuel truck outside the main gate; all had caught fire, and one by one their gas tanks also exploded.

"That's where the lab is, over there," said Daniel, pointing to a three-story building several hundred yards away.

"Where's the plane?" Jack asked.

"Across there." Daniel looped his hand as if throwing a rock. "It's the third hangar. Almost right across from us. The others are empty."

"Let me catch my breath," said Cara.

"If we had a mortar we could take it out from here," said Jack.

"You find one in the grass?" asked Daniel.

"Not yet."

Cara couldn't see past the backs of the buildings to the hangar. She tried correlating the map Daniel had drawn in the Fiat to what lay before her, but nothing seemed to fit. The runway was well beyond this clump of buildings, and the airplane they were to escape in nearly a mile and a half beyond that, near a secondary runway.

"Follow me then," said Daniel. "We're going to get wet."

Wet was an understatement. They tramped through twenty yards of swamp that came nearly to Cara's knees before coming to solid ground. The clothes Jack had bought for her at the old lady's were warm and fit well, but they sagged with the added weight of the water, holding her back. Her side, meanwhile, was cramping; her ribs screamed murderously. The others had to pause twice to let her catch up. Finally, they stopped behind a low pile of cement blocks next to a road behind the lab buildings.

"All right. You guys wait here," said Daniel. "I'll be right back for you."

"Wait, wait, wait," said Jack, grabbing him as he leapt up. "Where are you going?"

"I have to go get the chip for the radar resonator. It's in that office building." Daniel pointed toward a squat brick structure twenty yards away. "Take me a minute."

"Wait. Why are you doing that? The weapons are over there, right?"

"That was my mission, Jack. That's why I'm here."

"I thought you were supposed to shoot down the plane."

"We can do both, right?"

"I don't know that we can," said Jack. "What if you're caught?"

"I'm not going to get caught. Have some faith, Jacky."

"I do, Danny," said Jack flatly. "Which building has the weapons?"

"There." Daniel nodded his head and pointed to a

prefab concrete structure three stories high angled to their left. There were three buildings between it and the offices where Daniel said he was going. "Wait for me. You'll never get in by yourself."

"I just want to know where the hell it is when you get nailed."

"I'm not getting nailed."

"We're coming with you."

"How am I going to explain you?"

Jack frowned, but he had to agree. "We'll come to the back of the building."

"I'm going through and around the front to the other lab. I work here, Jack, remember? I don't have to sneak around. That would be suspicious, especially with that commotion."

"Fine. We'll come with you to the back door," insisted Jack. "Once we see you're inside, we'll go over to the other building and wait for you to let us in."

"Okay, that's good," said Daniel.

"You okay?" Jack asked Cara.

Cara nodded. She needed to tell Jack something was wrong, but before she could think of how to do it, he jumped to his feet and followed his brother.

Daniel trotted north across the field, paralleling a large, two-story warehouse shed made of metal. Cara tried to stop Jack, but he was running too fast and her side was tugging at her.

The grenade launcher had been stashed beneath the front dashboard of the Fiat. Apparently it had been jarred loose when Daniel tried pushing the ambulance through the gate, because it practically dropped into her hands as she dove out when the shooting started.

Why the hell hadn't they mentioned it when Jack started asking about other weapons to use against the plane?

And why did Daniel try to push the ambulance in?

She hadn't been close enough to hear what they were saying, but the guards seemed merely annoyed, not ready to shoot.

Just bad judgment? Panic? He knew his brother was in the back of the ambulance. Was he trying to protect him if the guards began firing?

Or was he trying to get them to kill him?

Why was he separating himself from them now?

A crumbling concrete road ran behind the buildings. They ran to it, stopping short behind a warren of discarded oil drums. The cans were covered with rust and some were oozing with a dark viscous liquid. The dank smell of shaved metal and oil ate at her nose and mouth.

"Be careful of the drums," said Daniel. "There's no telling what's in them."

"What do we have in the way of guards?" Jack asked.

"No way of knowing, with this commotion," said Daniel. He pointed to the office building. "Usually, there are only two guards down here. In the morning, they're always at that corner, watching the front of the labs and the hangar."

"All right. Good luck."

"Hey, it's not luck." Danny held his hand out. Jack slapped it. They could have been kids planning a Halloween trick on a nasty neighbor.

Who was the trick really on?

Cara caught her breath as Daniel trotted toward the back of the building. When he reached it, he took something from his pocket—a cigarette. He pretended he was just finishing a smoke, tossing it aside as he pulled open the door.

"Wait," whispered Cara as Jack rose to start for the other building. "Do you trust him?"

"Yeah, I trust him," said Jack.

"You thought he was a traitor. That's why you came to Russia, right?"

Jack looked at her as if she were speaking in tongues.

"Jack." Cara grabbed the stubby barrel of the empty launcher in his hand. "This gun was under the dashboard of the Fiat. Why didn't they tell us about it?"

"You think he's setting us up?"

"I don't know what to think. I don't understand why they didn't tell us about the grenade launcher. And your brother seems awful sure of himself."

"That's Danny. He was always cocky."

"How do we know there's an armory in that building? How do we know anything? Think about it." She pressed her knee against the dirt, steadying herself. "Why keep guns in a lab building?"

"Why not?" asked Jack. His eyes bore into hers. "They have to be somewhere. It makes sense if they figured the technicians would need them if there was a real fight."

Despite his confident voice, she could tell he was teetering, unsure what to believe.

"What about the grenade launcher?"

"I don't know," he said. "Maybe they knew and he didn't. I didn't trust the guy who said he was a CIA agent. Or maybe they just didn't have grenades and they thought going back on the base was stupid. I do."

"So why are we here?"

"Because he's my brother. There's no other choice."

"Yes, there is, Jack."

Cara touched his arm, but he turned his head toward the building, rising.

"Let's go," he said.

Cara pursed her lips, then rose and began following him to the back of the other building.

Chapter Seven

Beijing, China

From the outside, the Concorde III bore little resemblance to the original, with the exception of its downward-pointed beak. The craft was considerably larger and fatter, with stubby delta wings mounted low toward the rear of the craft. There were no windows, not even for the pilots, who used video cameras and a host of infrared and radar sensors to see the world around them. The plane's skin was a smooth piece of molded titanium-ceramic, specially invented for the aircraft. The top section bulged slightly, accommodating tubes for the super-cooled hydrogen that fueled the cryogenic engines; condensation wafted from the top of the fuselage in thin wisps, forming a kind of saintly halo around the top of the plane as it was fueled. The engines themselves were housed in triangular flares below the long belly. What with the glowing white surface, stubby wings, and a triple-planed tail section, the plane looked like something out of a 1950s comic book.

Inside, it reminded Buzz of an old-fashioned English men's club gone high-tech—thick leather club chairs were grouped in the main passenger area, each with its own flat DVD/video monitor folding up out of the floor next to it. Buzz, being led through the plane on a private tour by the French first officer before the flight, wondered if the seating was a permanent arrangement. If it were, tickets would have to cost ten thousand dollars apiece, since there were only four groups of six chairs apiece. Even counting the small crew area in the rear, which on this flight was reserved for security personnel doubling as waiters, there were seats for less than sixty people.

In lieu of windows, passengers could select one of eight exterior views on the video monitor at their seat, including a "fuselage pan," which allowed for a 180-degree view from the belly of the craft. The computer could zero in on sectors, magnifying them enough to read the logo on a baseball cap at twenty thousand feet. Only a decade before, such an ability would have made the plane a rival for the Aurora Mercury, America's top-secret hydrogen-powered spy plane. Satellite television feeds and the Web could be tapped into from the leather chairs, thanks to the keyboards that were part of the fold-up trays on the left side of the chairs. Of course, these were intended to supplement passengers' own laptops and palm-computers, which could be plugged into power supplies and video outputs at the bottom of the flat screens.

The mini-workstations included two external phone lines per chair, necessary since even satellite-based cell systems were rendered inoperable by the materials used in the plane's hull and its speed and heat in the air. The Concorde had what amounted to its own phone switching network, complete with antenna and transmitter in the tail section; the arrangement opened vast possibilities for industrial espionage, something that under other circumstances Buzz would have spent considerable time contemplating.

As it was, he had difficulty feigning interest as he trailed the plane's first officer into the cockpit. The plane's control suite was as advanced as anything in the world, including the newly updated B-2 bomber and the F-22, bragged the tour guide. Buzz nodded politely, watching over the Frenchman's shoulder as he sat in the copilot's seat and fired up a demonstration program on the command computer. There was not one gauge or dial in the cockpit; everything was glass or touch screen. Even powering the engines and steering could be done by touching the viewers or speaking into the voice module, though the traditional steering yoke and throttle bar were included "for old time sake," joked the first officer.

"Very nice," said Buzz, glancing at his watch. He was beginning to worry that he was going to miss his update call, scheduled for eight a.m. local time.

Five minutes from now. And his secure phone was with his aide back at the limo.

"Going to be some flight," said the first officer cheerfully. His words had only the barest hint of his native accent; if anything he sounded British. "Our escorts are already airborne. I can show you their locations on the screen if you'd like."

"Actually, I'd like to get some breakfast," said Buzz, trying to make a polite excuse to leave.

But that was the way his luck was running. The man blanched, and Buzz remembered that he had actually met him in the VIP breakfast lounge at the terminal—where, of course, he had already eaten. But there was no way to retract the faux pas. The Frenchman moved quickly to pop the crew hatch. As Buzz walked down the ribbon-festooned exit ramp, he realized he'd be the last one handed a parachute if the plane got shot down.

His aide had driven out near the plane on the tarmac. He stood between the car door and the driver's seat, waving the phone. With his wide, beefy shoulders and shaved head, he looked a little like a gnome—though he was six-three and nearly as tall as Buzz.

"Eagleton," said the DDO, taking the phone and sliding into the car.

"Blitz," said the Professor. "What kept you?"

"I got tied up," said Buzz. "Listen, Professor, I'm waiting for another call."

"I am your other call," said Blitz. "Blue ran into problems."

"What are you talking about?"

"I know you've been out of touch. I get the Code YG transcripts, so I thought to alert you. I told your desk man I would handle it."

Communications about Blue weren't supposed to be on Code YG, which was a communications channel devoted to normal CIA station operations. Unless something really bad had happened.

Really, really bad.

"Blue seems to have been wiped out. They missed their check-in and there have been reports of some sort of incident in the town near the base," said Blitz.

The fact that an NSC member was privy to information about one of his operations before he was would ordinarily have shorn the last shred of reserve and discipline from Buzz's demeanor—in other words, he would have gone apeshit ballistic. But the events of the last two days had pushed him well past that state, and the DDO stood mute.

"We're scrambling to get direct satellite surveillance of the airfield so we can confirm if Shadow R takes off. The F-14s are ready," said Blitz cheerfully. "And you know, I've been rethinking the possibilities and I think that if the attempt on the Concorde is successful, we stand to gain. In fact, it's almost desirable, except for the loss of life."

"Not if there's a world war," sputtered Buzz.

"That possibility is overrated."

"No, it's not."

"Do you want to cancel the flight?"

"No," said Buzz quickly. "We can't."

"Of course we can," said Blitz. Buzz pictured him holding his hand over the phone and laughing hysterically.

"If the President wants to stop the flight, that's his call," Buzz said.

"Your choice," said Blitz.

He might just as well have said, "Your funeral."

"God speed," added Blitz.

"Oh thanks, Professor. Thanks." He killed the circuit, and sat still for a moment, watching through the windshield as a large Chinese band began to play near the airplane. The dignitaries began filing from the nearby terminal building, walking down a long red carpet.

Buzz handed the phone out to his aide and pulled himself out of the car.

"All right. Let me go kowtow to the Vice President," he said.

"Uh, call came while you were on the tour," said his assistant. "Vice President came down with the flu. Looks like you're the U.S. delegation."

"Gee, what a shock," said Buzz.

Chapter Eight

Norabk, Western Siberia

Jack dove to the ground as he reached the back corner of the building, sliding down head-first to peer around the corner and up the alley between the two buildings. He heard a truck moving in the front, then saw two guards.

Jack pulled back as Cara ducked down behind him.

"What?" she asked.

"Guards." He edged back for another look. The men were roughly twenty feet away, talking, holding their weapons anxiously; one had a pistol, the other a rifle.

"What now?" Cara asked.

"We wait for them to go."

"How long will that be?"

"Not long, I hope," he said. He crawled back, making sure to keep his head pressed to the ground at the corner. One of the guards had moved.

Suddenly, the man in view raised his pistol and took a step away from the alleyway, shooting as he walked.

At Danny?

Jack started to get up, ready to rush him with the empty grenade launcher, anger overcoming reason. Then he heard the man laugh. The other said something about chasing rabbits, shouting and laughing. He fired too.

"What the hell are they doing?" Cara hissed as Jack pulled back to her.

"I think they're just screwing around. They may be drunk."

"This early?"

"Occupational hazard out here," he told her. "They said something about rabbits. I didn't get much of it."

Cara pushed over him to listen at the corner. Even covered with mud in the clothes of a peasant boy, her body was beautiful.

"You're right," she said. "They're saying something about the idiots at the front gate, blowing up the gasoline truck because they got nervous."

Jack crawled back and saw the guard who'd been at the head of the alley walking away.

"Okay, let's go," he told her, dashing across the open space. He reached the other side in three long strides, throwing himself on the ground and turning just in time to see Cara pirouette in the open space behind the building. She spun so fast that Jack's only thought was that she had inexplicably decided to dance.

Before he could tell her to quit fooling around, he heard the crack of a pistol. Jack got to his feet and pressed against the ribbed steel of the building. A truck motor roared nearby, drowning out everything else. Cara, only a few feet from him in the alley, crumpled to the cement, one arm thrown out, one tucked in.

His legs got numb, waiting. Finally a shoulder appeared in the space before him, then an arm and a back and a head. A man in a striped airborne T-shirt stood over Cara, pistol in hand. Slowly he aimed the gun at her head. Jack knew he should wait—he wanted to wait until the second man showed himself, he intended to wait until it was prudent to attack, but instead he sprang forward, throwing the butt of the empty grenade launcher against the base of the man's skull.

The guard fell away. Something flashed across the corner of Jack's vision and he ducked down and charged into it, slamming into the stomach of someone nearly as tall as he was. They fell, the grenade launcher flying and the second soldier's rifle falling to the side as they grappled. The soldier cursed and tried to bite him. Jack managed to wedge his elbow in the man's chest, levering it against him; the Russian rolled to the side, flailing with his arms and fists and kicking desperately. He spun on top of Jack, pinning his arms as he tried to grab for his fallen gun. Jack swept the weapon into his hands, but felt the stock being pulled from his fingers. His arms screamed with pain, and he felt as if he were being sucked into the cement beneath his body. The man's sweat gagged him like poisonous gas; Jack choked and the rifle flew upwards, stolen from him. It arced back down like a sledgehammer and Jack shoved his shoulder away, dodging the worst of the blow as he slid to the left. He rolled up and felt a heavy thud in his side, the Russian's boot or the butt of the gun—he didn't stop to find out. He cringed as he hunched to his knees, expecting another blow.

When it didn't come in the half second he expected it to land, Jack opened his eyes. The man's face loomed over his, eyes wide in frenzy, mouth foaming with blood. Then the man, shot through the brain twice, collapsed next to him. Cara, her face contorted with pain, was a few feet away, holding the first soldier's pistol in her hand. Her other arm was limp at her side.

"Is that the plane?" she asked, motioning with her head behind him. The words were barely distinguishable from each other, slurred by the pain of her wound.

Jack turned and saw a black shape being pushed across the front of the buildings. It had a scoop nose and a canopy, but he didn't wait to see the rest; two men with guns began running toward them from the hangar across from the alley. He picked up the rifle and pressed the trigger. Only two or three bullets stuttered out before the clip was empty, but it was enough to send the men back around the corner for cover.

"Come on," Jack said, pulling Cara to follow him back toward the building where Daniel had gone.

"The plane," she said.

"Give me the pistol."

"It's out of bullets," she yelled, but she gave it to him anyway, struggling to keep up as he ran toward the door of the building. Jack heard shouts and vehicles revving their motors. He pried the door open with his fingers, throwing himself inside, surprised when he wasn't met with gunfire.

A flight of steel stairs led up and down, with crash doors on each level. Jack guessed down, and started loping down the stairs, Cara following. He stopped midway, hearing a commotion above. Cara pushed around him as Jack tiptoed down to the landing and went beneath the stairs. He steadied the pistol upwards, covering the figures that were emerging one and a half stories above.

"It's empty," she reminded him, her voice halfway between snarl and whisper.

Three men were coming down the stairs. One was his brother. The other two were in Russian Army uniforms.

Cara had been right.

No—the Russians were holding guns on Daniel. One said something in Russian Jack couldn't understand.

"They're accusing him of being an American spy," whispered Cara. "They're going to kill him down in the basement. Something about a traitor's death."

Time stretched out as Jack watched the trio descend. He waited, trying to be patient, knowing he could use the pistol as a prop—the Russians wouldn't know it wasn't loaded.

Wouldn't help if they started shooting first.

As Daniel reached the bottom step Jack started to come out. But before he could, Daniel swirled around and reached to wrestle the gun out of his captor's hand. The gun fired and the man fell; Jack grabbed for the second man's leg through the side railing, pulling him down. The man pitched over and Danny tumbled on top of him, somehow managing to hold onto the pistol in the somersault. There were two quick shots; both Russians tumbled to the floor as the stairwell filled with smoke. An alarm began ringing above.

Cara scooped up the second man's pistol as Danny pulled open the basement door.

"We have to get out of the building," Jack told him.

"I still have to get the box," Daniel said. "They stopped me before I reached it."

"Jesus. Come on," said Jack. "The plane's moving out of the hangar."

"No, you come on," said Daniel, pulling away as Jack reached to stop him.

Jack followed as his brother turned in the hallway ahead and started up a new set of stairs. Jack caught up on the second floor, trotting alongside as they ran down the hall, Cara behind them. The rooms, all open, looked like they belonged in a college, with lab benches, computers, microscopes, and elaborate exhaust hoods. Danny ran to a set of lockers at the far end of the hall; he pulled one open and fished out a box at the bottom. It was no bigger than a cigarette pack.

"That's it?" asked Jack.

"Three chips. Yeah, pretty amazing work," said Daniel. "The guts are all I need."

"We've got company," said Cara, dropping to her knee as she spun around. The door at the far end of the hall opened. As it did, she leveled the pistol and fired three bullets into the space. The roar and smoke shook Jack so hard he slipped back against the lockers.

Either Cara had hit the person trying to come through the door, or she'd made him change his mind. The door slammed closed.

"We can get out through here," said Danny, hammering at the locked door at the near end of the corridor with the handle of his gun.

"Shoot the lock," said Jack.

"Oh, yeah," said Daniel. He started to laugh.

"Jesus, come on," said Cara.

It took Daniel two shots to blast the door open. Jack kicked it free with his leg and followed Daniel across the room.

"We can get to the roof from the window," yelled Daniel as he ran. He smashed the glass with the gun, knocking out the pane and stepping onto a fire escape. It was a short climb to the top.

Three Ural trucks filled with soldiers were driving on the pavement below; Jack caught a glimpse of the plane moving toward the corner of the far hangar.

It was so strange he forgot everything, stopping and standing as he stared. The front of the plane seemed normal enough, though it had been smoothed out considerably from the stock version and was covered with black radar-evading material. But instead of a tail and rear stabilizer, the black plane had a circle-shaped wing with thin fins extending toward the fuselage, around what Jack guessed was the exhaust. The front wings had sharp notches in them, as if a giant with scissors had cut them down.

"Here, there's a machine gun over here! And rifles!" Cara yelled. "Come on, come on!"

She was stooped over a set of sandbags at the far end of the roof beyond a warren of exhaust vents. A 7.62mm PK had been set up in a defensive position covering the approach from the back of the building along the main road. Jack ran and leapt over the sandbags, rolling next to Cara, who was struggling with the loading mechanism of the gun. Daniel had disappeared.

"We have to put bullets in it," she said.

"Yeah, okay," said Jack. There were large boxes of belted rimmed cartridges and a firing mechanism that looked roughly like an old M60, but Jack had never used the gun before. As he bent down to examine it, a head rose over the building's roof behind him, then a shoulder, then an assault rifle. Cara let go of the machine gun's wooden carrying handle and picked up her pistol, waiting until the soldier stepped on the roof before she fired. The man dove back over the side.

"Come on, come on," yelled his brother from the ground. "A truck. Come on."

Jack struggled, but couldn't get the machine gun loaded, his fingers jamming against the feed mechanism at the top.

"I thought your brother said there were only a dozen troops here," said Cara, running to look for Daniel.

"Yeah. He never could count very well," Jack said. He heard shouts from the far side of the building where they'd come over.

"There's a truck down there," shouted Cara.

"Go!" said Jack, grabbing the twenty-pound machine gun by the oblong hole in its wooden stock. He scooped up two boxes of ammo and ran to the side of the roof. A drainpipe led down to the ground right next to the truck.

Cara waited for him. She fired her pistol again, then gave him the weapon and started down, obviously in agony from her wounded arm.

When nothing appeared behind him, Jack pushed the pistol into his belt, then started downwards. He had the PK in his hand and the ammo boxes under his curled arm. About a third of the way to the ground he began to slip; he just barely managed to let the PK and ammo fall instead. The gun and its rounds clattered against the hood of the old Zil 130 open-backed truck as Daniel got it started.

The rear tail panel and two-thirds of the truck's wooden slats along the sides were gone, but the motor roared steadily and the old Zil began lumbering slowly backwards as Cara managed to get the machine gun into the rear bed. Jack dove in over the side; he and she slammed together, but somehow managed to stay in the truck as it moved down the pockmarked alleyway. It was pointed in the wrong direction, but there was no room to turn around.

"Hey!" yelled Daniel. "Take this."

Jack looked toward the cab. Daniel had found a rifle on the passenger-side floor and was holding it out the open back window to Jack. It was an AK-47 with a full banana clip.

Jack saw the tears in Cara's eyes as he looked up from the gun.

"It hurts," she said.

"It'll be okay." Jack touched her gently, then pushed away, setting the machine gun on its tripod as the truck roared toward the back of the buildings, circling back around.

"I only have one of the bullet boxes," she said in a voice barely audible over the poorly muffled engine.

"Can you load it?" yelled Jack.

"I don't think so," she said, but she bent down to it anyway, trying to move a shell into the action at the top of the weapon.

Jack lost his balance as the Zil turned the corner into a narrow alley, accelerating around the corner and out into the clear. The runway lay just ahead; the MiG was taxiing into position under its own power. Jack realized it had already been fueled and was about to take off.

"Ram it!" he shouted, banging on the top of the truck cab as Danny accelerated.

The plane was at least a hundred yards away, too far for them to catch. He pulled up his AK-47, firing wildly as the Zil bounced over the cracks and weed-strewn concrete. He could see the arc of his bullets, a thin gray stream chipping against the ground just in front of the plane, then edging up, edging toward the thin, bare metal and several hundred gallons of jet fuel.

Fire erupted from the rear of the plane. Jack felt the rifle pop empty, felt something satisfying in his chest—he'd gotten the son of a bitch.

But he hadn't. The fire was the burst of a rocket pack beneath the MiG's wings, helping it accelerate for a quick takeoff. It emerged from a furrow of smoke and shot ahead on the long runway, stuttering and then climbing like a missile, free.

Chapter Nine

Norabk, Western Siberia

Adrik felt the plane shake the rocket packs from her wings as the MiG climbed steadily away from the runway. He clamped his attention tightly around the cockpit, cranking in his landing gear, steadying the stick, and then checking the throttle, moving through his instruments, gluing his eyes not on the sky but on the artificial horizon at the center of the Black Eagle's control panel. The attack was behind him and no longer a worry. He was going up and he was going perfect; he had three hundred meters, four hundred, five. Gravity eased her grip on his chest and legs, and the pilot flew the reworked MiG as if she were a stallion galloping up a long, steep hill.

When he reached 1,500 meters, he began to pull the plane into a banking turn. He knew he was truly safe; if the troops that had broken into the base had had surface-to-air missiles, they would have fired them already.

He did not know exactly what had happened, but he was not surprised there had been an attack. Lev and the other generals undoubtedly had been caught off guard, but his flight crew's preparations and his own habits were more than enough compensation. By now the technicians were undoubtedly jumping into their foxholes and behind their sandbags, fighting off the attackers. Bashkin had seen to the preplaced defenses for the technical crew yesterday; he was much more competent than Adrik had ever believed.

The Bear, of course, was still on the ground; it was possible that his takeoff had been detected. The premature start of the mission meant that Adrik would have to conserve his fuel and delay his arrival at the intercept point, but such problems were not important.

His canopy and radar were clear. The government had made a major miscalculation in attacking the base without air support—and apparently without scrambling fighters to intercept him. Lev had predicted that any response by the Russian government would be uncoordinated, so in that much at least he was right.

Adrik had to be on his guard, however. The stealth characteristics of his plane were an important asset, but he was not invisible. Radio B lost its potency around ten thousand meters, allowing the best interceptor radars to detect him at close range. And while the heat signature of his plane had been greatly reduced, it was still an attractive target to advanced heat-seeking weapons. A properly equipped air-defense fighter could find and destroy him, given the right circumstances.

Of course, the fighter's pilot would have to fly better than Adrik to do so. This would be difficult.

Adrik leaned his head to the cockpit glass, straining

to see the base he had just left. One of the fuel trucks back near the hangars exploded, sending an immense finger of flame upwards. One of the buildings back near the hangar had smoke pouring from the top. But the rest of the base appeared deserted; he could see no armor column, no array of troop carriers and attack helicopters. The government had been able to mount only a pathetically small force to attack them, no more than a company or two of men.

Perhaps Lev and the White Bears would prevail after all. It would be good for his brother. It would be good for Bashkin and his wife and the millions of Siberians whose fates had been trampled for so long by the various masters of the Kremlin. Finally they would take their lives back.

Adrik slipped his hand away from the stick and carefully saluted the base and all the men who remained. He had not expected to feel this. He had not expected to think of Lev or Colonel Bashkin or Masha at this moment. He had not expected to feel such emotion for them. It swept through his body like adrenaline, and he felt almost giddy as he checked his course.

Was he like Masha? Did he want justice? Justice from the Russians, for the dead? What did that mean?

Had he crossed into thinking of himself as a Siberian? His people had come from Russia; he was as Russian as anyone walking the Moscow streets. Or was it even more abstract—was he feeling the difference between justice and revenge?

Adrik had always thought justice was not something to be won from the government, or by killing a bully or an oppressor. It was not something won by power or might. Justice, he thought, was an arbitrary thing, vague and unreachable, as whimsical as fate. Justice was the way the world worked without humans; justice was beyond them. Justice was the vast march of history toward some goal a person could barely glimpse, much less affect.

But now he thought perhaps there was some part of justice that wasn't arbitrary. Perhaps a person who acted correctly would have it, or feel some part of it. A person who fulfilled his duty—that might be enough.

Justice would not bring his children back or change the past. It would not bury the frozen bodies floating in the wild Siberian rivers. But if there was some portion of it that was attainable, it would be within his grasp in a few short hours nonetheless.

Chapter Ten

Norabk, Western Siberia

Jack wedged his finger against the trigger of the automatic rifle even though he knew it was too late. Bullets snapped through the clip like the roll of drumsticks on a snare, the reverberation shaking down into the heels of his feet as if his body were hollow.

They'd lost. The MiG was gone, no matter how many bullets he pissed into the sky.

All this way.

Jack pulled the butt of the gun against his side, cursing himself, seeing for an instant the face of his father, drawn and white, lying helpless on a bed halfway across the world.

He'd tried to play the hero and he'd screwed everything up.

"Jack! Jack! There's another gun!"

He snapped his head around to Cara, who was pointing to a pile of sandbags near the access ramp.

A machine-gun emplacement. Another PK, more ammo, a cache of more rifles under a plastic sheet.

What was the use? The MiG was gone. They might as well die here.

A round of small-arms fire from the hangar area behind them snapped Jack out of it. His brother had stopped the truck and Cara was already in the middle of the sandbagged position, grabbing the rifles. He jumped down and grabbed two fresh boxes of ammo for the machine gun. As he dove back into the truck, he saw six or seven soldiers running across the concrete apron toward them.

"Get us out of here!" he yelled at his brother. As the Zil lurched back into motion, Jack smashed open the ammo and tried to slide a clip into the gun. He'd never shot a Russian machine gun, and while there were some similarities with an American SAW or Squad Automatic Weapon—namely, they were both serious meat-grinders—by the time he managed to get the gun loaded the Siberians were peppering the rear of the truck with rifle fire. Cara fired a few rounds and sent them hunkering to the ground just as Jack pressed the trigger on the big gun; the barrel literally bounced up and down with the first few shots, and he found himself ramming it forward, muscling the weapon and yelling at himself to get control, screaming that he wasn't going to die in Siberia. He finally got a good burst off and saw one of the men writhing in pain as the Zil veered across the end of the runway and turned hard. He swung the barrel through the space where the wood planks should have been but didn't have a shot.

"Tell Danny to get us to that plane," he told Cara as the Zil bumped off the apron. "Tell him we got to get the hell out of here."

"He is," she said. "We have to go that way." She jerked her hand forward, pointing back toward the hangar area over Jack's shoulder, toward the front of the truck. "We have to go across this log road to the macadam. There's a fuel truck there," she said. "See it?"

They were three thousand yards away from it. Jack hoisted the machine gun and slammed it against the top of the cab, had Cara help him steady it. But twenty pounds of bouncing energy wouldn't have been easy to aim even if the road were smooth, and the gun nearly flew away the second he opened fire.

"Fuck," he yelled, pulling it toward him. The barrel was scorching and he screamed as the smallest part of it touched the nail of his pinkie. He slammed the whole thing down again and fired, one eye actually closed, his weight down on the back of the gun. The bullets bounced as wildly as the Zil.

And then the fuel truck exploded. In the next second they reached a solid roadway again and Daniel stepped on the accelerator, racing forward on the far access road past a row of Soviet-era dormitories that lacked roofs and at least half of their bricks. Jack and Cara tumbled backwards, jumbled in smoke and confusion and adrenaline. Jack had no idea what was happening; somehow he got an AK-47 into his hands and emptied the clip, reloaded, burned another. Whether he was actually aiming at anyone, he couldn't have said.

As Jack's head imploded with chaos and his lungs triple-pumped, an image of his father crashed through everything else, a strange, peaceful memory, and it was this that saved him from hyperventilating into unconsciousness. It was a shard of something that had seemed insignificant at the time, a small bit of experience that wasn't anything special but now crystallized in his head, formed an eye in the hurricane around him and helped him, made him calm down.

"Breathe slowly," his father was telling him. "Watch the hawk circle and be quiet. You'll see him strike."

Jack had come home from the Army and wanted advice on what to do next, and that was what he got—a lesson in watching hawks, no help at all.

But it saved him now. He breathed slowly, forcing his mind to settle down, forcing the jangled shapes back into solid images.

They were nearing the road to the back portion of the base where their escape plane was. There were no defensive positions or troops in the dormitory ruins, which continued along this road for another hundred yards before the swamp resumed. No one was guarding the road beyond that, at least no one he could see; the only thing between them and the auxiliary runway on the left was a small guardhouse.

But as they neared the turnoff for the access road, a BRDM-1—a Soviet-era armored vehicle equipped with a missile launcher and heavy machine gun—turned the far corner behind them near the start of the dormitories. Jack spun back in time to see a large missile steam from the top. The warhead—an AT-1 designed as an antitank weapon—sliced overhead and crashed through a building nearby.

Jack pulled the machine gun into position and loaded it as quickly as he could manage, even though its bullets were useless against the truck's plates. A small jeep was moving to try and cut them off at the end of the road, hoping to keep them bottled up here; Danny accelerated and rammed the front corner of the jeep, careening onto the access road as the armored car fired another of its missiles. This one landed with a loud thud in the swamp beyond; Jack lost his balance as the truck accelerated again, shooting past the buildings and momentarily in the clear. He got to his knees and emptied the PK's long string of thick bullets into the front of the jeep, which was stuck now at the intersection with the access road. The armored car would have to either push it out of the way or go around it into the swamp.

The boneyard with their escape plane was about a mile away, straight ahead. The runway the MiG had used, empty now, was to Jack's right. The hangar and lab area was almost directly behind him. Black smoke from the two tankers they'd blown up circled over them. Something else had caught fire in one of the buildings; men were running all around, and it seemed obvious that the defenders still didn't know exactly what they were up against.

A truck, or maybe the armored car, pushed the destroyed jeep out of the way and began following them. They had maybe a half-mile lead. Jack turned to the front of the truck; the gate was down across the roadway ahead, but he couldn't see if anyone was in the guardhouse next to it.

He turned to get the PK and put it back on the roof, planning to pepper the shack. Cara was sitting cross-legged around a metal eye hook on the truckbed, gripping it tightly with one hand. Her other arm was wounded and seemingly limp. She had a rifle tucked under one of her legs.

"You hurt?" he asked.

She shook her head.

"Think you can help me with the machine gun?"

She let go of the hook, holding onto him as he threw the gun onto the cab roof. But as they neared the post, Jack saw that it was abandoned and the expanse of concrete behind it empty.

Two tankers were parked in the distance; a large, propeller-driven plane sat at the end of the runway that began on the left. Dozens and dozens of planes, silver bodies glittering as the sun burst through a low range of clouds, lined a dirt and gravel road straight ahead. Some were covered with tarps; others looked brand-new; many were in various stages of obvious disrepair, picked bones rotting in heavy spring air.

"Duck!" Jack yelled to Cara as his brother crashed through the wooden barrier.

As they crashed through, the ground to the right bubbled; mud flew through the air in a giant geyser.

Jack just barely kept his balance. He twisted and saw the armored car, gaining.

"Stop the truck," he yelled to his brother. "Back up and block the road."

Daniel had already had the same idea, slamming the brakes and wheeling around in a circle. Cara flew into Jack's legs as the truck skidded around and then jack-knifed across the road.

By the time they were back on their feet and climbing off the truck, Daniel had torn off his shirt and was stuffing it into the gas tank.

"You got matches?" Daniel yelled.

Jack remembered the lighter he had gotten at the Circus. He tossed it to his brother and began running with Cara toward the gray, weed-strewn tarmac.

The truck exploded before he'd gotten more than a few feet. But there was Daniel, right beside him, pulling ahead even. He wasn't running like a pudgy guy in his thirties; he was the high school football star again, running the quarterback option. He led the way toward the runway and the row of abandoned planes.

The armored car had stopped, but only temporarily. It lowered a set of belly wheels and began moving again, gingerly edging toward the truck. Either its weight was too great to brave the wet area of swamp near the guardhouse, or the area was mined. Even so, it wouldn't take it too long to push the truck away. In the meantime, one of the car's crew had climbed atop and set up the BRDM's 12.7mm machine gun. Bullets sprayed the pavement, ricocheting in a sharp burst, then stopping.

"Let's take that plane," shouted Jack, pointing to an immense silvery craft at the edge of the runway. It was less than thirty yards away, its massive body propped on thin stilts that connected to huge wheels.

"That's not ours," said Danny.

"The owners won't mind."

Another burst from the armored car sent them diving to the ground. Jack grabbed Cara. She was shaking; her eyes were glazed. She seemed to be in shock.

The armored car hit the back of the truck with a loud crunch.

"Our plane's down there," said Daniel, half crawling, half scooting back along the ground to them.

"We're not going to make it," Jack said. "We're taking that one or we're not taking anything."

"Jack, no," said Daniel. "Come on."

Jack had to let go of Cara to stop his brother; she rolled to the ground with a moan.

"Danny. Look—there's no guards or crew. Come on. Shit. That armored car is going to be here in a minute."

"They use that plane as a shadow for the MiG," Daniel told him. "It's huge. It's twice as big as the one I was going to fly."

"Fine, let's go."

"You going to shoot me if I don't?"

Jack hadn't even realized he had a pistol in his hand. Somewhere along the way he had gotten it from Cara.

"No, Jesus. You're my brother. Don't even joke."

The engine of the armored car roared as it crashed into the Zil again.

"I don't know if I can fly it," Daniel said. "I was trained on that one plane. That's all I know."

The familiar face faded into something Jack had seen before, long, long before and often, without recognizing it. His brother was afraid.

"You can do it," Jack told him. "You can do anything. You're a fucking genius."

Whether it was the words or the roar of the gun atop the BRDM, Daniel tucked his head down and began running for the large plane. Jack turned to help Cara up, but she was already on her feet, running after his brother. Jack caught up, dodging past an empty jeep as the trio ran toward the tail of the plane.

It was only as he ran that he realized how big the plane truly was. Even from twenty yards away, the thin cigar shape of the fuselage made the body seem deceptively small. The plane sat high off the ground on long supports beneath each wing and at the nose. A metal ladder pointed upwards into the open nose-gear bay—the only way in.

Something zipped nearby, then something else.

The armored car was firing again.

No, it was someone with a rifle in front of him, someone shouting. Danny was on the ground. Cara was on the ground.

The plane was guarded after all. Two soldiers were crouched behind the wheels on the left side, shooting at him. Above them were massive, four-bladed double-banked propellers from one of the car-sized engines.

Danny rolled on the ground.

Dead.

"No!" Jack screamed, and he pushed the pistol toward the guard on the left side of the wheel, twenty feet away, maybe fifteen, leaping over his brother's prostrate body and almost literally throwing a bullet into the bastard who'd just killed Danny.

Except Danny wasn't dead. Jack realized he was still moving as the soldier with the rifle fired again, then slumped back. Jack dove to the ground, his pistol clicking empty. The other guard jumped up and Jack tried pushing himself toward the first man's AK-47. Before he could reach it a burst of gunfire caught the standing soldier and spun him around, dancing him into the boggy ground beyond the cement.

"Let's go, let's go!" Danny yelled behind him. He threw a pistol to the ground and pulled at the ladder, struggling with it before Jack managed to get there and help. Cara came running to them.

"Shit," she said. "You're hit," she said.

As he started to ask her where, his legs slipped out from under him and he fell back against the ladder, tumbling to the cement. His brother said his name in a voice that sounded like his father's. Then Jack couldn't hear anything, and his eyes saw only darkness.

Chapter Eleven

Norabk, Western Siberia

Cara knew she was on the edge of shock, her brain out of whack with her body. Things were moving so fast they streaked in front of her, then so slow it was like time had stopped. They were inside the mammoth plane. Jack had passed out, the side of his head creased by a bullet and his pants leg caked with blood. She helped Daniel steady him on his back and watched him climb ahead of her on the ladder, the thin aluminum sides shaking and groaning with the weight. She then pulled herself up after them, blood swirling in her head and her stomach fluttering. She saw that the ladder wasn't attached and threw it down when she reached the top, watched it bounce on the cement and roll onto the leg of one of the dead soldiers. Belatedly, she realized she should have pulled it up with her into the access compartment, but she didn't have the strength to jump to the ground and climb back.

Something snapped behind her. She rose and saw that Daniel was pulling the lever that controlled the hatch, snapping it shut. There was a narrow passage behind him leading up into the forward crew station and cockpit. She followed him as he pulled his brother onto the flight deck, propping Jack against the side panel of the backup navigator's station before leaping to the pilot's seat.

The cockpit was a mass of gear, old-fashioned levers and flight controls elbowing much newer video tubes and displays. Cara turned her attention momentarily to Jack, trying to make him comfortable on the steel deck as his brother made sense of the controls. She found a sweater and propped it beneath his head, found another and used it to clean the side of his head, even though it was made of rough wool.

The plane began to shake with a high-pitched whine. Daniel had started one of the engines.

"The armored car," he yelled, pounding the controls and retrieving a second whine. "It's coming. There was a gun or a cannon or something at the back of the plane. Can you make it work?"

Cara's training in Naval Intelligence had included two or three lectures on Russian long-range patrol aircraft—of which the TU-95 and relatively similar TU-142 were the prime and only examples. But the sum total of her knowledge about the plane was buried beneath years of lint. And even if she had been lucky enough to get a full year's course in the plane, the large, 1950s-era warplane came in infinite variations; each plane had undergone numerous refinements and alterations. The subsonic turboprop's main virtues were dependability and stability; the Russians used the four-engined mammoth for everything from strategic bombing to maritime patrol and reconnaissance. Like others in the Russian inventory, this particular plane was a grab bag of original and updated equipment, with the front navigator's station replaced by radar and ECM equipment, which were worked from bench consoles behind the pilot in the extended cockpit. The plane had a twin-barreled cannon in the rear, ostensibly for defense against air-to-air attacks, though as a practical matter essentially useless against a savvy attacker using missiles from a distance.

It would chew through the armored car, though.

Cara pushed herself toward the back as the plane trembled with a fresh engine igniting. She skirted the rear hatchway and bomb bays, clambering down the long, ribbed tunnel to the open gunner's compartment at the rear. The station was up a short set of metal steps just inside an open hatchway. She reached the steps as the plane jerked sideways, vibrating itself into motion. Cara fell back against the side blister, tumbling against the thick glass. She threw herself toward a metal spar, scrambled forward and up into the high-backed bare metal seat that half folded, half spun in the small space at the rear of the plane.

Slipping into the seat was like climbing into a phone booth. Flat panels of glass formed the sides and rear of the gunner's station; the rear view was a bit wider than the panel itself, but the side views were narrow triangles. The armament control panel had a video aiming display that was glowing lime green, apparently in ready mode; a white grid was ghosted over it but was obviously safed, with a large dotted triangle across it. Cara had actually had a few days' worth of familiarity training with Soviet weapons systems, most notably the highly effective Zsu-23 radar-guided antiaircraft cannon, but even if she remembered those sessions well, it would have been difficult to immediately translate the experience to this system. A pair of radar displays flanked the forked manual yoke; buttons and switches were arrayed in an inexplicable jumble around them. Cara pulled the yoke up and to the right, but nothing happened. She jammed her arms down, leaning against the handle as if it were the end of a seesaw. But as far as she could tell, nothing happened.

Cara's eyes flew across the panel, desperate to make some sense of the weapon. She assumed that its normal mode of operation was by radar, and that the control yoke was used to designate targets on the screen. But nothing happened as she flung the yoke back and forth; there was obviously some sort of safety mechanism that kept it from firing or at least targeting objects on the ground.

There had to be some way of killing the radar controls. But how? She hit a switch on the left side of the console; at the same time the plane jerked forward, and it took a second for her brain to disassociate the two things. She caught a glimpse of something moving on her right; it was the armored vehicle turning the corner from the access road. Four or five men jumped from it, fanning out and then pointing at the Bear. The machine gun at the top of the BRDM winked yellow and red. The thick glass of the Bear's rear gondola dulled the colors, washing them out like an old-fashioned computer game. Cara stared for a moment longer, hardly realizing that she was under fire. Then all of a sudden her fingers began slamming against the panel switches again, desperate to find something that would activate the cannon. The radar screen on the right side of the panel flashed; she felt something that grinding beneath her feet, and a series of red lights flashed on the panel directly in front of the yoke. Beneath the lights were rocker switches, each with its own Cyrillic letter. She began pushing them indiscriminately, pulling on the yoke with her other hand to see if she had managed to hit the right combination. The switches apparently affected the radar screen—the ghosted crosshairs changed color, pulsing around a dark green shape at the center as the turret moved. She had locked the target but the gun still wouldn't fire. The safety was still on.

The gun barrels swiveled to stay aimed at the front of the armored car as the plane moved, but all the curses in the world wouldn't get the cannons to fire.

Cara studied the control panel. An override would be put in a convenient place, but somehow safeguarded so it couldn't be accidentally hit. That would mean it would be fairly high on the panel, isolated, and maybe caged.

There was a large knoblike switch on the far right, beyond the screen, protected by a hinged metal screen.

As she reached for it, the Bear veered sharply to her left. Cara wrapped her fingers through the metal like a rock climber gripping a narrow nub. She pulled upwards and saw the cement below her pulverizing itself into steam, chewed up by the large-bore machine gun on the BRDM. She yanked at the caged control, felt something give way—blood began pouring from the tip of her finger; she'd ripped two of her nails and a good part of the flesh right off. Ignoring the pain, she banged at the cage, saw finally that it was locked at the top. The armored car winked again and something banged off the side of the plane.

There was just enough space between the cage wire to slip her mangled forefinger through. She pushed it in, wiggling against the bottom of the switch. It swung in and the gears beneath her were grinding again. The plane was moving and now something rocked the Bear hard; she pulled her right hand from the cage and at the same time grabbed the yoke handle with her left, squeezing against the red trigger.

The space before her seemed to disintegrate into something red; she had both hands on the yoke and something exploded below her. The Bear's twin 23mm cannons were spitting out rounds; she could see the stream of green tracers and grayish-black bullets flailing the concrete a hundred yards away. She pushed the yoke to the right and the small turret at the back of the plane dutifully followed. The thick stream of shells moved toward the armored car, sailing far over its turret. She pulled down and saw the BRDM's gun winking red at her. And then the cannon bullets she had unleashed crawled downwards into the metallic flesh of the vehicle, chewing through the soft face of the truck. She tried to release the trigger but couldn't, felt herself lifted off her feet, tumbling against the control panel and then falling off to the side, tossed like a crumpled piece of paper. Cara felt cold and for a second wondered if she were dead, or if the plane had been hit, then realized that they were moving through the air, the big plane pulling off the strip and up toward the clouds.

Chapter Twelve

Norabk, Western Siberia

His father opened his eyes as Jack walked into the hospital room. Jack saw that he was smiling.

"I'm sorry it took so long," Jack told him. "It was a CIA operation. Danny was never a traitor. The whole thing was planned."

"You have questions?" said his father.

"I do," said Jack. He stood next to the bed, staring down at his father's face. He hadn't seen it so peaceful, so full of color, in weeks—maybe much longer. The liver had been eating at him for months and years before he'd finally given in and gone to the doctor.

"You have questions?" repeated his father.

He had so many questions he couldn't think of which one to ask. Did his father really like Danny better? Why? How had he managed to raise them by himself after their mother had died? Why did he never offer Jack advice about the FBI—about practically anything? Why did he like to take long walks in the woods, hunting birds with cameras, walking and listening and holding his breath?

"You have questions?"

Jack shook his head. He looked across from the bed and saw the monitors, their lines running flat across the screen.

Something snapped hard above him, loud and fresh like the wind popping a sail taut. Jack opened his eyes and realized he was in the cockpit of the plane. A shell or something had just sailed over the fuselage and they were moving, rumbling down the runway. Daniel was sitting in the pilot's seat, frantically working the controls.

"Danny," said Jack.

"I could use some help up here," said his brother.

Jack pulled himself to his feet, struggling over the long center console and writhing around into the copilot's seat. There was a thunderous roar in the rear of the plane and Jack felt his stomach moving backwards, then hung on as the big Russian Bear left the concrete.

"Fuckin' A," said Danny. "Fuckin' A."

Jack hadn't heard him use that expression since Little League. "What am I doing?" he asked.

"That over there, I think, is the radio. Those switches on your right. I don't want you to transmit, but see if you can figure it out," said Danny. He pointed to the long knobs on the console between them. "Don't touch these; they're our engines."

"No problem."

"Shit. Can you believe I'm flying this thing?"

"No," said Jack.

Daniel looked at him and laughed. "Yeah. Fuckin' A."

The yokes in front of the two pilots were similar to the controls in airliners. The Antonov that Daniel had been trained to fly also had four engines, and while the planes had more differences than similarities, the main flight controls and instruments were close enough that he had a rough idea of what he was doing.

And that was going to have to do.

The Bear harkened back to a primitive era. While that might limit her capability as a bomber, it made her considerably easier to fly than most planes a third of her size. She climbed slowly but steadily upwards, the clocklike altimeter at the side of the instrument clusters screwing past two thousand meters as Cara pushed into the cockpit behind them.

"Jack. Are you okay?" she said.

"Yeah," he told her. The few markings near the radio controls were in Cyrillic. "You think you can help me with some of these words?"

"First things first," she said, pulling down a large box off the back wall. It plopped down on the deck, and it wasn't until she opened it that Jack realized it was a first-aid kit.

"You okay?" he asked.

"It's you I'm worried about. Your leg's shot to hell. There's enough blood on the floor here to fill a bathtub."

Jack looked down at his right leg. It was fine.

His left pants leg, though, was shredded and sodden black.

Cara ducked between the console. Something set his calf on fire and he yelled in pain.

"Peroxide," she said as he screamed. "At least I think so."

"Keep it down. You're making me nervous," said Daniel.

Jack bit back some of the pain as Cara wrapped his leg. "I know it's an ace bandage," she said. "But it'll have to do. I don't see any more gauze."

"It didn't hurt until you cleaned it," he told her.

"The fact that it hurt means it was dirty," she said. "You're probably in shock."

"You don't look too good yourself," Jack told her.

"Let me see your head," she said, laying her fingers gently against his temple.

Jack thought of kissing her. He leaned toward her, but the pressure of her finger against his wound tore him away.

"Sorry," she said. "You got a bullet across your scalp. It just creased the side. You're damn lucky."

"He always was," said Daniel.

"Danny shot the bastard," said Jack.

"No, you got him," said Daniel. "He just took a long time to fall. By the time I started shooting he was going down."

"Where are we going?" Cara asked.

"As soon as somebody finds the maps I'll let you know," said Daniel. "This is our bearing." He pointed to the small compass at the right side of his instrument display. "We're going south. One of those control areas back there is probably a navigator's station. I'm not sure which one and I don't know how sophisticated it will be. There was a GPS unit in the Antonov, but I don't expect we'll find that here."

"If we know how fast we're going and the direction, we can find a position," said Cara.

"Yeah, if we find a map," said Daniel.

"Can't we follow that MiG?" Jack asked.

"Not likely," said Daniel.

"We have to warn the Concorde. If we can get close enough to the flight, they can divert."

"I'm going to be lucky to just keep us in the air."

"We have to," said Jack. "We can do it."

"Maybe we can get them on the radio," said Cara. "All we have to do is get close to them. Fifty, forty miles and they'd probably pick us up."

"Have to be closer than that," said Daniel.

"If we just head toward Omsk, we should find them. Maybe we can figure out how to use the radar," said Jack.

Daniel shook his head. "I'm not even sure how much fuel we have. Or where the hell we are. I doubt I can land this thing. Hell, Jacky, I'm surprised I got it off the ground."

"If you don't know how to land it," Jack said, "it doesn't matter where we go, does it? Omsk is almost due south of us. If we just fly straight, we won't be far wrong."

"Where were you supposed to fly?" asked Cara.

"There's an airfield in southern Ukraine," said Daniel. "If I can find it."

Jack leaned across the wide hump of controls to his brother. He saw for the first time that sweat was pouring down his hands, dripping from his forearms.

"You can do it, Danny," he said softly. "I know you can. You're a fuckin' genius."

"No, I'm a schmuck," said Daniel. "And a coward."

Jack started to laugh, but Danny shook his head.

"I am," said Daniel.

"You wanted to take out the plane. That's why we're here," Jack told him. "With all we've been through, we have to give it one more try. We don't want to fail. Not after all that."

Daniel turned and looked at him. "No," he said in a whisper. Then he began turning the yoke gently, angling the plane southwards.

Chapter Thirteen

Over Southwestern Siberia

Crow studied the right video screen, examining its God's-eye-view rendering of his plane and the approaching Concorde. The Chinese J-10 escorting the plane was riding two-thirds of a mile off the Concorde's left wing, parallel to Crow's parking spot behind the right wing. The J-10—a Chinese-Israeli attempt at an F/A-18, with excellent flight characteristics but less avionics capabilities—jittered a bit in the display. Crow was so on edge his fingers tightened around his control stick. They were nearly a half hour away from where the MiG could reasonably be expected, but Crow felt the back of his neck tickle with perspiration.

F1 had spent the past two hours corralling off more malfunctions in the winged-together programming; the computer was now running at about sixty-five-percent capacity. Apparently the problems were being magnified by a short circuit in the wiring used to cut the landing gear off from the computer. Or at least F1 thought so.

The computer seemed to be complaining that it wasn't equipped with a soldering iron. Every so often error codes appeared in place of airspeed projections for detected aircraft on the tactical situation screen; Jack had to toggle the screen into a different mode and then back to clear the problem. Mechanically, at least, the plane was perfect—with the exception of the still-lit landing gear indicator. She responded to her pilot's directions with crisp precision.

Ordinarily the buzz of the big engines behind him would help Crow focus his attention, zone himself into the plane the way an athlete zoned in during competition. But as he lined up for the rendezvous with the Concorde he was too much on edge, off balance, feeling awkward in his seat, awkward in his flight suit—it was as if his body had subtly changed shape, upsetting his sense of reality. Crow knew intellectually that it was all anticipation and tension, but he was powerless to do anything about it. It had been a long time since he'd felt this way—in Vietnam, in the Gulf, maybe the first time he'd sat in an F-15 Eagle. He knew it would pass; the mind-blank had.

The J-10 jittered again in the display, acting as if it was having trouble holding position in the face of heavy turbulence. Crow asked F1 for a summary of weather conditions on his left MUD. Ordinarily the request was answered immediately. Now it took nearly twenty seconds as the onboard computer shuffled resources to make the proper satellite queries. A graphical cross section of the wind currents and a summary of other conditions aloft finally appeared on the monitor.

Clear sky with unlimited visibility. Wind mild and consistent.

If the display was to be believed, there was not much in the sky to be upsetting the Chinese escort. Maybe it was bouncing in the Concorde's slipstream, upset by unpredictable vortices thrown off by the plane's stubby delta wing and throbbing engines.

A good theory, except that now the big airliner fluttered as well.

"Concorde Flight, this is Raptor. I have three-point-two minutes to visual range and intercept. Do you copy?" Crow said, contacting the plane for the first time.

"Affirmative, Raptor," replied one of the plane's copilots in a very proper British accent. Four different officers were crammed into the flight deck, selected as much for language skills as flying ability. The plane could fly itself from hangar to hangar. "We see you at thirty thousand feet, approaching at five hundred sixty-seven knots."

The pilot read Crow the Concorde's flight data, which jibed with what the Raptor's sensors had already supplied. The plane was cruising at 25,000 feet, flying at six hundred knots or nautical miles an hour, just below the speed of sound and well under its capabilities. Partly, this was for the benefit of its Chinese escort, which was nearing the end of its flight radius anyway; the J-10 couldn't sustain Mach-plus speeds for any meaningful length of time. The same was true of the Russian Sukhoi, due to rendezvous two minutes after Crow. In fact, the Concorde wasn't going supersonic again until the Ural Mountains.

Assuming they made it that far.

The J-10 blinked again.

"Raptor to Concorde Flight, how's your weather?" Crow asked.

"We have clear conditions," said the copilot. "Top day for the beach."

The J-10 disappeared from the screen.

Shot down?

Something like panic prickled Crow's chest, panic and then denial—the stealthy MiG wasn't supposed to be here. His throat constricted and his lungs began double-pumping. In the same instant his hand jumped to the throttle bar, shoving the Raptor into giddyap mode as his right hand jerked the control stick to the left, his mind plotting a shortcut to the intercept before the computer could bounce it onto the screen.

The F-14s were a considerable distance away. They'd never get here in time.

"Raptor, please advise," said the Concorde copilot. "We show you deviating from briefed course at a high rate of speed."

The J-10 had been less than a quarter mile off the Concorde's wing. Were they blind? Or just oblivious? Why the hell hadn't they taken evasive maneuvers?

Crow punched his mike button to ask when the J-10 blinked back into the display, precisely in position.

Then the screen's black, red, and green colors turned blank azure.

It was another computer error, by far the most serious of the flight.

"Raptor?"

"Affirmative Concorde, I was closing to intercept to, uh, miss a bit of turbulence I was encountering." He stumbled for a logical reason for changing course, not wanting to alert them to his problems, let alone his nervousness or its cause. Blaming the weather was lame and patently false, but the Concorde copilot merely announced that they were holding their planned course. Most likely he thought Crow was just showing off.

The right MUD flicked back as F1 once again worked its magic, correcting problems on the fly. The diagnostics program listed error codes on the left display, then announced that it was working with only sixty-one percent of its normal resources.

The redundancy built into the system had its limits—sixty percent. Beyond that, vital systems would be affected and the computer could no longer be counted on to help him fly the plane.

It was better to kill F1 now rather than have it wig out on him at the worst possible moment, Crow realized. Even if it meant he'd be on his own when the MiG appeared.

The damn thing had hung with him this far. Couldn't it last another hour?

If the available CPU and memory units went below sixty percent, would the voice module go down? If so, he'd face the possibility of having no instruments at all—the only way to kill F1 was with a verbal confirmation.

Without F1, there'd be no tactical hints, no comprehensive analysis of the enemy's plans. The radar wouldn't be enhanced, anomalies would go undetected—it would be up to his eyes and the standard radar set. He'd have to figure out when to fire his pitifully small store of BBs on his own.

Do it. Before some other malfunction made it impossible to take the system off-line.

Crow spoke the coded instruction. F1 asked for confirmation.

"Sorry, buddy," he said.

It was the last thing the artificial copilot heard. The screens realigned into stock configuration, giving him his radar and flight data, losing the situation plot as well as the stream of error messages. For a brief second, Crow felt as if he'd jettisoned a backseater.

Then he turned his attention back to the windscreen, where the Concorde's lights glowed red, tiny pinpricks stretching into orange-yellow amoebas as Crow began banking to get into escort position.

A second set of lights broke away from it, slightly behind and below. The J-10.

Crow nudged his nose upwards, sliding into position behind the Concorde's right wing. As he glanced down at the instruments, he realized that the landing gear light that had bugged him from takeoff had finally burnt itself out.

Chapter Fourteen

Over Southern Siberia

The Concorde and its three escorts were all using active radars to scan the sky around them. The signals were like massive search beacons, drawing Adrik to them. He watched them on his passive radar plot, translating the vectors into a situation map in his head. The Concorde was proceeding precisely as scheduled. He dialed down the volume on his radio, which was set to intercept its Russian-language transmissions; he didn't want to be distracted. The radar would tell him all he needed to know.

Adrik approached his target's flight path at precisely forty-five degrees, carefully counting off the seconds until the sharp turn that would send him south behind it. His aim was to fall in about fifteen miles behind the Concorde and then steadily draw closer. Assuming that he had not been detected at five miles—a fair assumption—he would then choose between a rapid or gradual close, zeroing in on the target's tail. He needed to get relatively close for the MiG's cannon to work; while in theory the GSh-23's effective range was approximately one thousand meters, he knew he had to be perhaps half that to be sure of hitting his victim.

While the MiG could accelerate quicker than the Concorde from subsonic speed, the advantage was fleeting. The big airliner was far more powerful once its engines were pushed to the max. He had gone though the possibilities for days and days, mapping different strategies depending on what the Concorde did. Level acceleration would be the most difficult to deal with—at five miles distance it would reduce Adrik's time on-target to approximately five seconds. If the Concorde began to climb, however, the envelope increased; if it dove—which Adrik assumed would be the pilot's most likely response, instinctively trying to duck under his fighter cover—Adrik's advantage would multiply exponentially. The lower it was, the slower the Concorde had to go.

Every half mile closer before starting the attack would make Adrik's task ten times easier. But it didn't matter. He was going to succeed, even if he had only five seconds' worth of the enemy in his HUD aiming screen. Five seconds was an eternity, enough to fire nearly 250 rounds of ammunition.

The MiG only carried two hundred.

And if he were detected beforehand? Now, for instance? Now when he was still nearly fifty miles from the airliner?

He would sweep into the attack, pressing his MiG toward the nose of the Concorde. He was above the enemy plane, with nearly five thousand feet of altitude to play with. His aim would be to break the airliner from its escorts, slashing high to send it into a dive.

Then he would twist toward its tail, hanging with it, inching closer and closer, until at last he could press the trigger and release himself, release himself from the memories that haunted him, no matter how hard he tried to concentrate on the plane or the task before him.

His girls, next to each other on the bed, their hair carefully combed, their dresses spotless.

Having drowned them and then carefully laid them out, his wife had stood against the wall of the room as she shot herself. They were the last thing she saw before she died.

She didn't have to explain why or how she'd done it, telling them to take their baths together, holding them down in the basin with her large hands pressed gently yet firmly against their heads. Anna must have struggled, though by then perhaps both girls were too weak. Their poor bodies, so white, so pure, so tiny, would have grown red and then purple beneath the water. Their black hair would have floated to the top of the water, washed by their mother's tears.

There is no food.

That was all the note in her hand said.

Adrik's eyes narrowed as the passive radar plot showed the Concorde and its escorts passing in front of him. He leaned forward in his seat, one hand on the throttle and the other on the stick, willing away the ten seconds that remained before he would push the MiG into the sharp turn, relentlessly closing in on his fate and his justice.

Chapter Fifteen

Over Southern Siberia

The one thing they couldn't figure out was the radio.

Actually, there were a lot of things about the large Russian plane Jack, Daniel, and Cara couldn't decipher, but the radio was the most glaring. Daniel did, however, seem fairly comfortable at the controls, even though his hands continued to sweat. He helped Jack with the rudimentary elements of the radar system, enough to see that there was a large plane to their southwest.

"That's probably one of the Russian escorts, maybe a monitoring plane," said Daniel, looking at the small scope in the right quadrant of the control panel between them. "Because it's too far north and flying too slow to be the Concorde. Plus it's going in the same direction we are."

"You sure?" Jack asked.

"Of course not."

"What do you think, Cara?" Jack asked. She was sitting at one of the stations behind him.

When she didn't answer, Jack got up from the seat and saw her leaning against the console, gasping for breath. She was pale and her eyes had narrowed into slits.

"You okay?" he asked.

"I'm just so tired," she said weakly.

Jack squeezed out from behind the controls and eased his way to her.

"I'm just so tired," she repeated. Her hair hung in flat yellow strings around her ears and her injured arm drooped into her lap. The top third of her shirt was blotched brown and red, a massive triangle of caked blood. He'd helped her clean her arm, but the real pain was coming from her ribs, which she'd hurt jumping into the garbage train.

"Maybe we should put your arm in a sling," he suggested, touching it gingerly. "What do you think?"

"I'm just tired, Jacky," she told him. "Let me rest."

Before he could say anything else, Cara's eyes rolled into the back of her head and she fell limp into his arms. Jack eased her to the floor. The softest thing he could find to use as a pillow was the sweater that was stained with his blood. Balling it up, he slid it beneath her head. Then he pulled over the first-aid kit. There were three Syrettes of what he guessed was morphine.

Should he give her one?

Maybe she was just tired; he was exhausted himself. Her face looked pained, but she was at least sleeping. He decided to hold off. He pulled off the jacket he'd been wearing and propped it around her as a blanket; then he sat at the seat where she had been. He began flipping the toggles and switches, trying various combinations until the screens popped to life. This was a backup navigator's station with enhanced radar and com gear, but only static came through the headphones no matter what buttons he hit.

"What are you doing?" asked Daniel.

"Maybe one of these things will tell them we're here."

"Jack, this sucker is so damn big everybody in the world's going to know we're here."

"The shells from the armored car must have taken out the radio," said Jack.

"Yeah, that's what I think."

"You know, that's one of the things that bugs me about you."

"Huh?"

"You didn't think that at all or you would have said it before. I thought of it, and you're taking credit."

Daniel turned back from the pilot's seat. "You're nuts, Jacky."

"No I'm not," he said, going back to the radar controls. He found a switch that gave the main display a wide-angle view. Four blips appeared on the screen at the far end. The Russian system displayed squiggly characters next to each one.

"Hey, I think I have this radar working. And I think that's the Concorde," said Jack. He flipped the switch back and forth; the group of planes were now on the far end of the close view. "Shit, I think it's there. There's four planes at least, one big sucker and three smaller ones. That would be right, wouldn't it?"

"Got me," said Daniel.

"Let's figure that it's them," said Jack. "Um, the bearing, right? It's southeast of the plane on our scope up there, yeah, I can see them moving toward it. Yeah, there are definitely ID letters and some numbers like they're bearings or something."

The plane began bucking as he spoke. They were turning. Hard.

"What the hell are you doing?" he asked his brother.

"I'm going to try and get out in front of them, make them fly south."

"Why?"

"The further south they go, the further away from the MiG."

"Shit. Don't make us crash." Jack could see the sky through the cabin windows above. They were nearly thirty thousand feet above the earth; the air stretched into a blue nothingness ahead.

The plane rocked as Daniel leveled off.

"Don't touch anything," said his brother as Jack got back into the copilot's seat next to him. "Especially the throttle controls."

Jack glanced at the long levers that separated them. "I'm not going to," he said. "Can you go any faster?"

"Let me fly, okay? I'm doing pretty good."

"I'm not arguing. I was just wondering if we can go any faster."

"It bucks when I pick up speed," said Daniel. His face was flushed. "I don't know if it's the altitude or if there's something wrong with the motors or what."

"Relax," said Jack.

"I'm trying. Why don't you leave that and go see if you can figure out how to work the gun," said Daniel.

"What? You think I'm going to shoot the MiG down?"

"Maybe," said Danny. "Or maybe we can warn the others."

"Do I make you nervous?" he asked his brother.

Danny snorted, but then he turned to his brother with a very serious look. "Yeah. You do."

"Why?"

"Because—I don't know. I feel like you're Dad, watching me, waiting for me to screw up."

"Me? Me?"

"Yeah," said Daniel. He was dead serious.

"Geez, you never screwed up. You were the golden one."

"No. You were Dad's favorite."

"No, I wasn't," said Jack.

"You think maybe we can discuss this a little later?" said Daniel. He turned back to the front, checking his heading against the compass. The small radar screen on the console now showed the group of four planes Jack had seen on the other display.

"You were Dad's favorite," Jack said. "That's why he sent me to get you back."

"No. He sent you because he trusted you. He didn't trust me."

"That's not true," said Jack. "Shit, man. First of all, he thought you were in trouble."

"He bought the cover story."

"No, he bought the phone call. Somebody called and pretended to be you. God, Danny, how can you say he didn't like you better? He bailed you out with all that gambling money."

"No, he didn't."

"He didn't pay the money you owed?" Jack was angry with himself, but couldn't stop the words from frothing out. He'd wanted to say them for so long, and even though they were besides the point now, he couldn't keep them back.

"Dad wouldn't," said Daniel. "Really, Jacky, I got my hands full. You think you can figure out that gun or not?"

Jack stood up. "Yeah. Get us close enough to the MiG and I'll shoot it down."

"Great."

"Yeah, great," Jack spat back. He climbed from behind the chair, aware that he was acting like a nine-year-old but unable to do anything about it except leave his brother be.

Chapter Sixteen

Over Southern Siberia

Crow felt it at the base of his neck, the thin point of a stiletto tickling him beneath the flight suit, poking past the sweat and flesh. He twisted around, trying to catch a glimpse between the Raptor's twin tail fins.

Nothing but sky.

It was there, though. He turned his eyes back to the front and thumbed his radar through its sweeps. Still blank.

It was there and getting closer. He felt it.

He pushed slightly on the rudder pedal, holding his position. The ligaments in his knee felt like they were steel wool, rubbing against the bones.

His radar picked up a large, unidentified plane rumbling toward his flight path several miles to the west of the Russian AWACS plane. With F1 off-line, the Raptor couldn't provide a detailed analysis, but the

AN/APG radar kicked out a code identifying the target as a TU-95 Bear, a large and old Russian bomber.

Crow studied the radar scope's projection on the MUD. The Bear was definitely on an intercept for the Concorde flight path.

Diversion?

Maybe Shadow R was hiding behind the big plane.

Dumb move if the modified MiG really was as capable as Dr. Blitz had told him. The Bear was already drawing attention—the Russian AWACS hailed it, demanding it fly out of the area.

The Bear could easily be carrying missiles.

If so, it hadn't begun targeting them—the Raptor's radar warning receiver was clear.

F1 would have examined the Bear more carefully. It could have told him if there were weapons beneath the plane's wings, or if a bomb bay were open. It could have predicted what the big bomber would do if it were, indeed, hiding something like an air-to-air missile.

No sense worrying about lost friends now.

The TU-95 had to be here to divert attention. It wasn't answering the Russian controller's hails.

Crow could use this as pretense to call for the F-14s. Get them in here now.

And if it was just a bluff to cause an incident?

Better than a shoot-down.

As Crow pushed the radio control to dial in the F-14s, he felt something behind him once more. He jerked his head around, straining past the ejector seat, saw something, then found a black spec, a dot of something that could have been a piece of dust on the glass.

Except he knew it wasn't.

Crow slapped the stick, heart pounding and head clearing as he moved to cut off the interceptor.

Chapter Seventeen

Over Southern Siberia

Adrik nudged his control stick to the right as the American plane sheered across his path. The F-22 was a distraction, nothing more. He had an immense energy advantage on the Concorde, flying higher and faster than the airliner; all he had to do was push into cannon range.

Less than ten seconds. The Raptor slashed back, directly in front of him; Adrik nudged to the left and found the American was now matching his position perfectly. Adrik pulled his nose up, then pushed down, unable to shake him. The pilot was either extremely good or extremely lucky; perhaps both.

There was a sure way to get rid of him. Adrik edged his stick to the left, watching as the fat double tailplane of the American fighter slid into his targeting HUD. He squeezed his finger on the trigger, slapping a quick burst of shells into the Raptor's wing. The plane danced away, and Adrik dove for the Concorde, still seemingly oblivious to his attack. The targeting computer counted down the distance to target in the HUD—3500 meters, 3000, 2500.

The tail of the airliner grew fat. Then something flashed in front of his windscreen, and before Adrik could think about it he had jerked his stick hard right, narrowly avoiding a collision with the F-22.

Chapter Eighteen

Over Southern Siberia

Crow pulled the big plane into a tight roll, barely missing the MiG as he whipped his wings over, losing just enough momentum to fall behind his prey. He fought off the swirling pressure of gravity as he gyrated into firing position behind the enemy, the reversal complete. He pumped two quick bursts into the whirling circle of the MiG, then held back as his yawing target jinked to the west and began climbing. Crow had trouble twisting his wings off the top of a climb and spinning to stay behind the MiG as the enemy lost speed.

Except that the MiG wasn't where he thought it was, spinning itself and slicing to the north, rolling again and pitching around, determined to point its nose back on the Concorde. Crow had to take his turn wider to keep the MiG in front of him; he was out of firing position and had to coax more throttle to catch up.

The MiG had fallen below the Concorde and had a good angle for a rear-quarter attack on the airliner, which was just starting to accelerate. Crow pulled his nose toward the MiG's path, lining up a quick snap-shot. He pumped his trigger as he dove past the enemy's path, but the tracers edged over the black plane's wing. In the same moment the MiG began firing on the Concorde.

Crow managed to pull his nose back up in time to have the MiG flutter perfectly into the targeting pipper of his screen.

He had him.

He felt his body relax, all his energy flowing to his finger. He nailed the trigger and three rounds spurted from the gun, three rounds into the dark shadow of the enemy plane.

Then nothing. He'd used all his bullets.

Chapter Nineteen

Over Southern Siberia

For the most part, Buzz had ignored the others sitting around him in the circle of leather-upholstered chairs from the moment the Concorde III taxied down the runway. They were all low-ranking government officials. The French and Russian Ministers of Transportation sat directly across from him, ordering drinks nonstop. The man on his left was the Mayor of Beijing; he'd apparently gone to school in San Diego and kept asking questions about restaurants and bars there that Buzz had never heard of.

Buzz felt he should be sitting with the Russian and Japanese Premiers and the French Vice President at the head of the cabin; he was, after all, the ranking member of the American delegation. Surely a spymaster and future Senator from the world's sole superpower was on a level with those bozos.

Buzz had choked back his bile, if not his hubris, paying more and more attention to his personal television screen as the flight progressed. He had the fish-eye view selected; while the distortion took some getting used to, it gave him a complete 180-degree view of the sky from the tail of the plane. He could see the two escorts—Russian in front, American behind the right wing—clearly enough to read the small crew caution markings on their fuselages.

Which meant he could see plainly that neither had missiles beneath their wings, as per the Russians' instructions.

Buzz knew roughly where the danger area began, and felt his pulse jumping as they neared Omsk. Even so, he didn't realize what was happening when the Raptor suddenly rolled to its left behind them; he thought the plane had malfunctioned. It wasn't until red and green tracers lined the video screen that Buzz knew they were under attack.

He gripped the arms of his seat as the big jetliner took a downward swoop. The plane rocked and there was a whirling sound beneath him. Buzz groped for the seat belt in the crevices of the thick chair cushion as the airliner groaned through an evasive maneuver. The whirling sound grew into a thunder as the plane began to accelerate. As he pulled the belt around his stomach, Buzz felt himself thrown backwards in his seat, the Concorde bucking wildly and then beginning to dive downwards. The pilot announced a flight emergency and asked for calm with a voice that sounded anything but.

Buzz stared at the screen, looking for the American interceptor, but his eyes caught a black hole first, a black hole moving to the right of the Concorde and below, slashing toward them. Shadow R, the object of so much planning and maneuvering over the past several months. Until now, it had been mostly a work of imagination, the product of artists' renderings and partial satellite views. He was surprised by how small it looked, barely a dot against the gray surface of the Raptor, flying in close pursuit. The planes seemed to fall away, then rise over them—Buzz, his stomach reeling, realized it was the Concorde that was taking the violent turns. The cabin filled with the voices of men demanding to know what the hell was going on.

Buzz stared at the dark, shadowy plane that angled toward them from below. It began spitting green tracers through the air. It was no further than a mile away, perhaps even closer. The fact that it had been able to get so close proved Buzz had been right to worry about it—it vindicated his infiltration plan. The implications of Shadow R—which made advanced stealth technology available to anyone with half a million dollars and an old MiG-21—would change strategic thinking for a generation, perhaps even more. He'd foreseen the problem and dealt with it, the hallmark of a great leader.

And now he just might be killed by it. As he watched the tracers arcing into the right wing of the Concorde, Buzz felt an intense shudder consume the plane.

Chapter Twenty

Over Southern Siberia

Adrik began to fire just as the Concorde started to dive. His momentum was wrong and he couldn't roll back to hold his position, and had to settle for a quick squeeze as he kicked his wings over.

And then he realized he had a more serious problem. The American F-22 was armed. It caught part of his left wing before he jerked away.

Adrik didn't care if he was shot down—his flight would end with a crash in any event—but he cared very much about destroying the Concorde first. The airliner was proving more maneuverable and possibly resilient than he'd thought, though not nearly as fast. He lost sight of it momentarily as he dodged the American interceptor. Adrik lost sight of his enemy as he threw the plane into a scissors-style loop to his left. He guessed that the Raptor pilot would tuck back, using his plane's bigger engine to follow through the unwinding ribbon; it was the way all Western pilots flew, trained to take advantage of their technology.

Adrik nosed down hard. It was a tactic that depended entirely on crossing expectations, since he left himself open and vulnerable as he groped to recover, but a dogfight was as much a contest of minds as planes. Gravity hit him hard, the MiG's ancient rivets and new welds groaning as he yanked his stick to recover, but he felt good—and even better when the Concorde popped back into view ahead, lower than before, possibly wounded. He grinned, lining up the shot. Then some instinct took over, and he dropped his left wing, breaking off but not quite quickly enough—the Raptor pilot had hung with him, not surprised at all.

He was dead meat, fat in the other pilot's targeting screen.

But the American inexplicably flew over him, either lacking enough forward energy to maneuver properly or suddenly very stupid. But Adrik did not waste time trying to decipher the blunder. He jinked downward, free to return his attention to his target. The Concorde was descending; he had only to make a concerted attack and he would accomplish his mission. He began to accelerate, pushing away the distractions.

A warning sounded on his panel. He looked at the RWR: long-range Doppler radar, American type. From two or three planes, probably F-14s if the detector was to be believed. At the moment he was invisible to them. The F-22 had a strong radar image, of course, but fortunately it had no missiles to target him with.

Unless it was using its radar to paint him for the F-14s.

They appeared out of range; at least his indicators showed no launch yet.

The Raptor crossed ahead, cutting off his approach

to the Concorde. He needed to get around it, and quickly, before the other planes arrived and he was overwhelmed. He scanned ahead and began plotting a dive, then saw the silver glow of a huge plane from the north.

A TU-95 Bear. Turning near the Concorde's flight path, several thousand feet above. It began angling parallel to the airliner's path.

It was the plane he had practiced with yesterday. Its crew had obviously gotten it into the air with the hope of helping somehow.

It was arriving at a fortuitous time. Its radar signature was a big barn he could hide in as he swung around for his final attack. Adrik pushed the MiG into an arc toward the plane, his hard breath a steady rhythm as he felt his confidence growing.

Chapter Twenty-one

Over Southern Siberia

The MiG climbed to the north and Crow followed around, aiming to keep himself between the enemy interceptor and the Concorde's tail while his radar painted the target for the Navy F-14s. The leader of the F-14 flight called the shot and then tried to ask something, maybe to ask if he should fire more missiles, but Crow was too busy, overwhelmed by the rush of the fight and the need to sort out what was around him. He notched down the throttle, adjusting his speed to stay behind the Concorde, which apparently had been hit—two dark gray smudges ran back across the right wing, as if a giant hand had reached for it.

The MiG was heading for the TU-95. Crow cursed as the radar bleeped and lost contact, confused as much by the signal of the larger plane as Shadow R's gizmos.

The missiles would be lost.

Crow pushed the Raptor ahead, trying to anticipate the MiG's next move. Its pilot was good, damn good—an improviser.

The Bear was swinging around ahead, tacking to parallel their course as the Concorde, now five thousand feet below and to the south, caught up. The EW hadn't detected any weapons radar from the big Russian bomber yet.

The MiG suddenly darted to the north, climbing out from behind the Bear in a maneuver that seemed to defy gravity, whipsawing itself both to the north and upwards. Crow pulled his stick hard, aiming to keep himself between the MiG and the Concorde. The enemy plane swooped further out than he thought it would, continuing to climb—it might have been a matter of perception, Crow's fatigued eyes failing to gauge the fighter's momentum or speed correctly, but for an instant the MiG seemed to be giving up and running away.

No. He was going to use the Bear for the final attack. He knew he was being tracked by the Raptor; he might even know the F-14s were on their way. He was going to hide in the bigger plane's radar image until the last minute, then cut through it for the final attack.

He'd outthought Crow, pulling him ahead and confusing his radar again.

Or was he trying to draw the others away from the Bear? If the TU-95 had a heat-seeker in the bomb bay, another mile and the airliner would be dog meat.

Shit.

Crow could have taken it out with a half-dozen rounds. Now all he could do was yell.

Or ram it.

The Concorde and Bear lumbered toward each

other. Ten seconds, maybe five, and it would be in range.

Crow reeled the Raptor over, pointing his nose at the bomber's fuselage.

Chapter Twenty-two

Over Southern Siberia

Going back through the unpressurized fuselage tunnel into the rear of the plane, Jack felt his stomach rolling in the opposite direction. He lost his balance and fell against one of the spars. His teeth vibrated with the roar of the massive turboprops outside and his head seemed to break in half as he hit the metal.

He was going to give up—he hurt all over and he was numb with cold and he needed to sleep, needed to just close his eyes and wake up on a beach somewhere, with a waiter humping drinks down to him. He didn't care about his brother, he didn't care about Cara, he didn't care about his father. There wasn't anything more he was going to do or could do or would do; they had to get over the border and somehow land the plane, crash the damn thing on the ground if they had to, and the hell with the rest of the world. His job was screwed, but the truth was it had been screwed months before; he'd been manipulated by Buzz and the rest of them, just an inconsequential pawn, and he didn't care anymore. He'd spend the rest of his life as a traffic cop in a sleepy Jersey town and damn them all. He just wanted to sleep now.

If the plane had been smoother or quieter, maybe Jack would have fallen into the deep pit he longed for. But his head jostled and his stomach rolled, and Jack found himself back on his feet, groping his way toward the rear gondola. His fingers folded into tight hooks by the time he reached the door to the compartment; he couldn't work the handle at first and jostled against it, trying to get it open. Finally there was an enormous hiss—he stepped backwards as the panel flew around. Jack dove through, thinking it might close on him at any second. There was another loud hiss and wind blew all around him, as if he were outside; he pounded a lever in the steel frame on the side, then saw he could slip the door closed, resealing the compartment. When it closed, he felt as if he'd found a warm cocoon.

The gunner's station sat at the top of a short run of steel steps beyond the rear lower blister and a folded jump seat. He'd thought it would be like something out of *Twelve O'Clock High* or *Memphis Belle*—a machine gun with maybe a hard seat attached. But the antiaircraft station was considerably more modern, with a control panel more like *Star Trek*. A narrow aiming yoke sat in front of a computer screen and a green and yellow checkerboard of push buttons and lights. Heat rose furiously from the radiator unit near the floor; Jack felt himself starting to sweat as he sat in the seat.

Danny had told him to come back here just to get rid

of him. But there might be something he could do with the gun—assuming he could figure out how to work it.

Right. Shoot down the Concorde yourself. That would be special.

Jack examined the panel and screen. It was like an arcade game—you moved the yoke and pressed the trigger to designate targets.

Assuming you could tell what the hell was what.

There were several switches and a small oscilloscope-type control on the left; to the right was a caged pull-up switch that was undoubtedly some sort of safety. It had blood on it and was pulled upright.

The manual override Cara had used to fire.

The airplane began banking hard, and Jack fell into the seat. Through the flat glass window above the panel he saw the monstrous white beak of the Concorde as it approached a few hundred yards away. Jack grabbed the gun yoke to steady himself and heard the turret winding below him. He glanced down, just to make sure his finger wasn't on the trigger lever.

The gun's aim was marked by a triangular pipper in the aiming screen. The pipper moved with the yoke; the switches changed resolutions.

The Concorde passed by below with a shudder that hurled the Bear up on its keel. Jack grabbed at the control panel as the plane buffeted. Through the rear window he saw a large gray plane coming toward them from a few miles away. Oddly, the sun threw its shadow above it in the opposite corner of the window.

It took a few seconds for Jack to realize the black dart wasn't a shadow but a plane—the modified MiG. It was crossing behind the Bear, arcing into a dive.

The MiG was rendered as a small black shadow at the far edge of the aiming screen. Jack pulled the yoke, trying to bring the triangle to the blotch. The pipper flew wildly and the turret below the seat ground away. He got it and pressed the wedge of the gun, felt it burp, and saw a stream of bullets falling away, far below, a useless shot.

Jack caught himself against the panel again as the Bear shook with more turbulence. The MiG got bigger; it wasn't a smear, but a plane now, heading right for them.

If he could throw the gun into radar mode, he could designate the target and let the radar do the work. This close it could never miss.

Jack pushed the caged switch down with one hand and swung the yoke desperately with the other, the pipper flashing as he pressed the designator trigger. The gun began whirling and shooting, seemingly on its own, tracers flying wildly above and then in the direction of the MiG.

Chapter Twenty-three

Over Southern Siberia

Crow was about five seconds from crashing into the TU-95's wing when he saw the MiG plunge downwards in a desperate roll. The Raptor's EW yelped that the Bear had activated its targeting radar. In the next half second a stream of cannon fire raked the MiG from the rear of the bomber.

The TU-95 was trying to take out Shadow R.

Son of a bitch. It was on his side.

Crow tucked his wing, sheering off inches from the Bear's fuselage as he dove to follow the MiG below the long belly of the bomber. The Bear lost its target and stopped firing, but it had already broken Shadow R's attack. The MiG hadn't been damaged severely, if at all—it yo-yoed in a sharp, five-or-six-g twist designed to shake the Raptor's pursuit and send the American in front of him. But Crow was ready. He homed in on his enemy's tailpipe, hanging with him for the kill. He pressed his finger against the trigger, hoping that he'd been mistaken before, hoping he still had a few slugs left in his gun.

He didn't. It had taken him thirty years to get into position to avenge himself, and all he could do was close his eyes and curse.

It ought to make him feel better, knowing how far he'd come in those thirty years. The fat target in his windshield was proof that he had mastered every test. Even if he didn't shoot down the target, he'd accomplished his mission—the Concorde was now more than three miles away, accelerating like a demon. The cryogenic engines were cranking so hard even the Raptor would have trouble catching her.

Crow ought to feel like whooping. But instead he felt frustration and anger. He had the MiG fat in his windshield, hanging with it as it accelerated in a futile dash toward the airliner. His radar, his eyes—he had it, but he was powerless to do anything but curse.

Thirty years of fatigue, not triumph, weighed against him. His knees were like sharp, jangled pieces of metal pressing in both directions against his calves and thighs.

The bastard was going to get away.

Something echoed in his ear, a radio call from long ago.

Fox One.

Fox One. Radar missile under way.

The F-22's radar had the bastard locked and the F-14s were so close now they could probably use their own cannons.

Crow pushed the Raptor down toward safety as the silver BB flashed into the top corner of his windshield, growing long and shuddering and then puffing into a gray fist that enveloped the back edge of the MiG's wing. For a second nothing moved, the universe painted into place. Then Crow's plane resumed its sweeping plunge, pirouetting upwards at the end of the arc.

At the same time the MiG began tumbling in the opposite direction, its metal vaporizing with a quick flash, glowing white, then turning deep black, a few flames licking at the fuselage as both wings sheered off and the fuselage spun toward the brown-green earth twenty thousand feet below.

Chapter Twenty-four

Over Southern Siberia

Buzz saw Shadow R explode and made a fist, waving it through the air so wildly that he almost smashed the video screen. He looked up and realized that not only was everyone in his group looking at him, but so were most of the dignitaries in the rest of the plane. He smiled, pulled down his suit jacket, and undid his seat buckle. He stood and addressed them in his best speech-making voice.

"Gentlemen, I want to assure you that this incident will do nothing—*can* do nothing—to detract from the bright future that we are all embarked on here today. A new era is at hand—an era of peace, prosperity, and cooperation."

Buzz paused, gathering his breath. The words had sprung to his mouth unbidden, but sounded damn good. He was about to continue—he'd say something about commercial possibilities and then call the stewards forward for a round of drinks, maybe—when the plane's pilot came over the sound system announcing that the emergency was now under control. They were continuing for Moscow. The Concorde had sustained some slight, superficial damage to one of the wings; as a precaution, they would remain at their present altitude and speed.

Buzz nodded as the man explained, more or less, what had happened, leaving out the capabilities of Shadow R and neglecting to mention that the Americans had shot down the plane, not the Russian interceptor that had scurried away or the TU-95 that had lumbered into the dogfight and admittedly gotten a few potshots in. But Buzz figured this was immaterial—it could be corrected on the ground at the press conference, where what was said would be carried live across the planet.

And especially back to Maine.

It had to be done subtly, though. He didn't want to piss off D'Amici unnecessarily; otherwise the President might forget his promise to stay out of the campaign.

He had promised, hadn't he? That was what his cryptic remark meant, wasn't it?

Buzz sat down in the seat, noticing for the first time that his shirt was soaked through with sweat. He'd have to change that before the press conference, look fresh as a flower for the cameras.

Muff his hair a little. Rugged, not ruffled. That was what he needed.

Shouldn't have shaved before takeoff.

The steward appeared over his chair, asking if he'd like a drink.

"Double bourbon on the rocks," he said reflexively. Then he remembered the press conference. He called the man back. "Make it a single bourbon," he said, "with a little water."

Chapter Twenty-five

Over Southern Siberia

Jack wasn't exactly sure what had happened until he got back into the cockpit. He knew Shadow R had exploded, but he wasn't sure whether he had gotten it with the Bear's cannon. He'd seen the tracers loping toward the wing, but then lost sight of it until it blew up.

Danny set him straight as soon as he mentioned that he though he might have shot it down.

"Missile got it," Daniel told Jack as he plopped himself back in the copilot's seat. "One of the sensors started going nuts and I thought we were goners. Then I saw it. Boom."

"Boom."

"Your shooting probably helped, though."

"Gee, thanks."

"Fuckin' A." Danny laughed. Either he'd run out of

sweat, or he was feeling much more confident about flying the airplane.

"Still pissed?" Jack asked.

"Nah. Not so much. You did okay." Danny turned from the controls to look at him. "Sometimes you get on my nerves. Especially when I'm nervous to begin with."

"Yeah. I'm sorry. It worked out, though."

"If we land."

"If we land." Jack started laughing. Danny started laughing too, even though both of them knew it wasn't much of a joke.

Cara was stretched across the entrance to the flight deck, her head resting on her arms and Daniel's jacket.

"She came to and started talking, right after the MiG blew up," said his brother. "Then she dropped back to sleep. She's gorgeous. I think she's in love."

"Hands off," snapped Jack.

"I meant with you, asshole."

Jack didn't say anything. He felt like someone was slowly draining the air from his lungs, deflating his whole body.

"Look, I'm sorry I was freaking back there," said Daniel. "I mean, sending you out of the cockpit. And, uh—the whole thing. Telling you that you screwed it up outside the base."

"I did screw it up." Jack crossed his arms in front of him. "But you should have trusted me to begin with."

"I told them you'd try to rescue me."

Jack was genuinely surprised. "You told them that?"

"Yeah."

"Danny, were you really panicking?"

"Shit, yeah. I may later again. You don't think I know what I'm doing, do you?"

"You act like you do."

"Yeah, that's what it is. An act," said Daniel.

"No. Not really." Jack pushed himself to the side of the seat, turning to look at his brother. "Where have you been, man?"

"Where have I been? Siberia."

"Yeah, but where have you been? Since college."

"I've been around."

"Fuck, Danny, you used to be everything to me. You were my big brother. We hardly see you, Bree and me. And Dad."

"Well, you know. It's tough."

"No, I don't know."

"Dad and me don't always get along."

"Why? What'd he do?"

"Nothing." Danny shifted uncomfortably in the seat. "He just, you know, he makes me feel bad. But he's right."

"About what?"

"I can tell he thinks I let him down."

"No, he doesn't," said Jack.

Daniel concentrated on the plane's control wheel. A large plane with American insignia was pulling alongside; the pilot was waving. Daniel waved back.

"American," he mouthed, gesturing madly. "Jack, mime something for this guy so he doesn't shoot us down."

It took them a while to make the other pilot understand. He was flying a brand-new plane, a high-tech F-22, which Jack vaguely recognized from news reports. The pilot gestured that he would lead them down.

At least that was what he seemed to be saying.

"We'll follow," Jack tried to tell him.

"As best we can," Danny said.

"You think he understands?" Jack asked.

"Who knows what anybody understands," said Danny as Jack returned to the copilot's chair. "Man, my back is stiff."

"Yeah. I could use a beer."

"Ten beers."

"Dad used to say that," said Jack.

"Still does," said Daniel.

"I don't know, Danny. He's going to die. He may already be dead."

Neither one of them said anything else for a while. Daniel finally broke the silence by pointing out some of the equipment; he'd figured out the landing gear, knew where the flaps were so they could be set, and thought that if he used reverse thrust he would land easily. Or at least the crash would be pretty quick.

"You'll get it," said Jack.

"The last few years haven't been that good," Daniel said abruptly. "I've been kind of stagnant."

"Yeah, but you're rich."

Daniel laughed. "Jack, you think I'd be freezing my butt off in Siberia if I were rich?"

"That Teflon thing—"

"My share of that was less than two hundred thousand. It was a lot of money, but it's all in the house. Hell, I still have a monster mortgage. And by the way, it's a poly-fiber ceramic, not plastic. And definitely not Teflon."

"Oh."

"Why do you think they came to me about this stealth thing?"

"I don't know," said Jack.

"Because they know I haven't done anything for ten years. I was a washed-up numb-nut. I looked like a genius, but I was worthless."

"Bullshit." Jack felt himself getting angry and

defensive, as if Daniel was being criticized by someone other than himself. "You don't know anything about stealth materials?"

"I didn't say that." For just a second, Danny's scowl returned. "I haven't done anything since the poly-fiber, and that really was just luck. The last five years—some of my staff jobs barely paid for groceries, and the research posts have been nonexistent. I have a noncompete agreement because of the invention, and that's been a pain in the ass."

"You gamble again?"

"That was a college thing," said Daniel. "A mistake." He shook his head and shrugged. "It's my fault. I haven't lived up to expectations. Not mine. Certainly not Dad's."

"Who could?"

"You."

"Me?" Jack laughed. "I'm a lousy FBI agent who'll probably be canned for screwing up a covert operation. They knew about you because of me. That's what happened, isn't it?"

"I don't know," said Daniel. "This guy from the White House showed up at a cocktail party one day, asking me questions. He turned out not to be from the White House."

"Buzz?"

"No. He introduced me to Buzz. I got a long a speech about patriotic duty and family loyalty and all this crap. He said he thought real highly of you, so I must be okay."

"When did this happen?"

"A year and a half ago. They told me I couldn't say anything. They did promise me a bonus for this, at least. We'll see if they deliver."

"They better," said Jack.

"At first I was just consulting, then I was going to go on a team as a spy—I think I was a spy, it was supposed to be a scientific exchange, so maybe it wasn't even that. Then two months ago everything changed."

"No. Buzz was planning this all along. That's why I was transferred out of B-3," said Jack. "That son of a bitch."

Jack realized that there had been a lot of questions about his brother during one of the otherwise routine security checks before his next-to-last trip to Russia. Buzz or someone else must have been looking to penetrate Shadow R and stumbled across just the dupe. Possibly an offhand comment about how smart Daniel was, how gung ho and prep-star cocksure of himself he'd always been, had given them the idea to approach him. His being a football star in high school would have impressed Buzz.

The gambling had come up during one of the security checks on Jack himself.

Shit, he'd set his brother up.

"Why'd you do it, Danny? Why'd you go?" he asked.

"I wanted to be a hero, Jack."

Daniel looked at him, then back at the front of the plane.

"You're not going to tell Dad I'm broke, are you?" Daniel asked.

"You're not broke, not if they pay you for this, right? And anyway, who cares?"

"I don't want him to think I'm a failure."

"Yeah, well, me neither."

"Nobody ever said you were."

"Damn straight. Neither one of us." Jack pulled himself upright in the seat. The earth looked like a brown blanket pockmarked with black blotches of acne. "But we sure as shit could use a ton of fucking big-time beers."

"Sounds like a plan," said Daniel, turning the wheel slightly to keep the F-22 in the middle of the windshield.

IV

"If thou doest well, shall not thou be accepted?"

Gen. 4/7

Epilogue

New Jersey

As a little girl, Cara had been fascinated by hospitals, maybe because they'd seemed so mysterious and important, doctors and nurses walking quickly through doors and immensely complicated machines being rushed to and fro. Now she had had her fill, having spent the last two weeks in them—first to recover from her own wounds, then with Jack and his family, waiting for his father to die.

Not that they put it that way. Technically there was still hope he might get the liver he needed to continue. But it was obvious to everyone, including Jack's dad, that wasn't going to happen. His score was too low and it was likely even a new organ wouldn't save him; the rest of his body was pretty far gone. And besides, no one was lifting a finger to help him get a transplant.

It seemed to her that Buzz owed Jack and Daniel

some serious string-pulling. But their father had told them he didn't want any favors, and Jack had refused to ask Buzz, insisting that he wouldn't go against his dad's wishes. And besides, he said, the DDO had no influence with anyone outside the CIA anyway.

Cara doubted that, especially now. Buzz had made the rounds of every morning news program and done two stints on *Larry King Live* and one on the PBS news hour. He was basking in the aftermath of what the press now called "The Concorde Incident," with capital letters and appropriate graphics. There were rumors that he was running for Senator or Governor in Maine.

Despite the hype and ominous theme music, the media didn't know the half of "The Concorde Incident." Much of what they did know was wrong: The official version had the F-22 Raptor tracking Shadow R from the moment it took off. The F-14s "just happened" to be on a routine training mission several hundred miles away and were diverted at the last minute. The Raptor pilot had become an instant hero—a gray-haired, aw-shucks guy who didn't say much except that he was just doing his job, same as he had for nearly thirty years.

Jack and Daniel weren't mentioned at all, which was just as well. Jack had been given an extended, open-ended vacation, officially listed as a paid bereavement leave. His bosses had assured him everything would be worked out as soon as he was ready to come back to work. Cara had some doubts about that, but it was the kind of thing that had to play itself out, and at least for the immediate future Jack didn't seem to be giving it much thought. What he did seem to be thinking of was her—he'd visited her nearly every day at the hospital, which meant shuttling back and forth between her in Maryland and his father in New Jersey. Cara realized that part of the attraction was the fact that they had gone through so much together; she worried that it might be temporary—but in the meantime wanted to push it as far as she could. She already liked his family, Bree especially. They'd accepted her so much in the past week she almost felt married.

Almost. That was getting *way* ahead of things.

Cara took a long drag on the cigarette—a habit she'd picked up from Bree, as a matter of fact—and began walking back up the sidewalk toward the main entrance. Jack came through the automatic door, turned the wrong way, then saw her.

"Hey," he said, watching her walk.

"Hey back," she said.

He gripped her around the chest in a hug a bit too tightly; the ribs were still mending and she had given up the Nortab just yesterday.

"Sorry," Jack told her, letting go.

"I'm okay."

"I think you ought to come up now," he said. "He's fading."

Cara caught Jack's arm and pulled him away from the door. She stepped back and looked into his face, worn but calm.

"Are you okay?" she asked.

"Leg's fine."

"I don't mean your leg."

"Yeah, I'm okay."

"You doing the macho silent thing?"

The corners of Jack's mouth slid up in a weak smile. He shook his head. "No, you know, it's been coming so long, you get used to it."

"Your father loves you."

"Never used that word." Jack half winced, half nodded, serious but not defensive about his family, not protective or jealous or angry. He'd come to accept his father's impending death, and accepted his brother's somewhat aloof ways, which contrasted so greatly with his sister's, but not his, not so much.

They'd been a tight group growing up after Jack's mother died. They had to feel deeply for each other to make it, yet the two boys had been taught—or inherited, or invented—a way of relating that used ellipses instead of direct feelings. They were quiet about things, and that pushed them in odd ways. Under pressure as a kid, Daniel had cracked, gotten in over his head with the gambling.

No, the gambling was just a symptom. The real problem had wedged itself in there, aggravated their relationship. He was afraid he didn't measure up, but didn't, couldn't, tell his brother about it, and certainly not his dad.

Jack had the same fear, but it drove him in a different way.

They were beyond it now. Both of them.

Daniel had landed the huge plane without help, even figuring out how to use the propellers to slow the plane as it touched down. When they landed, he just got up and got off—no fanfare, no high-fives.

Jack too. Just a job. Pretty much what the pilot had said.

What they said was not necessarily what they felt. It paid to look at what they did.

Their father had been a difficult and demanding man, but one who cared a great deal, their reference point for everything. It would be difficult for them, even as adults, to go on without him.

But they would. That too was something they'd been taught, or inherited, or invented.

"You know, he called Danny Jack just now," Jack said."Just goes to show."

"Show what?"

Jack held out his hands in a shrug. "I don't know."

"He's always cared a lot for you, Jack. He told me how proud he's always been of you."

Jack nodded.

"It was hard for him to say that to you," she added. "Especially to you."

"Yeah, he's not that kind of guy." Jack gave her cigarette a disapproving look. "Listen, you coming up with me or what?"

"I am," she said, tossing the cigarette and sliding her arm around his.